James Cook

A Collection of Voyages round the World Performed by Royal Authrity - Containing a Complete Historical Account of Captain Cook's First, Second, Third and Last Voyages.

Vol. III

James Cook

A Collection of Voyages round the World Performed by Royal Authrity - Containing a Complete Historical Account of Captain Cook's First, Second, Third and Last Voyages.
Vol. III

ISBN/EAN: 9783337192228

Printed in Europe, USA, Canada, Australia, Japan

Cover: Foto ©Raphael Reischuk / pixelio.de

More available books at **www.hansebooks.com**

Voyages round the World:

PERFORMED

By ROYAL AUTHORITY.

Containing a complete HISTORICAL ACCOUNT of

Captain COOK's

First, Second, Third and Last

VOYAGES,

UNDERTAKEN

For making New Discoveries, &c. *viz.*

His FIRST—in the *Endeavour*, in the Years 1768, 1769, 1770, and 1771, in the Sourthen Hemisphere, &c.

His SECOND—in the *Resolution* and *Adventure*, in the Years 1772, 1773, 1774, and 1775, for making further *Discoveries* towards the South Pole, and round the World.

His THIRD and LAST—in the *Resolution* and *Discovery*, to the *Pacific Ocean*, in the Years 1776, 1777, 1778, 1779, and 1780, in the Northern Hemisphere, &c. Comprehending the Life and Death of *Capt. Cook*, &c. Together with *Capt. Furneaux's* Narrative of his Proceedings in the *Adventure* during the Separation of the Ships in the Second Voyage, in which Period several of his People were destroyed by the Natives of *Queen Charlotte's Sound*.

TO WHICH ARE ADDED

Genuine Narratives of *other Voyages of Discovery round the World, &c.* viz. those of Lord BYRON, Capt. WALLIS, Capt. CARTERET, Lord MULGRAVE, Lord ANSON, Mr. PARKINSON, Capt. LUTWIDGE, Mess. IVES, MIDDLETON, SMITH, &c. &c. Including the Substance of all the most remarkable and important *Travels* and *Journeys*, which have been undertaken at various Times to the different Quarters of the World.

THE WHOLE COMPREHENDING

A full Account of whatever is curious, entertaining, and useful, both by Sea and Land, in the various Countries of the known World.

Being the most elegant and perfect Work of the Kind.

Illustrated with a vast Number of Copperplates finely engraved by the most eminent Masters.

This EDITION is compiled from the AUTHENTIC JOURNALS of several Principal Officers and other Gentlemen of the most distinguished *naval* and *philosophical* Abilities, who sailed in the various Ships.

VOL. III.

A NEW, AUTHENTIC, and COMPLETE ACCOUNT and
NARRATIVE, of

A VOYAGE Round the WORLD,

UNDERTAKEN and PERFORMED

By the Hon. Commodore (now Admiral) BYRON,

In his Majesty's Ship the DOLPHIN, accompanied
by Capt. MOUAT in the TAMAR Sloop.

Undertaken principally for making Discoveries in the
SOUTHERN OCEAN, between the Cape of GOOD HOPE,
and the MAGELLANIC STRAITS;

And Containing, among a Variety of other interesting Particulars,

A genuine Account of the Straits of Magellan, and of
the gigantic Race of People called Patagonians; also
a Survey of several Islands discovered in the Southern
Hemisphere; together with a minute, circumstan-
tial, and full Description of the several Places, People,
Animals, Vegetables, and Natural Curiosities, discovered and seen in the Course of this remarkable
Voyage; which was begun on the 3d of July 1764,
and compleated the 9th of May, 1766; containing
a Period of a little more than Twenty-two Months,
and included in the Year 1764, 1765, and 1766.

CHAP. I.

*Extraordinary Preparations made, and Precautions used,
for this Voyage—Names of the two Ships, Number of
Men, &c.—Circumstances previous to hoisting the broad
Pendant, and our setting sail—The Dolphin takes in her
Guns at Long Reach, and is there joined by the Tamar
Frigate—They sail from the Downs, and arrive at Ply-
mouth—Anchor in the Sound—Passage from Plymouth to
Madeira—Observations on this Island—Run from hence*

to St. Jago one of the Cape de Verd Iflands, and anchor in Port Praya—Obfervations on the Ifland and Port—They make the coaft of Brazil, and enter the Harbour of Rio de Janeiro—Obfervations—Departure from this Port, bound, as we thought, to the Eaft Indies—Orders made known, which were to go on Difcoveries to the South Sea—The Dolphin and Tamar make Cape Blanco, Penguin Ifle, and the Harbour of Port Defire—The Dolphin in Danger of being loft at this laft Place—Obfervations on the Harbour and adjacent Country—Departure from Port Defire in fearch of Pepy's Ifland—Anchor on the Coaft of Patagonia, ten Leagues within the Mouth of the Straits of Magellan—An Account of the extraordinary Stature of fome Inhabitants feen there—Proceed up the Straits of Magellan to Port Famine—An Account of the Harbour, Coaft, and Inhabitants—A Defcription of the Country, particularly the Woods, and the beautiful Sedger—Favourable and pleafing Circumftances during our Stay here.

A.D. 1764. HIS prefent Majefty, very early in life formed a plan of diftinguifhing his reign, by patronizing the profecution of New Difcoveries in the unknown regions of the Southern Hemifphere; and we have been told, that he declared his intention, foon after he came to the crown, of appropriating a great part of his revenue for that particular purpofe. In 1764, orders were given for carrying this laudable defign into execution; in confequence of which, on the 18th of April, preparations were made to fit out the Dolphin fhip of war, and the Tamar frigate, for a fuppofed voyage to the Eaft-Indies. The Dolphin was a fixth rate, mounting 24 guns, and had three lieutenants, 37 petty officers, and 150 feamen on board; the Tamar mounted 16 guns, having on board three lieutenants, 22 petty officers, and 90 feamen. The honourable Commodore (now Admiral) Byron was appointed commander in chief, in the Dolphin, and the command under him, of the frigate, was given to Capt. Mouat. Both of thefe veffels were fitted out

for

for the purpose of making difcoveries of countries hitherto unknown, within the high fouthern latitudes, convenient for navigation, and in climates adapted to the production of commodities ufeful in commerce, particularly in the Atlantic Ocean, between the Cape of Good Hope, and the Straits of Magellan. The inftructions from the Admiralty-board to the commodore, likewife directed him to make an accurate furvey of Pepy's Ifland, and thofe which had been named by Sir John Narborough, Faulkland's Iflands, in honour of lord Faulkland ; which, though firft difcovered, and fince vifited by Britifh navigators, had never been fufficiently examined, fo as that an accurate judgement might be formed of their coafts, natives, and productions. Great care was taken, and extraordinary precautions ufed in preparing for this voyage. The bottom of the Dolphin was fheathed with copper ; as were likewife the braces and pintles for the ufe of the rudder, which was the firft experiment of the kind, that had ever been made on any veffel. On the 14th of May, being ready for fea, fhe left the dock, when we received a number of men from the old hulks, which had been for fome time ufed to receive on board materials for the ufe of the fhip. The next day we got in our mafts, and with all expedition poffible, began to put up the rigging ; the greateft part of the hands being now, from the time of her leaving the dock, principally employed in receiving the ftores, and in fhipping the ableft feamen, till the 9th of June, when we flipt our mooring, and failed for Long Reach, where we received our guns, and were joined by our intended confort, the Tamar frigate.

On the 14th, we received on board a pilot for the Downs, and at fix o'clock, A. M. weighed anchor with little wind, and with our boats a-head : our draught of water forward being then 15 feet fix inches, and abaft 14 feet fix inches. At feven o'clock the Dolphin ftriking the bottom, fwung round ; however, the ground being very muddy, it foon gave way, and this accident was attended with no other confequence, than her lying

in

in the mud about two hours. This circumstance at our first setting out, which occasioned only a small delay, instead of checking the ardour of our men, served only to inspire them with hopes of meeting with fewer crosses in the prosecution of their voyage. On the 16th we anchored in the Downs, and moored the ship. During our continuance here, we sent the pilot on shore, and received from Deal a large twelve-oared barge for the service of our ship, with a quantity of fresh beef and greens. This day the Tamar passed us for Plymouth, and on the day following we received the honourable Capt. Byron on board.

Thursday the 21st, we weighed and sailed from the Downs; and in the night had a violent squall of wind, which, at that season of the year, might be reckoned rather uncommon. On the 22nd, at eight o'clock, A. M. we anchored in Plymouth Sound, and saluted the admiral with 13 guns; and at nine, having received a pilot on board, sailed into Hamouze, and lashed alongside the Sheer Hulk. As the Dolphin had taken the ground, the men on board were, according to orders, employed in getting out the guns and booms for docking; it being thought advifeable to examine if she had sustained any damage, when it appeared, that the ship had happily not received any hurt. On the 28th she came out of dock, and having replaced her guns and stores, we sailed into the sound, where we moored, and found the Tamar lying between the island and the main, having unhung her rudder, to repair some small damage she had sustained. While we remained at Plymouth, our men received two months pay advance, in order to enable them to purchase necessaries; a privilege granted to all his Majesty's ships bound to distant ports; at which time the inhabitants on shore have the liberty of coming on board to sell them shirts, jackets, and trowzers, which are termed slops. After a stay of four days, the honourable John Byron, our Commodore, hoisted his broad-pendant, he being, as was reported, appointed commander in chief of all his Majesty's ships in the East Indies. Immediately upon this a signal

was

was made for failing, by firing a gun, and loofing our top fails, which being fet, and another gun fired, we took our departure from Plymouth on the 3d of July, having his Majefty's frigate, the Tamar, in company.

On Wednefday the 4th of July, we fhaped our courfe, with a fine breeze, for the ifland of Madeira, during which run, we had the vexation of obferving, that our confort was a very heavy failer. On Thurfday the 12th, in the evening, we defcried the rocks near Madeira called the Deferts, from their defolate appearance; and on the 13th we came to an anchor in Funchiale Bay; fo named from the great abundance of a beautiful kind of fennel that grows on the fhore. It is on the fouth part of the ifland, and at the bottom is the city of the fame name, feated on a fmall plain, from which three rivers run into the fea, forming an ifland called Loo Rock, it being entirely barren. Upon this is placed a caftle, and the town is alfo defended by a high wall, and a battery of cannon. This ifland is compofed of one continued hill of a confiderable height, extending from eaft to weft; the declivity of which on the fouth-fide is interfperfed with vineyards; and in the midft of this flope are the country-feats of the merchants, which add greatly to the beauty of the profpect. The air is fo temperate, that the inhabitants feel little inconvenience from heat and cold, there being here a perpetual fpring, which produces bloffoms and fruit throughout the year. The foil is fo fertile, that it produces more corn than any of the adjacent iflands of double the extent. The grafs fhoots up fo high, that they are obliged to burn it; and when they plant fugar canes in the afhes, in fix months time they will produce a confiderable quantity of fugar. The ifland abounds with fine cedar-trees, and almoft all kinds of rich fruits, particularly grapes as large as our common plumbs; but all the fine fruits are too lufcious to be eaten in any great quantities. The natives are faid to make the beft fweet-meats in the world: they excel too in preferving oranges, as alfo in making marmalades

4

malades and perfumed pastes. The sugar made here
is not only remarkably fine, but has the smell of vio-
lets; and the wine of this island will keep better in
long voyages and in hot countries, than that of any
other place in the known world, on which account
great quantities of it are bought up for the use of ships,
and exported to the West Indies. Their convents have
a venerable appearance, from their age and structure.
Some of the nuns belonging to them are handsome,
and, at particular hours, have the liberty of conversing
with strangers, through a double barred gate. Their
chief employment consists in making curious flowers of
all sorts, little baskets, and other trinkets, in needle-
work, which they sell to their visitors, and the money
is appropriated to the use of the convents. Notwithstanding the extraordinary fertility of the island, provisions of all kinds are very dear, the inhabitants living chiefly on fruit and roots. There are some hogs
and fowls; but they cannot be procured without great
difficulty, except by way of exchange for old cloaths,
which in whatever condition, or of whatever kind, are
eagerly sought after by the poor among the natives.
While we continued here, we were supplied with fresh
beef, very indifferent of the kind, as their bullocks,
either from want of sweet pasture, or from nature, are
both lean, and under the common size. On our arrival
in the road of Funchiale, we found the Ferrit and
Crown sloop lying at anchor, who saluted our Commodore on his hoisting the broad-pendant, the fort also
returned our salute with eleven guns; and on the 14th,
Commodore Byron waited on the governor, by whom
he was received with great politeness; and on the day
following the governor returned his visit at the house
of the consul. Having taken in our water, wine, and
other refreshments for the use of both the ships companies, on the 19th we began to prepare for proceeding
on our voyage.

On Friday the 20th, we took leave of the governor
by firing eleven guns, which compliment he returned
from the citadel; and at three o'clock, A. M. we
weighed

weighed anchor and fet fail, in company with his Majefty's fhips the Crown, Ferrit, and Tamar. It is ob-
fervable, that in leaving this ifland fhips are in a manner becalmed, till they get four or five leagues to the
leeward, where they are fure to find a brifk trading
wind. The next day we made the ifland of Palma,
one of the Canaries. We now parted company with
the Crown and Ferrit, and on the 22d fpoke with his
majefty's fhip Liverpool from the Eaft Indies, by whom
we fent letters to England. This day we examined our
water-cafks, and concluded, we were under a necefflity
to touch at one of the Cape de Verd iflands for a
frefh fupply. On the 26th, our water being foul and
ftinking, we were obliged to have recourfe to a kind
of ventilator, which forced the air through the water in
a continued ftream, whereby it was purified. On the
27th in the morning, we made the ifle of Sal, one of
the Cape de Verds, when obferving feveral turtles on
the furface of the fea, we hoifted out our boat, in order
to ftrike fome of them, but they all difappeared before
our people were within reach of them. Indeed we had
little chance of catching any forts of fifh, for none of
the finny tribe would come near the fhip, becaufe fhe
was fheathed with copper.

On Monday the 30th, at two o'clock P. M. we faw
the ifland of St. Jago; and at three came to an anchor, about a mile from the fhore, in the bay called
Port Praya, in nine fathoms water, having faluted a
fmall fortification belonging to the Portuguefe, who returned the compliment. At this time it was near the
rainy feafon, which, when fet in, renders this harbour
very unfafe; for a rolling fwell from the fouthward
makes a frightful furf on the fhore, and every hour a
tornado may be expected, which at times is very furious, and may produce fatal confequences to fhipping; on which account no veffel comes here after the
15th of Auguft, till the rainy feafon is over, which is
in the month of November. St. Jago is the largeft and
moft fruitful of all the Cape de Verd iflands; and notwithftanding its being rocky and mountainous, the valleys

leys not only produce Indian corn, but fruits of various
kinds, and plenty of cotton. The ifland has four
towns, befides Ribeira Grande, the capital, in which
refides the governor, Oviodone, and bifhop. Moft of
the priefts are negroes, as indeed are far the greateft
part of the inhabitants, there being only about three
whites to forty blacks, who have fcarce cloaths fufficient to cover their nakednefs. There are but few
foldiers, and thofe, to outward appearance, are moft
indigent wretches. A fhip no fooner arrives, than the
natives flock from all parts of the ifland with different
kinds of provifions; and thefe they exchange for old
clothes, particularly black, on which they fet the
higheft value, and for a mere trifle of that kind, you
may be provided with a fufficient quantity of turkeys,
geefe, fruit, and other neceffary articles of fea-ftock.
But, however wretched thefe people may appear at
the firft view, they live in the greateft plenty, and
from the fertility of the foil, enjoy not only the neceffaries, but what, in other places would be efteemed the
luxuries of life. Having by this time got on board a
fupply of water, frefh provifions, and fruit, we unmoored, fignal having been made for our departure.

On Thurfday, the 2nd of Auguft, we got under
fail, and put to fea, with the Tamar in company. Soon
after, the fcorching heat, and unceafing rain, affected
the health of our crew, many of whom began to fall
down in fevers, notwithftanding the commodore took
the utmoft care to make the men, who were wet, fhift
themfelves, before they laid down to fleep. On the
8th we loft a good deal of way, by fhortening fail till
the Tamar came up, who had her topfail yard carried
away. In thefe hot latitudes, fhips generally take fifh
in plenty, but we were not able to catch one, the caufe
of which difappointment, we have already noticed.

On Thurfday, the 11th of September, we defcried
Cape Frio, on the coaft of Brazil, in the 23d degree
of fouth latitude, and the 42nd deg. 20 min. W. longitude from London. The next day, about noon, we
entered

entered the harbour of Rio de Janeiro, and anchored in eighteen fathoms water, Fort St. Acroufe bearing S. E. half S. a remarkable peak, in the form of a fugar-loaf, prefenting itfelf to our view on the larboard fide, at the fouth by eaft, and Snake's Ifland, which is the largeft in the harbour, appearing clofe by the town at W. N. W. and the north end of the town at W. half N. On the 14th, we received a pilot on board, and ran in between the ifland and main, not a quarter of a mile from the fhore, and at noon faluted the citadel with eleven guns, which were immediately returned. Our firft care was to get on board frefh provifions for the fhips companies, which began to be in great want of them, efpecially of greens, the fcurvy having already made its appearance among the men on board. On the 19th, our Commodore vifited the governor, who received him in ftate, putting the guard under arms: the nobility conducted him to the viceroy's palace, while 15 guns were fired in honour of the Britifh flag; his excellency afterwards returned the vifit, and was received by the commodore on board the Dolphin, in a manner fuitable to his high rank. On this occafion all hands manned the fhip, ftanding on the yards with their arms extended juft to touch each other; and a falute was given with 15 guns, which was returned by an equal number from the citadel. On the 9th of October, Lord Clive, in the Kent Indiaman, paid Commodore Byron a vifit, when he likewife received the fame compliment, both at his coming on board, and his going away. The fame day a pilot came on board to conduct us into the road, and at fix o'clock P. M. we weighed, and fet our fails; but having little wind, we were obliged to come again to an anchor, and wait till the next morning, during which time we had an opportunity of making a few obfervations on the harbour, which feems capable of receiving an hundred fail of fhips in good anchorge, with fufficient room for them to ride in fafty. The town of Rio de Janeiro is commodioufly feated at the back of Snake's ifland, which being not above five hundred yards from it, commands, from the fortifications erected on it, every thing that can possibly come to annoy the town; and there are several other islands at the entrance fortified with different batteries. These fortifications appear so formidable in the eyes of the Portuguese, that they are so vain as to think, the whole power of Europe would not be sufficient to deprive them of their possession; yet we may safely affirm, that six sail of our men of war of the line would be able to destroy all their batteries in a few hours.

From the 15th of September to the 18th of October, our men were employed in watering, wooding, caulking, &c. We had six Portuguese caulkers to assist our carpenter, who were paid at the rate of six shillings sterling per diem, though it is certain, that one of our English caulkers would do as much in one day, as they could do in three; but though slow and inactive, they perform their work very completely. In this port the air is refreshed by a constant succession of land and sea breezes; the former comes in the morning, and continues till towards one o'clock, and soon after is regularly succeeded by a strong sea-breeze. These contribute to render the port very healthy and pleasant, and are justly esteemed so salutary, that the negroes term the sea-breeze the Doctor. The soil of Brazil is generally fertile, it producing a variety of lofty trees fit for any use, many of them unknown in Europe; and the woods abound with rich fruits, among which are a considerable number that are neither known in Europe, nor in any parts of America. Oranges and lemons grow here in as great plenty, as nuts in our woods in England. The sugar-cane flourishes here in the utmost perfection, and great quantities of excellent sugar, indigo, and cotton, are exported from hence into Europe. Great quantities of gold are also found by the slaves, numbers of whom are employed in searching for it in gullies of torrents, and at the bottom of rivers; and this country is also famous for its diamonds. With respect to the animals of Brazil, all the horses, cows, dogs and cats are said to have been brought from Europe:

3

rope: among thofe natural to the country are a great variety of monkeys, Peruvian-fheep, deer and hares; the racoon, the armadillo, the flying fquirrel, the guano, the opoffum, the ant-bear, and the floth. Among the fowls are many parrots, parroquets, macaws, and other birds remarkable for the beauty of their plumage; with a great variety of finging birds, and feveral fpecies of wild geefe, wild ducks, common poultry, partridges, wood-pigeons and curlews. However, the country of Brazil is no lefs remarkable for the multitude, the variety, and incredible fize of its fnakes, and other venemous reptiles. In Rio de Janeiro the viceroy is invefted with the fame power over the natives, as the king of Portugal enjoys over his fubjects in Lifbon. The inhabitants, who are of a brown complexion, have a great number of negro flaves, which they purchafe in the public markets, where they are chained two and two together, and generally driven round the town to be expofed to view. The women here are very fwarthy, and have difagreeable features; but thofe of a fuperior rank are feldom feen, as they are never fuffered to go out of doors but by night. The Portuguefe are naturally of fo jealous a difpofition, that ftrangers, merely by looking at their women incur their refentment, and are in danger of fuffering by that fpirit of revenge, which univerfally prevails in this country; on which account the women are obliged to be always on their guard. Indeed, they here feldom enter upon matrimony; but when tired of each other, they feparate by mutual confent, and then endeavour to find out another paramour to fupply the place of the former. As foon as the evening approaches, the Portuguefe of this city go their rounds, and enter upon fcenes of debauchery, which we may venture to affirm are as frequent and flagitious as thofe between the inhabitants of Lifbon. Rio de Janeiro is feated near the fide of a number of high hills, from whence to the fouthward is a very large aqueduct, which fupplies the whole town with water. This aqueduct, which extends acrofs a deep valley, confifts of above fifty arches placed in two rows, one upon another,

ther, and in some parts rise upwards of a hundred yards from the bottom of the valley. By this means the water is conveyed into two fountains, from whence the inhabitants fetch all they want. These stand opposite the viceroy's palace, which is a stately stone building, and the only one in the whole city that has windows; the other houses in the town having only lattices. At the further end of the palace stands the jail for criminals, which from its structure, and the multiplicity of its iron grates, is far from adding any beauty to the palace, to which it joins. The churches and the convents are extremely magnificent, and calculated to strike the passions of the people who resort to them. On the altar pieces, and other parts of those structures, are many fine figures of our Saviour, the Virgin Mary, the Apostles, and other saints. In these churches a great number of friars and monks of different orders are constantly employed to celebrate mass to as many as happen to assemble; the churches being always open, and wax tapers kept continually burning; whence, in passing by these structures, all those of their persuasion pay due reverence, by pulling off their hats, and crossing themselves, with every other token of respect. In almost every corner of the streets are niches, in some of which are placed crucifixes, and in others some saint, dressed in linen and silk, or other stuffs. The cathedral and Jesuits College, which are the most manificent buildings in the city, may be seen from the harbour, and form an agreeable distant prospect. A considerable trade is carried on here by a number of merchants who reside in the city. Every year at least forty or fifty sail of ships come from Lisbon, and different parts of the Brazils, besides some ships that trade to Africa, and the small craft that frequent the neighbouring ports. The European ships bring leather, linen, and woollen cloths, coarse and fine bays, serges, hats, stockings, thread, biscuit, iron, hardware, pewter, and all kinds of kitchen furniture, with other commodities; and in return carry from thence sugar, tobacco, snuff, brasil, and other dying and me-

dicinal

dicinal woods, fuftic, raw hides, train oil, &c. With
refpect to their food, it muft be acknowledged, that
their beef is very indifferent, as through the exceffive
heat of the weather, they are obliged to eat it foon after
killing, which is performed in the following manner :
they drive a number of bullocks into an inclofed place,
and then throwing a rope over that they intend to kill,
take him out from among the reft, and confine his head
down by means of the rope, when a negro butcher
coming behind him, cuts the hamftrings of his hind
legs, and when the beaft falls, he fticks a knife in his
head exactly between his horns. Thefe cattle are fo
wild and unmanageable, that few, except negro but-
chers, chufe to encounter them ; and yet they are fo
fmall, that when the fkin, offal, &c. are taken away,
they in general do not weigh more than two hundred
and a half. Such are the ingenious remarks of our
journalift, who was an officer on board the Dolphin ;
and our readers will, perhaps, remember, that we have
given a full and complete account of the Brazils, and
Rio de Janeiro, in the 7th and fome of the following
pages of this work.

While we continued at the Brazils, yams were ferved
to the fhip's company inftead of bread, at two pounds
a day each man : but we procured fugar, tobacco, and
other commodities at a very reafonable price. Fowls
and hogs are however very dear, the chief food of the
negroes being fifh and Indian corn, the latter of which
they cultivate in great quantities, and plenty of the
former they catch out at fea, they having a confiderable number of fifhing canoes, in which they go out
in the morning, affifted by the land-breeze, which, as
we have before obferved, rifes regularly at that time,
and return in the evening with the fea-breeze, which is
no lefs invariable. In this port they have not only a
yard for building fhips, but a convenient ifland, where
they can heave down a veffel of any fize. A Spanifh
South-feaman was obliged to put into this port, while
we lay here, in order to heave down, and repair the damage fhe had fuftained. During our ftay, Commodore
Byron

Byron lived on fhore, having a commodious houfe fitu-ated on the top of a hill to the northward, where the viceroy and others paid him frequent vifits, and fhewed him all the refpect, that a ftranger of his rank could poffibly claim. The following piece of information may be of fervice to future navigators, particularly to thofe of our own nation.—"The Portuguefe, at Janeiro, practice every artifice in their power to entice away the feamen from the fhips which touch there; and if by cajoling or intoxicating them, they can get any men within their power, they immediately fend fuch up the country, and keep them there till the fhip to which they belong has left the place. By thefe arts, five men from the Dolphin, and nine from the Tamar, were feduced; the latter were recovered, but the former were effectually fecreted." All hands were now, being the 16th of October, employed to complete the fitting the Dolphin and Tamar for fea, having all the reafon pof-fible to believe, that we were bound to the Eaft-Indies, and that we fhould now proceed to the Cape of Good Hope, the fcheme having been fo well concerted by the Commodore, as even to deceive Lord Clive, who preffed him with great importunity to allow him to take his paffage in the Dolphin, we being in much greater readi-nefs for fea than the Kent, which had befides the mis-fortune to have many fick on board : but to this the Commodore could not confent; yet flattered his lord-fhip with the hopes of his taking him on board on their meeting at the Cape.

On Saturday, the 20th, we left this port, and the coaft of Brazil, bound as we thought for the Cape of Good Hope, but when at fea, by fteering to the fouth-ward, we to our great furprize found our miftake; and on the 22nd, we were relieved from our fufpenfe ; for a fignal being made for the commander of the Tamar frigate to come on board, he and our own company were informed, that the Commodore's orders were to go on difcoveries into the South Sea : a circumftance that, from the manner of which it was received, fur-nifhes the greateft reafon to believe, that no one on
board

board had before the least notice of the voyage in which they were now engaged. To this information the Commodore added, that the good behaviour of our company, by order of the lords of the Admiralty, would be rewarded, with double pay, and other emoluments. This declaration was received with marks of the highest satisfaction; the crew promised obedience to the commodore as to any orders he should give, and expressed their willingness to do all in their power for the service of their country. Some French writers have given a forced and very malevolent turn to this generous conduct; but the daring spirit which characterizes British seamen is too well known, for any one to suppose, that an increase of pay was necessary to prompt them to do their duty in perilous service: and the instances of disinterested generosity which distinguish the British nation, cannot leave the true motive which actuated the board of admiralty, when it thus distributed its bounty, any ways equivocal, or exposed to the misconstruction of invidious men. To make the acquiescence of the French sailors, under the inattention of their government, when M. de Bougainville failed round the world, an occasion for casting a reflection on the English sailors, for the contrary conduct of government, in a similar circumstance, bespeaks a species of mean subtlety, which can disgrace none but those who practice it, and which the spirited rivalship of that polished nation does not countenance.

On Monday, the 29th, it blew a violent hurricane, and during the storm we were obliged to throw four of our guns overboard. It continued all night, but subsided on the morning of the 30th, when we made sail, and being arrived in latitude 35 deg. 30 min. S. we found the weather exceeding cold, though at this time the latter end of October, which answers to our April, in the northern and temperate zone, and we were besides sixteen degrees nearer the line than at London. A little more than a week before, we had suffered intolerable heat, so that such a sudden change was most severely felt. The seamen, having supposed, that they

were

808 COMMODORE BYRON'S VOYAGE

were to continue in a hot climate during the whole
voyage, had difposed of all their warm cloathing at the
ports where we had touched, as alfo their very bedding;
fo that now, finding their miftake, and being pinched
with cold, they applied for flops, and were furnifhed
with the neceffary articles for a cold climate.

On Friday the 2nd of November, the Commodore
delivered to the lieutenants of both fhips their commif-
fions, they having hitherto acted only under verbal orders from him. On the 4th, the fhip was furrounded
with vaft flocks of birds, among which were fome
brown and white, and feveral pintadoes, fomewhat
larger than pigeons. We alfo in latitude 38 deg.
53 min. S. and in 51 deg. W. longitude, faw a quantity of rock weed, and feveral feals. On the 10th, we
perceived the water difcoloured; and the next day we
ftood in for land, being in latitude 41 deg. 16 min. S.
and in 55 deg. 17 min. W. longitude. On the 11th,
we fteered all night S. W. by W. and on Monday the
12th, we found ground at the depth of 45 fathoms: our
latitude was 42 deg. 34 min. S. longitude 58 deg. 17
min. W. About four o'clock, P. M. our people in the
forecaftle called out, " Land right a-head!" At this
time it was exceeding black round the horizon, and we
had a good deal of thunder and lightening : the commodore himfelf imagined what we firft defcried to be
an ifland, which feemed to rife in two rude craggy hills;
the land adjoining to it appeared to run a long way to
the S. E. We were now fteering in a S. W. direction,
and founded in 52 fathoms water. Our commander
thought himfelf embayed, and entertained little hope
of getting clear before night. We now fteered E. S. E.
the land ftill keeping the fame appearance, and the
hills looking blue, as they generally do at a fmall diftance, when feen in dark rainy weather. Many on
board afferted, that they faw the fea break upon the
fandy beaches, but after having made fail about an
hour, what had been taken for land, in a moment
vanifhed; and, to the aftonifhment of every one, proved
to have been a mere *deceptio vifus*, which feamen
                                                    call

call a fog-bank. Thefe delufions are frequently occafioned by ridges of clouds, and fometimes, in the
higher latitudes, by an extraordinary quality of the air,
to be accounted for only by the doctrine of refraction.
Others have been equally deceived by thefe kind of il-
lufions.   The mafter of a veffel, not long fince made
oath, that he had feen an ifland between the weft end of
Ireland and Newfoundland, and even diftinguifhed the
trees that grew upon it; yet it is now well known, that
no fuch ifland exifts, at leaft it could never be found,
though feveral fhips were afterwards fent out on purpofe
to feek it.   And Commodore Byron was of opinion,
that if the weather had not cleared up foon enough for
us to fee what we had taken for land difappear, every
man on board would freely have made oath that land
had been difcovered in this latitude of 43 deg. 46 min.
S. and in 60 deg. 5 min. W. longitude.   This falfe
appearance was fucceeded, on Tuefday the 13th, by
a fudden and tremendous hurricane.   Notwithftanding
the weather was extremely fine, in the afternoon the
fky grew black to windward, and a noife was heard,
which refembled the breaking of the fea upon a fhallow
beach.   The birds were obferved flying from the
quarter whence the ftorm iffued, and fhrieking through
the apprehenfion of its approach.   It was not poffible
to make the neceffary preparations before it reached us.
The fea rolled towards us in vaft billows covered with
foam.   Orders were inftantly given to hawl up the fore
fail, and let go the main fheet; but before we could
raife the main tack, the Dolphin was laid upon her
beams.   We now cut the main tack, for it was impoffible to caft it off, upon which, the main fheet ftruck
down the firft lieutenant, much bruifed him, and beat
out three of his teeth.   The main-top fail not being
quite handed was fplit to pieces.   The Tamar fplit her
main-fail, but being to the leeward, fhe had more time
to prepare; and had not fufficient warning been given
by the agitation of the fea, the Dolphin muft have been
overfet, or her mafts would have been carried away.
It was the opinion of all our people, that had this ftorm

approached with lefs warning, and more violence, or had it overtaken us in the night, the fhip muft have been loft. Our Commodore thought this guft of wind more violent than any one he had encountered; it lafted about twenty minutes, and then-fubfided. It blew, however, hard all night, and on the 14th, we had a great fwell. The fea alfo appeared as if tinged with blood, owing to its being covered with fmall red cray-fifh, of which great quantities were taken up in bafkets by the fhip's company.

On the 15th, our three lieutenants and the mafter were fo ill as to be incapable of doing their duty ; but the reft of our hands were in good health. Our latitude this day was 45 deg. 21 min. and longitude 63 deg. 2 min. E. On the 16th, we fhaped our courfe for Cape Blanco, agreeable to the chart of it, laid down in Anfon's voyage; and after many hard gales of wind, on the 17th, we faw the Cape, and for two days ftrug-gled hard to reach Port Defire. We now ftood into a bay to the fouthward of the Cape, but could find no port. On the 20th, we made Penguin Ifland, and as Port Defire was faid to be three leagues to the N. W. of it, a boat was fent out, and having found it we ftood in for land; and anchored four miles from the fhore.

On Wednefday the 21ft, we weighed in order to enter the harbour of Port Defire; but found it very rocky, and not above a quarter of a mile from fide to fide. On our failing up, the wind was at S. S. W; directly in our favour, and the weather being remarka-bly temperate, all our boats were round the fhip; but on a fudden the wind came about to the N. E. which being directly againft us, we made all poffible hafte to get our fails furled; but being within the harbour we could not return, and the tide of flood running with exceffive rapidity, we were obliged to let go both anchors, and before we could bring her up, fhe took the fhore. This was followed by a cold rainy night, rendered more melancholy and gloomy by the reflection, that the boats were all driven to fea, where every perfon

in

in them would probably perish, and that we ourselves had no reason to expect our ever getting off, as both the wind and tide were against us, but that we should be obliged to live, or perhaps perish, on this defert coast of Patagonia, several hundred leagues to the southward of any European settlement; but at length, to our great joy, our twelve-oared barge providentially drove into the harbour, by which means the ship was preserved, for without this timely assistance she must have perished, we having no boat to carry out an anchor. After many attempts, we carried out our stream anchor, which, when the tide turned, enabled us, by weighing our other anchors, to get into the middle of the harbour, where, with the Tamar in company, we moored both ships: but as it blew very hard, we were obliged to take down our yards and topmasts. Mean while two of our boats had been driven on shore, and the men suffered extremely from its raining very hard all night: but notwithstanding this they returned the next day. As to our long boat, it was carried many leagues out to sea with only two men in it; we had therefore little prospect of seeing them again; but on the 23d they returned with the boat into harbour, though they were almost starved to death with the severity of the cold and want. On their first appearance we sent a boat to their assistance, which brought them on board.

This harbour is not much more than half a mile over. On the south shore is a remarkable rock, rising from the water in the form of a steeple, which appears on entering the harbours mouth. Abreast of this rock we lay at anchor in seven or eight fathoms water, moored to the east and west, with both bowers, which we found extremely necessary, on account of the strong tide that regularly ebbs and flows every twelve hours. Indeed the ebb is so rapid, that we found by our log line it continued to run five or six knots an hour; and in ten minutes after the ebb is past, the flood returns with equal velocity: besides, the wind generally blows during the whole night out of the harbour. It is also necessary to observe, that the ground is far from afford-

ing

ing good anchorage; for as it principally confifts of light fand, it is not to be depended on, and if one anchor fhould ftart, while the tide is rufhing in, the fhip would immediately take the fhore, before the other anchors would poffibly bring her up. However it may be fairly conjectured, that there is firmer anchorage farther up the harbour, efpecially for a fhip that requires only a fmall draught of water; for on fending our boats two or three leagues up, they found good anchorage and lefs tide. On the north fhore, about four or five miles above the before mentioned rock, there are fome white cliffs that rife to a great height, and at a diftance nearly refembling chalk, though their whitenefs is merely owing to great flocks of birds voiding their dung upon them. The country all around is likewife interfperfed with rocks, high and craggy, but between each precipice the ground is covered with long and coarfe grafs. The valleys form a barren comfortlefs profpect, in which there is nothing to entertain the eye but great numbers of wild beafts and birds, and many large heaps of bones that lie fcattered about, efpecially by the fide of every ftream of water. But we faw no Indians, nor the leaft fign of the human fpecies. Among the animals we found near the fhore a great number of feals of different fizes. Thefe live both on the land and in the water, and are fo fierce that they cannot be encountered without danger. The head has fome refemblance to that of a dog with cropt ears, but in fome it is of a rounder, and in others of a longer make. They have large eyes, and whifkers about the mouth: their teeth are extremely fharp, and fo ftrong, that they can bite a very thick ftick in two. Though without legs, they have a kind of feet or fins, which anfwer the different purpofes of fwimming and walking; thefe have five toes like fingers, armed with nails, and joined together with a thin fkin like thofe of a goofe; by the help of which they fhuffel along very faft through the fand, or over the fmall rocks on the fhore. Their fkins, which are covered with fhort thick hair, are black, but frequently fpotted with different

colours,

colours, as white, red, or grey, and are often manufactured into caps, waistcoats, tobacco-pouches, and the like. The old ones, which are about eight feet long, make a hoarse barking, somewhat like a dog, and the young ones mew like a cat. The largest of them will yield about half a barrel of oil; and their skins, if properly cured, would be of considerable value. Some of our men used to eat the young ones, and their entrails were thought by them as good as those of a hog. Here are likewise great numbers of guanicoes, a kind of wild deer, called by some Peruvian sheep, their backs being covered with a very fine soft wool. They have a long neck, and the head resembles that of a sheep; but they have very long legs, and are cloven footed like a deer, with a short bushy tail. These are as large as a middle sized cow, and when freed from the skin and offal, weigh about two hundred and a half. Their flesh is excellent, either fresh or salted, and after so long a voyage, was very serviceable in refreshing our seamen. They herd together in companies of twenty or more, and the method we pursued in killing them was by sending a party of men in the night, who searched for them by the springs of water to which they resort; and there lying in ambush among the bushes, they had an opportunity of shooting them at their pleasure; yet these animals, when sensible of danger, suddenly escape; for they are very swift of foot. In this place are also hares of a prodigious size; for they weigh, while alive near 20 pounds, and, when skinned, are as big as a fox. These are chiefly inhabitants of the valleys. With respect to the feathered race, here are a great number of ostriches, but not near so large as those in Africa. These birds, which are remarkable for the length of their necks and legs, and the shortness of their wings, have been considered by naturalists as holding the same place among birds, as camels do among beasts. Their small head has some resemblance to that of a goose, and their plumage consists of grey feathers covering the back as far as the tail, but those on the belly are white. They have four toes on each
foot

foot, one behind and three before; and from the shortness of their wings, are unable to raise their bodies from the ground; yet by their help they will run with amazing swiftness. We found great quantities of their eggs, some of which are of an enormous size. There is here also another extraordinary large bird, which we called the wild eagle, whose body is about the size of a large turkey of 30 pounds weight. They have a very stately appearance, and are of a dark brown hue, intermixed with different coloured feathers; but what is most curious in these birds, is their having a crown on their heads, and a ring of feathers round their necks. The barrels of the large feathers, or quills in their wings, are each half an inch in diameter, and their wings when extended reach 14 feet from point to point. The penguin, which is also found here, is about the size of a goose; but instead of feathers is covered with a kind of ash-coloured down. Its wings, which resemble those of young goslins, are too short and unfledged to permit it to fly, but are of use to it in swimming, and also to assist it in leaping along upon the ground. These birds appear heavy and inactive upon land, where they seem regardless of danger, and are easily knocked down with a stick; yet are active enough upon the water. Their flesh, however, is disagreeable, on account of its having a fishy taste; but their eggs are very good. In the evening they retire to the rocks near the sea, where they stay till the morning. But to return to the history of our voyage.

On Saturday the 24th, both ships being safely moored in the harbour, the commodore went on shore and shot a hare, weighing 26 pounds, and saw others which appeared to be as large as fawns. Landing again on the 25th, he found the barrel of an old musquet, with the king's broad arrow on it, and an oar of a singular form. The musquet barrel had suffered so much by the weather, that it might be crumbled to dust between the fingers; it was probably left there by the Wager's people, or by Sir John Narborough, when he was in these parts. Here were some remains of fire, but no inhabitants

inhabitants could be discovered. This party shot several wild ducks, and a hare, which ran two miles before it dropped, with the ball in its body; the flesh of which animal was of an excellent flavour, and as white as snow. Here they found the skull and bones of a man; and caught a young guanicoe, very beautiful, and which grew very tame on board, but died a short time afterwards. On the 27th, we discovered two springs of tolerable good water; and on the 28th, a tun of it was brought on board; but it is to be observed, the mineral qualities of these springs unfortunately prevented their being of any use to us in supplying our ship with water; and we could not even find a quantity of pure wholesome water fit for our present use. We had sunk several wells to a considerable depth, where the ground appeared moist, but upon visiting them, had the mortification to find, that, altogether, they would not yield more than thirty gallons in 24 hours. On the south shore the rocks are not so numerous as on the north side; and there are more hills and deep valleys; but they are covered only with high grass, and a few small shrubs. Hence this is but a bad place to touch at, by any ship that is under the necessity of wooding and watering. This day, when a party went on shore, they saw such a number of birds take flight, as darkened the sky, nor could the men walk a step without treading on eggs; and as the birds hovered over their heads at a little distance, the men would knock down many of them with stones and sticks. After some time they dressed and would eat the eggs they had carried off, though young birds were in most of them. They saw no traces of inhabitants on either side the river, but numerous herds of guanicoes, which were exceeding shy. The surgeon of the Dolphin, one of the party, shot a tyger-cat, a small, but very fierce animal. Some of the crew being sent on shore for water, on the 30th, two of them discovered a large tyger lying on the ground. The animal taking no notice of them, they threw stones at him, but could by no means provoke him. He remained on the spot, and continued

2   stretched

stretched on the ground, till their companions, who were a little way behind them, came up, and then he walked away very leisurely.

During our stay at this place, our men were employed in fitting and completing the ship for sea; and the carpenters were particularly obliged to fish our mainmast, which had been damaged at the head. Others, as has been already mentioned, were employed as rangers to go in search of water, though without success; but when they were on this duty, they had a double allowance of brandy, and small tents were erected on shore for their own use. Before our departure, we also sunk two casks, one of them on the north shore from the place of anchorage, a-breast of the rock in form of a steeple. The other cask was sunk on the south shore, two miles and a half to the S. S. W. of the steeple rock, and near a gentle declivity, on which we erected a post twelve feet high from the ground, with a piece of board nailed across it by way of mark. At length having equipped the ship for sea, and received proper ballast from the shore, signal was made for sailing. Our crew were greatly refreshed by the provisions they met with at this place, having had the flesh of the guanicoes served three times a week, which they found to be delicious food; and this, doubtless, contributed greatly to their continuing in a good state of health, as were also all on board our consort the Tamar: besides a perfect unanimity subsisted between the officers and men of both ships, who maintained the most friendly intercourse with each other, whenever they had an opportunity. On Saturday, the 1st of December, our cutter being thoroughly repaired, we took her on board, and on the 2nd, we struck our tents, which had been set up at the watering-place. This bears about S. S. E. of the steeple rock, from which it is distant about two miles and an half.

On Wednesday, the 5th, we unmoored, and between five and six in the evening weighed. We now got under sail, having fair and pleasant weather, and steered out E. N. E. with a favourable gale at N. N. W. directing

recting our courfe from Port Defire, in fearch of Pepy's Ifland, faid to have been feen by Cowley, who lays it down in latitude 47 deg. but makes no mention of its longitude. In our charts it is laid down in longitude of 64 deg. from the meridian of London, bearing E. by S. of Cape Blanco ; and it received its name in honour of Samuel Pepys, Efq. fecretary to James duke of York, when lord high admiral of England; who pretended, that it had not only a good harbour, in which a thoufand fhips might fafely ride at anchor, but that it abounded with wild fowls, and was extremely convenient for wooding and watering; but after many unfuccefsful attempts to difcover this ifland, in order to procure a frefh fupply of wood and water, we had the mortification to find, that all our endeavours were in vain and ineffectual. We were therefore obliged to defift from the fearch, and on the 11th, at noon, the Commodore refolved to ftand in for the main, both fhips being in want of wood and water. Having changed our courfe, large whales were obferved to fwim frequently about the fhip, and birds in great numbers flew round us. On the 15th, being in latitude 50 deg. 33 min. S. and in 66 deg. 59 min. W. longitude, we were, about fix in the evening, overtaken by the hardeft gale at S.W. that the Commodore had ever been in, with a fea ftill higher than any he had feen in going round Cape Horn with lord Anfon. The ftorm continued the whole night, during which we lay to under a balanced mizen, and fhipped many heavy feas.

On Sunday the 16th, at eight o'clock A. M. it began to fubfide ; at ten we made fail under our courfes; and on the 18th, in latitude 51 deg. 8 min. S. and in longitude 71 deg. 4 min. W. we faw land from the maft head. Cape Virgin Mary (the north entrance of the Strait of Magellan) bore S. 19 deg. 50 min. W. diftant nineteen leagues. The land, like that near Port Defire, was of the downy kind, without a fingle tree. On the 19th, we ftood into a deep bay, at the bottom of which appeared a harbour ; but we found it barred, the fea breaking quite from one fide of it to the other. At low water it was rocky and almoft dry; and we had only fix fathom when we ftood out again. In this place we obferved porpoifes, which were milk white, with black fpots, purfuing the fifh, of which there were great numbers.

Thurfday, the 20th, we had little wind with thunder and lightning from the S. W. at four o'clock A. M. we faw an extremity of land belonging to Cape Fairweather, extending from S. to W. We were now at the diftance of four leagues from the fhore; when founding, we found twenty-five fathoms water, with foft ground, and the latitude of the Cape to be in 51 deg. 30 min. S. We never fteered above five or fix miles from the fhore, and in paffing between the laft-mentioned Cape and Cape Blanco, we had no founding with twenty-five fathoms line. The coaft here appears in white cliffs, with level buff land, not unlike that about Dover and the South Forelands. We now came in fight of Cape Virgin Mary, from which we were diftant five leagues, and alfo the land named Terra del Fuego. We found the coaft to lie S. S. E. very different from Sir John Narborough's defcription; and a long fpit of fand running to the fouthward of the Cape for more than a league. We had very fair weather all the morning, and at three o'clock P. M. Cape Virgin Mary bore N. W. half N. About two leagues to the weftward, a low neck of land runs off from the cape; we approached it without danger, and at fix, anchored with the beft bower in fifteen fathoms water, at which time the cape bore N. half E. about feven miles; but the Tamar was fo far to leeward, that fhe could not fetch the anchoring ground, and therefore kept under way all night. On the 21ft, at three o'clock A. M. we weighed, and again got under fail; and at fix the extremes of Terra del Fuego appeared, extending from the S. E. by S. to the S. W. by S. four or five leagues diftant. At eight we perceived a good deal of fmoke iffuing from different quarters, and, on our nearer approach faw plainly a number of people on horfeback. This is the coaft of Patagonia, and the place where the half ftarved remains

of

of the crew of the Wager, as they were paffing the
ftrait in their boat, after the lofs of the fhip, faw a
number of horfemen, who waved what appeared to
them like white handkerchiefs, inviting them to come
on fhore. Mr. Bulkley, the gunner of the Wager, who
publifhed an account of her voyage and misfortunes,
fays, that they were in doubt whether thefe people were
Europeans, who had been fhipwrecked on the coaft, or
natives of the country about the river Gallagoes. At
ten o'clock, we anchored in fourteen fathoms on the
north fhore, and faw Cape Virgin Mary, which appeared
over the low neck of land to the E. N. E. and Point
Poffeffion to the W. by S. We were now about a mile
from the land, and had no fooner came to an anchor,
than we faw with our glaffes a number of horfemen,
abreaft of the Dolphin, riding backward and forward,
and waving fomething white, as an invitation for us to
come on fhore. Immediately our twelve oared boat
was hoifted out, which was manned with the commodore, Mr. Marfhal, the fecond lieutenant, the journalift, to whom we are indebted principally for the hiftory of this voyage, and a party of men all well armed.
Mr. Cumming, our firft lieutenant, followed in the fix
oared cutter.

On our firft approaching the coaft, evident figns of
furprize were vifible among fome in our boat, on feeing
men of a moft enormous fize, to the number of about
five hundred; while others, perhaps, to encourage the
reft, obferved, that thofe gigantic people were as much
furprized at the fight of our mufquets, as we were at
feeing them; though it is highly probable they did not
know their ufe, and had never heard the report of a
gun: however, this was fufficient to remind us, that
our fire-arms gave us an advantage much fuperior to
that derived from ftature and perfonal ftrength. The
people on fhore as we advanced kept waving and hallooing; but we could not perceive they had among
them weapons of any kind. When we had rowed
within twenty yards of the fhore, we lay on our oars,
and obferved fome on foot near the beach, but the

greater

greater part were on horseback, drawn up upon a stony
spit, which ran a good way into the sea, and where it
was very difficult to land, the water being shallow,
and the stones very large. They now shouted with
great vociferation, and by their countenances seemed
eagerly desirous of having us land. After the most
amicable signs which we were capable of understanding, or they of giving, a signal was made for them to
retire backwards, to a little distance, with which they
readily complied. The commodore now held a short
consultation with his officers on the propriety of landing, when one, fired with the thoughts of making a
full discovery in regard to these Indians, made a motion to approach nearer and jump on shore, but the
commodore objected to it, and would not suffer any
man to go before himself. In a short time we attempted
to land, most of our boat's crew being up to the middle in water. The commodore, regardless of such
kind of difficulties, pushed resolutely on, and, having
with great intrepidity leaped on shore, drew up his
men upon the beach, with the officers at their head,
and ordered them not to move from that station, till he
should either call or beckon to them. Commodore Byron now advanced alone towards the Indians; but perceiving they retreated as he advanced, upon this he
made signs, that one of them should come forward.
These being understood, one who appeared afterwards
to be a chief, advanced towards him. His stature was
gigantic, he being nearly seven feet high. Round one
of his eyes was a circle of black paint, and one of
white round the other: the rest of his face was painted
with various colours, and he had the skin of some wild
beast, with the hair turned inwards, thrown over his
shoulders. His hair was long and black, hanging down
behind. The commodore and Indian chief having
paid their compliments to each other, in a language
mutually unintelligible to the person to whom it was
addressed, they walked together towards the main body
of the natives, few of whom were shorter than the
above-mentioned standard, and the women large in
proportion.

proportion. Mr. Byron now made signs for them to
fit down on the ground which they did, and the old
men chanted fome ftrains, in a moft doleful cadence,
with an air of ferious folemnity. The eyes of no one
perfon were painted with the fame colours, fome being
white and red, and fome black and white. Their teeth
are remarkably even, well fet, and as white as ivory.
Our commodore, who had the precaution to take with
him on fhore a number of trinkets, fuch as ftrings of
beads, and the like, in order to convince them of our
amicable difpofition, diftributed them with great freedom, giving to each fome as far as they went. He then
took a whole piece of green ribbon, and putting the
end into the hands of the firft Indian, he continued it
to the next, and fo on as far as it would reach; while
none of them attempted to pull it from the reft, and
yet they feemed more delighted with it, than with the
beads. When the ribbon was thus extended, he pulled
out a pair of fciffars, and cut it between each two of
thofe who held it, leaving about a yard in the poffeffion
of each, which he afterwards tied about their heads.
It was remarked, that though the prefents were infuf-
ficient to fupply them all, not one preffed forward from
the ftation affigned him, nor feemed to envy the fuperior good fortune of his neighbour. They were now
fo delighted with the different trinkets, which they
had an opportunity of viewing, as the beads hung round
their necks, and fell down before on their bofoms, that
the commodore could fcarcely reftrain them from carefs-
ing him, particularly the women, whofe large and maf-
culine features correfponded with the enormous fize of
their bodies. We faw fome infants in their mothers arms,
whofe features, confidering their age, bore the fame proportion to thofe of their parents. Except the fkins which
thefe Indians wore, moft of them were naked, a few
only having upon their legs a kind of boot, with a
fhort pointed ftick faftened to each heel, which ferved
as a fpur. Some of their women had collars round
their necks. Among them was one of the gigantic
fize, and moft difagreeably painted, who had her
hair

hair adorned with beads of blue glafs, hanging in two divifions down before her fhoulders; fhe had alfo bracelets of pale gold, or brafs, upon her arms. From whence this finery could be procured was a fubject of wonder, as from their great amazement at firft feeing us, we conjectured, that they had never beheld any of our dwarfifh race before. It may, however, be concluded from the accounts of Sir John Narborough, and others, who have taken notice of thefe Indians, that they doubtlefs change their fituation with the fun, fpending their fummer here, and in winter removing farther to the north, in order to enjoy the benefit of a milder climate. Hence Sir John and others have related, that they faw men of an uncommon fize, at leaft eight or ten degrees more to the northward; whence it may be reafonably conjectured, that during one part of the year, they may have fome intercourfe with the Indians bordering on the Spanifh fettlements, and that from them they might have purchafed thefe ornaments. There are thofe who may defpife the fondnefs of thefe Goliah-like Indians for glafs, beads, and other trifles which among civilized nations are held in no eftimation; but fuch fhould remember, that, in themfelves, the ornaments of unpolifhed and civil life are equal, and that thofe who live nearly in a ftate of nature, have nothing that refembles glafs, fo much as glafs refembles a diamond; the value which we fet upon a diamond, therefore, is more capricious than the value they fet upon glafs. The love of ornament feems to be a ruling paffion in human nature, and the fplendid tranfparency of glafs, and the regular figure of a bead excite pleafing ideas. The pleafure which a diamond gives among us is, principally, by its being a mark of diftinction, thus gratifying our vanity, which is independent of, and frequently over-rules natural tafte, which is gratified by certain lines and hues, to which we give the name of beauty: it muft be remembered alfo, that an Indian is more diftinguifhed by a glafs button or bead, than any individual among us by a diamond; though, perhaps, the fame facrifice is not made to his

4   vanity,

vanity, as the poffeffion of his finery is rather a teftimony of his good fortune, than of his influence or
power in confequence of his having what, as the common medium of all earthly poffeffions, is fuppofed to
confer virtual fuperiority, and intrinfic advantage. One
of the Indians fhewed our commodore the bowl of a
tobacco pipe, made of red earth, and by figns intimated that he wanted fome tobacco, none of which they
had among them.   On this the commodore beckoned
to the feamen, who ftill remained drawn up on the
beach, three or four of whom inftantly running forward, the Indians were alarmed, and jumping up in
an inftant were preparing to retire, as it was fuppofed,
to fetch their arms. The Commodore therefore ftopped
the failors, directing one of them only to come forward, when he had got all the tobacco they could mufter
among them.   This reftored good harmony, and all
the Indians refumed their places, except an old man
who fung a long fong, at nearly the conclufion of which
Mr. Cumming brought the tobacco.   This gentleman,
though fix feet two inches high, was himfelf aftonifhed
at the diminutive figure he cut among the ftrangers, who
were broad and mufcular in proportion to their height.
Their language appeared to us to be nothing more than
a jargon of founds, without any mixture of the Spanifh
or Portuguefe, the only European tongues of which it
was poffible for them to obtain any knowledge, and with
which it is probable it would have been mixed, had they
any immediate intercourfe with the Spaniards or Portuguefe of South America.   We muft not omit, that
before our landing, the greateft part of thefe Patagonians were on horfeback, but on feeing us gain the
fhore, they difmounted, and left their horfes at fome
diftance.   Thefe horfes were not large, nor in good
cafe, yet they were well broken, and very fwift, but
bore no proportion to the fize of their riders.   The
bridle was a leathern thong, with a fmall piece of wood
that ferved for a bit, and the faddles refembled the pads
in ufe among the country people in England.   Their
women rode aftride, and both men and women without
                                          ftirrups;

stirrups; yet they galloped fearlessly over the spit upon
which we landed, the stones of which were large, loose
and slippery. These people looked frequently towards
the sun with an air of adoration, and made motions
with their fingers, in order to make us sensible of any
particular circumstance they wanted us to understand.
They appeared to be of an amiable and friendly disposition, and seemed to live in great unanimity among
themselves. After they had been presented with the
tobacco, they made signs for us to go with them to the
smoke which we saw at a distance, and at the same time
pointed to their mouths, as if intimating an inclina-
tion to give us refreshment; but their number at present
being so greatly superior to ours, and it being not im-
probable, that still greater multitudes might surround
us unawares from the inland country, our commodore,
who was equally remarkable for his prudence and
bravery, thought it not adviseable to venture any farther from the water side, and therefore intimated, that
he must return to the ship, on which they sat down
again, apparently much concerned. At length, after
making signs that we would depart, with the most
plausible promises, by gestures, of returning again to
them from the ship, we left these Patagonian Indians,
who were so distressed and afflicted at our departure,
that we heard their lamentations for a considerable time
after. When the commodore took his leave of them
they kept their seats, not one offering to detain, or
follow him. Another officer on board the Dolphin,
in his account of these extraordinary people, adds, that
they all appeared to be very sagacious, easily understood
the signals or intimations which our people made to
them, and behaved with great complacency and good
nature. Such is the informations we have received
from the papers of our journalist, whose veracity required no proof among those who have had the pleasure
of his acquaintance; but as evidences in corroboration
of his assertions, and the truth of the facts, we shall in-
sert here the following account of the Patagonians,
which we have received from a gentleman, who was also

an

an officer in one of the ships, and on shore at the same
time with our author.

The Dolphin having entered ten or twelve leagues
into the mouth of the straits of Magellan, the men on
deck observed thirty or forty people of an extraordinary
stature, standing on the beach of the continent, who
looking attentively on them, made friendly signs, by
which they seemed to invite them to come on shore;
while others who stood aloft, discovered with their
glasses a much greater number, about a mile farther up
the country; but ascribed their apparent size to the
fogginess of the air. The ship happened at this instant
to be becalmed; the honourable Mr. Byron, thinking
no time would be lost by going ashore, resolved to land,
in order to see these Indians, and learn what he could
of their manners; he therefore ordered a six-oared boat
for himself and officers; and one of twelve oars to be
filled with men and arms, as a security, in case there
should be any attempt to surprize or injure him, or any
of those who went with him; though the people on
shore did not seem to have any thing like an offensive
weapon among them. On the commodore's landing, in
company with his lieutenant, he made signs to the Indians, who were crowding round him, to retire, which
they very readily did, to the distance of thirty or forty
yards. He then, attended by his lieutenant, advanced
towards them, about twenty yards, and their number
was soon increased to upwards of five hundred men,
women, and children. Several civilities at this time
passed on both sides, the Indians expressing their joy
and satisfaction, by singing uncouth songs, shaking
hands, and sitting with looks of pleasure, with their
wives and children round the commodore, who distributed among them ribbons, and strings of beads, with
which they appeared highly delighted. He tied necklaces round the necks of several of the women, who
seemed to be from seven to eight feet high; but the
men were for the most part about nine feet in height,
and some more. The commodore himself measures
full six feet, and though he stood on tip-toe, he could

but juſt reach the crown of one of the Indians head, who was not, by far, the talleſt among them. The men are well made, broad ſet, and of a prodigious ſtrength. Both ſexes are of a copper colour; they have long black hair, and were covered partly with ſkins, which were faſtened about their necks by a thong; the ſkins worn by the men being looſe, but the womens were girt cloſe with a kind of belt. Many of the men and women rode on horſes, which were about fifteen hands and a half high, all of them aſtride; and they had among them ſome dogs which had a picked ſnout like a fox, and were nearly of the ſize of a middling pointer. Theſe friendly people invited the commodore, and all thoſe who were landed, to go with them up the country, ſhewing a diſtant ſmoke, and pointing to their mouths, as if they intended to give us a repaſt; and in return, the commodore invited the Indians to come on board, by pointing to his ſhip; but neither of them accepted of the other's invitation, and therefore having paſſed two hours in an agreeable converſation, carried on wholly by ſigns, they parted with all the marks of friendſhip. The country (obſerves this gentleman) is ſandy; but diverſified with ſmall hills, covered with a ſhort graſs, and with ſhrubs, none of which, as Sir John Narborough has long before remarked, is large enough to make the helve of an hatchet.

Another gentleman on board has favoured us with an account that exactly tallies with the above, with theſe additional circumſtances. That when they were ten or twelve leagues within the ſtraits, they ſaw through their glaſſes many people on ſhore of a prodigious ſize: which extraordinary magnitude they thought to be a deception, occaſioned by the hazineſs of the atmoſphere, it being then ſomewhat foggy; but on coming near the land, they appeared of ſtill greater bulk, and made amicable ſigns to our people to come on ſhore. That when the ſhip failed on to find a proper place of landing, they made lamentations, as if they were afraid our people were going off. He alſo ſays, there were near ꟷꟷ of them, and about one third of the men on horſes

4   not

not much larger than ours; and that they rode with their knees up the horses withers, having no stirrups. That there were women, and many children, whom some of our people took up in their arms and kissed, which the Indians beheld with much seeming satisfaction. That by way of affection and esteem, they took his hand between theirs, and patted it; and that some of those he saw were ten feet high, well proportioned, and well featured; their skins were of a warm copper colour, and they had neither offensive nor defensive weapons. He also says, that they seemed particularly pleased with lieutenant Cumming, on account of his stature, he being six feet two inches high, and that some of them patted him on the shoulder, but their hands fell with such force, that it affected his whole frame.

There is nothing about which travellers are more divided, than concerning the height of these Patagonians. M. de Bougainville, who visited another part of this coast in the year 1767, asserts, that the Patagonians are not gigantic; and that what makes them appear so, is their prodigious broad shoulders, the size of their heads, and the thickness of all their limbs. Some time before the hon. Mr. Byron made this voyage, it was the subject of warm contest among men of science in this country, whether a race of men upon the coast of Patagonia, above the common stature, did really exist; and the contradictory reports, made by ocular witnesses, concerning this fact, tended greatly to perplex the question. It appears that, during one hundred years, almost all navigators, of whatever country, agree in affirming the existence of a race of giants upon those coasts; but during another century, a much greater number agree in denying the fact, treating their predecessors as idle fabulists. *Barbenais* speaks of a race of giants in South America; and the *Unca Garcilassa de la Vega* in his history of *Peru*, is decisively on the same side of the question. For *quenado* lib. 1. chap. 13 and 14, records the American traditions concerning a race of giants, and a deluge

which

which happpened in remote times, in these parts. Magellan, Loaisa, Sarmiento, and Nodal, among the Spaniards; and Cavendish, Hawkins, and Knivet, among the English; Sebald, Oliver de Noort, le Maire, and Spilberg, among the Dutch, together with some French voyagers, all bear testimony to the fact, that the inhabitants of Patagonia were of a gigantic height: on the contrary, Winter, the Dutch admiral Hermite, Froger, in De Gennes's narrative, and Sir John Narborough, deny it. Sir Francis Drake, who sailed through the straits, says nothing concerning it; and his silence on this head can only be accounted for on the supposition, either that he saw no inhabitants on the coast in his passage, or that there was nothing extraordinary in their appearance. To reconcile these different opinions, we have only to suppose that the country is inhabited by distinct races of men, one of whom is of a size beyond the ordinary pitch, the other not gigantic, though perhaps tall and remarkably large limbed; and that each possess parts of the country separate and remote from each other. That some giants inhabit these regions can now no longer be doubted; since the concurrent testimony of late English navigators, particularly Commodore Byron, Captains Wallis and Carteret, gentlemen of unquestionable veracity, establish the fact, from their not only having seen and conversed with these people, but even measured them. But it is time now to proceed with the history of our voyage.

On Friday the 21st of December, at three o'clock P. M. we weighed, and worked up the strait of Magellan, which is here about three leagues broad, not with a view to pass through it, but to take in a proper stock of wood and water, not chusing to trust wholly to the finding of Falkland's Islands, which we determined afterwards to seek. At eight in the evening we anchored in 25 fathoms water, at the distance of three miles N. N. E. from Port Possession, in view of two remarkable hummocks, which Bulkley,

ley, from their appearance, diftinguifhed by the name
of the Affes Ears. On the 22nd, at three o'clock
A. M. we weighed and fteered S. W. by W. about
four leagues, when the water fhoaled to fix fathoms
and a half, we being then over a bank of which no
notice has hitherto been taken, and full three leagues
from the fhore; but in two or three cafts of the log-
line, it deepened to 13 fathoms. When the water
was fhalloweft, the Affes Ears bore N. W. by W.
and the north point of the firft narrow W. by S. diftant
fomewhat more than five miles. We now fteered
S. W. by S. two leagues to the firft narrow, as it is
ufually called, which brought us through. This narrow is about three miles over, and is the narroweft
part of the ftraits; and through it a regular tide runs
with great rapidity. In this run we faw an Indian
upon the fouth fhore, who kept waving to us as long
as we were in fight; alfo fome guanicoes upon the
hills. The land is on each fide furrounded with
thefe; but the country is entirely barren without a
a fingle tree, yet we here obferved great quantities of
fmoke from different parts of the fhore. The courfe
of the firft narrow to a little fea, or the found, is
S. W. by W. about eight leagues. The land on each
fide is of a moderate height, and rather higheft on
the north fhore, but runs low towards the fecond
narrow. On founding from the firft to the fecond
narrow, we found from 20 to 25 fathoms water, with
good anchorage; and it was there about feven leagues
from the north fhore to the ifland of Terra del
Fuego. At the entrance or eaft end of the fecond
narrow lies Cape Gregory, which is a white cliff of a
moderate height; and a little to the northward of
it is a fandy bay, in which you may ride in eight
fathoms water, with very good anchorage. When
abreaft of Cape Gregory we fteered S. W. half W.
five leagues, through the fecond narrow, having a
depth of water from 20 to 25 fathoms. We went
out of the weft end of this narrow about noon, and
fteered three leagues fouth for Elizabeth's Ifland.

At

At this part of the narrow on the fouth fhore, is a white headland, called Sweepftakes Foreland. The wind being right againft us we anchored in feven fathom. The ifland bore S. S. E. about a mile diftant, and Bartholomew's Ifland bore E. S. E. In the evening fix Indians came down to the water-fide, and continued for fome time waving and hallooing to us, but feeing their labour fruitlefs, they went away. Between the firft and fecond narrows the flood fets to the S. W. and the ebb to the N. E. but being paft the fecond narrow, the courfe with a leading wind is S. by E. three leagues between St. Bartholomew's and Elizabeth's Iflands, where the channel is one mile and a half over. The flood fets through to the fouthward with great vehemence and rapidity, fo that when near, it appears like breakers, and the tide round the iflands fets different ways.

On Sunday the 23d we had very moderate weather, but hazy, with intervals of frefh breezes. In the morning we weighed, and worked between the two iflands: we got over on the north fhore before the tide was fpent, and anchored in 10 fathom. St. George's Ifland bore N. E. by N. diftant three leagues; a point of land, which we named Porpoife Point, N. by W. diftant five miles, and the fouthernmoft land S. by E. diftant about two miles. In the evening we again got under fail, and fteered S. by E. and at ten o'clock we anchored about a mile from the north fhore, in 13 fathoms. Sandy Point now bore S. by E. diftant four miles; Porpoife Point N. N. W. three leagues, and St. George's Ifland N. E. four leagues. On the 24th, we fent the boat to found between Elizabeth's and St. Bartholomew's Iflands, and found it a very good channel, with deep water. On this occafion we faw a number of Indians, who hallooed to us from Elizabeth's Ifland. Both the men and women were of the middle fize, well made, and with fmooth black hair. Their complexion was olive-coloured, and their bodies were rubbed over with red earth, mixed with greafe. They are very

active

active and swift of foot. Their cloathing consists of skins of seals, otters, and guanicoes, sewed together in a piece about four feet square, and wrapped round their bodies. They have likewise a cap made of the skins of fowls with the feathers on; and upon their feet were pieces of skin to answer the purpose of shoes: besides, some of the females had pieces of skin fastened round their waists. The women however had no caps, but wore a kind of necklace formed of shells. Several of the men had nothing wrapped round them, but were entirely naked. This day the Commodore, accompanied by his second lieutenant landed upon Sandy Point, where they found plenty of wood, with exceeding good water, and for four miles of their walk the shore was very pleasant. A fine level country is over the point, and the soil to all appearance is extremely rich. The ground was covered with different kinds of flowers, that perfumed the air with their fragrance, among which, where the blossoms had been shed, we saw berries innumerable, even the grass was intermixed with peas in blossom. In this luxuriant herbage, a multitude of birds were feeding, which on acount of their uncommon beautiful plumage, we called painted geese. In our walk from Sandy Point, which was more than 12 miles, we saw no part of the shore where a boat could land without great danger, the water being every where shoal, and the sea breaking very high. In little recesses of the woods, and always near to fresh water, we discovered a great number of wigwams, belonging to the Indians, which had been very lately occupied, for in some of them the fires were scarcely extinguished. Plenty of wild celery, and a variety of plants, were seen in many places, the utility of which to seamen in a long voyage is well known. We returned in the evening to the ships, which we found at anchor in Sandy Bay, in 10 fathoms water, and at the distance of about half a mile from the shore. During our absence, some of our men were employed in hauling the seine, and in three hours

had

had caught a great quantity of fish, of an extraordinary size; among which were sixty large mullets. A shooting party had good sport; for the place abounds with geese, teal, snipes, and other birds. This excellent food was, especially at this time, very acceptable, for the keen air of this place had made our people so hungry, that they could have eaten three times their allowance. By a good observation we found our latitude to be 53 deg. 10 min. S.

On Tuesday the 25th, being Christmas-day, we weighed at eight o'clock, A. M. and with little wind, steered S. by E. along-side of the shore between two and three miles, but had no founding with a line of 40 fathoms. Every thing here was in the greatest perfection, with respect to the appearance of the trees, and the verdure of the lands, which in different places afford a most enchanting prospect; and many parts of the shore have pasture for sheep or cows, which in such long voyages are generally on board. At this time of the year, the sun is 17 hours above the horizon, these islands being situated nearly at the same distance from the equator, as the middle part of Great Britain, only one to the south, and the other to the north. In sailing towards the South Pole, the same alteration is found as in steering towards the north, till you run between 60 and 70 degrees, when the westerly winds generally prevailing in the southern ocean, and blowing very furiously in the months of April, May, June, July, August, and September, there is no probability of sailing round the cape in these months, for which reason ships seldom attempt it, unless in the proper season. At three P. M. we cast anchor in 18 fathoms water, Sandy Point bearing N. N. W. three leagues and the south point of Fresh Water Bay, S. E. half E. two miles. The tide here runs very slow, but rises considerably by the shore, where we observed it to flow 16 feet. The land here is diversified with woods, and abounds with water; in some places it rises very high, and is covered with perpetual snow. On the 26th we weighed, and steered S. S. E. for Port Famine. The

northernmost

northernmoft point, called St. Anne's, at noon, bore S. by E. half E. diftant three leagues. A reef of rocks runs out from this point S. E. by E. about two miles; and the water will fuddenly fhoal from 60 to 20 fathoms, at the diftance of two cables length from the reef. The point itfelf is very fteep, and care muft be taken in ftanding into Port Famine, for the water fhoals very fuddenly, and at more than a mile from the fhore there is but nine feet water, when the tide is out. Soundings will foon be got by hauling clofe round St. Anne's Point; but when there is no more than feven fathoms, it will not be fafe to go farther in.

On Thurfday the 27th, we anchored at noon in Port Famine. Our fituation was extremely eligible, for we were fheltered from all winds, except the S. E. which feldom blows, and was a fhip to be driven on fhore in the bottom of the bay, fhe could not receive any damage, for it is all fine foft ground. In this harbour may be found a confiderable quantity of excellent wood, either green or dry, the latter lying along the fhore on both fides the ftraits, which are almoft covered with the trees that have been blown down from the banks, and drifted by the high winds. Thefe trees are fomewhat like our birch, but are of fo confiderable a fize, that the trunks of fome of them are two feet and a half in diameter, and 60 feet in length. Many of thefe were cut down for our carpenter's ufe, who found, that when properly dried, they were very ferviceable, though not fit for mafts. As to drift wood, there is a quantity fufficient to have furnifhed a thoufand fail.

Port Famine obtained its name from a party of Spaniards who had planted a colony on the fhore; but for want of a regular fupply of provifions, were ftarved to death. There are ftill fome remains of buildings, though they are now almoft covered with earth. We faw them on a hill, that has been cleared of wood, and which is not far from where our fhips lay. The river Sedger difcharges itfelf into the bay. This river is about half a cable length broad at the entrance, and is juft navigable for boats. In going into it we met with

No. 26.   5 N

two flats, one on the starboard-side, and the other on
the larboard, which we discovered at half ebb; these
render it somewhat difficult to go up the river, except
after half flood, when it may be navigated with great
pleasure and ease, by keeping in the middle of the
channel. About two miles up the river it is not above
30 yards over, at which place we found on our right,
a fine gravelly steep beach, so that the boats had
the convenience of coming along-side of it, in order
to receive the water casks, which we found to be
excellent. The Commodore, with a party, went up the
river four miles, but could proceed no farther, the
trees which had fallen across the stream impeding
the boat's way; one of the stumps of them having made
a hole in her bottom, she was immediately filled with
water; but, with difficulty they hauled her on shore,
and contrived to stop the leak, so that they made a
shift to return in her to the ship. This river has perhaps as beautiful an appearance as it is possible for the
most luxuriant fancy to conceive. Its agreeable windings are various; and on each side is a fine grove of
stately trees, whose lofty heads jut over the river; and
form a pleasant shade. Some of them are of a great
height, and more than eight feet in diameter, which is
proportionably more than eight yards in circumference;
so that four men joining hands could not compass
them; among others, we saw the pepper-tree, or
winter's-bark, in great plenty. To complete this delightful spot, the wild notes of different kind of birds
are heard on all sides, and the aromatic smell of the
various sorts of flowers which adorn its banks, seem to
unite in gratifying the senses of the inchanted stranger.
The flowers with which in many places the ground is
covered, are not inferior to those that are commonly
found in our gardens, either in beauty or fragrance.
Such are the charms which nature has lavished on a
spot, where the Indians alone can behold its beauties;
while they are probably insensible of those attracting
scenes, which persons of the most improved taste might
contemplate with no small pleasure; and were it not
for

for the feverity of the cold in winter, this country, by
cultivation, might be made the finest in the world.
The leaves of the trees, the dimensions of whose trunks
we have already noticed, resemble those of our bay-trees.
The rind is grey on the outside and pretty thick. This
is the true winter's bark, a name which it obtained from
its being brought in the year 1567, from the Straits of
Magellan, by Mr. William Winter. This bark, on
being taken off the tree and died, turns to the colour
of chocolate. It has an acrid, burning, pungent taste,
and is esteemed an excellent remedy against the scurvy.
It is however extremely fragrant, and the tree, when
standing, has a strong aromatic smell. We frequently
made use of the bark on board our ship in pies, instead of pepper, and being steeped in water it gives a
very agreeable flavour. These trees are likewise found
in the woods, in many other places in the straits, and
also on the east and west coasts of Patagonia. The land
in the woods, in some places, consists of gravel, in
others of sand, and in others of good brown earth; but
old fallen trees and underwood obstruct the passage
through them. These woods near the shore, extend
up the files of very high hills, but the mountains
further within land rise much higher, and their barren
rugged summits covered with snow, are seen peeping
over the hills next the shore. Indeed, the land on each
side the shore rises to a great height, particularly on
the island of Terra del Fuego, on the south side of the
straits, where there are high barren rocks covered with
everlasting snow. These have a black dreary aspect,
and must have a considerable influence on the air,
which they render cold and moist. This evidently appeared even while we were there, though this was
their midsummer, when every thing must naturally be
in the highest perfection. But notwithstanding the
weather, when the sun shone out, was very warm, yet
it was unsettled, and we had frequently heavy rain
and thick fogs. In the woods are innumerable parrots, and other birds of the most beautiful plumage.
We shot every day geese and ducks enough to serve

two

the commodore's table, and that of several others: we had, indeed, plenty of fresh provisions of all kinds, particularly fish, of which we caught such numbers as supplied our men three times a week. We must not omit here, that we saw many Indian huts, built with small branches of trees, and covered with leaves and mud, but we never met with a single inhabitant. The country between this and Cape Forward, which is distant about three leagues, is exceeding fine : the soil appears to be very rich, and there are no less than three pretty large rivers, besides many brooks. While we continued in this port, the commodore and a party went one day to Cape Forward. Upon setting out we intended to have gone farther ; but the rain having fell very heavy, we were glad to stop at the cape, and make a good fire to dry our clothes. The Indians had departed so lately from this place, that the wood, which lay half burnt, was still warm. Soon after our fire was kindled, we perceived another on the Terra del Fuego shore, a signal, probably, which we did not understand. The rain having abated, we walked over the cape, and found the strait to run about W. N. W. The hills as far as we could see, were of an immense height, very craggy, and covered with snow from the very base upwards. The commodore having ordered a tent to be erected on the borders of a wood, and near a rivulet, three seamen were stationed there to wash linen, and they lay in the tent. One evening, soon after they had retired to rest, they were awakened by the deep and hollow roarings of some wild beasts which approached nearer every moment. Terrified with apprehensions of being devoured, they made and kept up a blazing fire, round which the beasts walked at a small distance till dawn of day, when they retired. We did not credit this story, for the relators could not tell us what kind of beasts they saw, only they were very large; yet it must be acknowledged, that, at different times, when on shore, we tracked many wild beasts in the sand, but never saw one. And as we were returning through the woods, we found two very large skulls,

which,

3

which, by the teeth, appeared to have belonged to some beasts of prey, but of what kind we could not guess.

CHAP. II.

The Dolphin and Tamar steer back from Port Famine in search of Falkland's Islands—Arrive at Port Egmont—Observations on this Port and the adjacent country—Run from Falkland's Islands to Port Desire, and through the Straits of Magellan as far as Cape Monday—The Florida Storeship happily discovered—A strange Sail makes her Appearance, and follows the Dolphin, which proved to be the Eagle, commanded by M. Bougainville—A Description of different Parts of the Straits—Passage from Cape Monday into the South Sea—The Dolphin in a critical Situation—Observations on Tuesday Bay—Enters the Pacific Ocean—And touches at Masa-Fuero—Observations on this Island.

WE began this New-year in Port Famine, where we enjoyed every A.D. 1765. blessing, which after so long a voyage we had reason to expect. We had fish, wood, and water, in abundance: both our ship and the Tamar were in good condition, and the success of our voyage, with the continued kindness of our commodore, kept our men in high spirits. Having compleated the wood and water of both ships, and provided every necessary that was wanted, on Friday the 4th of January, we weighed, and set sail from Port Famine, standing over to the Island of Terra del Fuego, where we saw great quantities of smoke rising from different quarters, which we supposed to be raised by various parties of Indians. The intention of the commodore was now to steer back again in search of Falkland's Islands. With this view on the 5th, we held on our course N. W. by N. four leagues, and then three leagues north, between Elizabeth

beth and Bartholomew Iflands, after which we fteered
N. E. half E. from the fecond narrow to the firft, being a run of eight leagues. We proceeded through
the firft narrow againft the flood ; but the tide of flood
fetting ftrong to fouthward, drove the fhip directly
towards the fouth fhore, which might have proved of
fatal confequence to the fhip ; for as we were under
a very high rocky cliff in 50 fathoms water, if there
had happened a fudden fquall of wind, we muft have
been inevitably loft : however, the flood fet us back
again into the entrance of the firft narrow, and we caft
anchor in 40 fathom, within two cables length of the
fhore. On the 6th, at one o'clock, A. M. we weighed,
and had a pleafant northerly breeze with the tide of ebb ;
but this breeze foon abating, the tide fet the fhip to the
N. W. and at five fhe took the ground on a fand
bank of 15 feet, which reduced us to no fmall extremity ; but providentially, in about half an hour,
fhe fwung by the force of the tide into deeper water.
This fhoal, not mentioned by any former navigators,
is very dangerous, as it lies directly in the track between Cape Virgin Mary and the firft narrow, and juft
in the middle between the north and fouth fhores.
It is more than two leagues long, equally broad, and
in many places very fteep ; fo that fhould a fhip ground
upon it in a hard gale of wind, fhe would probably
foon be beat to pieces. When we were upon this bank,
Point Poffeffion bore N. E. diftant three leagues, and
the entrance of the narrow S. W. diftant two leagues.
About fix o'clock, A. M. we anchored, and at noon
worked with the ebb tide till two, but finding the
water fhoal, we came again to anchor, about half a
mile from the fouth-fide of the bank : at which time
the Affes Ears bore N. W. by W. diftant four leagues.
On the 7th, about eight o'clock, A. M. we weighed
and fteered about half a mile S. E. by E. We now
got our boats out, and towed the fhip into the deepeft
water in the fouth channel ; by which means we anchored in 14 fathoms, the tide of flood making ftrong
againft us ; and then being for the diftance of half a
mile

mile round us encompaffed with fhoals, that had only eight feet water, we fent our boat to found, in order to find a channel; and after being difappointed more than once, we at length weighed for the laft time, and left the coaft.

On Tuefday the 8th, by obfervation we found ourfelves in latitude 51 deg. 50 min. We now brought to for the Tamar, who had come through the north channel, and was fome leagues aftern of us. This day we had ftrong gales from the weftward: and in the forenoon a moft violent fquall of wind which fprung our main-maft, but effectual methods were taken immediately by our carpenter to fecure it. On the 9th, we were in latitude 52 deg. 8 min. S. and in 68 deg. 31 min. W. longitude, at which time Cape Virgin Mary bore S. 83 deg. W. diftant 33 leagues. On the 10th, our courfe was N. 18 W. for 13 leagues; and our latitude 51 deg. 31 min. S. longitude 68 deg. 44 min. W. On the 11th, our courfe was N. 87 E. for 33 leagues. Cape Virgin Mary bore S. 73 deg. 8 min. W. and Cape Fairweather W. 2 deg. S. This day we had ftrong gales at S. W. accompanied with a great fea. In the evening we efpied land, but our confort being fome leagues aftern, we wore fhip, and made an eafy fail off. On the 12th, at day break, we ftood in again, and at four o'clock recovered fight of the land a-head, which was taken for De Werts Iflands, and at the fame time we faw other land to the fouth, which appeared to be a confiderable number of iflands near each other, fome of them feeming very low, and almoft even with the furface of the water, and which we judged to be what are called in the charts New Iflands. Intending to ftand in between thefe, we found the land which appeared to be unconnected, was joined by fome low ground, and formed a deep bay. When hauling out of this we difcovered a long low reef of rocks, ftretching out for more than a league to the northward of us, and another between that, and what we had taken for the northermoft of De Werts Iflands. This land confifts chiefly of mountainous and barren

rocks,

rocks, except the low part, which is not feen till you approach near it, and the whole has very much the appearance of Staten Land. Birds and feals abound here, and we faw large whales fpouting round the fhip. When we were near enough to difcern the low land, we found ourfelves wholly embayed, and had it blown hard at S. W. fo high a fea muft have rolled in, as would have made it impoffible to keep clear of the fhore; we mention thefe particulars, that all fhips may hereafter avoid falling into this bay. At noon we obferved in latitude 51 deg. 27 min. S. and in 63 deg. 54 min. W. longitude.

On Sunday the 13th of January, at day-break, we ftood in for the north part of the ifland by the coaft of which we had been embayed. Being about a league to the eaftward, it fell calm, and poured down torrents of rain, after which a moft uncommon fwell came from the weftward, and ran fo high, and with fuch velocity, that we expected every moment it would fet us very faft towards the fhore, as dangerous as any in the world, and we could fee the furge breaking at fome diftance from it mountains high; very fortunately for us a frefh gale fprung up at S. E. with which, to our great joy, we were able to ftand off, and we would advife every one, who may hereafter come this way, to give the north part of this ifland a good birth. We now brought to in latitude 51 deg. S. and in 63 deg. 22 min. W. longitude.

Monday the 14th, we difcovered a flat ifland covered with tufts of grafs as large as bufhes. We continued our courfe along the fhore fix leagues farther, and then faw a low rocky ifland, bearing S. E. by E. and diftant about three leagues from the land we were coafting, which here forms a very deep bay, and bears E. by N. of the other ifland on which had been feen the long tufts of grafs. During the night we ftood off and on, and on the 15th, at three o'clock, A. M. we ftood in towards the land, and hoifted out our boats to found.. Thefe were gone till noon, when they returned with the agreeable news of having found a fine convenient

bay,

bay, entirely secure from the fury of the winds, with its entrance lying to the northward. The land is on each side very high, and the entrance, which is half a mile broad, not in the least dangerous, there being nothing to obstruct the passage, and the depth is from seven to 13 fathoms, with soft muddy ground. The shore of this bay is not encompassed with sunken rocks or sands; nor is there the least danger in approaching it. In passing on the starboard-side, many fine small bays and harbours open to the view, and to the third of these, which we entered, and found of great extent, the name was given of Port Egmont, in honour of the right honourable the earl of Egmont, first lord of the Admiralty, under whose direction this voyage was principally undertaken. The mouth of it is S. E. distant seven leagues from the low rocky island, which is a good mark to know it by. At the distance of about two miles from the shore, there is about eighteen fathoms water; and about three leagues to the westward of the harbour, there is a remarkable white sandy beach, off which a ship may anchor till there is an opportunity to run in. We moored in 10 fathoms, with fine holding ground. This harbour is so commodious, that we think it proper to give a particular discription of that and the adjacent country.

Port Egmont is surrounded by a range of islands, perfectly disjoined, and each placed in a convenient and agreeable situation. There are three different passages into this port, one from the S. W. another from the N. E. and the third from the S. E. and this last we found capable of receiving a ship of the greatest burthen. This harbour is of such capacity, as to be able to contain the whole royal navy of England, which might lie here in perfect security. As the adjacent country has all the requisites for a good settlement, it is probable, that was it added to the crown of Great Britain, it would in time become a most flourishing spot. There are here many cascades of water, which are so conveniently situated, that by bringing casks along-side the shore, many of them may be filled at once. One

inconvenience, however, attends this place, which is that there are no trees; but this is of small consequence; for in the proper season of the year, young trees might easily be brought through the straits to these islands, where there is no doubt but they would grow and prosper. On our first arrival we sowed the seeds of turnips, radishes, lettuces, &c. and before we left the harbour many of them began to spring up very fast, and we have since heard, that some persons who arrived here after our departure, eat of those roots and salad. It must however be acknowledged, that the wheat which we also sowed, being put into the ground at an improper season, though it sprang up, did not come to perfection. This we learnt from a person who lately came from hence in one of his Majesty's ships of war. The pasture ground of this island is so rich, that the grass rose as high as our breasts, which rendered our walking rather troublesome. We cut down great quantities of it for the use of our sheep. It is not to be doubted, but that was this country to be properly examined, many valuable discoveries might be made with respect to its vegetables and minerals; for upon a slight survey of the hills, we found a kind of iron ore, and have some reason to believe, that if an exact scrutiny was made, other ores might be found of greater value. On our first going on shore, the water side was entirely covered on every side with different kinds of birds, of very beautiful colours, and so tame, that in less than half an hour we knocked down as many as we could conveniently carry away in our boats; particularly white and painted geese, a great number of penguins, cape hens, and other fowls. Those which we called painted geese, were nearly of the size of ours, only of a different colour, having a ring of green feathers on the body, and spots on different parts, with yellow legs. A stranger would scarcely forbear smiling at this time upon seeing our ship, for never was any shop in Leadenhall-market so plentifully supplied with poultry, and the men in every part were busily employed in picking them. As by experience we found they had a strong
taste

taste from their feeding upon sea-weeds, small fish, and particularly limpits, of which there are great plenty as large as oysters, we found out a new method of dressing them, which rendered even these fowls extremely palatable: so that we had as much provisions, and of the nicest sorts, as we could desire. The method we pursued, was by cutting them into pieces over night, and letting them lie in salt-water till the next day, and after being thus purged by lying in soak, we made them, with a sufficient quantity of flour, into pies. Besides these fowls, we met with a prodigious quantity of ducks, snipes, teal, plover, small birds, and fresh-water geese, which last, living entirely by the fresh ponds, have a most delicious taste, and are not inferior to those we are accustomed to eat in England. They are entirely white except their legs. We frequently sent two of our men in search of them, who were sure to bring home half a dozen, or more, which they found a sufficient load, being not a little encumbered by the height of the grass. We found also a great number of seals, some of them very large, and several men were employed on shore, at a place we called Blubber's Bay, from the number of those animals we killed, for their oil: for when boiled they yielded a sufficient quantity of it for the ships companies to burn in lamps, while the men preserved their skins for waistcoats, and other uses. We were not surprised at meeting with such a great number of seals, when we afterwards found that they had sometimes 18 or more, at a litter. Sea-lions of a prodigious size are also found on the coast. The commodore was once unexpectedly attacked by one of these, and extricated himself from the impending danger with great difficulty. We had many battles with this amphibious animal, the killing one of which was frequently an hour's work for six men: one of them almost tore to pieces the commodore's mastiff dog by a single bite. The master having been sent to sound the coast, four very fierce animals ran after the boat's crew till they were up to the middle in water, and having no fire-arms, they were obliged to put off from the shore. The next day the commodore

and

and his party faw a fea-lion of an enormous fize, and the crew being well armed inftantly engaged him. While they were thus employed, one of the other animals pofted towards them; but a ball being inftantly lodged in his body, he was foon difpatched. Five of thefe creatures were killed in their attempts to feize the men, whom they always purfued the moment they got fight of them. They were of a mixed fhape, between a wolf and a fox, moft like the latter, but of the fize of the former. They burrow in the ground like a fox, feed on feals and penguins, and are very numerous on the coaft. The failors, in order to be rid of fuch difagreeable intruders, fet fire to the grafs, which burnt fo rapidly, that the country was all in a blaze for a few days, and thefe animals were feen running to feek fhelter from the fury of the flames. On the north-fide of this harbour is the principal ifland, to which we frequently went on fhore, on account of its fituation, and the fine profpect it afforded from a prodigious high hill, which cannot be afcended without difficulty; but on gaining the fummit, the great fatigue of afcending it, is fully recompenced, by the delightful view it commands of the fhips at anchor, with every part of the harbour; of the three paffages into Port Egmont; the fea which furrounds you on every fide; and all the adjacent iflands, which are upwards of fifty, fmall and great, all of which appeared covered with verdure. While we lay in this harbour the crew breakfafted on portable-foup and wild celery, thickned with oatmeal, which made a very nutritive mefs.

On Wednefday the 23d, the commodore, with the captains of the Dolphin and Tamar, and the principal officers went on fhore, where the Union Jack being erected on a high ftaff, and fpread, the commodore took poffeffion of this harbour, and all the neighbouring iflands, for his Majefty King George the Third, his heirs and fucceffors, by the name of Falkland's Iflands. The colours were no fooner fpread, than a falute was fired from the fhip. Our feamen were very merry on the occafion, a large bowl of arrack punch being carried

on

on fhore, out of which they drank, among many other toafts, Succefs to the difcovery of fo fine a harbour. It was the opinion of the honourable Commodore Byron, that thefe iflands, are the fame land to which Cowley gave the name of Pepys's Ifland, and as the commodore feems not to entertain a doubt in his own mind, we fhall lay before our readers, the reafons he has been pleafed to give the public in fupport of his opinion.

" In the printed account of Cowley's voyage" (obferves Commodore Byron) he fays, " We held our courfe S. W. till we came into the latitude of 47 deg. where we faw land, the fame being an ifland, not before known, lying to the weftward of us: it was not inhabited, and I gave it the name of Pepys's Ifland. We found it a very commodious place for fhips to water at, and take in wood, and it has a very good harbour, where a thoufand fail of fhips may fafely ride. Here is great plenty of fowls, and, we judge, abundance of fifh, by reafon of the grounds being nothing but rocks and fands." To this account there is annexed a reprefentation of Pepys's Ifland, in which names are given to feveral points and head lands, and the harbour is called Admiralty Bay; yet it appears that Cowley had only a diftant view of it, for he immediately adds, " the wind being fo extraordinary high that we could not get into it to water, we ftood to the fouthward, fhaping our courfe S. S. W. till we came into the latitude of 53 deg." And though he fays, that " it was commodious to take in wood," and it is known that there is no wood on Falkland's Iflands, Pepys's Ifland and Falkland's Ifland may, notwithftanding, be the fame; for upon Falkland's Iflands there are immenfe quantities of flags with narrow leaves, reeds, and rufhes, which grow in clufters, fo as to form bufhes about three feet high, and then fhoot about fix or feven feet higher: thefe at a diftance have greatly the appearance of wood, and were taken for wood by the French who landed there in the year 1764, as appears by Pernetty's account of their voyage. It has been fuggefted, that the latitude of Pepys's Ifland might,

might, in the manufcript from which the account of Cowley's voyage was printed, be expreffed in figures, which if ill made, might equally refemble 47 and 51; and therefore as there is no ifland in thefe feas in latitude 47, and as Falkland's Iflands lie nearly in 51, that 51 might reafonably be concluded to be the number for which the figures were intended to ftand: recourfe therefore was had to the Britifh Mufeum, and a manufcript journal of Cowley's was there found. In this manufcript no motion is made of an ifland not before known, to which he gave the name of Pepys's Ifland, but land is mentioned in latitude 47 deg. 40 min. expreffed in words at length, which exactly anfwers to the defcription of what is called Pepys's Ifland in the printed account, and which here, he fays, he fuppofed to be the Iflands of Sebald de Wert. This part of the manufcript is in the following words: " January 1683, This month wee were in the latitude of 47 deg. and 40 min. where wee efpied an ifland bearing weft from us, wee having the wind at N. E. wee bore away for it, it being too late for us to goe on fhoare, wee lay by all night. The ifland feemed very pleafant to the eye, with many woods, I may as well fay, the whole land was woods. There being a rock lying above water to the eaftward of it, where were an innumerable company of fowles, being of the bigneffe of a fmall goofe, which fowles would ftrike at our men as they were aloft: fome of them wee killed and eat: they feemed to us very good, only tafted fomewhat fifhly. I failed along that ifland to the fouthward, and about the S. W. fide of the ifland there feemed to me to be a good place for fhipps to ride; I would have had the boat out to have gone into the harbour, but the wind blew frefh, and they would not agree to go with it. Sailing a little further, keeping the lead, and having 26 and 27 fathoms water, until wee came to a place, where wee faw the weeds ride, having the lead againe found but feaven fathoms water. Fearing danger went about the fhipp there, were then fearefull to ftay by the land any longer, it being all rocky ground, but the harbour feemed to be a good place for

3   fhipps

shipps to ride there; in the island seeming likewise to have water enough.; there seemed to me to be harbour for 500 saile of shipps. The going in but narrow, and the north-side of the entrace shallow water that I could see, but I verily believe that there is water enough for any shipp to goe in on the south-side, for there cannot be so great a lack of water, but must needs scowre a channell away at the ebbe deepe enough for shipping to goe in. I would have had them stood upon a wind all night, but they told me they were not come out to go upon discovery. Wee saw likewise another island by this that night, which made me think them the Sibble D'wards. The same night we steered our course againe W. S. W. which was but our S. W. the compasse having two and twenty degrees variation easterly, keeping that course till we came in the latitude of three and fifty degrees."

In both the printed and manuscript account, this land is said to lie in latitude forty-seven, to be situated to the westward of the ship when first discovered, to appear woody, to have an harbour where a great number of ships might ride in safety, and to be frequented by innumerable birds. It appears also by both accounts, that the weather prevented his going on shore, and that he steered from it west-south-west, till he came into latitude fifty-three: there can therefore be little doubt but that Cowley gave the name of Pepys's Island after he came home, to what he really supposed to be the island of Sebald de Wert, for which it is not difficult to assign several reasons; and though the supposition of a mistake of the figures does not appear to be well grounded, yet, there being no land in forty-seven, the evidence that what Cowley saw was Falkland's Islands, is very strong. The description of the country agrees in almost every particular, and even the map is of the same general figure, with a strait running up the middle. The two principal islands have been probably called Falkland's Islands by Strong, about the year 1689, as he is known to have given the name of Falkland's Sound to part of the strait which
divides

divides them. The journal of this navigator is still unprinted in the British Museum. The first who saw these islands is supposed to be Captain Davies, the associate of Cavendish in 1692. In 1594, Sir Richard Hawkins saw land, supposed to be the same, and in honour of his mistress, Queen Elizabeth, called them Hawkins's Maiden Land. Long afterwards they were seen by some French ships from St. Maloes, and Frezier probably for that reason, called them the Malouins, a name which has since been adopted by the Spaniards." So much for the dispute concerning the discovery of these celebrated islands, which the Spaniards now enjoy unmolested, while to England only remains the empty honour of having discovered, explored, and given them a name.

We had now completed our watering, surveyed the harbour of Port Egmont, and provided every necessary for our departure. This evening the smith came on board, he having been employed on shore, in making and repairing iron work for the use of the ship. We continued in the harbour till Sunday the 27th, when at eight o'clock A. M. we left Port Egmont, and sailed with the wind at south-south-west. But we were scarcely out at sea, when it began to blow hard, and the weather became so extremely hazy, that we could not see the rocky islands. We now most heartily wished to be safe anchored in Egmont harbour; but, contrary to our expectations, in a short time the weather cleared up, though it blew a hard gale all the day. At ten o'clock, after having run along the shore east, about five leagues, we saw a remarkable head-land, which was named Cape Tamar. Five leagues farther we passed a rock, and called it Ediftone. We now sailed between this and another head-land, to which was given the name of Cape Dolphin, in the direction of east-north-east, five leagues farther. The distance from Cape Tamar to Cape Dolphin, is about eight leagues, and from its having the appearance of a sound, it was called Carlisle Sound, though it is since known to be the northern entrance of the strait between the two principal islands.

We

We steered from Cape Dolphin along the shore east, half north, to a low flat cape, or head-land, and then brought to. During the course of this day, the land we saw was all downs, having neither trees nor bushes, but large tufts of grass in various places. It may not be improper here to take notice, that as in most of the charts of Patagonia, an island is described by the name of Pepys's island, as hath already been mentioned, where travellers have asserted, that they have seen trees in abundance, and many rills of water; but that after several attempts in the latitude where it was said to be discovered, no island nor any sounding could be found; in justice to the pretended discoverers of that and other imaginary islands, we here beg leave again to observe, that they probably had no intention to deceive, for on this coast, where you meet with frequent gales of wind, and thick foggy weather, we found the banks of fogs were apt to deceive even an accurate observer, and make him mistake them for land. Thus we ourselves have frequently imagined, that we saw land very near; but suddenly a breeze of wind springing up, our supposed land disappeared, though we did not think ourselves above a league and a half from it, and convinced us of our mistake by opening to our view an unbounded prospect. So easily does the mind of man, when set on one particular object, form to itself chimerical notions of its darling pursuit, and when harrassed, as we will suppose, by the distresses that frequently attend an enterprize of this nature, make an imaginary discovery of land, where nothing but a thick fog, and a vast extent of sea, are to be found.

On Monday the 28th, at four o'clock, A. M. we made sail, and steered east-south-east, and south-south-east to two low rocky islands, about a mile from the main; and to a deep sound between these, we gave the name of Berkley's Sound. About four miles to the southward of the south point of this sound, the sea breaks very high, on some rocks that appear above water. The coast now wore a dangerous aspect; rocks and breakers

No. 27.   5 P   being

being at a confiderable diftance from the fhore, and in
all directions; and the country appeared barren and defolate, much refembling that part of Terra del Fuego
which lies near Cape Horn.   The fea rifing here very
high, we tacked and ftood to the northward, to prevent
our being driven on a lee-fhore.   Having now run no
lefs than feventy leagues of this ifland, we concluded,
it muft be of confiderable extent.   Some former navigators have made Falkland's iflands, to be about two
hundred miles in circumference, but in the opinion of
our Commodore, they are near 700 miles.   At noon
we hauled the wind and ftood to the northward, the
entrance of Berkley's Sound bearing at three o'clock,
S. W. by W. fix leagues off; and in the evening we
ftood to the weftward, the wind having fhifted to the
S. W.   On Tuefday, the 5th of February, at one o'clock
P. M. we again made the coaft of Patagonia, bearing
S. W. by S. fix leagues diftant.   At two we paffed by
Penguin Ifland; and at three ftanding towards the harbour of Port Defire, which was two leagues diftant, we
to our great fatisfaction, difcovered the Flora ftorefhip,
which had been fitted out at Deptford, and had on
board a great quantity of new baked bread, packed in
new cafks, befides brandy, flour, beef, and all fuch neceffary provifions and ftores for the ufe of our two fhips.
This veffel, whofe arrival was fo opportune for the profecution of our voyage, was difpatched by the lords of
the Admiralty, with as much fecrecy as the Dolphin,
with refpect to the ignorance of the men on board as to
their place of deftination.   When fhe firft failed from
Deptford, fhe was fitted out for Florida; nor did the
mafter know, till he arrived fouthward of the line, that
he was ordered to recruit the Commodore's veffels.   We
had for fome time paft been uneafy, concluding that
this fhip had probably met with fome accident that had
obliged her to return: but her appearance agreeably removed all the anxiety we had felt from this groundlefs
conjecture; and indeed it was very happy for us, that
we fell in with her at this juncture, which was the more
feafonable, as for fome time we had been reduced to a
                                                    fhort

short allowance of certain articles of provisions, which she was able to supply us with; but had this not been the case, a worse consequence must have ensued, namely, that of being obliged to steer to the Cape of Good Hope, in order to purchase provisions, and consequently losing our voyage; as by this delay it would be too late for us to attempt a passage into the South Sea, either by passing the straits of Magellan, or doubling Cape Horn, consequently an end would be put to all our discoveries, and the expence of fitting us out be thrown away. At four o'clock P. M. having anchored in Port Desire, the master of the store ship came on board the Dolphin, bringing a packet from the lords of the Admiralty to the Commodore. This person was a midshipman in his Majesty's service, and was to have a commission as soon as he found the Commodore. He had been several days in search of Pepys's Island; but was like us obliged to desist, and having crossed the latitude in which it was supposed to lie, had met with a storm that had greatly damaged his masts and sails. In the evening the master of the Florida left the Dolphin, and by order of the Commodore, our carpenters attended him on board his own ship, to repair the damages she had sustained. During our run from Falkland's islands to Port Desire, the number of whales about the Dolphin rendered our navigation dangerous. One blew the water upon our quarter deck, and we were near striking upon another; they were of an uncommon size, much larger than any we had yet seen.

On Thursday the 7th, the night proved very tempestuous; when both the Tamar and Florida made signals of distress, having been driven from their moorings up the harbour. They were got clear of the shore with great difficulty, as they were the next night, when they both drove again. Finding the storeship was in constant danger of being lost, the design of unloading her in this harbour was given up, and the Commodore determined to take her with him into the strait. Capt. Mouat of the Tamar having also informed us, that his rudder was sprung, it was secured with iron clamps in

the

the best manner he could, there being no timber to be found proper for making her a new one. Having by the thirteenth completed the repairs of our respective ships, we made ready to leave this port, as by the rapidity of the tide, the boats could have little or no communication with the store ship: it was therefore resolved to sail back to the eastward, and take in our stores at one of the Ports we had before visited. One of our petty officers, well acquainted with the strait, and four of our seamen, were put on board the Florida, to assist in navigating her, and she was ordered to make the best of her way to Port Famine. On the 14th, we put to sea, and when, a few hours after, abreast of Penguin island, we got sight of the store-ship a long way to the eastward. On Saturday the 16th, about six o'clock, A. M. Cape Fairweather bore W. S. W. distant five leagues; and on the 17th, we hauled in for the strait of Magellan, and at six o'clock A. M. Cape Virgin Mary bore S, distant five miles. On the 18th, we passed the first narrow. To our great surprise, in the morning of the second day after we left Port Desire, we discovered a strange sail, which our Commodore apprehended might be a Spanish man of war of the line, who was come to intercept us; and in consequence of that surmise, boldly gave orders, that all on board the Dolphin and Tamar should prepare to give her a warm reception, by firing all our guns, and then boarding her from both ships: but while we were bringing to and waiting for her, it grew dark, and we lost sight of her, till the next morning, when we saw her at three leagues distance, and found she still followed us, while we sailed towards Port Famine. She even came to an anchor when we did. We were now employed in getting up our guns, having only four upon deck, which had been used for signals, the rest having for a considerable time before lain in the hold. We soon however got fourteen upon deck, and then came to an anchor, having the Tamar a-stern, with a spring on our cable; and that we might give her as warm a reception as possible, we removed all our guns to one side, pointing to the place

where

where the veffel muft pafs.   While we were thus bufily
employed in taking all the meafures prudence could
fuggeft to defend us from an imaginary danger, an accident that happened to the ftore fhip fhewed that we
had nothing to fear, and that the veffel againft which
we were arming ourfelves, ought not to be confidered
as an enemy; for while the Florida was working to
the windward, fhe took the fhore, on a bank about
two leagues from our fhip.   About the fame time the
ftrange veffel came up with her, and feeing her diftrefs
caft anchor; and immediately began to hoift out her
boats to give her affiftance; but before they had reached
the ftore-fhip, our boats had boarded her, and the commanding officer had received orders not to let them
come on board; but to thank them in the politeft manner for their intended affiftance.   Thefe orders were
punctually obeyed, and with the aid of our boats only,
the ftore-fhip was foon after got into deep water.   Our
people reported, that the French veffel was full of
men, and feemed to have a great many officers.   At
fix o'clock in the evening, we worked through the
fecond narrow; and at ten paffed the weft end of it.
We anchored at eleven off Elizabeth Ifland, and the
French fhip did the fame, in a bad fituation, fouthward
of St. Bartholomew's Ifland, whereby we were convinced fhe was not well acquainted with the channel.

On Tuefday the 19th we weighed, and at fix o'clock,
A. M. we fteered between Elizabeth and Bartholomew
Iflands, S. S. W. five miles, when we croffed a bank,
where among the weeds we had feven fathoms water.
This bank is fituated W. S. W. about five miles from
the middle of George's Ifland.   To avoid danger, it
is neceffary to keep near Elizabeth's Ifland, till the
weftern-fhore is but a fhort diftance, and then a fouthern
courfe may be failed with great fafety, till the reef,
which lies about four miles to the northward of St.
Anne's Point, is in fight.   The Frenchman ftill followed
us, and we thought fhe came from Falkland's Iflands,
where is a French fettlement, to take in wood, or that
fhe was on a furvey of the Strait of Magellan, in which
we

we were now failing.   On the 20th, we hoisted out our
boats, and towed round St. Anne's Point into Port
Famine.   Here we anchored, at six in the evening, and
soon after the French ship passed by us to the southward.   During our stay in this port, we were principally
employed, in receiving provisions from the store ship,
and in compleating our wood and water.   On the 25th,
finding that both the ships had received as much stores
and provisions as they could possibly stow, the commodore sent home all the draughts of the places he had
caused to be taken, by the store-ship, with express
orders, that if they were in any danger of being boarded and examined by any foreign ships, their first care
should be to throw the plans and pacquets into the sea.
On taking leave of the Florida, our boatswain, and all
that were sick on board the Dolphin and Tamar, obtained leave to return in her to England; the commodore in the mean time, declaring openly to the crew
in general, that if any of them were averse to proceeding on the voyage, they had free liberty to return ;
an offer which only one of our men accepted.   We now
with the Tamar failed from Port Famine, intending
to push through the strait before the season should be
too far advanced.   At noon we were three leagues diftant from St. Anne's Point, which bore N. W. three or
four miles from Point Shutup, which bore S. S. W.   Point
Shutup bears from St. Anne's Point, S. half E. and they
are about four or five leagues asunder.   Between these
two points there is a flat shoal, which runs from Port
Famine before the river Sedger, and three miles to the
southward.   At three o'clock, P. M. we passed the
French ship, which now anchored in a small cove.
She had hauled close to the shore, and we could see
large piles of wood cut down, and lying on each side
of her.   Upon our return to England, we learnt this
ship was the Eagle, commanded by M. Bougainville,
and that her business in the strait was, as the commodore had conjectured, to cut wood for the French
settlement in Falkland's Islands.   From Cape Shutup
to Cape Forward, the course is S. W. by S. distance

seven

seven leagues. At eight in the evening we brought to, Cape Forward bearing N. W. half W. diftant about a mile. This part of the ftrait is eight miles over, and off the cape we had 40 fathoms within half a cables length of the fhore.

On the 26th, at four o'clock, A. M. we made fail, and at ten we kept working to windward, looking out at the fame time for an anchoring-place, and endeavouring to reach a bay about two leagues to the weftward of Cape Forward. An officer was fent into this bay to found, who finding it fit for our purpofe we entered it, and at fix o'clock, P. M. anchored in nine fathoms water. On the 27th, at fix o'clock, A. M. we continued our courfe through the ftrait, from Cape Holland to Cape Gallant. This cape is very high and fteep, and between it and the former cape is a reach, three leagues over, called Englifh Reach. Five miles fouth of Cape Gallant is Charles's Ifland, of which it is neceffary to keep to the northward. We fteered along the north fhore, at the diftance of about two miles. Eaftward of Cape Holland is a fpacious fandy bay, called Wood's Bay, in which there is good anchorage. The mountains on each fide the ftrait are more defolate in appearance than any others in the world, except perhaps the Cordeliers, both being rude, craggy, fteep, and covered from the bottom to their fummits with fnow. From Cape Gallant to Paffage Point, diftant about three leagues, the coaft lies W. by N. by compafs. Paffage Point is the eaft point of Elizabeth's Bay, and is low land, off which lies a rock. Between this and Cape Gallant are feveral iflands, fome very fmall; but the eaftermoft, Charles's Ifland, is fix miles long: the next is called Monmouth's Ifland, and the weftermoft, Rupert's Ifland: this lies S. by E. of Point Paffage. Thefe group of iflands make the ftrait narrow: between Port Paffage and Rupert's Ifland, it is not more than two miles over, and it is advifeable for navigators to go to the northward of them all, keeping the north-fhore on board.

On Wednefday the 27th, at fix o'clock, P. M. we
ftood

stood in for Elizabeth's Bay, and anchored in ten fathoms, good ground. In this bay there is a good rivulet of fresh water. On the 28th, we met with exceffive gales from the W. N. W. which blew with such violence, that we were driven three leagues to the eastward, where we cast anchor on the top of a rock, in 13 fathoms and a half water, a cable's length from the bay: but soon after we parted, or rather started our ftream anchor, and fell off the rock: it was very dark, and the ship still kept driving with her whole cable out, and was in the greatest danger of being lost; however, we let go both bowers in 17 fathoms water. The wind still continued to blow very hard, and the ship was so near the rocks, that the boats could but just keep clear of the furf off the shore: but that providence which had hitherto attended us, ftill continued to be our friend, and preserved us from impending destruction; for the next morning we hove in the cable of our ftream-anchor, both the flukes of which were broke; and being thus rendered useless, it was thrown overboard. We now with our gib and stay-sails ran out into 10 fathoms, till we were exactly in the fituation from whence we had been driven, where we anchored with our best bower.

On Friday the 1st of March, at five o'clock, A. M. we weighed, attended with light gales and moderate weather. At seven passed Muscle Bay, a league to the westward of Elizabeth's, on the southern shore. At eight we were two leagues W. by N. of this bay, and abreast of Bachelor's River, which is on the north shore. A league from hence lies the entrance of St. Jerom's Sound, which we passed at nine. In our course along this coast we saw a smoke, and soon after discovered a great number of Indians in detached parties, some of whom, on seeing us, put their canoes into the water, and made towards our ship. When within musket shot, they began a most hideous shouting, and we hallooed, and waved our hands, as signals for them to come on board; which after having frequently repeated, they did. On entering the ship they surveyed it with no

2   small

small signs of astonishment, as if they had never seen a vessel of the like kind before. These Indians were in general of a middling stature, and of a very brown complexion, with long black hair, that hung down to their shoulders. Their bodies were covered with the skin of some animals unknown to us; but many of the poor wretches had not a sufficient quantity to cover their nakedness. We trafficked with them, or rather gave them abundance of things, particularly cloaths, which they seemed to receive with thankfulness: they were also exceeding fond of the biscuit, which we distributed among them pretty freely, though they appeared rather unwilling to part with any thing in return. Some of these people had bows and arrows, made of such hard wood, that it seemed almost impenetrable; the bows were not only exceeding tough and smooth, but wrought with very curious workmanship; and the string was formed of a twisted gut. The arrows, which were about two feet long, were pointed with flint shaped like a harpoon, and cut with as great nicety, as if they had been shaped by the most exact lapidary; and at the other end a feather was fixed to direct its flight. They have also javelins. These Indians seem to be very poor and perfectly harmless, coming forth to their respective employments at the dawn of day, and when the sun sets, retiring to their different habitations. They live almost entirely on fish, and particularly on limpets and muscles, the latter of which they have in great plenty, and much larger than those we met with in England. Their boats are but indifferently put together: they are made chiefly of the bark of trees, and are just big enough to hold one family: when they land, being very light, they haul them upon shore, out of the reach of the tide, and seem very careful in preserving them. In the structure of some of these boats no small degree of ingenuity is evident. They are formed of three pieces, one at the bottom, which serves for the keel and part of the sides, and is fashioned both within and without by means of fire; upon this are placed two upper pieces, one on each side, which are sewed toge-

No. 27.　　　　5 Q　　　　　　ther,

ther, and to the bottom part, like a seem sewed with a needle and thread. All their boats in general are very narrow, and each end formed alike, both sharp, and rising up a considerable height. These Indians are very dexterous in striking the fish from their canoes with their javelins, though they lie some feet under water. In these instances, they seem to shew the utmost extent of their ingenuity; for we found them incapable of understanding things the most obvious to their senses. On their first coming aboard, among the trinkets we gave them were some knives and scissars, and we tried to make them sensible of their use; but after our repeated endeavours, by shewing the manner of using them, they continued as insensible as at first, and could not learn to distinguish the blades from the handles. There are plenty of seals in this part of the straits, but we did not meet with many fowl, owing doubtless to the intense cold, nor did we find the woods infested with any kind of wild beasts. On sailing to the westward we found an irregular tide, which sometimes ran 18 hours to the eastward, and but six to the westward; at other times, when the westerly winds blew with any degree of strength, it would constantly run for several days to the east. At intervals we had hard gales of wind, and prodigious squalls from the high mountains, whose summits are covered with snow. The straits are here four leagues over, and it is difficult to get any anchorage, on account of the unevenness, and irregularity of the bottom, which in several places close to the shore has from 20 to 15 fathoms water, and in other parts no ground is to be found with a line of 150 fathoms. We now steered W. S. W. for Cape Quod. Between this and Elizabeth's Bay is a reach about four miles over, called Crooked Reach. In the evening of the 4th, we anchored abreast of Bachelor's River, in 14 fathoms. The entrance of the river bore N. by E. distant one mile, and the northernmost point of St. Jerom's Sound, W. N. W. distant three miles. About three quarters of a mile eastward of Bachelor's River lies a shoal, upon which there is not more than six feet

water

water when the tide is out: it is diftant about half
a mile from the fhore, and may be known by the weeds
that are upon it. We here faw feveral Indians difperfed in different quarters, among whom we found a
family which ftruck our attention. It was compofed
of a decripid old man, his wife, two fons and a daughter.
The latter appeared to have tolerable features, and an
Englifh face, which they feemed defirous of letting us
know; they making a long harangue, not a fyllable of
which we underftood, though we plainly perceived it
was in relation to the woman, whofe age did not exceed
thirty, by their pointing firft at her, and then at themfelves. Various were the conjectures we formed in regard
to this circumftance, though we all agreed that their
figns plainly fhewed that they offered her to us, as being
of the fame country. In one particular they appeared
to be quite uncivilized, for when we came up to them,
they were tearing to pieces and devouring raw fifh. On
the 5th, we fent the boats a-head to tow, but could not
gain a bay on the north fhore, which appeared to be
an excellent harbour, fit to receive five or fix fail; we
were therefore obliged to caft anchor on a bank, with
the ftream anchor, Cape Quod bearing W. S. W. diftant about fix miles. An officer was now fent to look
out for a harbour, but he did not fucceed.

On Wednefday the 6th, we moored in a little bay
oppofite Cape Quod; and the Tamar, which could not
work up fo far, about fix miles to the eaftward of it.
This part of the ftrait is only four miles over, and its
afpect dreary and defolate beyond imagination, owing
to the prodigious mountains on each fide of it, which
rife above the clouds, and are covered with perpetual
fnow.

On Thurfday the 7th, at eight o'clock we weighed,
and worked with the tide. At noon, Cape Quod bore
E. by S. and Cape Monday, the weftermoft land in
fight on the fouth fhore, W. by N. diftant ten leagues.
The tides here are very ftrong, and the ebb fets to the
weftward, with an irregularity for which it is very
difficult to account. At one the Tamar anchored op-

5 Q 2   pofite

posite Cape Quod, in the bay we had just left; and in the evening we anchored in a small bay on the north shore, five leagues to the westward of Cape Quod. The marks to know this bay are two large rocks that appear above water, and a low point, which makes the east part of the bay. The anchorage is between the two rocks, the eastermost bearing N. E. half E. distant about two cables length, and the westermost, which is near the point, W. N. W. half W. at about the same distance: there is also a small rock which shows itself among the weeds at low water, and bears E. half N. distant about two cables length. Should there be more ships than two, they may anchor farther out in deeper water. We found in this part of the strait few birds of any kind, and but a small quantity of muscles along the shore; and though we sent out our boat into a bay to haul the seine, it returned without success, not any fish being to be found. However, we frequently found great quantities of red berries, somewhat resembling our cranberries, which being wholesome and refreshing proved of considerable service to the ship's company. They are about the size of an hazle nut, and the chief provisions of the Indians in these parts. On the 8th, we found abundance of shell-fish, but saw no traces of people. In the afternoon, the commodore went up a deep lagoon under a rock, at the head of which was a fine fall of water, and on the east-side of it several small coves calculated for the reception of ships of the greatest burthen. He returned with a boat load of very large muscles. On the 9th, we got under way, at seven o'clock, A. M. and at eight saw the Tamar very far astern. We now stood to the N. W. with a pleasant breeze at S. by E. but when abreast of Cape Monday Bay, the wind took us back, and continued from six o'clock to eight, at which time Cape Monday Bay bore E. half N. six leagues. On the 10th, at six o'clock, A. M. Cape Upright bore E. by S. distant three leagues. From Cape Monday to Cape Upright, which are both on the south shore, and distant from each other about five leagues, the course is W. by N. At ten a violent
storm

ftorm of wind came on, which was very near effecting
our deftruction; for it was very thick rainy weather,
and we fuddenly difcovered funken rocks on our lee-
bow, juft appearing above the furface of the water, at
the diftance of about half a mile from us. We tacked
immediately, and in half an hour it blew fo hard, that
we were obliged to bear up before the wind, and go in
fearch of an harbour. We were foon after joined by
the Tamar, who had been fix or feven leagues to the
eaftward of us all night. At fix in the evening we
came to anchor in a bay, in 16 fathoms water; but
the anchor falling from the bank into 50 fathoms, the
fhip almoft drove on fhore; happily the anchor clofing
with a rock brought us up. We now weighed, and on
the 11th fteered into a proper anchoring place, on a
bank, where the Tamar was riding, entirely furrounded
with high precipices, where we lay not more than two
cables length from the fhore. There is a bafon at the
bottom of this bay, within which is ten fathoms, and
room enough for fix or feven fail to lie in perfect
fecurity. Having at this time heavy fqualls of wind,
attended with much rain, the commodore, with a
generofity that endeared him to the crew, diftributed
as much cloth among the failors as would make all of
them long waiftcoats; a prefent highly acceptable at
this feafon of the year, and the more fo, as the officers
and men, on leaving England, from their expecting to
fail directly to India, had provided no thick cloathing.
And that no partiality might be fhewn to thofe on
board his own fhip, he ordered a fufficient quantity for
the ufe of Capt. Mouat's company in the Tamar.

On Tuefday the 12th, while we were employed in
fearching after wood and water, the Tamar's boat was
fent to the weftward, with an officer from both fhips,
to look for harbours on the fouthern fhore. On the
14th, the boat returned with the agreeable news, that
they had found feveral bays, particularly five between
the fhip's ftation and Cape Upright, where we might
anchor in fafety. When the commodore heard this,
in order to encourage his men in the difcharge of their
duty,

duty, he ordered a double allowance of brandy to be given to every one on board, which, with their warm fear-nought jackets, provided by government, proved both comfortable and salutary; for some hills, which, when we came first to this place, had no snow on them, were now covered, and the winter of this dreary and inhospitable region seemed to have set in at once. Those in the boat, during their absence, were benighted, and obliged by distress of weather to land, and take shelter under a tent which they had taken with them. They saw a number of Indians employed on the shore, in cutting up a dead whale, which scented the place for some distance around, it being in a state of putrefaction. This they supposed was designed for food, seeing they cut it in large slices, and carried them away on their shoulders to another party at a distance, who seemed employed round a fire: however it is equally probable, that like the Greenlanders, they might be making oil for their lamps against the approaching severity of winter. One of the officers told us, that near Cape Upright some Indians had given him a dog, and that one of the women had offered him a child which was sucking at her breast, but for what purpose he could not say. How much soever by their appearance, and manner of life, these seemingly forlorn rational beings may be degraded in the eyes of Europeans, we ought not from this trifling incident, to attribute to them such a strange depravity of nature as makes them destitute of affection for their offspring; or even to think that it can be surmounted by the necessities or wants attending the most deplorable situation; a notoriety of facts and universal history are against even a supposition of this kind. On the 15th, at eight o'clock, A. M. we made sail, and in the afternoon we anchored on the east-side of Cape Monday, in Wash Pot Bay. The pitch of the cape bore N. W. distant half a mile, and the extreme points of the bay from E. to N. by W. The nearest shore was a low island between us and the cape, from which island we lay about half a cable's length. We

had

had at this place frequent showers of rain and hail, with the air all the time excessive sharp.

On Saturday the 16th, at six o'clock, A. M. we unmoored, and at eight a strong current set us to the eastward. In this perplexing situation were we driven about from place to place, losing perhaps in a few hours, what we had been six days and nights working to the westward; for when the wind continues with violence there is no regular tide ; but on the contrary, a constant westerly current running two miles an hour. Perceiving we lost ground, we came to an anchor, but finding the ground to be rocky we weighed again ; and every man on board the rest of the day, and the whole night, continued on deck, during which time the rain poured down in unremitting torrents. Notwithstanding this incessant labour, on the 17th, we had the mortification to find we had been losing way on every tack, and at nine o'clock, A. M. we were glad to anchor in the very bay we had left two days before. It continued to rain, and blow violently for two days longer, so that we began to think, without a favourable wind, it would be our ill fortune to spend the winter quarter in one of these coves. The commodore had sent out a boat to sound the bay on the north shore, but no anchorage could be found. On the 21st, we set sail, the wind veering from S. W. by W. to N. N. W. we worked to windward with continual squalls, which at intervals obliged us to clue all our sails. In the mean while the Tamar, whom till this time we had never lost sight of, by a favourable breeze, got a few leagues to the westward, where she lay two days in good anchorage. Harrassed as we were by continual disappointments, to add still more to our vexation and concern, we found our men were attacked by the scurvy, which had made its appearance on many of them ; however, by the assistance of vegetables, and the extraordinary care of the commodore, who caused portable soup to be served to the sick, and twice a week to the whole ship's company, on Fridays with pease, and on Mondays with oatmeal ; and who with the

greatest

greateſt humanity never ſpared to diſtribute from his own table, whatever might be of uſe for the recovery of thoſe attacked by this dreadful diſorder, it was prevented from raging with any great inveteracy. On the 22d, to our great joy we made way, the current ſetting to the weſtward. At ſix in the evening, we anchored in a commodious bay on the eaſt-ſide of Cape Monday, where the Tamar lay in 18 fathoms. We found this place very ſafe, the ground being excellent. It is remarkable, that notwithſtanding the late ſeverity of the weather, added to their inceſſant labour, the crew of both ſhips, in general, retained both health and ſpirits.

On Saturday the 23d, at eight o'clock, A. M. we again ſet ſail, and in a few hours opened the South Sea, which rolled in with a prodigious ſwell. At four in the afternoon, we anchored about a league to the eaſtward of Cape Upright, in a good bay, with a deep ſound at the bottom, by which it may be known. On the 24th, the boat was ſent to the weſtward, with the ſecond lieutenant, in ſearch of an harbour, at which time we had continued rains, and cold unhealthy weather, with ſtrong gales from the N. W. At ſix in the evening the boat returned without having been able to get round Cape Upright. On the 25th, the boat was ſent again with arms, and a week's proviſions, beſides materials for erecting a tent, in caſe they ſhould land, and find it neceſſary to make uſe of it. In the evening they returned, having been about four leagues, and had found two anchoring places, neither of them very good ; upon which we weighed, and on the 20th, ſtood to the N. W. to windward of Cape Monday. The ſtraits here are four or five leagues over, and the mountains ſeemed to be ten times as high as the maſt head of our ſhip, but not much covered with ſnow. We continued under ſail, till the wind increaſing, and a violent ſea from the weſtward coming on, we were obliged to lie to under our cloſe reefed top-ſails. At four in the afternoon, the weather became very thick, and in leſs than half an hour we ſaw the ſouth ſhore,

at

at the diftance of about a mile, but got no anchorage; we therefore tacked, and ftood over to the north fhore. At eleven we faw the land on the north fhore, at which we were much alarmed; when to heighten the danger of our fituation,. the fky fuddenly became dark and lowering, and the noife of the waves, which we plainly heard dafhing againft the precipices, feemed to foretel the difafter which we thought ourfelves near experiencing; but at the very inftant, when we expected immediate deftruction, by hoifting out our head fails, our fhip veered round on the other tack, and left the breakers, on which we made fail with our head to the fouthward. During this critical fituation, from which we had been fo providentially delivered, the officers and men united in doing their utmoft, to extricate us from the impending danger, and behaved with that alacrity and intrepidity, which fo ftrongly characterize thofe who compofe our naval force, who juftly merit this transient teftimony to their honour. We now made a fignal for the Tamar to come up, fuppofing her cafe to be equally defperate with our own: however fhe foon failed a-head, firing a gun, and fhowing lights whenever fhe faw land. Our fituation was now very alarming; the ftorm increafed every moment, the weather was exceeding thick, the rain feemed to threaten another deluge, we had a long dark night before us, we were in a narrow channel, and furrounded on every fide with rocks and breakers. By the violence of the wind, our mizen-top-fail was fplit from the yard, and rendered entirely ufelefs. During this tempeftuous night we parted company with our confort. We now brought to, keeping the Dolphin's head to the S. W. but there being a prodigious fea, it broke over us fo often, that the whole deck was almoft under water. After bending a mizen-top-fail, and repairing as well as we could the damages our fhip had fuffered, on the 27th, about five in the morning, to our inexpreffible joy, the day began to dawn upon us; but the weather was fo hazy, that no land could be feen, though we knew it could not be far diftant, and it might be clofe under our lee. We therefore made a signal for the Tamar to come under our stern, which having done, we bore away, and, at seven, both ships came to an anchor in Cape Monday Bay, about one mile to the eastward, with the small bower, in 23 fathoms water, and veered out to a whole cable. We had twice in this perplexing traverse been within four leagues of Tuesday's Bay, at the western entrance of the strait, and had twice been driven back 10 or 12 leagues by the fury of opposing storms. When the season is so far advanced as it was when we attempted the passage through this strait, it is a most difficult and dangerous undertaking, as it blows a hurricane incessantly night and day, and the rain is as violent and constant as the wind, with such fogs as often render it impossible to discover any object at the distance of twice the ship's length. Our commodore, after attending to the necessary refreshments of his officers and men, who had endured the greatest fatigues, thought proper to name the high-land, which we had so miraculously escaped, Cape Providence. It rises to a very great height, and projects to the southward, being situated about four or five leagues from Cape Monday, but upon the opposite shore. On the 28th, finding our cables much damaged by the rocks, we condemned our best bower, and cut it into junk. We also bent a new one, which we rounded with old rigging eight fathoms from the water. In the mean time the Tamar had parted from her anchor, and was drove over to the east-side of the bay. She was brought up at a small distance from some rocks, against which she might otherwise have been dashed to pieces. On the 29th, at seven o'clock, A. M. we weighed and set sail, but, at intervals, were attended with hard squalls, from the westward, with heavy rains. While we were working to windward, the Tamar, steering by the south coast, ran a-ground, and made the signal of distress, by firing a gun, and hoisting her ensign in the mizen-shrouds ; on which we stood again into the bay, bore down to her assistance, and hoisted out our boats.

We

We sent anchor hawsers, with which they soon hove her off, and she came to anchor near us in Monday Bay.

On Saturday the 30th, the winds were so violent as perfectly to tear up the sea, and carry it higher than the top-masts. The storm came from W. N. W. and was more furious than any preceding one. A dreadful sea rolled over us, and dashed against the rocks with a noise like thunder. Happily, we did not part our cables, of which we were in constant apprehension, knowing the ground to be foul. Finding the ship laboured much, we lowered all the main and fore-yards, let go our small bower, veered a cable and a half on the best bower, and having bent the sheet cable, stood by the anchor all the rest of the day. On the 31st, about one o'clock, A. M. the weather, though somewhat moderate, continued till midnight to be dark, rainy, and tempestuous, when soon after the wind changed to the S. W.

On Monday the 1st of April, we had soft and moderate gales; yet still the weather continued thick, attended with heavy rain. At eight o'clock, A. M. we weighed our best bower, and found the cable much wounded in several places, which we thought a great misfortune, it being a fine new cable that had never been wet before. On the 3d, an officer was sent from each ship in the Tamar's boat, in quest of anchoring places on the south shore; and at the same time an officer was sent in our commodore's cutter, to explore the north shore. On the 4th, the cutter returned, with an account of having found a proper anchoring place to the west of the north shore. The commanding officer had met with a party of Indians, whose canoe was of a construction not observed before, being composed of planks sewed together. These Indians had no other covering than a piece of seal-skin thrown over their shoulders. Their food, of the most indelicate kind, was eaten raw. One of them tore a piece of stinking whale's blubber with his teeth, and then gave it his companions, who followed his example. One of these Indians, observing a sailor asleep, cut off the hinder

5 R 2   part

part of his jacket with a sharp flint. About eight o'clock A. M. we got under sail, and at six in the evening anchored in the bay, on the southern shore, which had been discovered, proposing to take in wood and water. While we lay here, several of the natives made a fire opposite to the ship; on which we invited them to come on board, by all the signs we could devise; but as they would not comply, the Commodore went on shore in the jolly-boat, and made them presents of several trifles, which much pleased them. He likewise distributed some biscuits among them, and was surprized to remark, that if one fell to the ground, not a single individual would offer to take it up without his permission. In the mean time some of the sailors being employed in cutting grass for the few remaining sheep we had on board, the Indians instantly ran to their assistance, and, tearing up the grass in large quantities, soon filled the boat. We were much delighted with this token of their good will, and we saw they were pleased with the pleasure the commodore had expressed on the occasion. When he returned to the ship, they followed him in their canoe, till they came near the Dolphin, at which they gazed with the most profound astonishment. Four of them were at length prevailed on to venture on board; and the Commodore, with a view to their diversion, desired one of our midshipmen to play on the violin, while some of the seamen danced. The poor Indians were extravagantly delighted; and one of them, to testify his gratitude, took to his canoe, and fetching some red paint, rubbed it all over the face of the musician; nor could the Commodore, but with the utmost difficulty, escape the like compliment. When they had been diverted some hours it was hinted to them, that they should go on shore, which they at length did, though with the utmost reluctance.

On Sunday the 7th, at six o'clock, A. M. we weighed, and got under sail with the wind at E. S. E. At this fortunate change of weather joy appeared in every countenance, and never were people in higher spirits. For six weeks we had been beating to windward, having been

been several times driven back, and narrowly escaped the greatest dangers; but we now flattered ourselves, that we should shortly arrive in the Pacific Ocean, the ultimate end of our wishes; but at eleven o'clock the wind ceased, and the current drove us two leagues, Cape Upright bearing S. E. five leagues, on which we came to with the stream anchor, in 110 fathoms water. At four o'clock, P. M. the boat belonging to the Tamar, which had, as we mentioned, been sent out some time before, returned from the westward, having been to the southward of Cape Desiada, on the south shore, and found many convenient places for anchorage; but the people in the boat were much fatigued by their long and laborious rowing. On the 8th, at two o'clock, A. M. we set sail, with the wind at W. by N. and at eleven, came to an anchor in a very good bay, between Cape Upright, and Cape Pillar. In this bay we found plenty of excellent fish not much unlike our trout, only of a more red cast. We here met with good anchorage, entirely secure from any winds from the N. N. W. to the S. E. and here you may sail with equal safety and pleasure, having from 14 to 20 fathoms muddy ground. About four in the afternoon, the wind came to the S. E. which gave us high satisfaction. We instantly weighed and sailed from the bay, in order to proceed to the westward. On standing out we saw the Tamar at anchor in Tuesday Bay, which lies on the south shore; but the wind suddenly veering round from the S. S. E. to the S. W. in a very heavy squall, attended with rain, obliged us to carry sail to get to an anchor in that bay; and the night approaching fast, the Tamar kept burning false fires, to direct us into it: but in order to enter, we were obliged to make several tacks under close reefed top-sails, in very great disorder, having rocks on each side: however we at last came to an anchor, with the small bower, in 12 fathoms; but the wind blew so strong, it was some time before we could get our sails handed.

Tuesday Bay is by far the finest we saw in these straits. It is capable of containing a number of large ships, which may ride in the greatest security, with good
ground,

ground, at not more than 25 fathoms water, free from rocks and fands. Into this bay Sir John Narborough recommends all fhips to anchor, that are bound to the weftward. Indeed we found no difficulty in being fupplied with good wood and water, and with excellent fifh in large quantities. Along the fides of the rocks are beautiful cafcades of water, with which the cafks may be filled with the greateft convenience. On the 9th, at fix o'clock, A. M. we weighed, leaving this fine bay, and failing to the W. N. W. We paffed Cape Pillar on the fouth fhore, with a fine gale from the S. E. where the ftraits are about nine leagues over. At ten, having now no occafion to be continually founding, for fear of fhoals and funken rocks, we got our long boat, yawl, and fix oared cutter under the half deck, with the 12 oared cutter under the booms; and fecured the hatches, bulk heads of the quarter deck, and forecaftle. At four in the afternoon we reached the extremity of the ftraits, where the diftance from Cape Victory on the north-fhore, to Cape Defiada on the fouth fhore, is 12 leagues, bearing from each other about N. and S. The whole length of the Straits of Magellan, in which we had been detained, chiefly by contrary winds, from the 17th of February to the 9th of April, is from Cape Virgin Mary to Cape Defiada, with every reach and turning, no more than about 116 leagues. We were now to leave the cold climate, and the tempeftuous feas of this fouthern latitude, juft after the time of the autumnal equinox, with the dreadful hurricanes that muft unavoidably attend the approach of winter, and to fteer joyfully to the northward, warmed with the hopes of meeting with calmer feas, and milder climates. But notwithftanding the difficulties and fufferings we experienced in paffing the ftraits of Magellan, when the weather we met with was beyond all defcription dreadful, yet the commodore prefers this paffage to going round Cape Horn, which he had twice doubled, and he recommends it to future navigators, to be at the eaftern entrance of the ftrait in the month of December, at which time he thinks even a fleet of fhips

might

might navigate it fafely in about three weeks. He juftly obferves, that the facility with which wood and water are to be obtained, the vaft plenty of vegetables, and the abundance of fifh, which may be almoft every where procured, are advantages highly in favour of this paffage. On our entering the Pacific Ocean, we found a great fwell running from the S. W.

On Friday the 20th, we defcried the ifland of Mafa Fuero to the weftward. The commodore thought it more advifeable to touch here, than at the ifland of Juan Fernandes; it being rather more fecure than the latter, from any difcoveries which the Spaniards might make of our defigns; in confequence of which our voyage, and all farther difcoveries might have been prevented. Mafa Fuero lies in the latitude of 33 deg. 28 min. S. and in 84 deg. 27 min. W. longitude from London. On the 27th, we had a diftant view of the ifland, the land of which rifes to a great height. Our cutter was fent afhore to find a place to anchor in, but returned at four in the afternoon without fuccefs, but caught a great number of fifh. They had no foundings with 100 fathoms line. On the 28th, however, we came to an anchor on the eaft-fide of the ifland, in 24 fathoms water, at which time the extremities of the ifland appeared on the S. and N. W. The tops of the mountains are not always to be feen, they being in fome parts covered with clouds, which hang hovering over them, and the air on their tops being feldom clear. At eleven in the morning we fent out our boat, with an officer, to find out a convenient place to wood and water in on fhore.

The furface of this ifland is very irregular; but the valleys have a beautiful verdure, and their fides are full of trees from the top to the bottom. At a great diftance indeed thofe beauties are not vifible, but when within a mile or thereabouts, they form a moft delightful profpect. The goats, which we faw in great numbers, were fo fhy, that we found it difficult to get near them, efpecially within the diftance of a mufquet fhot; however, we made a fhift to kill fome, and we thought
them

them to be excellent food, particularly the kids. We obſerved a remarkable circumſtance, with reſpect to two of them which we ſhot, they having had their ears ſlit when young. It is probable that the men who were ſent on board the Tryal Sloop by lord Anſon, to examine into the ſtate of this iſland, had more ſerious employment than that of ſlitting the ears of the goats; and it appears much more probable, that ſome ſolitary Selkirk had dwelt here, who, like his nameſake, at Juan Fernandes, when he caught more than he wanted, marked, and let them go. However, during our ſtay at this place, we ſaw no traces of any human being. Round the ſouth-ſide of the ſhore, we found a red earth, impregnated with large veins of gold colour. The ſhores are every where very ſteep, and near them you cannot find leſs than from 24 to 50 fathoms. We found it every where difficult to get on ſhore, it being full of rocks and large ſtones, with a very great ſurf. Round the iſland we met with great quantities of fiſh, ſuch as cavalies, bream, maids, and congers of a particular kind: with a ſingular ſort of fiſh called chimney-ſweepers, ſomewhat like our carp, only larger. There is another ſpecies of valuable fiſh which we called cod. It is not exactly like our cod in ſhape, but the taſte is equally agreeable. We likewiſe found a great number of cray-fiſh, which were ſo large as to weigh eight or ten pounds each. We ſaw a multitude of ſharks, one of which was near carrying off one of our men. As the great ſwell would not permit the boat to approach the ſhore, he was ſwimming a caſk to it; but the ſailor who was always left to take care of the boat, ſaw the ſhark within a few yards of his companion, juſt ready to ſeize upon him, and called to him to haſten aſhore, which, through his great fright, he could hardly reach. The boat-keeper having the boat-hook in his hand, ſtruck at the ſhark with great force, but without any viſible effect. The dog-fiſh we met with here are very miſchievous, and deſtroy abundance of the ſmaller ſort of fiſh: they frequently obliged us to haul in our lines, for when near, no other fiſh are to be found. Beſides
these

thefe, the fhore is generally crouded with feals, and fea-lions. The dog-fifh does not appear to have the leaft refemblance of a dog, or any other animal, and there-fore it is difficult to determine the derivation of its name. It has a roundifh body, and inftead of fcales, is covered with that rough fkin ufed by joiners and cabinet-makers for polifhing wood, generally known by the name of fifh fkin. Its back is of a brownifh afh-colour; but its belly is commonly white, and fmoother than the reft of its body. The eyes are covered with a double membrane, and the mouth armed with a double row of teeth. It has two fins on the back, with fharp prickles ftanding before them. It brings forth its young alive, and is never very large, feldom weigh-ing more than 20 pounds. The fea-lion has fome re-femblance to a feal, but is of a much larger fize, for thefe animals, when full grown, are from 12 to 20 feet in length, and from 8 to 15 feet round. The head is fmall in proportion to the body, and terminates in a fnout. In each jaw they have a row of large pointed teeth, two thirds of which are in fockets: but the others, without them, are moft folid, and ftand out of the mouth. They have fmall eyes and ears, with whifkers like a cat, and fmall noftrils, which are the only part deftitute of hair. The males are diftinguifhed by having a large fnout or trunk, hanging five or fix inches below the end of the upper jaw, which the females have not. The fkin of the fea-lion is covered with a fhort light dun coloured hair, but his fins and tail, which when on fhore, ferve him for feet, are almoft black; the fins or feet are divided at the ends like toes, but are joined by a web, that does not reach to their ex-tremities, and each toe is furnifhed with a nail. They are fo extremely fat, that on cutting through the fkin, which is near an inch in thicknefs, there is at leaft a foot of fat before you come to either lean or bones; and yet they are fo full of blood, that if deeply wounded in 10 or 12 places, there inftantly gufhes out as many fountains of blood, fpouting to a confiderable diftance. Their flefh refembles in tafte that of beef; and their fat, on being melted, makes good oil.   The males are of a much larger size than the females, and both of them continue at sea all the summer, and coming ashore at the beginning of winter, stay there during that season, when they engender, and bring forth their young, having commonly two at a birth, which they suckle with their milk.   On shore they feed on the verdure that grows near the water: and sleep in herds, in the most miry places they can find, with some of the males at a distance, who are sure to alarm them, if any one approaches, sometimes by snorting like horses, and at others by grunting like hogs.   The males have frequently furious battles about their females.

This island is usually called by the Spaniards, the Lesser Juan Fernandes, it being about 22 leagues to the W. by S. of the island more frequently called by that name: and is termed Masa-Fuero, from its being at a greater distance from the continent.   In his way to this place, the Commodore was not far from the spot, where he had endured the extremity of wretchedness 24 years before, when he was a midshipman, under Captain Cheap, on board the Wager, a frigate of 28 guns, one of the squadron which was commanded by Commodore Anson, in his memorable expedition to the South Sea, and which was wrecked on the shore of an island on the coast of Chiloe.   In many respects this island and that of Juan Fernandes resemble each other: the shore of both is steep, and for the most part have little fresh water; but no spring was here found comparable to that of the watering place at the Greater Juan Fernandes: they are both mountainous, and adorned with a variety of trees, which with the different bearings of the hills, and the windings of the valleys form, even from the sea, the most rude, and at the same time the most elegant prospects.   None of the trees of the greater Juan Fernandes are large enough for any considerable timber, except the myrtle, the trunks of some of which are of such a size, as to be worked 40 feet in length.   But the goats of the greater Juan Fernandes are much fewer in number than at Masa-Fuero;
the

the Spaniards having placed no dogs on the latter
ifland, in order to deftroy them. With refpect to
the plenty of excellent fifh, and the number of amphibious animals, as feals and fea-lions, which line the
fhores of both, they perfectly refemble each other. In
Mafa-Fuero are many cafcades, or fine falls of water,
pouring down its fides into the fea. But our ftay here
was fo fhort, and we were fo feldom on fhore, that we
had neither leifure nor opportunity to view this little
ifland with the accuracy and precifion that might be
wifhed, and that was abfolutely neceffary for taking a
full view of the delightful fpots which we faw, with the
confufion that neceffarily attends a diftant profpect.
The greateft difadvantage belonging to this ifland is
that of not having fuch a commodious harbour, as the
ifland of Juan Fernandes.

.While we were taking in water for the fhips, whenever our men found any great furf, they by order of the
Commodore, fwam to and from the boats in cork
jackets; for he would by no means admit of their going
into the water without putting them on, he being fully
fenfible that when properly fecured on the body, the
perfon who ufes them cannot poffibly fink, or fuffer any
confiderable inconvenience, if he does but take care to
keep his head above the furface of the water, which
is eafily done. But thefe jackets afforded no defence
againft the fharks, which were often very near the
fwimmers, and would dart even into the very furf to feize
them: our people however providentially efcaped them.
One of thefe voracious fifh feized a large feal clofe to
one of the watering boats, and devoured it in an inftant; and the commodore faw another do the fame,
clofe to the ftern of the fhip. The following little
adventure alfo took place while we lay off this ifland.
The gunner and one of the feamen, who were with
others, on fhore for water, were left behind all night,
being afraid to venture in the boat, as the fea ran high.
The commodore being informed of this circumftance,
fent them word, that as blowing weather might be
expected, the fhip might be driven from her moorings

in

in the night; in which cafe they would infallibly be left behind. This meffage being delivered, the gunner fwam to the boat; but the failor faying, he had rather die a natural death than be drowned, refufed to make the attempt: and taking a melancholy farewel of his companions, refolved to abide his fate; when juft as the boat was going to put off, a midfhipman took the end of a rope in his hand, and fwam on fhore, where he remonftrated with the difconfolate tar on the foolifh refolution he had taken, till having an opportunity of throwing the rope, in which was a running knot, round his body, he called to the boats crew to haul away, who inftantly dragged him through the furf into the boat; he had, however, fwallowed fo much water that he appeared to be dead; but by holding him up by the heels, he was foon recovered; and on the day follow-ing was perfectly well.

Having taken in as much wood and water as the weather would permit, the furf fometimes fwelling in fuch a manner, as to prevent our boats coming near the fhore, we thought of leaving the ifland; but before our departure, in the evening of the 29th, the com-modore removed Captain Mouat from the Tamar, and appointed him Captain of the Dolphin, all flag-officers having a commander under them. This occafioned feveral other changes. Mr. Cumming our firft lieu-tenant, was appointed Captain of the Tamar, and we received in his room Mr. Carteret, her firft lieutenant. The commodore alfo gave Mr. Kendal, one of the mates of the Dolphin, a commiffion as fecond lieute-nant of the Tamar. After thefe promotions, on the 30th, we weighed, and fteered along the E. and N. E. fide of the ifland, but could find no anchoring place; we bore away therefore, with a frefh breeze at S. E. and at noon the center of the ifland was diftant eight leagues in . rection of S. S. E.

CHAP.

CHAP. III.

The Dolphin and Tamar continue their course from the Island of Masa-Fuero westward—Arrive off certain beautiful Islands, named the Islands of Disappointment, because no places of anchorage could be found—The natives of these Islands described—King George's Islands discovered—Another Island is seen, and called the Prince of Wales's Island—A description of these islands—Also a particular account of the inhabitants, and of several incidents that happened while the ships were exploring them—The Island of Danger passed—The Duke of York's island discovered—Another new Island found, which receives the name of Byron's Island—The Persons and behaviour of the Indians described.

ON the first of May, being Wednesday, we continued to steer N. by W. but on the 2nd, at noon, we altered our course, and steered due west, with the view of falling in with an island, which is laid down in the charts by the name of Davis's Land, in latitude 27 deg. 30 min. S. but on Thursday the 9th, the commodore laid aside his design, being in latitude 26 deg. 46 min. S. and in 94 deg. 45 min. W. longitude; and, having a great run to make, he determined to steer a N. W. course, till he should fall in with a true trade wind, and then to search for Solomon's Islands; but the discovery of both these spots of land was reserved for a future navigator; for the commodore, in crossing the southern ocean, missed of the islands, which have since been named the Society Isles; and about the same distance to the southward of the Marquesas, discovered by Mendana, a Spaniard, in the year 1597, and afterwards explored by Captain Cook. We had hitherto enjoyed a continued series of fine weather; but the nearer we approached the line, the crew began to fall down with the scurvy very fast, and every day, to the end of this month, brought with it an increase of that dreadful disorder. On the 10th, and following

day,

day, we faw feveral dolphins and bonettas round the ship, and obferved a few birds which had a fhort beak, all their bodies being white, except the back, and the upper part of their wings. On the 14th, in latitude 24 deg. 30 min. S. and in 97 deg. 45 min. W. longitude, we faw more of thefe birds, and feveral grampufes, from whence imagining we might approach toward fome land, we kept a good look out, but found our expectations difappointed.

On Thurfday the 16th, two remarkable birds, as large as geefe, with white bodies, and black legs, were obferved flying very high, from whence it was conjectured that we had paffed fome main-land, or iflands, to the fouthward of us; for the laft night we obferved, that, notwithftanding we had a great fwell from that quarter, yet the water became quite fmooth for a few hours, after which the fwell returned. On Wednefday the 22nd, being in latitude 20 deg. 52 min. S. and in 115 deg. 38 min. W. the fwell from the fouthward was fo great, that we expected every minute, to fee our mafts roll over the fhip's fide; to prevent which, and to eafe the fhip, we hauled more to the northward. This day we caught, for the firft time, two bonettas, and were vifited by fome tropic birds, larger than any we had feen before. Their whole plumage was white, and they had in each of their tails two long feathers.

On Sunday the 26th, we were in latitude 16 deg. 55 min. S. and in 127 deg. 55 min. W. longitude, when we faw two large birds about the fhip, all black, except their necks and beaks. The feathers of their wings and tails were long, yet they flew very heavily. We fuppofed them, from this laft circumftance, to be a fpecies that did not fly far from the fhore. We had imagined, that before we had run fix degrees to the northward of Mafa-Fuero, wefhould have been favoured with a fettled trade wind to the S. E. but the winds ftill continued to the north, though we had a mountainous fwell from the S. W. On the 28th, two other birds, one black and white, and the other brown and white, would have fettled on the yards, but were intimidated

timidated by the working of the ship. On the 31st, our people began to fall down with the scurvy very fast, which made us wish for land. At length after a passage of 31 days,

On Friday the 7th of June, at one o'clock, A. M. the Tamar made the signal of seeing land; on which we brought to till day light; and in the mean time flattered ourselves with the pleasing hopes of getting some kinds of refreshments, of which we stood in great need, especially for those who were sick; and we knew, that the islands, which are situated within twenty degrees of the line, are frequently well stored with fruit of all kinds. Soon after day-break, we had the pleasure of seeing a low small island covered with beautiful trees, and on sailing to the leeward, we were regaled with the smell of the finest fruits. The poor wretches who were able to crawl upon deck, stood gazing on this little paradise, which however nature had forbidden them to enter, with sensations which cannot easily be conceived. They saw cocoa-nuts in abundance, the milk of which is perhaps the most powerful antiscorbutic in the world; and to increase their mortification, they saw the shells of many turtles scattered about the shore. These refreshments, for want of which they were languishing to death, were as effectually beyond their reach, as if there had been half the circumference of the globe between them; for an officer, having been quite round the island, reported, that no bottom could be found, within less than a cable's length from the shore, which was surrounded, close to the beach with a steep coral rock; and that, at the distance of three quarters of a mile from the shore, no soundings could be had within 140 fathom of line. Besides, had we at one place cast anchor in 45 fathoms, the surf upon the shore was so great, that the ship would have been in great danger of being stranded. This island lies in the latitude of 14 deg. 5 min. S. and in 145 deg. 4 min. W. longitude from London. It extends 12 miles in length; and in the body of the island is a good deal of water, which was, we apprehend,

2   washed

washed over the banks, as some of them appeared to
have been broken. We soon perceived it was inhabited,
for we saw numbers of Indians upon the beach, with
spears in their hands, that were at least 16 feet long.
They ran along the shore, abreast of the ships, dancing,
hallooing, and shouting in the most hideous manner.
They frequently brandished their long spears, and then
threw themselves backwards, and lay a few minutes
motionless, as if they had been dead; doubtless meaning to signify thereby, that they would kill whoever
should presume to go on shore. Notwithstanding various signs of amity and good-will were made them by
our people in the boat, nothing could abate their hostile
disposition. They made in their turn signs for us to
be gone; and always took care, as the boat sailed along
the shore, to move in the same direction, and accompany it; and though the men saw some turtle at a distance, they could get at none, as those Indians still kept
opposite to them. The sailors were eager to fire on the
brave defenders of their native soil, but their officers
withheld them from such a wanton act of cruelty; and
as no anchorage could be found, the commodore
thought it most adviseable to steer to the adjacent
island. These Indians are of a very black complexion,
with well proportioned limbs, and seemed to be extremely active, and fleet of foot to an astonishing degree.
Their women, who were only to be distinguished by
their bosoms, had something twisted round their waists,
and hanging down from thence, to hide what nature
taught them to conceal, as had also the men; and this
was their only cloathing. They altogether amounted
to about 50 in number; and to the S. W. we could
perceive their huts, under the shade of the most lovely
grove we ever saw. While sailing along shore, we took
notice, that in one place the natives had fixed upright
in the sand two spears, to the top of which they had
fastened several things that fluttered in the air, and that
some them were every moment kneeling down before
them, as we supposed, invoking assistance of some in-
visible being to defend them against their invaders.

Among

Among other figns of good will that they could devife, our men threw them bread, and many other things, none of which they vouchfafed fo much as to touch, but with great expedition hauled five or fix large canoes, which we faw on the beach, up into a wood. When this was done they waded into the water, and feemed to watch for an opportunity of laying hold of the boat, that they might drag her on fhore.

On Saturday the 8th, the boats having reported a fecond time, that no anchoring ground could be found about this ifland, we worked, at fix o'clock, P. M. under the lee of the other ifland, which lay to the weftward of the former, and fent out our cutter to found for a place to anchor in. We now obferved feveral other low iflands, or rather peninfulas, moft of them being joined one to the other by a neck of land, very narrow, and almoft level with the furface of the water, which breaks high over it. Here, to our great difappointment, no refrefhments could be procured, owing to the inacceffible nature of the coaft; and we faw a much greater number of Indians furrounding the fhore, who, with fpears of equal length, followed us in like manner, feveral hundreds of them running about the coaft in great diforder; and at the fame time we beheld the ifland covered with a prodigious number of cocoa-nut, plantain, and tamarind trees. Having waited fome time with great impatience for the return of our cutter, we fired a gun, as a fignal for our men to come on board, which terribly alarmed the Indians, who feemed to confult among themfelves what meafures it would be moft prudent for them to take. They kept abreaft of the boats, as they went founding along the fhore, and ufed many threatening geftures, to deter them from landing. Their canoes they dragged into the woods, and at the fame time the women came with great ftones in their hands, to affift the men in preventing, what they doubtlefs thought to be, our hoftile intentions. The cutter returned near noon, bringing much the fame account of this as of the other ifland, there being no foundings at a cable's length from the shore, with a line of 100 fathoms. This gave us inexpressible concern, as we had now 30 sick on board, to whom the land air, the fruit and vegetables, that appeared so beautiful and attractive, would have afforded immediate relief and returning health. Finding it impossible to obtain those tempting refreshments which hung full in our view, we quitted, with longing eyes, this paradise in appearance, to which the name was with propriety given of the Islands of Disappointment. Continuing our course to the westward, on the 9th we saw land again, at the distance of seven leagues, W. S. W. At seven o'clock, P. M. we brought to for the night. In the morning of the 10th, being within three miles of the shore, we found it to be a long low island, with a white beach of a pleasant appearance, covered with cocoa-nut and ocher trees, and surrounded with a rock of red coral. We stood along the N. E. side, within half a mile of the shore, and the natives, on seeing us, made great fires, and ran along the beach, abreast of the ships in great numbers, armed like the natives of the islands we had last visited, and like them, they appeared to be a robust and fierce race of men. Over the land we could discern a large lake of salt-water, which appeared to be two or three leagues wide, and to reach within a small distance of the opposite shore. Into this lake we observed a small inlet, about a league from the S. W. point, where is a little town seated under the shade of a fine grove of cocoa-nut-trees. The commodore immediately sent off the boats to sound; but they could find no anchorage, the shore being every where perpendicular as a wall, except at the mouth of the inlet. We stood close in with the shore, and saw hundreds of the natives ranged in good order, and standing up to their waists in water: they were all armed, like those we had seen in the other islands, and one of them carried a piece of mat, fastened to the top of a pole, which we imagined was an ensign. They made a loud and incessant noise; and in a little time, many large canoes came down to the boats, but with no friendly intentions, for we soon perceived their

4

main

main defign was to haul our boats on fhore. One of them went into the Tamar's boat, and with the greateft adroitnefs feized a feaman's jacket, and jumping overboard with it, never once appeared above water, till he was clofe in fhore among his companions: another got hold of a midfhipman's hat, but not knowing how to take it off, he pulled it downwards, inftead of lifting it up; fo. that the owner had time to prevent his taking it away. Our feamen bore thefe infults with much patience, as tranfgreffions of the fimple children of nature.

Finding about noon, that there was no anchorage here, we fteered along the fhore to the weftermoft point of the ifland, and when we came to it we faw another ifland, bearing S. W. by W. at about four leagues diftance. We were now about one league beyond the inlet, where we had left the natives; but they were not contented with our having quietly left them; for we now obferved two large double canoes failing after the fhip, with about 30 men in each, all armed after the manner of their country. The boats were a good way to leeward of us; and the canoes paffing between the fhip and the fhore, feemed to chace them with great refolution. Upon this the commodore made a fignal for the boats to fpeak with the canoes, which they no fooner perceived, than they turned towards the Indians, who being inftantly feized with a fudden panic, hauled down their fails, and paddled away at a furprizing rate. The boats, however, came up with them; but notwithftanding the dreadful furf that broke upon the fhore, the canoes pufhed through it, and were inftantly hauled upon the beach. Our boats followed them, when the natives, dreading an invafion of their country, prepared to defend it with javelins, clubs, and ftones: upon feeing this our men fired, and killed two or three of them; one of whom who ftood clofe to the boats, received three balls, which paffed quite through his body; yet he afterwards took up a large ftone, and died in the action of throwing it. The Indians carried off the reft of their dead, except this

one

one man, and made the beft of their way back to their
companions at the inlet. The boats then returned, and
brought off the two canoes they had purfued. One of
them was 32 feet long, and the other fomewhat lefs :
both were of a very curious conftruction, and muft have
been formed with prodigious labour. They confifted
of planks exceedingly well wrought, and in many places
adorned with carving; thefe planks were fewed together,
and over every feam there was a flip of tortoifefhell, very
ingenioufly faftened to keep out the weather. Their
bottoms were as fharp as a wedge ; and the boats being
very narrow, two of them were joined laterally together
by a couple of ftrong fpars, fo that there was a fpace of
about eight feet between them. A maft was hoifted in
each, and a fail was fpread between the mafts : this fail was
made of matting, and remarkable for the neatnefs of its
workmanfhip. Their paddles alfo are very curious, and
their cordage as good, and as well made as any in
England, though it appeared to be made only of the
outer covering of the cocoa-nut. When thefe veffels
fail, feveral men fit on the fpars which hold the canoes
together. The furf which broke high upon the fhore,
rendering it impoffible to procure refrefhments for the
fick, in this part of the ifland, we returned back to the
inlet, in order to try what more could be done there ;
but the boats being fent to found the inlet again, returned, and confirmed their former account, that it
afforded no anchorage for a fhip. While the boats
were abfent, a great number of the natives were feen
upon the fpot where we had left them in the morning,
who feemed very bufy in loading and manning fome
canoes which lay clofe to the beach. The commodore,
thinking they might be troublefome, and being unwilling to have recourfe to the fanguinary means which had
before been ufed, fired a fhot over their heads, which
produced the intended effect, for they inftantly difperfed. Juft before the clofe of the evening, our boats
landed, and brought off a few cocoa-nuts, but faw none
of the inhabitants.

On Tuefday the 11th, in the morning, the commodore,

modore, with all the men who were ill of the scurvy, and capable of doing it, went on shore, where they continued the whole day. The houses were totally deserted, except by the dogs, who howled incessantly, from the time we came on shore, till we returned to the ship. The wigwams were low mean structures, thatched with the leaves of cocoa-nut trees; but they were delightfully situated in a fine grove of stately trees: many of which were such as we were entirely unacquainted with. The shore was covered with coral, and shells of very large pearl oysters, and the commodore firmly believed, that as profitable a pearl fishery might be established here as any in the world. In one of the huts was found the carved head of a rudder, which had evidently belonged to a Dutch long-boat. It was very old and worm-eaten. A piece of hammered iron, a piece of brass, and some small iron tools, were also found, all which had most probably been obtained from the same ship to which the boat belonged. The inhabitants of these islands were not over-burdened with cloathing: the men we saw were naked, but the women had a piece of cloth of some kind hanging from the waist as low as the knee. The cocoa-nut tree seems to furnish them with all the necessaries of life, particularly food, sails, cordage, timber, and vessels to hold water. Close to their houses we discovered buildings of another kind, which appeared to be burying-places. They were situated under lofty trees that gave a thick gloomy shade: the sides and tops were of stone, and they somewhat resembled in their figure, the square tombs with a flat top in our country church-yards. Near these buildings we found many neat boxes, full of human bones; and upon the branches of the trees that shaded them, hung a great number of heads and bones of turtles, and a variety of other fish, inclosed with a kind of basket-work of reeds. We here saw no venomous creature; but the musquetoes covered us from head to foot, and infested not only the boat, but the ship, being an intolerable torment. We observed a great number of parrots, and parroquets, with a variety of other birds, altogether
unknown

unknown to us. We faw alfo a beautiful kind of doves, fo tame, that fome of them frequently came clofe to us, and followed us into the Indian huts. The frefh water here is good but rather fcarce : the wells that fupply the natives being fo fmall, that when two or three cocoa-nut fhells have been filled from them, they are dry for a few minutes ; but as they prefently fill again, if a little pains were taken to enlarge them, they would abundantly fupply any fhip with water. We obtained cocoa-nuts and fcurvy-grafs in great quantities, which were moft ineftimable acquifitions, as by this time there was not a man on board who was wholly untouched with the fcurvy. All this day the natives kept themfelves clofely concealed, and did not even make a fmoke upon any part of the ifland, as far as we could fee. In the evening we all returned on board, highly pleafed with this day's amufement and work. This ifland lies about 67 leagues from the Iflands of Difappointment, in the direction of W. half S. and in the latitude of 14 deg. 29 min. S. longitude 148 deg. 50 min. W. The inhabitants feem to have fome notions of religion, as we faw a place, which we concluded to be appropriated to their manner of worfhip. A rude, but very agreeable avenue opened to a fpacious area, in which was one of the largeft and moft fpreading cocoas we faw in the place ; before which were feveral large ftones, probably altars ; and from the tree hung the figure of a dog adorned with feathers.

On Wednefday the 12th, we vifited another ifland which had been feen to the weftward ; and fteered S. W. by W. clofe along the N. E. fide of it, which is about fix or feven leagues long. This ifland makes much the fame appearance as the other, having a large falt lake in the middle of it. The fhip no fooner came in fight, than the natives repaired in great numbers to the beach, armed in the fame manner as thofe already defcribed, but not of fuch boifterous manners. The boats founded as ufual along the fhore, but had ftrict orders not to moleft the Indians, except it fhould be abfolutely neceffary in their own defence ; but on the

contrary, to ufe every gentle method in order to obtain
their confidence and good will. They rowed as near
the fhore as they durft for the furf; and making figns
of their wanting water, the Indians readily underftood
them, and directed them to run down farther along the
fhore, which they did, till they came abreaft of fuch a
clufter of houfes, as we had juft left upon the other
ifland. The Indians followed them thither, and were
there joined by many others. The boats immediately
hauled clofe into the furf, and we brought to with the
fhips, at a little diftance from the fhore; upon which, a
ftout old man, with a long white beard, came down
from the houfes to the beach, attended by a young
man, and appeared to have the authority of a chief or
king. On his making a fignal, the reft of the Indians
retired to a fmall diftance, and he then advanced to
the water's edge, holding in one hand the green branch
of a tree, and in the other grafping his beard, which
he preffed to his bofom. In this attitude he made a
long fpeech, or rather fong, for it had an agreeable
cadence. We were forry that we could not underftand
him, but to fhew our good will, while he was fpeaking, we threw him fome trifling prefents, which he
would neither touch himfelf, nor fuffer them to be
touched by others, till he had done. He then walked
into the water, and threw to us the green branch;
after which he took up the things which had been
thrown from the boats. Every thing having now a
friendly appearance, we made figns that they fhould lay
down their arms; and moft of them having complied,
one of the midfhipmen, encouraged by this teftimony
of confidence and friendfhip, leaped out of the boat
with his clothes on, and fwam through the furf to the
fhore, on which the Indians flocked round him, finging
and dancing as if to exprefs their joy, and began to
examine his clothes with feeming curiofity; they particularly fhewed figns of admiration on viewing his
waiftcoat; upon which he took it off, and prefented
it to them. This act of generofity had a difagreeable
effect; for he had no fooner given away his waiftcoat,

than

than one of the Indians untied his cravat, and the next
moment fnatched it from his neck, and ran away with
it. He therefore, to prevent his being ftripped, made
the beft of his way back to the boat. We were ftill
however upon good terms, and feveral of the Indians
fwam off to us, fome of them bringing a cocoa-nut, and
others a little frefh water in a cocoa-nut fhell. We
endeavoured to obtain from them fome pearls, but we
could not make ourfelves underftood. We fhould, however, probably have fucceeded better, had an intercourfe
of any kind been eftablifhed between us ; but unluckily
no anchorage could be found for the fhips. In the lake
we faw two very large veffels, one of which had two mafts,
and fome cordage aloft. To thefe two iflands the commodore gave the name of King George's Iflands, in
honour of his prefent Majefty. That which we laft
vifited lies in latitude 14 deg. 41 min. S. longitude
149 deg. 15 min. W.

On Thurfday the 13th, having continued our courfe
to the weftward, about three o'clock, P. M. we defcried
land, bearing S. S. W. diftant fix leagues. We immediately ftood for it, and found it to lie E. and W.
and to be about 60 miles in length. It is diftant from
King George's Iflands about 48 leagues, in the direction of fouth 80 deg. W. fituated in the latitude of
15 deg. S. and the weftermoft end of it in 151 deg.
53 min. W. longitude. We ran along the fouth-fide
of it, and the appearance of the country exhibited a
pleafant green furface ; but a dreadful furf breaks upon
every part of the fhore, with foul ground at fome diftance, and at about three leagues are many rocks and
iflots. It has a narrow neck of land running S. by W.
and N. by E. We faw a number of Indians, and feveral
canoes difperfed about different parts of the ifland, to
which was given the name of the Prince of Wales's
Ifland. From its weftern extremity, we fteered north
82 deg. W. and on the 16th at noon, obferved in latitude 14 deg. 28 min. S. and in 156 deg. 23 min. W.
longitude. The mountainous fwell from the fouthward,
which to this day we had loft, now returned ; and we
were

were attended with vaft flocks of birds, which in the
evening took their flight to the southward ; from which
appearances we concluded, more land lay in that direction ; the difcovery of which we fhould have attempted,
had not the ficknefs of the crews in both fhips been
an infuperable bar to fuch an attempt. On the 17th,
the fwell continued, and various kinds of birds flew
about the fhip ; fuppofing therefore land to be not far
diftant, we proceeded with caution, for the iflands in
this part of the ocean render navigation very dangerous,
they being fo low, that a fhip may be clofe in with them
before they are feen. Nothing material occurred on
the 18th and 19th. On the 20th, we found our latitude
to be 12 deg. 33 min. S. longitude 167 deg. 47 min. W.
The Prince of Wales's Ifland, diftant 313 leagues.

On Friday the 21ft, at feven o'clock, A. M. we again
faw land a-head, bearing W. N. W. and diftant about
eight leagues. It had the appearance of three iflands
from this point of fight; and the commodore took them
for Solomon's Iflands, feen by Quiros, in the beginning
of the 17th century, and very imperfectly defcribed by
him. But on our nearer approach, we found only a
fingle ifland, about 12 miles in length, furrounded with
fhoals and breakers, on which account it was named the
Ifland of Danger. The reef of rocks which we firft
faw, when we approached this ifle, lies in latitude
10 deg. 15 min. S. and in 169 deg. 28 min. W. longitude ; and it bears from this reef W. N. W. diftant nine leagues. From the Prince of Wales's Ifland
it bears north 76 deg. 48 min. W. diftant nine leagues.
As you run in with the land, you fee the fands, and
about feven leagues off from the moft eaftern parts of
the ifland, lies a ridge of rocks, near a quarter of a mile
in length, and when abreaft of thefe, the ifland bears
W. by N. We failed round the north end, and upon
the N. W. and W. fide faw innumerable rocks and
fhoals, which ftretched near two leagues into the fea,
and were extremely dangerous. But as to the ifland
itfelf, it had a more beautiful and fertile appearance
than any we had feen before, and, like the reft, abounded

No. 28.   5 U   with

with people and cocoa-nut trees. The habitations of
the natives we saw standing in groups all along the
coast. At a distance from this we observed a large
vessel under sail. It was with much regret that we
could not sufficiently examine this place, which we were
obliged to leave by reason of the rocks and breakers,
that surrounded it in every direction, which rendered
the hazard attending a minute survey, more than an
equivalent to every advantage we might procure.

On Sunday the 23d, having still proceeded in our
course to the westward, at nine o'clock, P. M. the
Tamar, who was a-head, fired a gun, and our people
imagined they saw breakers to the leeward; but we
were soon convinced, that what had been taken for
breakers, was nothing more than the undulating reflection of the moon, which was going down, and shone
faintly from behind a cloud in the horizon. We had
this day excessive hard showers of rain, on which we
seized such a favourable opportunity of filling our
casks with a fresh supply of water. This is performed
on board of ship, by extending large pieces of canvas
in an horizontal position, hanging them by the corners,
and placing a cannon ball, or any heavy body in the
center; by which means the rain running trickling
down to the middle, pours in a stream into the casks
placed under. In this manner the Manilla ships, during the long passages they make through the South
Seas, recruit their water, from the great showers of rain
which at this season of the year fall in these latitudes,
for which purpose they always carry a great number of
earthen-jars with them. On the 24th, we had moderate
fair weather, and at ten o'clock, A. M. we descried
another island, bearing S. S. W. distant about seven
or eight leagues. We found it to be low, and covered
with wood, among which were cocoa-nut trees in great
abundance. But though the place itself has a pleasant
appearance, a dreadful sea breaks upon almost every
part of the coast, and a great deal of foul ground lies
about it. A large lake is in the middle of this island,
and it is near 39 miles in circumference. It is about

four

four leagues in length from E. to W. nearly as much in breadth, and lies in latitude 8 deg. 33 min. S. and in 178 deg. 16 min. W. longitude from London. We failed quite round it, and, when on the lee-side, sent our boats out to sound for an anchoring-place. They returned with the unfavourable news that no soundings were to be got near the shore. However, having been dispatched a second time to procure some refreshments for the sick, they landed with great difficulty, and brought off about 200 cocoa-nuts, which to persons in our circumstances, were an inestimable treasure. They found on shore thousands of sea-fowl sitting on their nests, and so divested of fear, that they did not attempt to move at the approach of the seamen, but suffered themselves to be knocked down, having no apprehension of the mischief that was intended them. The ground was covered with land crabs; these were the only animals we saw, nor did we observe the least sign of any inhabitants; and it was supposed never before to have received the mark of human foot steps. The commodore was inclined to believe, that this island was the same that in the French charts is laid down about a degree to the eastward of the great island of Saint Elizabeth, which is the principal of Solomon's Islands, but being afterwards convinced of the contrary, he named it the Duke of York's Island, in honour of his late royal highness.

On Friday the 28th, we gave up all hopes of seeing Solomon's Islands, which we had expected to visit, and should certainly have found, had there been any such islands in the latitude in which they are placed in our maps. These islands are said to have been discovered by Ferdinand de Quiros, who represented them as exceeding rich and populous; and several Spaniards who have pretended that they were driven thither by stress of weather, have said, that the natives, with respect to their behaviour, were much like those of the continent of America, and that they had ornaments of gold and silver; but though the Spaniards have at different times sent several persons in search of these islands, it was always without fuccefs : which muft probably proceed, either from the uncertainty of the latitude in which they are faid to be found, or the whole being a fiction. There is indeed good reafon to believe, that there is no good authority for laying down Solomon's Iflands in the fituation that is affigned them by the French : the only perfon who has pretended to have feen them, is the above mentioned Quiros, and we doubt whether he left behind him any account of them, by which they might be found by future navigators.   However, we continued our courfe in the track of thefe fuppofed iflands, till the 29th, and being then 10 deg. to the weftward of their fituation in the chart, without having feen any thing of them, we hauled to the northward, in order to crofs the line, and afterwards to fhape our courfe for the Ladrone Iflands, which though a long run, we hoped to accomplifh, before we fhould be dif-treffed for water, notwithftanding it now began to fall fhort.   This day we obferved in latitude 8 deg. 13 min. S. and in 176 deg. 20 min. E. longitude.

On Tuefday the 2nd of July, at four o'clock, P. M. we difcovered an ifland bearing north, diftant fix leagues. We ftood for it till fun-fet, and then kept off and on for the night.   In the morning we found it to be a low flat ifland, of a moft delightful afpect, full of wood, among which the cocoa-nut tree was very confpicuous. However, we had the mortification to find much foul ground about it, upon which the fea broke with a threatening furf.   We fteered along the S. W. fide of it, which we judged to be about four leagues in length, and foon perceived that it was not only inhabited, but very populous.   Immediately about 60 canoes, or rather proas, put off to the fhips, none of which had fewer than three, nor more than fix perfons on board.   Thefe Indians had nothing of that fierce difpofition, which had, in many inftances, totally cut off all friendly in-tercourfe.   After gazing at the fhips for fome time, one of them fuddenly fprung out of his proa into the fea, and fwam to the Dolphin, then ran up the fides like a cat.   He had no fooner reached the decks, than fitting

down,

down, he burft into a violent fit of laughter; then ftarted up, and ran all over the fhip, attempting to fteal whatever he could lay his hands on; but, being ftark naked, he was always foiled. A feaman put him on a jacket and trowfers, which caufed great diverfion, as he difplayed all the antics of a monkey. At length he leaped over-board, with his new habiliments, and fwam back to his proa. The fuccefs of this adventurer encouraged feveral others to fwim to the fhip, and whatever they could feize they carried off with aftonifhing agility. Thefe Indians are tall, well-proportioned, and clean limbed; their fkin of a bright copper colour; their features exceeding regular; and their countenances expreffing a furprifing mixture of intrepidity and cheerfulnefs. Their hair is black and long, which fome wore tied up behind in a great bunch, others in knots: fome had long beards, fome only whifkers, and fome nothing more than a fmall tuft at the point of the chin. Except their ornaments, they were all ftark naked: thefe confifted of fhells very prettily difpofed, and ftrung together, and were worn round their necks, wrifts and waifts. All their ears were bored, but no ornaments were feen in them; though as the lobes of their ears hung down almoft to their fhoulders, it is highly probable, that fomething of confiderable weight is at times affixed to them by way of ornament. One man in the group appeared to be a perfon of confequence; he had a ftring of human teeth round his waift, which nothing that was fhewed him could induce him to part with. Some were unarmed, but others had a very formidable weapon, confifting of a kind of fpear, very broad at the end, and ftuck full of fhark's teeth, which are as fharp as a lancet at the fides, for about three feet of its length. The officers fhewed them cocoa-nuts, and made figns that they wanted more; but inftead of giving any intimation that their country furnifhed fuch fruit, they endeavoured to feize upon thofe they faw. To this ifland we gave the name of Byron's Ifland. It is feated in latitude 1 deg. 18 min. S. and in 173 deg. 46 min. E. longitude.

CHAP.

CHAP. IV.

The two Ships depart from Byron's Island—Cross the Equi-
noxial Line—Arrive at Tinian—Anchor in the very Spot
where Lord Anson lay in the Centurion—A Description
of that Island, with remarkable Incidents and Trans-
actions—Observations on the Indians, and the Construc-
tion of their Proas—They sail from the Ladrone Islands
—Touch at the Isle of Pulo Timoan.—An Account of the
Malays—Arrive at Batavia—A particular Description
of the State and Situation of this Country—Passage from
Batavia to the Cape of Good Hope—Observations during
our Stay there—Set sail and pass the Island of St.
Helena—The Tamar steers for Antigua in order to refit—
And the Dolphin on the 9th of May, 1766, anchors in
the Downs.

ON Wednesday the third of July, we sent out the
boats to sound, soon after we had brought to off
Byron's Island; when returned, they reported, that
there was depth of ground at 30 fathom, within two
cables length of the shore, but as the bottom was coral
rock, and the soundings much too near for a ship to lie in
safety, we were obliged to make sail, without having
procured any refreshments for our sick. We now steered
nearly due north, and crossed the line two degrees beyond the extremity of western longitude from London,
or in 178 deg. E. In our course, we saw great quantities of fish, but none could be taken, except sharks,
which were become a good dish even at the commodore's own table.

On Sunday the 21st, all our cocoa-nuts by this time
being expended, the men began to fall down again with
the scurvy. These nuts had, in an astonishing manner, checked the progress of this dreadful disorder:
many whose limbs were become as black as ink, who
could not move without the assistance of two men, and
who, besides being entirely disabled, suffered excruciat-
ing pain, had been in a few days, by eating these nuts,

so

so far recovered, as to do their duty, and even go aloft as well as they did before they were seized by this distemper. The favourable report which the writer of Lord Anson's voyage had made of Tinian, one of the Ladrones, (a range of islands so named by Magellan, on one of which he lost his life, in an encounter with the natives) induced our commodore to proceed to so friendly an asylum, as that was described to be, for diseased and exhausted mariners. Accordingly on the 28th, in latitude 13 deg. 9 min. N. and in 158 deg. 50 min. E. longitude; and being now nearly in the parallel of Tinian, we shaped our course for that island. On the 30th, we again saw land, which proved to be the islands of Saypan, Tinian, and Aiguigan, which are between two and three leagues distant from each other. On the 31st, we steered along the east side of them, and at noon, hauling round the south point of Tinian, between that island and Aiguigan, anchored at the S. W. point of it, in 16 fathoms water, on good ground, and in the very spot where Lord Anson lay in the Centurion, in August 1742. As soon as the ship was secured, the commodore went on shore to fix upon a place where tents might be erected for the sick, not a single man being at this time free from the scurvy, and many were in the last stage of it; yet not one on board had died since our setting out from England. We found several huts which had been left by the Spaniards and Indians the year before; for this year none of them as yet had been at the place, nor was it probable that they should come for some months, the sun being now almost vertical, and the rainy season set in. The commodore affirmed, that he never felt such heat, either on the coast of Guinea, in the West Indies, or upon the island of St. Thomas, which is under the line. The thermometer which was kept on board the Dolphin, generally stood at 86 degrees, which is but 9 degrees less than the heat of the blood at the heart, and had it been on shore, it would have rose much higher. After a spot had been fixed upon for the tents, six or seven of the men endeavoured to push through the woods, in search of the
beautiful

2

beautiful lawns and meadows defcribed in Anfon's voyage; but the trees ftood fo thick, and the place was fo overgrown with underwood, that they could not fee three yards before them; they were therefore obliged to be continually hallooing to each other, to prevent their being feparately loft in this tracklefs wildernefs.   As the weather was intolerably hot, they had nothing on but their fhoes, fhirts, and trowfers; and thefe were foon torn to pieces by the bufhes and brambles: at laft, however, they got through with incredible labour, and difficulty; but found the lawns entirely overgrown with a ftubborn kind of reed or brufh, in many places higher than their heads, and no where lower than their middles, which continually entangled their legs, and cut them like whipcord. During this excurfion, they were covered with flies from head to foot; and whenever they offered to fpeak, they were fure of having a mouthful, many of which never failed to get down their throats.   After having walked three or four miles they faw a bull, which they killed, and a little before night got back to the beach, as wet as if they had been dipt in water, and fo fatigued, that they were fcarce able to ftand.

On Thurfday the 1ft of Auguft, a party was difpatched to fetch the bull, and our people were employed in fetting up more tents.   As the commodore himfelf was very ill of the fcurvy, he ordered a tent to be pitched for himfelf, and took up his refidence on fhore, where we alfo erected the fmith's forge, in order to repair the iron work of both fhips.   We were likewife employed in getting the water cafks on fhore, and clearing the well at which they were to be filled.   This well we thought to be the fame the Centurion watered at, but it was the worft we had met with during the voyage, for the water was not only brackifh, but full of worms. Alfo the road where the fhips lay was a dangerous fituation at this feafon, for the bottom is a hard fand, and large coral rocks, and the anchor having no hold in the fand, is in perpetual danger of being cut to pieces. We did not perceive thefe difagreeable circumftances when we firft caft anchor, thinking then the ground to
be

be good; but finding the contrary after having moored, to prevent any bad confequences, we rounded the cables and buoyed them up with empty cafks. Afterwards finding the cables much damaged, we refolved to lie fingle for the future, that by veering away, or heaving in, as we fhould have more or lefs wind, we might always keep them from being flack, confequently from rubbing, and this expedient fucceeded to our wifh. At the full and change of the moon, a prodigious fwell tumbles in here; and it once drove in from the weft-ward with fuch fury, that we were obliged to put to fea for a week; for had our cable parted in the night, and the wind been upon the fhore, which fometimes happens for two or three days together, the fhip muft inevitably have been loft on the rocks. Thus had we arrived at this delightful ifland, after a paffage of four months and twenty days, from the Straits of Magellan, with this furprifing and happy circumftance, thatduring this long run, though many had great complaints of the fcurvy, from the falt provifions they had been obliged to live upon, yet through the care of the com-modore, in caufing the people to be fupplied at ftated times with portable foup, and the refrefhments we had obtained from feveral iflands, we had not buried a fingle man; and we had now, by being favoured with fair weather, an opportunity of fending our fick on fhore, into the tents, which fome of our men had foon pre-pared for their reception. But while we ftayed here two died of fevers; and in the commodore's opinion, from the almoft inceffant rains, and violent heat, during the feafon we were here, this beautiful and fertile ifland is one of the moft unhealthy fpots in the world. We frequently difpatched parties into the woods in fearch of cattle, which, from the account publifhedinthehiftory of Commodore Anfon's voyage, we expected to find in numbers; but to our difappointment, a few only were difcovered at a great diftance from the tents, fo very fhy, that it was difficult to get a fhot at them; and more fo to drag them fix or feven miles to the tents, the woods and lawns which we have already defcribed, being so thick, as greatly to obstruct our passage: for though the beasts themselves had made paths through these woods, we could not proceed in them without the greatest difficulty. During the first week we killed only three white bullocks, one of which our men could not bring down to the shore, before it was covered with maggots, and stunk most intolerably: nor was this the worst; for the sailors suffered such inexpressible fatigue as frequently brought on fevers, occasioned by the warmth of the climate, the prodigious number of flies by day, and the musquitoes by night: these last resemble our gnats in England, but are larger, more numerous, and much more troublesome. They were also in their march much embarrassed with centipieds, scorpions, and a large black ant, little inferior to either of them in the malignity of its bite. We had also to encounter with an innumerable number of other venomous insects, altogether unknown to us, by which we suffered so severely, that many were afraid to lie down in their beds: nor were those on board in a much better situation than those on shore: for numbers of these tormentors being conveyed to the ship by the wood, they took possession of every birth, and left the poor seamen no place of rest either below or upon the deck.

On Wednesday the 7th, we sent on shore to the tents, which was called the hospital, 16 of our ship's company; and the next day John Watson, our quarter-master, departed this life; and soon after died Peter Evans, one of the seamen belonging to the Tamar. This day we got our copper oven on shore, and baked bread, which we served to the sick; the whole being under the inspection of the surgeon. Poultry we procured upon easy terms, for the birds were in great plenty, and easily killed; but the flesh of the best of them was very ill tasted. Our principal resource for fresh meat was the wild hog, with which the island is well stocked. These animals are exceeding fierce, and a carcass of some of them frequently weighed 200 weight. They were killed without much trouble, but a black belonging to the Tamar contrived a method to ensnare them, so that we took great numbers of them alive, which was an unspeakable advantage. But being very desirous of procuring some beef in an eatable state, with less risk and labour, we sent a boat, upon the information of Mr. Gore, to the N. W. part of the island, where the cattle were very numerous. A party was also sent with a tent for their accommodation, who shot them; and they were immediately killed, cut up, and conveyed to the boats: however, sometimes such a sea broke upon the rocks that it was impossible to approach them, and the Tamar's boat lost three of her best men by attempting it.

This island of Tinian is situated in 15 deg. 8 min. north latitude, and 114 deg. 50. min. west longitude from Acapulco, in New Spain; and is 12 miles in length, but only half as much in breadth. It produces limes, four oranges, cocoa-nuts, bread-fruit, guavas, and paupaws in abundance; but we found no water-melons, scurvy-grass, or sorrel. The cocoa nut which we have so often mentioned in describing the new discovered islands, is one of the most beautiful, as well as the most admirable, of all the vegetable productions, and is also found in many other parts of the world, particularly in the East and West Indies. It is a species of the palm. The trunk is large, strait, and insensibly grows smaller from the bottom to the top. On the upper part of the trunk are the branches, which form a beautiful head. The fruit hangs in branches by strong stalks; some of which are always ripe, others green, and some just beginning to button; while the blossoms, which are yellow, are still in bloom. The fruit is of different sizes, and of a greenish colour: it is covered with two rinds, the outer composed of long, tough, brown threads; but the second is extremely hard, and has within it a firm white substance, in taste nearest to that of a sweet almond. The people of several countries eat it with their meat as we do bread, and squeeze out of it a liquor that resembles almond-milk, which on being exposed to the fire, is converted into a kind of oil, that is used both in sauces and in lamps.

In

In the middle of the nut is also a confiderable quantity of a clear cool liquor, that has the tafte of fugar-water, and when drank is very refrefhing. What is called the cabbage confifts of a clufter of many white, thin, brittle flakes, which have fomewhat of the tafte of almonds, and, when boiled, has a refemblance to the tafte of an Englifh cabbage, but is fweeter and more agreeable. But the moft remarkable fruit of this ifland is the bread-fruit, it being generally eaten by the Europeans who come here inftead of bread, to which it is even preferred. It grows upon a lofty tree, which, near the top, divides into fpreading branches, covered with leaves of a deep green colour, notched on the edges, and from 12 to 18 inches in length. The fruit which grows fingle on all parts of the branches, is feven or eight inches long, of an oval form, and covered with a rough rind, and when gathered green, and roafted on the embers, has its infide foft, tender, white, and crummy like bread. Its tafte comes neareft to that of an artichoke's bottom. This excellent fruit is in feafon eight months in the year. As it ripens it turns yellow, and growing fofter, has the tafte of a ripe peach, and a fragrant fmell, but is then faid to be unwholefome, and apt to produce the flux. The fifh, however, caught about this coaft appear to be unwholefome. Some of our officers after having eaten a difh of fine looking fifh, were taken ill with a violent purging and vomiting, which had like to have been attended with fatal confequences. Mr. Walter in his hiftory of commodore Anfon's voyage, obferves, that the few they caught at their firft arrival, had furfeited thofe who eat of them, and therefore the people on board the Centurion thought it moft prudent to abftain from fifh. This obfervation, added to our own experience, is a fufficient proof of their being prejudicial. Indeed, at firft, from taking the word furfeit in a literal fenfe, we concluded, that thofe who tafted the fifh, when the late Lord Anfon came hither, were made fick merely by eating too much of them; from which fuppofition we were led to think, that there could be no

reafon

reafon for a total abftinence with refpect to this kind
of food, but only a caution to eat with temperance.
However, we were foon made wifer by experience; for
though all our people eat fparingly of this fifh by way
of experiment, neverthelefs all who tafted them were
foon afterwards dangeroufly ill. Befides the above
mentioned fruit, this ifland produces cotton and indigo
in abundance, and would certainly be of great value if
it was fituated in the Weft Indies. The furgeon of the
Tamar, an ingenious and very judicious gentleman, enclofed a large fpot of ground here, and made a very
pretty garden; but our fhort ftay would not permit us
to derive any advantage from it. However, amidft
fuch plenty we enjoyed, the want of its produce might
very well be difpenfed with.

It is furprizing that an ifland thus abounding with
the neceffaries and luxuries of life, fhould be deftitute
of inhabitants, but it feems it was once populous; and
that an epidemical ficknefs having carried off multitudes of the inhabitants of this and the neighbouring
iflands, the Spaniards removed the reft to Guam, to
fupply the numbers that had died there, where lan-
guifhing for their native foil, and their former habitations, the greateft part of them died with grief. Indeed
we faw the ruins of their deferted town, which is now
over-grown with trees and bufhes. But though Tinian
is uninhabited, the Indians of Guam, and other of the
neighbouring iflands, frequently refort thither to jerk
beef, and carry it away. Thefe Indians are a bold,
ftrong, well limbed people; and if we may judge from
the admirable ftructure of their flying proas, the only
veffels they ufe at fea, they are far from being deficient
in point of underftanding. Thefe veffels move with
fuch amazing fwiftnefs, that it is generally allowed by
all who have obferved them with attention, that they
will run at leaft 20 miles an hour. The conftruction of
thefe proas is very remarkable, the head and ftern being exactly alike; but the fides very different, that intended for the windward fide being built rounding,
while the lee-fide is flat. The body is formed of two
pieces

pieces joined end ways, and neatly fewed together with bark: and as the ftrait run of her leeward fide, and her fmall breadth, would certainly caufe her to overfet, a frame called an out-rigger, is laid out from her to the windward, to the end of which is faftened a log, made hollow, in the fhape of a fmall boat: thus the weight of the frame balances the proa, and that, with the fmall boat, always in the water, prevents her overfetting to the windward. The veffel generally carries fix or feven Indians, two of whom fit in the head and ftern, who fteer the proa alternately, with a paddle, according to the tack fhe goes on; he in the ftern being the fteerfman; the reft are employed in fetting and trimming the fail, or bailing out the water fhe may accidentally fhip. Thus by only fhifting the fail, thefe veffels with either end foremaft, can, with aftonifhing fwiftnefs, run from one of thefe iflands to another, and back again, without ever putting about. While we lay at this place, the Tamar was fent to examine the ifland of Saypan, which is much larger than Tinian, rifes higher, and has a much pleafanter appearance. The Tamar anchored to the leeward, at the diftance of a mile from the fhore, and in 10 fathom water, with much the fame kind of ground as we had in the road of Tinian. Some of the Tamar's company landed upon a fine fandy beach, which is fix or feven miles long, and walked up into the woods, where they difcovered many trees very fit for top-mafts. They faw no fowls nor any tracks of cattle, but plenty of hogs and guanicoes: alfo large heaps of pearl oyfter-fhells thrown up together, and other figns of people having been there: poffibly the Spaniards may go thither at fome feafons of the year, and carry on a pearl fifhery. As we fhall have an opportunity of again mentioning thefe places in our accounts of other voyages, we here, for the amufement of our numerous fubfcribers, infert what other navigators, and judicious writers, have related both of the Philippine and Ladrone Iflands, both fituated in the Pacific Ocean, and at no great diftance from each other.

An

An Account of the Philippine, and Ladrone, or Marian Islands.

THE Philippine Islands are situate in the Chinesian Sea, part of the Pacific Ocean, between 114 and 130 degrees of eastern longitude, and between 5 and 19 degrees of north latitude, about 100 leagues S. E. of China. There are 1100 of them, and several very large. The chief of the most northerly of them is Manila or Luconia, which is the largest of the Philippines, and is situate in 15 deg. of north latitude, being about 400 miles long and above 180 broad in most places.

The capital of this island, and of all the rest, is the city of Manila, situate on a bay in the S. W. part of the island, being two miles in circumference, surrounded by a wall and other works, a very commodious harbour, but of difficult access, on account of the rocks and sands which lie before it; a castle defends the entrance.

The chief buildings are the cathedral, parish churches and convents; one of the religious houses is appropriated to the support of orphans, daughters of the inhabitants, who are provided for during their lives; or, if they chuse to marry, have a portion of two or three hundred crowns given them. Their churches, chapels, and altars, are richly adorned, and their processions on holidays as splendid as in Spain. The college of the jesuits here, as in most popish countries, is more magnificent than any of the rest.

The island of Luconia, or Manila, is esteemed healthful, and the water in it the best in the world. It produces all the fruits of warm climates, and has an excellent breed of horses carried thither from Spain. It is well situated for the Indian and Chinese trade; and the bay and port, which lies on the west-side of it, is a large circular bason of 10 leagues diameter, entirely land-locked. The city of Manila, which stands on the east-side, is large and contains several spacious

I   streets

ftreets and grand houfes; and at the beginning of the firft war with the Spaniards, in the reign of king George II. was an open place, only defended by a little fort; but confiderable additions have lately been made to its fortifications. The port peculiar to the city is that of Cabite, which lies two leagues to the fouthward, and here the fhips employed in the Acapulco trade are ftationed.

The city is healthfully fituated, and well watered, and has a very fruitful country in its neighbourhood; but it is fome difadvantage to its trade, that it is difficult getting out to fea to the eaftward, through fuch a number of iflands: here the Spaniards wafte abundance of time, and are often in great danger.

The trade from hence to China and India confifts chiefly in fuch commodities as are intended to fupply Mexico and Peru, namely, fpices, Chinefe filks, and manufactures, particularly filk ftockings, of which no lefs than 50,000 pair have been fhipped in one cargo, with vaft quantities of Indian ftuffs, callicoes and chints, which are much worn in America, together with other fmall articles, fuch as goldfmiths-work, &c. wrought at the city of Manila by the Chinefe, of which nation there are not lefs than 20,000 refiding there, as fervants, manufacturers, or brokers. All thefe articles are tranfported annually to the port of Acapulco in Mexico: this trade is not open to all the inhabitants of Manila, but is reftrained to the convents of Manila, principally to the jefuits, being a donation to fupport the miffions for the propagation of the Catholic faith. The tonage of each fhip is divided into a certain number of bales, all of the fame fize; and the convents have a right to embark fuch a quantity of goods on board the Manila fhips as the tonage of their bales amount to. The trade is limited by royal edicts to a certain value; according to fome, it fhould not exceed 600,000 dollars; but it is frequently known to amount to three millions.

The bulk of the people of Manila are of Chinefe or Malayan extraction, and there are fome blacks. The Spaniards, though feweft in number, have the govern-

ment

ment in their hands. The adjacent country is full of fine plantations, farms, and country-houses of the principal inhabitants. Upon the mountains, in the middle of the country, the people live in tents and huts, under the spreading trees. The plains are overflowed in the rainy season, the houses built upon high pillars; and the people have no communication but by boats during the rains, which usually fall in June, July, August, and September, and then happen terrible storms of wind and thunder. Earthquakes are frequent; the city of Manila has suffered several times by them; and from the volcanoes, which abound here, issue torrents of fire and melted minerals. These are the inconveniencies we meet with; but the fair season is for the most part exceedingly pleasant.

The city of Manila contains about 3000 inhabitants; and during the second war in the reign of king George II. was in the year 1763, taken by admiral Cornish and Sir William Draper. It was, however, stipulated to be ransomed; but the ransom-money hath never yet been intirely discharged. The priests take prodigious pains to make converts to the Romish faith, and have been pretty successful in their endeavours. The Indians pay a poll-tax; and a considerable sum of money is annually allowed for the support of female orphans, both of Spanish and Indian parents.

The complexions of the several people who inhabit these islands are very different. The blacks are as black as the Caffres of Afric, but differ from them in their features and long hair, and therefore are supposed to be of Indian extraction; and as they possess the mountainous and inaccessible parts of the country, it is conjectured, that they were the original inhabitants, and driven up thither by succeeding adventurers.

The descendants of the Malayans (inhabitants of Malacca) are very tawny, the Chinese not so dark, and the Spaniards are pretty near the colour of the Chinese. There is also a nation of painted people, called Pintados, who colour their skins like our ancestors the Picts.

No. 29. 5 Y The

The natives are for the moſt part of a moderate ſtature, and their features juſt ; the Spaniards have taught them to cloath themſelves, except the blacks, who only tie a cloth about their loins, and another about their heads, and uſually go bare-foot.

Rice and fiſh are moſt eaten by thoſe who live near the ſea-coaſts, and the mountaineers eat the fleſh they take in hunting, and the fruits of the earth, which grow ſpontaneouſly in great plenty. Their liquor is water, which they uſually drink warm as the Chineſe do. They have alſo palm-wine, and ſpirituous liquors diſtilled from the juice of the ſugar-cane, rice, &c. They bathe twice a day in cold water, either for health or diverſion, or both : plays are another diverſion, and they are entertained frequently with dancing and mock fights.

Theſe iſlands are extremely well ſituated for trade ; all the rich merchandize of India is ſent from hence to America, and the treaſures of Mexico and Peru are brought hither annually, by which exchange, it is ſaid, they make a profit of 400 per cent.

Few countries enjoy a more fruitful ſoil ; the people in many places live upon what the earth produces ſpontaneouſly, and the ſurface of the ground is exceeding beautiful ; the trees are ever green, and ſeldom without fruit.

Their neat cattle run wild in the mountains, and are hunted, as well as deer, wild hogs and goats. The monkies and baboons found here are very ſagacious : during the ſeaſon, when there is no fruit to be got, they go down to the ſea-ſide to catch oyſters ; that the fiſh may not pinch their paws, they put a ſtone between the ſhells, to prevent their ſhutting cloſe. Wax is ſo plentiful, that they make no other candles, and never burn lamps. Their bees are of ſeveral kinds, ſome of them very large, and make their combs in the woods, producing ſuch quantities of honey as would almoſt ſubſiſt the natives.

Medicinal and ſweet gums, iſſuing from the bodies of trees, are part of the produce : ſerpents of various kinds are

are found in thefe iflands; but the fathers who relate that fome of them are fo large, they will fwallow a ftag, horns and all, furely do not expect to be believed, any more than when they relate, that the leaves of trees are converted into infects; but the laft of thefe ftories may proceed from a miftake, for it is certain that fome in-fects depofit their eggs (as they do with us) upon the leaves of trees, which are hatched there, as is the cafe of the cochineal fly; and they might ignorantly imagine that thofe infects proceed from the leaf. The alligators are very dangerous; and the ignana, a kind of land alligator, does a great deal of mifchief. Among their birds are peacocks, parrots, cocatoes, and turtle-doves, which are very beautiful, fowls with black bones, and the bird tavan, which lays a number of eggs in trenches in the fand, and leaves them to hatch there. The faligan faftens her nefts to fome rock, as a martin does againft a wall, which diffolving into a kind of jelly in warm water, is efteemed delicious food. Here is alfo the xolo bird, which eats like a turkey; the camboxa is a well tafted fowl peculiar to thefe iflands. The herrero or carpenter, is a fine large green bird. It is called the carpenter, becaufe its beak is fo hard, that it digs a hole in the trunk, or fome large branch of a tree, in order to build its neft.

Their fruits are mangoes, plantains, bananoes, cocoas, tamarinds, caffia, and the cocoa or chocolate nut, which has been brought over from Mexico; oranges, lemons, and all manner of tropical fruits. The cinnamon and nutmeg-tree have been planted here; but degenerate, and are good for little.

A great deal of good timber and dying woods grow in thefe iflands; and the calamba, or fweet-wood, a kind of cane, grows in the mountains, which, if cut, yields a draught of water, and is of great fervice to the natives.

They have one plant that has all the properties of, and is ufed as a fubftitute for opium; of this the natives are very fond, and frequently intoxicate themfelves with it.

Flowers and fweet-herbs grow wild here, but they do

not

not cultivate them in their gardens, and there are abundance of medicinal, as well as poisonous herbs and flowers, which do not only kill those that touch or taste them, but so infect the air, that many people die in the time of their blossoming : on the contrary, these islands are providentially well furnished with antidotes, particularly the bezoar stone, which is found in the belly of a creature much like a deer ; and the root dilao, which is like ginger, and heals wounds made by any venomous beast, being bruised and boiled with oil of cocoas.

The tree camondog is so venomous, that the pilchards eating the leaves which fall into the sea die ; as will the persons who eat the poisoned fish. The liquor which flows from the trunk of this tree serves these people to poison the points of their darts which they blow through the trunks abovementioned : the very shadow of the tree is so destructive, that, as far as it reaches, no herb or grass grows, and if transplanted, it kills all the other plants it stands near, except a small shrub which is an antidote against it, and always with it : a bit of a twig of this shrub, or a leaf carried in a man's mouth, is said to be a security against the venom of the tree, and therefore the Indians are never without it.

The maka bukay, which signifies the giver of life, is a kind of ivy which twines about any tree, and grows to the thickness of a man's finger ; it has long shoots like vine branches, of which the Indians make bracelets, and esteem them a preservative against poison. There are many other trees and plants of extraordinary virtue in these islands ; among others, there is the sensitive plant, in all respects like a colewort, which growing out of a rock, avoids the touch, and retires under water : there is another that grows on St. Peter's Hill about Manila, which is not very tall, and has little leaves, which whenever it is touched, draws back and closes all its leaves together ; for which reason the Spaniards call it la vergin cosa, that is, the bashful.

There grows near Cathalagan, in the island of Samar, a plant of a surprising virtue, discovered by the fathers

of

of the society, as they tell us, of late years : the Dutch have also some knowledge of it, and, it is said, will give double the quantity of gold for it.   The plant is like ivy, and twines about any tree it grows near : the fruit which grows out of the knots and leaves resembles a melocotoon in bigness and colour, and within has eight, ten, or sixteen kernals as big as a hazel nut, each green and yellow, which when ripe, drop out of themselves.

The usual dose given of it is the weight of half a royal, that is the sixteenth part of an ounce, powdered and mixed in wine or water ; if it has no effect the first time, the dose is repeated, and is a powerful antidote against any poison, either of venomous herbs or darts which are used by the natives of Macassar, Borneo, and the Philippines.

The general language spoken in these islands is the Malayan tongue ; besides which, every people have a language peculiar to themselves.   They write on cocoa-nut leaves, with an iron style or pen ; and arts and sciences have been introduced by the Spaniards, the natives having nothing of this kind to boast of before their arrival.

All these islands, except Mindanao and Paragoa, are under the jurisdiction of a Spanish viceroy, who has governors under him in every other island and town of consequence, and the like courts are erected for the trial of civil and criminal causes, as in old Spain.   The archbishop of Manila, the bishops and their commissaries, determine ecclesiastical causes as in Europe ; but there lies an appeal from them to the pope's delegate, who resides in one of the islands.   The court of inquisition has also a commissary here.   But notwithstanding the Spaniards are represented as sovereigns of these islands, this must only be understood of the open country and the sea-coasts, in which there may be 300,000 souls : but these are not a tenth part of the inhabitants, the rest look upon themselves as a free people: every mountain almost is possessed by a different tribe, who make war upon one another, the Spaniards

seldom

seldom intermeddling in their quarrels. The Chinese were formerly so numerous here, that they disputed the authority of the Spaniards over them : it is computed that 40,000 of them resided in and about the city of Manila ; but the Spaniards compelled them to submit, and banished some thousands of them, the rest were permitted to remain here, to carry on their manufactures ; for they are almost the only artificers.

Their arms are bows, arrows, and lances or spears, broad swords, and tubes or trunks, through which they blow poisoned arrows, the slightest wounds whereof are mortal, if immediate remedies are not applied. They have cane shields also covered with a buffaloe's hide, and a head-piece for defensive arms.

These savages, as the Spaniards call them, worship one supreme God, and their ancestors, as the Chinese do, from whom most of them are descended ; they worship also the sun and moon, and almost every thing they see, whether animate or inanimate, groves, rocks, rivers, and one particular tree, which they would esteem it a sacrilege to cut down, believing the souls of some of their friends may reside in it, and that in cutting the tree they may wound a near relation. Instead of temples, they have caves, wherein they place their idols, and sacrifices to them. Some beautiful young virgins first wounds the victim with a spear, and then the priests dispatch the animal ; and, having dressed the meat, it is eaten by the company. Superstition prevails among them ; they have their lucky and unlucky days ; and if certain animals cross the way when they are going upon business, they will return home, and go out no more that day. The Spaniards tolerate them in their idolatrous worship ; and suffer them to game, on paying to the government 10,000 crowns per annum. They are also much given to a detestable vice : and did not imagine it to be a crime, till the Spaniards punished them for it.

The men purchased their wives here as in China ; and the marriage ceremony is performed by a priestess, who sacrifices some animal on the occasion ; after which, the
bride

bride is led home, and the whole concludes with an entertainment as at other places. They marry in their own tribe, and with their neareft relations, except the firft degree ; fome of them are confined to one wife, other tribes allow a plurality of women, and divorces for reafonable caufes on either fide. Children are either named after heroes or flowers, or from fome accidental circumftance that occurs at the time of their birth; but as foon as they marry, they chufe new names, and their parents are obliged to make ufe of their old ones.

The dead are wafhed and perfumed, wrapped in filk, and put in a clofe coffin, near which a cheft is placed that contains the arms of a man, or domeftic utenfils of a woman: mourners are hired to affift in making a difmal noife. They bury their dead as in China, and do not burn them : as foon as the body is buried, an entertainment is made, and all is converted to mirth and feftivity. In general, they mourn in black garments ; and fhave their heads and eye-brows.

The next Spanifh ifland to that of Manila is Samar or Philippina, between which and Manila is a narrow channel, called the Straight of Manila, the N. E. point whereof is called Spirito Sancto ; the ifland is near 400 miles in circumference, the chief town, Cathalagan, governed by a Spanifh alcade. The ifland of Sebu, which lies in 10 deg. S. latitude, is the place where Magellan firft fet up the Spanifh colours ; the chief town named Nombre de Dios, afterwards made a bifhop's fee, has in it a cathedral and feveral other churches and monafteries. The ifland of negroes lies weft of Sebu, and was fo named becaufe it is inhabited chiefly by blacks. Mindanao lies the moft foutherly of any of the Philippine Iflands, and is the largeft of them except Manila, being near 200 miles in length, and 150 in breadth It is poffeffed by people of different nations and different religions ; but the Mahometans, who are fituate on the fea-coafts, are much the moft numerous, whofe fovereign is ftiled Sultan of Mindanao. Thofe who poffefs the middle of the ifland are called Hillanoons, and another nation ftiled Solognes, are

fituate

situate on the N. W. coast. The air of this island is
not so hot as might be expected, being refreshed frequently by the sea breezes, and the periodical rains,
which lay the flat country under water. The winds
blow from the east, from October to May, and then
turn about and set westerly; next month the rains and
storms succeed; at first there are not more than two
or three showers a day; they afterwards come oftener,
with violent hurricanes and loud thunder, and the
wind continues westerly until November, during which
time they have such storms that trees are blown up
by the roots, the rivers are overflowed, and they do
not see the sun or stars sometimes in a week: about
August the air is very cool, the rain and wind are moderate in September, and in October the wind blows
from the east again, and it continues fair till April, and
sometimes May.

Mindanao, the capital city, lies on the south-side of
the island, in 123 deg. 15 min. of eastern longitude,
and 6 deg. 20 min. north latitude, near the mouth of
a river, and about two miles from the sea; the houses
being built on bamboo pillars, 16 or 18 feet above the
surface of the ground, on account of the annual floods,
when they have no communication with one another
but by boats. The city is about a mile in length,
built along the winding bank of the river; the Sultan's
palace is supported by 180 trees, and has 20 cannon
mounted in the front; and several of the nobility have
great guns in or before their houses. Large ships
cannot come up to the town, there being scarce 11 feet
water on the bar, at the entrance of the river.

The natives are held to be men of a sprightly genius,
but very lazy and indolent, and will rather thieve than
work; but none are more active when they find there
is a necessity for it; and there may be two reasons for
their lazy disposition, one from the heat of the climate, and the other from the tyranny of the government, no man being sure he shall enjoy what he acquires
by his industry.

The Mindanayans are of a low stature, and very
slender,

2

slender, of dark tawny complexions, black eyes and hair, flat faces, short noses, wide mouths, and black teeth, which they take abundance of pains to dye of that colour; and they wear the nails of their left hands almost as long again as their fingers, scraping and dying them with vermillion.

The men have a haughty mein, and yet are said to be very complaisant to foreigners, unless they are insulted, and then they seldom fail to resent the affront, and destroy their enemy by poison or a dagger, never hazarding their persons in a duel.

Their habit is a linen frock and drawers, and a small piece of linen cloth tied about their heads, but they go bare-foot: the complexion and features of the women are better than those of the men; but yet they too much resemble the other sex, and cannot be admired for their beauty; they wear a frock like the men, and a piece of cloth round their waists; the sleeves of the frock being large, and coming down to their wrists. Their hair is tied up in a roll at the hinder part of their heads. The men shave their heads, all but a lock that is left in the middle of the crown, like other Mahometans; their beards are very thin, being pulled up by the roots with tweezers. People of figure are cloathed in silk or fine callico; the women go bare-foot as well as the men, and adorn their arms and fingers with bracelets and rings. They are not restrained from conversing with their countrymen or foreigners.

The food of people of condition is flesh, fish, and fowl of all kinds, except hogs flesh, which the Mahometans never touch. The poorer sort content themselves with rice and sago. Rice is the principal part of the meal with all of them; they take it up with their hands, using neither knives or spoons; and their meat, whatever it be, is boiled to rags, that it may very easily be pulled to pieces with their fingers. They usually drink water, but make a pretty strong liquor with plantains; they wash before and after every meal, and bathe several times a day. Swimming is one of the chief diversions of the women, as well

as the men, to which they are ufed from their infancy.

Upon joyful occafions the dancing girls, as they are
called, are fent for to divert the company; but this
dancing confifts only in fkrewing themfelves into laf-
civious poftures, and addreffing their great men with
flattering fpeeches. They have plays and mock fights
alfo acted before them, and hunting of wild beafts is
their principal rural fport, in which their women par-
take; but their hunting is only driving the deer and
other game into an inclofure, from whence they cannot
efcape, and then fhooting at them.

Mindanao is a fruitful foil, well watered with rivers,
and their mountains afford excellent timber. Of the
libby, or fago-tree, there are large groves: the fago is
the pith of a tree which the natives eat inftead of bread,
and is frequently brought over to Europe, being fo
grained, that it is fometimes taken for a feed. They
have no corn but rice. Plantains, guavas, mangoes,
and all tropical fruits, abound here. Cloves and
nutmegs have been tranfplanted hither, and appear
fair to the eye; but it is faid they degenerate, and
the fruit is good for nothing: if thefe plants were
cultivated, poffibly they might equal thofe of the fpice
iflands.

Here are no beafts of prey in this ifland, but almoft
every other ufeful animal, fuch as horfes, cows, buffaloes, and hogs, with bunches over their eyes; here
are alfo fnakes, fcorpions, and other venomous infects; and the feathered kind are the fame as in
Manila.

The Malayan language is generally fpoken here;
and the Mahometans have the koran and books of
devotion, in the Arabic language. The liberal arts
do not flourifh here; they are forced to employ the
Chinefe to keep their accompts for them; nor have
they fo much as a clock or a watch in all the country,
but beat upon drums every three hours, that people
may know the time of the day. There are fcarce
any other working trades, except goldfmiths, carpen-

2   ters,

ters, and blacksmiths, who perform their work very well with the tools they have, for the smiths have neither vice nor anvil, nor the carpenters any saws, but when they have split their planks, plane them with the ax or adze. Their diseases are fluxes, fevers, and the small-pox; and some are affected with a kind of leprosy, or dry scurf, which covers the body, and itches intolerably.

The religion of the sultan, and those who inhabit the sea-coasts, is Mahometanism, and that of the inland people is Paganism, differing little from the Chinese. In allowing a plurality of wives and concubines, the Mahometans of this island imitate those of Turky, only they allow their women greater liberties, suffering them to converse freely with their acquaintance or strangers; but it is said they are so prejudiced against swines flesh, that one of their great men refused to wear a pair of shoes made by an European, when he was informed that the threads with which they were sewed were pointed with hogs bristles. They look upon themselves to be defiled, if they touch any thing which belongs to a hog; they durst not kill them lest they should be defiled by the touch of the weapon they make use of, which occasions these animals to multiply so fast, that the island is over-run with them. They are very glad to see the Europeans kill them, but must undergo several ablutions or washings, if they should happen to touch a man that had eaten its flesh.

The sultan of Mindanao is an absolute prince, and his throne hereditary; both the persons and purses of his subjects are in his power, and if he knows any of them abound in wealth, he borrows it of them. He has one great minister, in whom he lodges the administration of the government, both civil and military, to whom both natives and foreigners must apply themselves for liberty to trade. Their wars are chiefly with the mountaineers, who inhabit the middle of the island, with whom they are very cautious of coming to a general engagement; but when the armies are pretty

near,

near, they begin to entrench and cannonade each other, and will remain in the same camp some months, sending out parties to make incursions into the enemies country, and surprize defenceless places. Their arms are a crice or short dagger, and a broad sword, a spear, and bows and arrows.

The most considerable of the Philippines that have not been mentioned, are Mindora, S. W. of Manila : Panay, and Leyte, which lie north of Mindanao ; and the island of Paragoa, which lies very near the north part of Borneo, and is subject to one of the princes of that island.

Philippina was the first that was discovered of this cluster of islands, and consequently gave name to the rest. It lies between 12 and 14 degrees north latitude, and is the most fertile and pleasant of all the Philippines, exhibiting a scene of perpetual verdure; for here the sun is powerful, without being disagreeable.

The Ladrone Islands are situate in the Pacific Ocean, in 140 degrees of eastern longitude, and between 12 and 28 degrees of north latitude. Guam or Ignana, the largest, is situate in 13 deg. 21 min. north latitude, 7300 miles west of Cape Corientes in Mexico, according to Dampier. The other inconsiderable islands are, 2. Sarpanta. 3. Bonavista or Tinian. 4. Sespara. 5. Anatan. 6. Sarignan. 7. Guagam. 8. Alamaguan. 9. Pagon. 10. The burning mountain of Griga. 11. Magna. 12. Patas. 13. Disconocida ; and, 14. Malabrigo.

Guam is about 12 leagues long and four broad, lying N. and S. It is pretty high champaign land, sloping down towards the coast. The east-side, which is the highest, is fenced with steep rocks, on which the waves constantly beat, driven by the trade wind. The west-side is low land, in which are several little sandy bays divided by rocks.

The natives of Guam are of a good stature, have large limbs, a tawny complexion, black long hair, small eyes, thick lips, and are long visaged. They are sometimes afflicted with a kind of leprosy, otherwise the
country

country is healthful, especially in the dry season. The rains begin in June, and last till October, but are not violent.

The island produces rice and most tropical fruits, and one sort which Dampier has named bread-fruit, grows upon a tree like apples, and at its full bigness is as large as an ordinary foot-ball; it has a hard thick rind, and within a soft yellow pulp, of a sweetish taste; the natives eat it instead of bread, having first baked or roasted it in the embers: it is in season eight months in the year, and grows only in these islands.

Dampier relates, that when he was there (about the year 1700) there were not above 100 Indians upon the island, though he was informed there had been 3 or 400 sometime before: and the reason given why there was no more at that time was, because most of them had burnt their plantations, and fled to other islands on their being used ill by the Spaniards.

Their swift-sailing sloops, or flying proas, are the admiration of all that see them; the bottom of the vessel, or the keel, is of one piece, made like a canoe, 28 feet in length, built sharp at both ends, one side of the sloop flat, and the other rounding with a pretty large belly; being four or five feet broad, with a mast in the middle. They turn the flat side to the wind, and having a head at each end, sail with either of them foremast, and have never any occasion to tack. Dampier computed they would sail 24 miles an hour. The tide never rises above two or three feet at this island.

The writer of Lord Anson's voyage relates, that they arrived at the island of Tinian or Bonavista, one of the Ladrone Islands, which lies north of Guam, on the 27th of August, 1742, being situated in 15 deg. 8 min. north latitude, and 114 deg. 50 min. west of Acapulco in America. This island is 12 miles in length, and six in breadth, extending from the S. S. W. to N. N. E. The soil is dry and sandy, and the air healthful; the land rises in gentle slopes from the shore to the middle of the island, interrupted by valleys of an easy descent.

The

918 COMMODORE BYRON'S VOYAGE

The valleys and gradual swellings of the ground are beautifully diversified by the encroachments of woods and lawns; and the woods consist of tall spreading trees, celebrated for their aspect or their fruit; the turf of the lawns clean and uniform, composed of fine trefoil, intermixed with a variety of flowers; the woods, in many places, open, free from bushes, and under-wood, affording most elegant and entertaining prospects.

The cattle on this island were computed to amount to 10,000, (we suppose he means horned cattle) all perfectly white except their ears; besides which there were hogs and poultry without number. The cattle and fowls were so fat, that the men could run them down, and were under no necessity of shooting them. Their flesh is well tasted, and very easy of digestion.

About the beginning of the present century, this island was said to contain at least 30,000 inhabitants, when a dreadful mortality raging among them, prodigious numbers died, and the calamity prevailing with equal violence in the islands of Rota and Guam, the Spaniards obliged those that remained at Tinian to remove to Guam, in order to make good the deficiency by the number of the souls that had perished in that island; since which time, Tinian has been wholly uninhabited. The ruins of the buildings in Tinian, some of which are of a particular form, evince it to have been once a populous place. The island of Rota has not any thing in it that demands particular attention. Its chief produce is rice, which is cultivated by a few Indians, who live there undisturbed, but are subject to the Spanish governor.

Though the other islands are uninhabited, they are in general exceeding fertile, the air good, and the climate temperate. They also produce plenty of provisions; but they are seldom visited, on account of the great inconvenience arising from the want of water for anchorage. Tinian is more commodious in this particular, but even there it is very unsafe from June to October. In the month of September, the Tamar, one of Commodore

modore Byron's ships, met with an accident, that was attended with fatal consequences to two of her best seamen; she had, as usual, sent her boat on shore, when the surf suddenly rose so high as to fill the boat with water, by which means the men were dashed against the steep craggy rocks near the shore, and two of them drowned; and the rest who were six in number, with great difficulty escaped suffering the same fate, by swimming to shore, they being frequently repelled by the unusual swell which prevailed at that time.

Several other islands have lately been discovered to the eastward of the Philippines; and from them called the New Philippines, of which father Clan, in a letter from Manila (inserted in the Philosophical Transactions) gives the following account: that he happening to be at the town of Guivam, in the island of Samar, found 29 palars, or inhabitants of certain newly discovered islands, who were driven there by the easterly winds which blow in those seas from December to May. They had run before the wind for 70 days together, according to their own relation, without being able to make any land till they came in sight of Guivam: they were 35 persons, and embarked in two boats, with their wives and children, when they first came out, but several perished by the hardships they underwent in the voyage; they were under such a consternation when a man from Guivam attempted to come on board them, that all the people which were in one of the vessels, with their wives and children, jumped over board; however, they were at length persuaded to steer into the harbour, and they landed the 28th of December, 1696. They eat cocoa-nuts and roots which were brought them very freely, but would not touch boiled rice, the common food of the Asiatics. Two women, who had formerly been cast on shore from the same islands, were their interpreters; they related that their country consisted of 32 islands, and by the form of their vessels and sails their country seemed to be in the neighbourhood of the Mariana's, or Ladrone Islands; they related that their country was exceeding populous, and that

that all the islands are under the dominion of one king, who keeps his court in the island of Lamaree: the natives go half naked, and the men paint and stain their bodies, making several sorts of figures upon them, but the women and children are not painted; the complexion and shape of their face is much like those of the tawny Philippines or Malayes: the men wear only a cloth about their loins which covers their thighs, and another loose about their bodies which they tie before. There is little difference betwixt the dress of the men and women, but that the cloth which covers the women hangs a little lower on their knees; their language is different both from the people of the Philippines and the Ladrone Islands, and comes nearest to that of the Arabs: the women that seem most considerable among them, wear necklaces, bracelets, and rings of tortoiseshell. They subsisted themselves all the time they were at sea with the fish they catched, in a kind of wicker basket with a great mouth, ending in a point, which they hauled after them; and their drink was rain water, which they happened to be supplied with: they have no cows, or dogs, in their islands, and they run away at the sight of the one, and the barking of the other; neither have they any horses, deer, cats, or any four footed beasts whatever; or any land fowls but hens, which they breed up, and never eat their eggs: they were surprized at the whiteness of the Europeans, having never seen any people of this complexion, as they were at their manners or customs: it does not appear that they have any religion, nor do they use any set meals, but eat and drink whenever they are hungry or thirsty, and then but sparingly. They salute any one by taking him by the hand or foot, or gently stroaking his face: among their tools they have a saw made of a large shell, sharpened with a stone, having no iron or other metals in their country; and were surprised to see the many tools used in building a ship. Their arms are lances or darts, headed with human bones and sharpened. They seem to be a people of much life and courage, but of a peaceful disposition; and are well
proportioned,

proportioned, but not of a large fize. We now proceed with the narrative of our voyage.

On Monday, the 30th of September, after having been at the ifland of Tinian nine weeks, we found our fick pretty well recovered; and this day the tents were ordered to be ftruck, and to be brought, with the forge and oven, on board the fhips. We alfo laid in two thoufand cocoa-nuts, and a quantity of limes, for the ufe of the feamen, the commodore having experienced them to be efficacious antidotes againft the fcurvy. On Tuefday, the 1ft of October, we weighed and failed from Tinian and the reft of the Ladrone iflands. Having finifhed our bufinefs on which we were fent, by the difcovery of thofe iflands in the South-Seas, according to our original deftination, we bent our thoughts towards returning home, and it was propofed, fhould we be fo fortunate as to find the N. E. monfoon fet in, before we fhould get the length of the Bafhé Iflands, to touch at Batavia, which our commodore preferred to any port of China for recruiting his fhips, he being deterred from touching at the latter, and particularly at Canton, by the bafe and ungenerous ufage which Lord Anfon received there, after a voyage of much longer duration, and attended with a feries of the moft dreadful diftreffes and misfortunes, that called for pity and affiftance. We had very little wind this day and the next, till the evening, when it came to the weftward and blew frefh. On the 3d, in the morning we ftood to the northward, and made the ifland of Anatacan, remarkably high, and the fame that was firft fallen in with by Lord Anfon. On the 10th, we obferved in latitude 18 deg. 33 min. north, and in 136 deg. 50 min. eaft longitude. On Friday, the 18th, feveral land birds were feen about the fhips, which appeared to be very much tired: a very remarkable one was caught; it was about the fize of a goofe, and all over as white as fnow, except the legs and beaks, which were black: the beak was curved, and of fo great a length and thicknefs, that it is not eafy to conceive how the mufcles of the neck (which was about a foot long, and as fmall as that of a crane) could support it. We kept it alive about four months upon biscuit and water, but it then died, apparently for want of nourishment, being almost as light as a bladder. It was very different from every species of the toucan that is represented by Edwards: and, in the opinion of our commodore, has never been described. These birds appeared to have been blown off some island to the northward, that is not laid down in the charts. On Tuesday the 22nd, at six o'clock A. M. the northernmost of the Bashé islands, being Grafton's, bore south, distant six leagues. We proceeded without touching at this place, which was proposed, and steered westward again. By our reckoning, which however the experience of Captain Gore has since disproved, it lies in latitude 21 deg. 8 min. north, and in 118 deg. 14 min. east longitude. The principal of these islands are five in number, but we were induced not to touch at any one of them, on account of the dangerous navigation from thence to the straits of Banca. On the 24th, we were in latitude 16 deg. 59 min. north, and 113 deg. 1 min. east longitude. We therefore kept a good look-out for the Triangles, which lie without the north end of the Prasil, and occasion a most dangerous shoal. On the 30th, we found ourselves in latitude 7 deg. 17. min. north, and in 104 deg. 21 min. east longitude. This day we observed several large bamboos floating about the ship.

On Saturday the 2nd of November, we found by observation, our latitude to be 3 deg. 54 min. north, longitude 103 deg. 20 min east; and on the 3d, we came in sight of the island of Pulo Timoan, bearing S. W. by W. distant about twelve leagues. On the 5th, we anchored in a bay on the east side of the island, in sixteen fathoms water, and at about the distance of two miles from the shore. On Wednesday the 6th, we landed, in hopes of procuring fresh provisions, but found the inhabitants, who are Malays, a surly insolent set of people. On seeing us approach the shore, they came down to the beach in great numbers, each man having a long knife in one hand, a spear headed with iron in the other, and a dagger by his side. Notwith-

4   standing

standing thefe hoftile appearances, we landed, but could only purchafe about a dozen of fowls, a goat, and a kid; for which we offered them knives, hatchets, bill-hooks, and the like, which they refufed with great contempt, and demanded rupees in payment. Having none of thefe pieces, we were at a lofs how to pay for what we had purchafed, but recollecting we had fome pocket handkerchiefs, they accepted of them, though they took only the beft. Thefe people are well made but fmall in ftature, and of a dark copper colour. There was among them an old man, dreffed fomewhat in the fafhion of the Perfians, but all the reft were naked, except fome pieces of cloth, which were faftened with filver clafps round their waifts; and they wore kind of turbans, made up of handkerchiefs, upon their heads. We faw not any of their women, whom they probably took care to keep out of our fight. Their houfes are neatly built of flit bamboo, and raifed upon pillars about eight feet from the ground. Their boats are of an admirable good conftruction, and fome of them of large dimenfions. In thefe they probably trade to Malacca. This ifland is mountainous, woody, and produces the cocoa-nut, and cabbage-tree, in great abundance; but the natives would not permit us to have any of their fruit. We faw alfo fome rice grounds; but what may be the other productions of this ifland we cannot fay. In the bay is excellent fifhing, though the furf runs very high. We hauled our feyne with great fuccefs, but could eafily perceive that by fo doing we offended the inhabitants, who confidered all the fifh about the ifland as their own property. Two fine rivers run into this bay, and the water is excellent; we filled as many cafks with it as loaded the boats twice. Some of the natives brought down to us an animal, which had the body of a hare and the legs of a deer. One of our officers bought it; and we would have kept it alive, had it been in our power to have procured proper fuftenance; but this being impoffible, it was killed, and we found it excellent food. We ftaid here only two nights and one day, and all the time had the moft

6 A 2

violent

violent thunder, lightning, and rain we had ever known. This island of Pulo Timoan lies off the eastern coast of the peninsula of Malacca, in latitude 3 deg. 12 min. north, longitude 105 deg. 40 min. east. Finding that nothing more was to be procured at this place,

On Thursday the 7th, in the morning we set sail, and after arriving in the latitude of Pulo Condone, we had nothing but tornados, and tempestuous weather. On the 10th, at seven o'clock A. M. the east end of Lingen bore S. W. by W. distant twelve leagues. At noon we anchored with the kedge in twenty fathoms; and at one o'clock P. M. we saw a small island, which bore S. W. half S. distant ten leagues. On Monday the 11th, we weighed, and, having made sail, we descried some small islands, which we supposed to be Domines, bearing W. half N. distant seven leagues. At noon by observation we found our latitude to be 18 min. south. On the 12th, at ten o'clock A. M. we saw a small Chinese junk; and on the 13th, a small island, called Pulo Toté. At four o'clock, P. M. we came to an anchor, and saw a small sloop about four miles distant from us, which hoisted Dutch colours. In the night we had violent rain with hard squalls. On Thursday the 14th, we weighed, and at nine o'clock A. M. made sail. The vessel we had seen the day before still laying at anchor, we sent a boat with an officer to speak with her: the officer was received on board with great civility; but was much surprized at finding, that he could not make himself understood, for the people on board were Malays, without a single white man among them; they made tea for our men immediately, and in every respect behaved with great hospitality. This vessel was of a singular form; her deck was of split bamboo, and she was steered, not by a rudder, but by two large pieces of timber, one upon each quarter. This day the wind became more moderate and variable from N. N. W. to W. S. W. On the 15th, we set sail, and at two o'clock P. M. Monopin hill bore S. by E. distant ten leagues, having the appearance of a small island. It bears S. by W. from the seven islands, and is distant from them seven leagues, in the latitude of two deg. fouth. From the feven iflands we fteered S. W. by S. and foon after faw the coaft of Sumatra, bearing from W. S. W. to W. by N. diftant feven leagues. In the evening we anchored; and on the 16th, at four A. M. we continued our courfe S. by E. till the peak of Monopin Hill bore eaft, and Batacarang Point, on the Sumatra fhore S. W. in order to avoid a fhoal called Frederick Hendrick, which lies nearly midway between the Banca and Sumatra fhore. We then fteered E. S. E. and kept midchannel, to fhun the banks of Palambam River, and that which lies off the weftermoft point of Banca. When abreaft of Palambam River, we regularly fhoaled our water, and when we had paffed it, we deepened it again. We held on our courfe E. S. E. between the third and fourth points of Sumatra, which are about ten leagues diftant from each other. The high land of Queda Banca appeared over the third point of Sumatra, bearing E. S. E. From the third point to the fecond, the courfe is S. E. by S. at the diftance of eleven leagues. The high land of Queda Banca, and the fecond point of Sumatra bear E. N. E. and W. S. W. from each other. The ftrait is five leagues over, and the mid channel is twenty-four fathoms. At fix o'clock in the evening, we anchored; and at five in the morning on the 17th, we weighed, with a moderate gale at weft. On Tuefday, the 19th, we met with an Englifh fnow, belonging to the Eaft India Company, whofe captain with great generofity, prefented our commodore with a fheep, a dozen of fowls, and a turtle. This was a moft acceptable prefent, for we had now nothing to eat but the fhip's provifions, which were become very bad. Our beef and pork ftunk intolerably, and our bread was rotten and full of worms. In the afternoon we anchored, and fent a boat to found for the fhoals which lie to the northward of Lafipara, which ifland bore from us S. E. by S. diftant fix leagues. On the 20th we worked between the fhoals and the coaft of Sumatra, and having got through the ftrait, well known to navigators, on the 27th, we fteered between the iflands of Edam

and

and Horn, and entered the road of Batavia, where we anchored without the shipping.

On Wednesday the 28th, we moored nearer the town, and saluted the fort with eleven guns, which were returned. We here observed, that, since our leaving England, we had lost a day in our reckoning, by having steered westward a year; so that by the Dutch account this day was the 29th of November. We counted in this road more than one hundred sail great and small; among which was an English ship from Bombay, also the Falmouth man of war, which we found condemned and lying ashore, and all the men cleared for England, except the warrant officers, who were left here till the Lords of the Admiralty should think proper to recall them. A Dutch commodore belonging to their company is always stationed here, who in the eyes of his countrymen is a person of very great consequence. He thought fit to send his cockswain, a very dirty ragged fellow, who asked the commodore many impertinent questions, as whence we came, &c. at the same time pulling out a book, pen, and ink, in order to set down the answers; but our gentlemen being impatient to save him any more trouble, desired him immediately to walk over the ship's side, and put off his boat, with which he was graciously pleased to comply. The commodore went on shore, and visited the Dutch Governor at his country-house, by whom he was received with great politeness, and told, that he might take a house in any part of the city, or be lodged at the hotel. Any inhabitant of Batavia permitting a stranger to sleep, though but for a single night in his house, incurs a penalty of 500 dollars: the hotel being the only licensed lodging-house, the governor appoints the keeper of it, who was at this time a Frenchman. This hotel is the most superb building in the city, having more the air of a palace than an inn. During our stay at this place, we were supplied with good greens, fruits of all kinds, and plenty of fresh meat: we took also on board a great quantity of water, at the rate of five shillings a leager, or a hundred and fifty gallons. A ship of four hundred

dred and fifty tons, built at Bombay, was employed in caulking the Dolphin, and paying her bottom and sides with varnish. When we arrived here, we had not one man sick in either ships; but knowing Batavia to be more unhealthy than any other part of the East Indies, and as the rainy season was at hand, and our men could procure arrack at a very low rate, it was for these reasons resolved to make our stay as short as possible: however, we had an opportunity of enquiring into the state of this country, and we hope the following particular account of what we learnt will not be disagreeable to our friends and readers.

The island of Java, the capital whereof is Batavia, lies six degrees south of the line, and is divided from Sumatra, distant therefrom five leagues, by the straits of Sunda. It is supposed to be 420 miles in length extending almost due east and west; but its breadth, which is hardly any where more than 150 miles, is different in different places. On the north coast of Java are several good harbours, commodious creeks, and flourishing towns, with many islands near the shore. Though Java is situated so near the equator, few climates are more temperate and healthful at particular seasons, the east and west winds blowing all the year all along the shore, besides the general land and sea-breezes, but in the month of December the coast is very dangerous, on account of the violence of the westerly winds. In February the weather is changeable, with storms of thunder and lightning: and in May the rains are sometimes so violent, for three or four days together, that all the low countries are laid under water: one great convenience attends this disagreeable circumstance, which is that of destroying infinite broods of insects, that would otherwise destroy the fruits of the earth. Their sugar and rice ripen in July and October, which months not only furnish the inhabitants with all kinds of fruits, but with every necessary and luxury of life. The land, which is very fertile about the sea-coast, is finely diversified with hills and valleys, which, near Batavia, is highly improved by rich plantations, spacious canals,

and

and whatever can add to the charms of a country naturally pleasant and agreeable. But the Dutch have
made a very inconsiderable progress in the cultivation
of the country beyond the neighbourhood of that city,
the entrance to the inland parts being almost every
where obstructed by impassable forests, or by mountains,
whose heads seem to touch the clouds. Java produces
a great variety of fruit: there are here cocoa trees in
abundance; and in the plains is found a tree, whose fruit
is called jamboos, the juice whereof is used by the natives as an infallible remedy against the flux, which often
rages with great violence. The Indian forrel, which
has no resemblance to that in England, is eaten by the
inhabitants in large quantities with their salads, and its
leaves mixed with saw-dust of sandal wood is used as a
certain cure for the tooth-ach. Their fruits are, in general, very rich, particularly their pompions, the inside
of which are red, and taste not unlike our cherries.
With respect to their shape, they bear the nearest resemblance to an orange, but are of a much larger size; a
single one sometimes weighing eight or ten pounds.
This fruit, if left on the tree, continues in perfection all
the year round, and when gathered, will, with care, keep
four or five months. We thought them so excellent,
that we brought many of them to England. The
mango fruit rises from a white flower that grows on the
small twigs of a tree, every way as large as our English
oaks. Pepper and coffee also grow in the country, and
at a small distance from Batavia are several plantations
of sugar canes, from which is made a considerable
quantity of sugar. What is here called the Indian
oak, is as durable as any that can be found in Europe,
the wood being of such a consistence, as to be proof
against the worms, and, what is more, against the mice,
which will gnaw a passage through almost every other
sort of wood. The leaves of this tree boiled in water,
till one half of them is consumed, is, among the natives,
the general remedy against pleurisies. In short we were
told, that almost all sorts of garden stuff thrive in Batavia, and that those brought not only from Surat and

Persia,

Persia, but from Europe, yield near that city a great increase, so that their kitchen gardens produce pease and
beans, with roots and herbs sufficient for the consump-
tion of the inhabitants : however rice is the only corn
that grows in the island. The woods and forests of
Java abound with a prodigious variety of wild beasts,
as rhinoceroses, tygers, foxes, buffaloes, apes, wild
horses, jackals, and crocodiles. Their cows are nearly
as large as ours in England, and have generally two or
three calves at a time : their sheep are also nearly of the
size of ours. They have likewise a prodigious number
of hogs whose flesh is esteemed excellent, and far preferable to beef or mutton. Here are a variety of fowls,
particularly partridges, pheasants, wood-pigeons, wild
peacocks, and bats so large, that the body of one of
them is as big as that of a rat, and their wings when
extended reach at least three feet, from the extremity of
one to that of the other. With respect to reptiles, they
have many that are very pernicious, particularly scorpions, among which we saw several that were at least a
quarter of a yard in length; but those of a smaller size
are so common, that it is hardly possible to remove a
chest, a looking-glass, or a large picture, without finding them, and being in danger of suffering by their
sting. The same creature smothered in oil, and applied to the wound is a general remedy against their
poison. Besides these, there are a great number of
snakes of different sizes, from one foot in length to ten.
Among a variety of valuable animals useful to man,
there are none more plentiful than fish, of which there
are many kinds, and very good, as also a great number
of turtle.

The island of Java was formerly divided into several
petty kingdoms, which are at present united under the
jurisdiction of the king of Bantam, who is in the possession of the eastern part of the island, as the Dutch
are of the western, and some parts of the coast. The
natives of Java are, according to the Dutch, not only
proud beyond measure, but skilled in all the arts of im-
posture. Their faces are flat and of a brown cast, with

small

fmall eyes, like the antient Chinefe, from whom they
boaft their original defcent. The men, who are ftrong
and well proportioned, wear round their bodies a piece
of calico, which among the more wealthy is flowered
with gold. The women are in general fmall of ftature,
and have a piece of calico, which reaches from their
arm-pits to their knees. The principal part of them,
efpecially thofe near the coaft, are Mahomedans, and
the reft Pagans. In the weftern part of the ifland are
many towns, and in the eaftern, the cities of Balambuan
and Mataram are thofe in which the king of Bantam
refides, who is ftiled the Emperor of Java. Batavia
was formerly no more than an open village inhabited by
Pagans, and furrounded by a palifado of bamboos; but
fince the Dutch have eftablifhed a fettlement, it is become one of the fineft cities in the Indies. It lies in 5
deg. 50 min. fouth latitude, and is watered by many
fmall rivulets which unite into one ftream, before they
difcharge themfelves into the fea. The city is of a
triangular form, fortified with a ftone wall that has
twenty-two baftions, and four great gates, two of which
are exceeding magnificent. The harbour is very capacious, being large enough to contain a thoufand veffels
in perfect fecurity from the violence of the winds. It
is fhut up every night with a chain, through which no
fhip can pafs without permiffion, and paying a fixed duty,
to enforce which ordinances it is guarded by a ftrong
party of foldiers. The ftreets run in right lines, and
are moft of them thirty feet broad, and paved with
brick near the houfes. Fifteen of the ftreets have canals of water running through them, and over one of
thofe canals are four ftrong bridges, each confifting of
four arches twelve feet broad : but in the city there are
fifty-fix bridges, befides many draw-bridges without
the walls. The ftreets are fo crowded, that from four
in the morning till late at night it is difficult to pafs
through them, on account of the concourfe of people
continually engaged in bufinefs. We may obferve of
the public buildings, that the Chinefe hofpital is a
neat ftructure, fupported by a tax laid on marriages,

burials,

burials, and public shews, as well as the voluntary con-
tribution of the Chinese-merchants. In the same street
is a foundling-hospital, and also a building, in which
are lodged all the artizans in the Dutch East-India Company's service. The company have likewise a great
rope-yard, that employs a considerable number of the
poorer sort of people, who work under the shade of the
nut-trees planted on each side. To the west end of
this yard are the company's warehouses, for mace,
cinnamon, cloves, and other commodities. In the
castle which is of a quadrangular figure, built upon a
flat, are apartments for all the members of the council
of the Indies. The palace is within the walls of the
castle, and is appropriated to the use of the governor.
It is built with brick, but is extremely magnificent,
and loftier than the other buildings of the city. On
the top of the turret belonging to the palace, is placed
an iron ship curiously wrought, for the purpose of a
weather cock, which is so large that it may be seen some
leagues out at sea. Round the city forts are erected,
to protect the inhabitants of the plain from the incursions of the original natives, who before they were
erected, frequently came down upon the people, and
plundered their plantations. Among the principal
public buildings are a very handsome town-house, a
spinhuys, or house of correction; also four or five
churches for the Dutch Calvinists; besides a great
number of religious structures for the use of persons of
other religions. The garrison consists of foot; and
there is a troop of horse, as a guard for the company's
possessions lodged in the city: these men are of good
stature, and when drawn up in their uniform, make
no despicable appearance.

The inhabitants of Batavia are a compound of various
nations, among whom the Dutch are the most powerful and wealthy. Next to these are the Chinese, who
are, perhaps, the most ingenious cheats in the world.
They farm the excise and customs, and indeed are sure
to be concerned in every thing from which they have
a chance of deriving the least profit. They live under

a governor of their own, and drefs in the fame manner as thofe in China ; but wear their hair long and neatly braided, paying, in this laft circumftance, no manner of regard to the Tartarian edicts, which in China oblige the natives to cut off all their hair but one lock. It is remarkable that on the top of a mount of earth, underneath which lie the remains of one of their governors, ftands a table, whereon is placed a cup, into which the Chinefe fometimes put money and provifions as an offering to the foul of the deceafed. This is fituated in the midft of a grove, without one of the city gates. The Malayans, who are the next in riches and trade to the Chinefe, alfo live under a governor of their own. Their houfes are covered with leaves, and furrounded with cocoa-trees. Their drefs is the fame with the Chinefe, and they are generally chewing betel. The Mardykers, or Topaffes, are idolaters of various nations, who live both within and without the city, and feem to be a people of eafy difpofition, who accommodate themfelves without much difficulty, to the cuftoms and manners of the people among whom they refide. Their merchants carry on a confiderable commerce: others of them are of different trades, and particularly excel in gardening. They drefs in much the fame manner as the Dutch, and their houfes are of ftone, well built, and covered with tiles. Befides thefe, there are people of many other nations, all of whom have their different dreffes, cuftoms, manners, and places of religious worfhip. So that the inhabitants of this city make a more motly appearance than can be conceived by any who have not feen them. The roads about the city, for many miles, are as good as any in England : they are very broad, and by the fide of them runs a canal, fhaded with trees, which is navigable for veffels of a very large fize. On the other fide of the canal are gardens, and the country houfes of the citizens, (moft of whom keep their carriages, it being almoft a difgrace to be feen on foot) where they fpend as much of their time as poffible, the fituation being lefs unwholefome than the city, which is built on a

fwamp ;

swamp; and the trees, though they have a pleasant appearance, must undoubtedly prevent the noxious vapours that are perpetually arifing, from being difperfed, by obftructing the circulation of the air. Thus we have given a particular account of every thing we faw in Batavia worthy of obfervation; of which place the reader will find a ftill more circumftantial, full, and complete defcription, in the hiftory of Capt. Cook's firft voyage, page 273 of this work. We now prepared for our departure; and having fitted the Dolphin, taken in our water, and a fufficient ftock of frefh provifions, together with a quantity of rice and arrack,

On Monday the 10th of December, we weighed anchor, and fet fail with the Tamar in company, being faluted, on our leaving the road, by the Englifh fhip, the Dutch commodore and the fort. We paffed by the Thoufand Iflands, which extend along the north fide of Java, almoft to the weft point of New Guinea. Commodore Roggewein failing through the midft of them, and finding it impoffible to count them, gave them, we are told, the general name of the Thoufand Iflands. They are inhabited by a favage people of a black complexion, who are almoft naked, and thefe iflands are famous for producing a beautiful kind of bird, known among us by the name of the bird of paradife. We alfo paffed by a multitude of other fmall iflands, commonly called the Bed of Rofes. After which we entered the Straits of Sunday, where the land on each fide is very high, both on the fhore of the ifland of Sumatra, and that of Java, the paffage between which conftitutes the Straits of Sunday. The land of the laft mentioned ifland is very irregular, and the inhabitants extremely poor. They trafficked with us chiefly for old cloaths; and we had an opportunity of fupplying ourfelves with a great quantity of the fineft green turtle, fowls, and fruit of all kinds. The commodore bought for 10 rixdollars, as many turtle as weighed upwards of 1000 pounds weight, part of which he gave to our fhip's company, and also fent

a part

a part to that of the Tamar. On the 14th, at seven in the evening, we came to an anchor on the north-side of Prince's Island, which lies within the south entrance of the straits, in order to recruit our wood and water. We found this island well stocked with provisions of all kinds, and particularly fowls. The inhabitants are to all appearance free from the dominion of the Dutch ; though according to the accounts given by the natives, they often fall victims to their unprovoked cruelties, as they frequently seize them, and reduce them to the condition of slaves ; and even sell them in the same manner, as the negroes are purchased on the coast of Guinea. We lay off this island till the 19th, during which time, we repaired an inconsiderable damage the Dolphin had sustained, by having had some pieces of copper torn off the larboard bow, by the small bower anchor. This done, and having taken in as much wood and water as we could stow, we weighed, and, working to the windward, before night got without Java Head. By this time a putrid fever raged among our crew, whereof three of our hands died, and many others lay in so dangerous a condition that we had little hopes of their recovery. On the 25th, being Christmas-day, our people were in high spirits, and not a little troublesome ; but at this time we had an accident which gave us some concern. William Walter, a quarter gunner, was sitting asleep with a pipe in his mouth, and fell overboard ; when, notwithstanding all possible means were used to save him, he was never seen more. This unfortunate man was a very good seaman, and universally respected by the officers and all on board.

A.D. 1766.   On Monday the 10th of February, at six o'clock, A. M. we came in sight of the coast of Africa, in latitude 34 deg. 15 min. south, and in 21 deg. 45 min. east longitude. On the 12th, at three P. M. we made land to the eastward of Cape d'Aguilas, but had contrary winds for several days together. From hence the coast lies W. N. W. to the Cape of Good Hope, distant about 30 leagues. On the

13th,

13th, we passed between Penguin Island and Green Point, and at three o'clock, P. M. came to an anchor in Table Bay, with a fresh gale, working to windward under a close reefed main and top-sails, and there found some light Dutch ships and Indiamen, bound for Europe. In this bay the S. E. wind blew so strong, as to oblige us to lie with our yards and top-masts struck; and it was sometimes with the greatest difficulty that our boats reached the shore, through the violence of the squalls, which at particular times are here so great, as to drive ships from their anchors out to sea. On our entering the bay we saluted the fort, which compliment was immediately returned; and on Friday the 14th, the commodore waited upon the governor, who sent his coach and six to the water-side to receive him. The Cape is a most excellent place for ships to touch at; it is a healthy climate, a fine country, and abounds with refreshments of every kind. The company's garden is a delightful spot, and at the end of it is a paddock belonging to the governor, in which are kept a great number of very curious animals; among others were three fine ostriches, and four zebras of an uncommon size. The square, in which the old governor lives, is encompassed by many other grand buildings, besides what is appropriated to the use of that great officer, who here appears with the dignity of a prince. Our commodore during his stay, resided in a house adjoining to the governor's, where he had a centinel always at the door, and a serjeant who attended him whenever he went abroad. In the middle of this square is a very fine fountain, which supplies the greatest part of the town with water. The officers of both ships resided chiefly at Mr. Prince's, and as for a long time we had enjoyed no recreation, we now spent our time very agreeably. The people also on board had all leave to go on shore by turns, and they always contrived to get completely drunk with cape wine before they returned. This was chiefly owing to the civility of the inhabitants, who as they depend on the foreign ships who touch here, think it their interest to behave with good manners,

and

and extraordinary complaisance to all strangers. During
the time we continued at the cape, which was three
weeks, all on board both ships were supplied with fresh
mutton and beef; for provisions are so cheap, that a
sheep may be bought for a Spanish dollar, which, when
cleared of the offal, will weigh 50 or 60 pounds.
Their tails, which are remarkably large, are chiefly
composed of fat, which eats like marrow. Their skins
are not covered with wool, as ours in England, but with
a kind of down, intermixed with long hair. The bullocks are large, and used for the most part in teams,
for which they are preferred to horses; eight or ten of
them being harnessed together, and conducted by a
slave, who goes before to guide them. The horses are
small, but very spirited: and we were told an odd circumstance concerning them, which is, that they are never
known to lie down but when sick, and that this is an
infallible sign by which their owners know when they
are out of order.

With respect to the country in general, it is situated
in 35 deg. of south latitude, and in a temperate climate,
where the extremes of heat and cold are equally unknown. It abounds with the most beautiful landscapes,
the skirts of the mountains being interspersed with lofty
groves of the finest trees, and the valleys and plains consist of delightful meadow lands, adorned with a variety
of the most beautiful flowers, that fill the air with their
fragrance. The land also produces the finest vegetable
productions, and the richest fruits, while most of those
brought from the East and West Indies, flourish here
as well as in their native soil. One of the most beautiful, and a native, is the aloe, of which are many sorts,
seen not only in the gardens of the company, but in the
clefts of the rocks, and, it is said, that throughout the
year, one sort or other is continually in bloom. The Indian
gold-tree is likewise a remarkable curiosity, having gold-
coloured leaves speckled with red, with small greenish
blossoms. Here are also numbers of quince-trees, whose
fruit is said to be not only larger, but better than the
quinces of any other country in the known world. The

Dutch

Dutch have difcovered feveral excellent methods of preferving them, and not only make great quantities of marmalade for their own ufe, but fell it to the fhips that touch here for refrefhments. No country abounds with a greater variety of animals. Among the wild beafts are the elephant, the rhinoceros, and the buffalo, with lions, tygers, leopards, wolves, wild dogs, porcupines, elks, harts, goats of various kinds, wild horfes, the zebra, and many others. Among the moft extraordinary of thefe is a fmall animal, fomewhat larger than a fquirrel, with a head that has fome refemblance to that of a bear. It is called a rattle-moufe, from its frequently making a rattling noife with its tail. This is neither very hairy, nor very long. Its back is of a liver colour, and its fides nearly black. It purs like a cat, and lives for the moft part on trees, leaping like a fquirrel from one tree to another, feeding upon acorns, nuts, and the like. The feathered tribe are no lefs numerous; for befides many of thofe known in Europe, here are oftriches much larger than thofe we faw in the ftraits of Magellan, flamingoes, fpoon-bills, blue-birds, green-peaks, the long-tongue and many others. The flamingo is larger than a fwan, and a very ftately bird. Both the head and neck are as white as fnow, and the latter is confiderably longer than that of a fwan. The bill is very broad, and black at the point, and the reft of it of a deep blue. The upper part of the wing-feathers are of a flame colour, and the lower black; but the legs, which are much longer than thofe of a ftork, are of an orange colour, and the feet refemble thofe of a goofe. Though they live upon fifh, their flefh is both wholefome, and well tafted. The green-peak is all over green, except two red fpots, one on its breaft, and another on its head, and is a very beautiful bird. It feeds on infects, which it picks out of the bark of trees. The long-tongue is about the fize of a bull-finch, and his tongue is not only very long, but faid to be as hard as iron, and the end as fharp as the point of a needle; this being a weapon given it by the author of nature for its prefervation. The feathers

No. 30.   6 C   on

on the belly are yellow, and the reft fpeckled. At the Cape are alfo many forts of excellent fifh, a confiderable number of which are common in Europe, and others peculiar to thefe feas. The reptiles and infects are likewife extremely numerous, and among thefe are a variety of ferpents, fcorpions, and fome centipedes. Thus to counterbalance the advantage this country affords, from the abundance of ufeful animals, there are alfo thrown into the fcale many that are prejudicial and extremely dangerous; as if it was intended to fhew to man, that amidft the greateft bleffings and advantages beftowed on one of the moft enchanting fpots in the univerfe, it was neceffary to mix a certain pro-portion of evil, to reduce it more to a level with thofe countries that are in fome refpects lefs defirable.

Both our fhip and the Tamar by this time had re-ceived a frefh fupply of wood, water, and all neceffary ftores, and being completely fitted for failing to our native country, on Thurfday the fixth of March, our commodore took leave of the good old governor, and the next day we got under way, and failed with a fine breeze at S. E. On Sunday the 16th, at fix o'clock, A. M. we faw the rocks off the ifland of St. Helena, bearing W. by N. diftant about eight leagues; and at noon, in 8 deg. 16 min. fouth latitude, we obferved a ftrange fail which hoifted French colours, but in the evening ran her out of fight. We purfued our courfe without any thing material occurring till the 20th, when we were alarmed by the fhip's running foul of a whale or grampus, on which fhe ftruck her head, and then her larboard bow. This put the commodore and officers in no fmall confternation, left the Dolphin fhould have fuffered from the violence of the fhock, as we were at that time running at the rate of fix knots an hour; however we found the fhock, though a rude one, attended with no bad confequence. We perceived the fea near the place where the fhip ftruck, tinged with blood, by which we fuppofed the whale was killed, or at leaft deeply wounded. On Tuefday the 25th, we croffed the equator in longitude 17 deg. 10 min. and

the

the next morning Captain Cumming of the Tamar, made the fignal to bring to, and came on board the Dolphin to inform the commodore, that the rudder braces were broke from the ftern-poft, whereby the rudder was rendered intirely ufelefs: upon which the commodore fent his carpenter with affiftants on board the Tamar, who went to work upon a machine after the model of that which had been fixed to the Ipfwich, and Grafton, each of which fhips, at different times, fteered home from Louifbourg by the help of fuch a fubftitute for a rudder. This machine was completed in about fix days, and received fome improvements from the ingenuity of the conftructor: but it was thought better to fend the Tamar to Antigua, in order to refit; accordingly on the 1ft of April, the Tamar parted company with the Dolphin, fteering for the Caribbee iflands. In their paffage they found the difference of failing with the machine, to be only about five miles in forty-eight hours. After the departure of the Tamar, which was the firft time of our being feparated wholly from her fince our leaving England, and in latitude 34 deg. north, longitude 35 deg weft, we had a moft violent gale of wind, which drove us to the northward of the weftern iflands, and into latitude 48 deg. north, longitude 14 deg. weft. We came within two hundred leagues of the land, and fpoke with feveral fhips lately from England, who gave us very erroneous accounts of the bearing of the coaft. We had now a ftrong eafterly wind, which lafted feveral days, and the weather appeared to us piercing cold, from our having been, during fo long a time, ufed to a warm climate. However, we at laft had a favourable wind, and on Thurfday the 7th of May, faw the ifland of Scilly. On the 9th, in the morning, we arrived in the Downs, where we caft anchor; having been nine weeks running from the Cape of Good Hope, and fomewhat more than two and twenty months in the circumnavigation of the globe.

Thus ended a voyage, originally planned by his Majefty, George the Third, and which produced the difcovery of thofe iflands, that have lately engroffed the

attention

attention of the public. We have endeavoured to defcribe them, and our courfes with accuracy, and with truth and authenticity, that might juftly be expected from one who faw every thing of which we have given a defcription. By the affiftance of divine providence, and the tendernefs of our excellent commodore, in caufing the crews to be ferved with portable foup, and with the greateft humanity diftributing provifions to the fick from his own table, that dreadful difeafe the fcurvy was rendered lefs inveterate and fatal; and we loft, including thofe who were drowned, a very inconfiderable number of men, a number fo inconfiderable, that it is highly probable, more of them would have died, in the courfe of a year, had they ftaid on fhore. From our arrival at Spithead, till our leaving the fhip in the river, no boats were fuffered to come on board us, nor any an-fwers to be given to enquirers, with refpect to who we were, or from what port we were come, fo that a variety of conjectures were formed as to our late voyage. After having waited a few days, each man, according to the promife of the commodore, received double pay for his fervices, and had an opportunity of enjoying thofe comforts, which we, after an abfence of twenty-two months from our native country, might be fup-pofed ardently to wifh for.

A

A NEW, ACCURATE, GENUINE, and COMPLETE
HISTORY, of

A VOYAGE Round the WORLD,

PERFORMED

By Capt. SAMUEL WALLIS, Efq.

In his Majefty's Ship the DOLPHIN;

Having under his Command the SWALLOW Sloop and
PRINCE FREDERICK Store-Ship,

Of which Mr. CARTERET and Lieutenant BRINE
were appointed Mafters:

UNDERTAKEN PARTICULARLY

With a view to make Difcoveries in the SOUTH
SEAS:

Which remarkable circuit of the Globe was begun on
FRIDAY, the 22nd of AUGUST 1766, and compleated
on FRIDAY the 20th of MAY 1768, containing a Period of 637 Days, and included in the Years 1766,
1767, and 1768.

INTRODUCTION.

NEVER was there perhaps collected together in any
language, a more copious fund of rational entertainment than will be found in this comprehenfive and
complete work, of which the prefent voyage is a part.
To trace the progrefs of the difcoveries that have fuc-
ceffively been made, in paffing round the globe, muft
fill the reader's mind with fuch a variety of new information, as cannot fail to raife his wonder, and entertain
him with inexpreffible delight. In the courfe of this
work he is fafely conducted through regions that were
once

once thought inacceffible, and made acquainted with
countries altogether different from that wherein he
dwells.   Every page he reads will furnifh him with no-
velties, and every voyage will bring him nearer to that
unknown country, in fearch of which fo many able
commanders have been fent in vain.   The difcovery of
the weftern continent by Columbus, gave geographers
reafon to believe, that a like continent exifted fome-
where in the fouth.   Without fuch an equipoife they
could not conceive how the globe could preferve its ba-
lance. Magellhaens, a Portuguefe mariner, was the firft
who attempted to immortalize his name by the difcovery.
He paffed the ftraits, that to this day bear his name ; and
entered the Pacific Ocean, where no European veffel had
ever before failed.   He difcovered the Ladrone and Philippine ifles, and returned by the Cape of Good Hope,
having furrounded the whole earth, and proved to de-
monftration, the fpherical figure of the globe.   He was
followed by navigators of different nations, who, emu-
lous of his glory, fought to purfue the track he had
pointed out, with better fuccefs ; but the dangers they
encountered, and the difafters they met with, rendered
the difficulties that attended the profecution infurmountable ; many perifhed, and thofe who furvived were glad
to return home after a fruitlefs fearch.   The ill fuccefs
which attended thefe firft attempts threw a damp upon
the enterprize, and it remained long unnoticed, except
in the writings of the learned.   Some French geographers, fully perfuaded of the reality of fuch a continent,
endeavoured, a few years ago, to revive in their countrymen the fpirit of enterprize, with a view to derive
honour to their country, by compleating the difcovery ;
but the tafte for uncommon navigations among the
French feemed intirely extinct, and it was not till the
Dolphin and Tamar had failed from England that they
thought of renewing it.

    At this time, as we have elfewhere obferved, our moft
gracious Sovereign had formed the defign of diftinguifhing himfelf by patronizing the profecution of new
difcoveries in the unknown regions of the fouthern he-
                                                        mifphere ;

misphere; and surely nothing can more endear a British monarch to his maritime people, than a steady perseverance in this laudable resolution. The love of glory is a passion natural to kings: the conquerors of the world are placed before them as patterns, and they are encouraged by example to seek occasions for war to acquire a name. But how much more glorious is it to enlarge the earth with a new region, than to triumph in the conquest of some rival state!—to extend protection to a remote, and it may be a defenceless people, than to boast of levelling fortresses, and by a general carnage of friends and foes, become master of a few desolated towns, purchased at an expence, a thousand times greater than what is necessary to insure the success of new discoveries. Can there be any comparison between the glory of a successful enterprize, founded on the laudable motives of diffusing happiness through regions, whose inhabitants, for ought we know, are yet immersed in savage darkness; and that of engaging in a hazardous war, by which millions of treasure must be expended, and thousands of lives sacrificed? Is not the chance of succeeding in the first case much more probable than that of conquering in the other? And does not success in the discovery of the long sought region promise much greater advantage to a trading nation, than the conquest of any part of the earth on this side the globe? Did not the little Phœnician state reap more glorious harvest from the discoveries of its merchants, than Alexander could boast from all his conquests? Was it not the perseverance of the Princes Henry, John, and Emanuel, in supporting the expences of prosecuting new discoveries in the fifteenth century, that laid the foundation of the Portuguese greatness, whose territories in Europe are of no inconsiderable extent? But if the glory of aggrandizing a state, and perpetuating a name to posterity, be the first object of human ambition, where shall we look for a monarch, who, after having spread murder and desolation throughout the world, descended to the grave with that heart-felt satisfaction, that attended the Florentine merchant Americus Vespucius,

3

Vespucius, when he saw all Europe agreeing, with one consent, to transfer his name to more than a third part of the terrestrial globe?

The success which has attended his present Majesty's first essays, in the voyages we are now relating, though it has as yet produced no extraordinary advantages to compensate the sums expended in the prosecution of them, yet it has been such as to open the way to new islands, from whose inhabitants new arts may be learnt, and from whose productions new acquisitions may be made, both to the vegetable and fossil kingdoms, by which the boundaries of science may be enlarged, and the gardens of the curious enriched. Nor does it afford a small satisfaction to inquisitive minds, to be made acquainted with the genius, the arts, the various pursuits, the customs, the manners, the religious notions, the distinctions of rank, and the subordination that is to be met with among the people of various islands and countries, distinct from each other, and from us, in language, habits, learning, and ways of living. Who can read of the poverty and misery of the wretched inhabitants of Terra del Fuego, who have nothing but the skins of beasts thrown over them to defend them from the severity of the cold: natives of a most horrid climate; not better provided with food than with raiment; who can read the story of these forlorn creatures, without lamenting the condition of human beings, destitute as these appear to be, of every comfort and convenience, and exposed every moment to the piercing rigour of the climate, and the still severer cravings of unsatisfied hunger! On the contrary, who can think of these, while, at the same time, he is told of the pleasurable lives of those happy islanders, in the new discovered countries, who abound in flesh, fish, and fruits, even to profusion, without admiring the ways of providence, that, for purposes unknown to us, has so unequally bestowed its dispensations! In these voyages, when we read of men that eat men, not from hunger, but from savage ferocity, we shudder to think of the depravity of our nature, and are convinced of the necessity of bounding our passions

by

by wholefome laws, and of correcting the irregularities of our appetites by the reftraints of religion.

The variety of incidents that happened to our navigators, and in the courfe of their voyages, when hiftorically recited, afford a peculiar kind of entertainment, not to be met with in other productions of a different kind. The many fingular adventures, unforefeen dangers, and providential efcapes, that every fhip experienced in pafling round the globe, can only be conceived by thofe who read, and believed by thofe who have feen the wonders of the deep. Nothing can excite or gratify curiofity more than relations of marvellous events that happen in fucceffion, and in circumftances equally critical and important. There is not an object that prefents itfelf either by fea or land, but affords fome degree of ufe and fpeculation. The fifh that fwim about the fhip, and the fowls that prefent themfelves in the ocean, are indications by which the fkilful mariner avails himfelf, either to guard againft the ftorm, or to prepare for land; and our readers, as circumftances arife, either fhares his danger, or partakes of his refrefhment. We are now preparing for them new fubjects of entertainment; and being about to pafs again through the Straits of Magellan, into the vaft Pacific Ocean or South Sea, it may not be amifs to offer a remark on this immenfe body of water. It extends from the weftern coafts of North and South America, to the eaftern fhores of China, Tartary and Japan. From its moft weftern boundary between Peru and Chili, to its moft eaftern point at Cochin-China, it very near rolls over an extent of 180 degrees of longitude; and it is now fuppofed, by the moft accurate inveftigation that human fkill and fpirit will ever make, to reach quite to the South-Pole, and may poffibly be as extenfive towards the North; fo that this fea may be faid to embrace, within five degrees, an entire hemifphere of the globe of the world; to explore which, in a certain track, is the object of the voyage, undertaken by Captain Samuel Wallis. The hiftory of this we fhall now prefent to the view of our numerous fubfcribers, only obferving that Capt. Wallis in this circumnavigation of the globe, directed his course more weftwardly than any former navigator within the tropics.

C H A P. I.

Preparations for this Voyage, Inftructions, &c.—Names of the Ships and Commanders—Circumftances previous to their fetting fail from Plymouth—Paffage from thence to the Coaft of Patagonia—Capt. Byron's Account of the gigantic Natives confirmed, with fome additional Circumftances —The three Ships continue their Courfe through the Straits of Magellan—The Narrative of the Patagonians concluded—A particular and minute Defcription of the Coaft on each Side the Straits—The Places in which the Ships anchored during their Paffage, with an Account of the Shoals and Rocks that lie near them.

A. D. 1766. WHEN the prefent honourable Admiral Byron, then commodore, returned from his voyage round the world, Captain Samuel Wallis, Efq. was immediately appointed to the command of the Dolphin, in order to make another circuit of the globe, but particularly with a view to difcoveries in the Pacific Ocean, having the Swallow, a floop, mounting 14 guns, appointed to accompany him, the command of which was given to Mr. Carteret, a lieutenant under Commodore Byron, and who on his return was advanced to the rank of a mafter and commander. His complement was one lieutenant, 22 petty officers, and 90 feamen. The prince Frederick ftorefhip, was likewife put under Captain Wallis's command, whofe mafter was lieutenant Brine.

On the 19th of June, Captain Wallis, having received his commiffion, went on board the Dolphin, and the fame day hoifted the broad pendant, and began to enter feamen; but agreeable to his orders, he took no boys either for himfelf or any of his officers. The Dolphin

being

being now fitted for her intended voyage, the articles of war, and the act of parliament were read on board. On the 26th of July, she sailed down the river, and on Saturday the 16th of Auguft, at eight o'clock, A. M. anchored in Plymouth Sound. On Tuefday the 19th, Captain Wallis received his failing orders, with inftructions refpecting the Swallow Sloop, and the Prince Frederick ftorefhip; and this day we took on board 3000 weight of portable foup, and a bale of cork jackets. Every part of the fhip was filled with ftores of various kinds, even to the fteerage and ftate room; and an extraordinary quantity of medicines being provided by the furgeon, which confifted of three large boxes, and thefe were put into the captain's cabbin.

On Friday the 22nd, at four o'clock, A. M. the Dolphin, (on board of which was our journalift) departed from Plymouth, in company with the Swallow and Prince Frederick; and too foon, to our mortification, we found the Swallow to be a very heavy failor.

On Sunday the 7th of September, we had a view of the ifland of Porto Santo, due weft, and near noon came in fight of the eaft end of the ifland of Madeira. At five we ran between this and the Deferters, and at fix anchored in Madeira Road, about a mile from the fhore, in 24 fathoms water, with a muddy bottom. About eight the Swallow and Prince Frederick came alfo to an anchor. The next morning we faluted the governor with 13 guns, and the compliment was returned with an equal number. We failed from hence on the 12th, after having taken in beef, wine, and a large quantity of onions, as fea-ftores. On the 16th, when off the ifland of Palma, failing at the rate of eight miles an hour, the wind fuddenly died away, and for two minutes the veffel had no motion, though we were at leaft four leagues diftant from the fhore; and we found the fhip 15 miles to the fouthward of her reckoning. Saturday the 20th, we caught eight bonettas, out of a great number which furrounded the fhip, and this day we faw two herons flying to the eaftward. The Swallow parted from us in the night, between the 21ft and 22nd,

and

and on Tuesday the 23rd, at noon, the neareft land of
the ifland of Bonavifta bore from S. to W. S. W. and
the eaft-end bore at the fame time weft, diftant two
leagues. We now thought it neceffary to found, and
had only 15 fathoms, rocky ground; at the fame time
we perceived a great rippling, occafioned, as we fuppofed, by a reef; alfo breakers without us, diftant about
one league in the direction of S. E. We fteered between
the rippling and the breakers, and the Prince Frederick paffed very near the laft, in the S. E. but had no
foundings; yet thefe breakers are thought to be dangerous. On Wednefday the 24th, at fix o'clock, A. M.
the ifle of May bore W. S. W. diftant fix leagues; and
foon after our confort, the Swallow, joined company
again. At ten o'clock the weft end of the ifland of
May, one of the Cape de Verd iflands, bore north, diftant five miles; and at noon the fouth end of St.
Jago bore S. W. by W. diftant four leagues. Between
thefe two places we found a current, fetting to the fouthward, at the rate of 20 miles in 24 hours. At near four
o'clock, P. M. we caft anchor in Port Praya, in company with the Swallow, and Prince Frederick, in eight
fathoms water, upon fandy ground. During the night
we had much rain and lightning. On the 25th, we
obtained leave from the commanding officer at the fort,
to get water and other neceffaries. This being the fickly
feafon at this place, and the rains fo great as to render
it exceeding difficult to get any thing down from the
country to the fhips; the fmall pox being alfo at this
time epidemic; the captain detained every man on
board who had not had that contagious diftemper.
However, we caught abundance of fifh, and procured
a fupply of water, and fome cattle from the ifland.
We alfo found large quantities of wild purflain, which
was very refrefhing, either raw as a fallad, or boiled in
our broth with peafe.

On Saturday the 28th, we put to fea, and at about fix
o'clock, P. M. the peak of Terra del Fuego bore
W. N W. diftant 12 leagues. In the night we faw very
plainly the burning mountain. This day Captain
Wallis

Wallis ordered every man to be furnished with hook and line, that he might supply himself with fish ; and likewife to prevent infection, commanded that no man should keep his fish longer than 24 hours; for the captain had obferved that not only ftale, but even dried fish, had tainted the internal air of the ship, and made the people fickly.

On Wednefday the 1ft of October, we loft the true trade wind, and had variable gales. We were now in latitude 10 deg. 37 min. north. On the 3rd, we found a current run S. by E. at the rate of fix fathoms an hour, and on the 7th, the ship was 19 miles fouthward of her reckoning. On Monday the 20th, the crews of the three ships were ferved with oil, all the butter and cheefe being confumed; and orders were iffued, that, during the remainder of the voyage, they fhould be ferved with vinegar and muftard once a fortnight. On the 22nd we judged we were within 60 degrees of land, from the fight of a prodigious number of fea-fowls, among which was a man of war bird. This day we croffed the Equinnoctial Line, in longitude 23 deg. 40 min. weft from London. On Friday the 24th, orders were given for ferving our ship's company with brandy, and the wine was referved for fuch as might be fick. On the 27th, the Prince Frederick fprang a leak, and her crew were at this time fo fickly, through the fatigue of pumping, and the badnefs of their provifions, that Lieutenant Brine, her commander, was apprehenfive of not being able to keep company much longer, unlefs fome affiftance could be given him. The captain therefore fent a carpenter and fix failors on board, but had it not in his power to fupply her with better provifions. As the carpenter found he could do little towards ftopping the leak, the Dolphin and Swallow compleated their provifions from the ftore ship, and put on board her empty oil-jars, ftaves and iron-hoops. On Saturday the 8th of November, we were in latitude 25 deg. 52 min. fouth, and in 39 deg. 38 min. weft longitude from London ; and on the 9th, having feen a great number of albatroffes, we founded with 180
fathoms

fathoms of line, but had no ground. On the 12th, though the summer season in these climates, yet we found the weather so very cold, as to be obliged to have recourse to our thick jackets. On Wednesday the 19th, at eight o'clock, P. M. we saw a meteor of a very extraordinary appearance, in the N. E. which flew off in an horizontal line to the S. W. with amazing rapidity: it was near a minute in its progress, and left behind it a train of light so strong, that the deck was not less illuminated than at noon day. On the 21st, we were by observation in latitude 37 deg. 40 min. south, and in 51 deg. 24 min. west longitude from London. On the 22nd, we saw whales, seals, snipes, plovers, and other birds; with a great number of butterflies. Our soundings continued from 40 to 70 fathoms.

On Monday the 8th of December, at six o'clock, A. M. we descried land, having the appearance of many small islands. At noon in latitude 47 deg. 16 min. south, and in 64 deg. 58 min. west longitude, it bore from W. by S. to S. S. W. distant eight leagues. At eight o'clock, P. M. the Tower Rock, at Port Desire, bore S. W. by W. distant about three leagues. At nine Penguin Island bore S. W. by W. half W. distant two leagues, and on the 9th, the same island, at noon, in latitude 48 deg. 56 min. south, and in 65 deg. 6 min. west longitude, bore S. by E. distant 19 leagues. We remarked this day, that the sea appeared coloured by the vast quantity of red shrimps that surrounded the ship. The next day, at noon, Wood's Mount, near the entrance of St. Julian's, bore S. W. by W. distant three or four leagues, and our soundings were from 40 to 45 fathoms. On the 11th, we observed in latitude 50 deg. 48 min. south, and in 67 deg. 10 min. west longitude, when Penguin Island bore N. N. E. distant 58 leagues. On Saturday the 13th, in latitude 50 deg. 34 min. south, longitude 68 deg. 15 min. west, we were not more than two leagues distant from the extreams of the land. We found Cape Beachy Head, the northermost cape, to lie in latitude 50 deg. 16 min. south, and Cape Fairweather, the southermost cape, in

2   latitude

latitude 50 deg. 50 min. south.   On the 14th, we were by observation in latitude 50 deg. 52 min. south, and in 68 deg. 10 min. west longitude from London, at which time we were six leagues from the shore, and the extreams of the land were from N. W. to W. S. W. Penguin Island bore north 35 deg. east, distant 68 leagues.   On the 15th, at eight o'clock, the entrance of the river St. Croix bore S. W. half W. and the extreams of the land S. by E. to N. by E.   At eight o'clock, A. M. we were two leagues from the land.   That on the north shore is high, and appears in three capes; but on the south shore it is low and flat.   We had 20 fathoms quite cross the opening of the river, the distance from point to point being about seven miles; and afterwards keeping at the distance of about four miles from each cape, we had from 22 to 24 fathoms. Cape Fairweather, at seven in the evening, bore S. W. half S. distant four leagues.   We stood off and on all night, and had from 30 to 22 fathoms water.

On Tuesday the 16th, at noon, we observed in latitude 51 deg. 52 min. south, and in 68 deg. west longitude.   At one o'clock we were about two leagues from the shore.   At four, Cape Virgin Mary bore S. E. by S. distant four leagues.   At eight in the evening, we were very near the cape, and before nine anchored in a bay close under the south-side of the cape, in 10 fathoms water, bottom gravelly.   Soon after the Swallow and Prince Frederick come to an anchor between us and the cape, which bore N. by W. half W. and a low sandy point like Dungeness S. by W.   From the cape was a shoal, to the distance of about half a league, which may be easily known by the weeds that are upon it. This day we saw several men riding on the shore, who made signs for us to land.   Accordingly the next day, being the 17th, Captain Wallis ordered the signals for the boats belonging to the Swallow and Prince Frederick to come on board, and in the mean time we hoisted out our own.   We had observed the natives to remain opposite the Dolphin all night, shouting aloud, and keeping up large fires.   Our boats being all manned and

and armed, and having with us a party of marines, about six o'clock we reached the beach, the captain having left orders with the master to bring the ship's side to bear upon the landing place, and to keep the guns loaded with round shot. Captain Wallis with Mr. Cumming and several officers now landed; the marines were then drawn up, and the boats were brought to a grapling near the shore. The captain having made signs for the Indians to sit down, he distributed among them combs, buttons, knives, scissars, beads, and other toys. The women were particularly pleased by a present of some ribbons. He then intimated that he should be glad to accept some guanicoes and ostriches, in exchange for bill-hooks and hatchets, which were produced, but they were either really or designedly ignorant of his meaning. Captain Wallis measured several of those Indians; among whom the tallest was six feet seven inches; others were one and two inches shorter; but the general height was from five feet ten to six feet. They are muscular and well made, but their hands and feet very small in proportion to the rest of their bodies. They are clothed with the skins of the guanico, sewed together into pieces about six feet long, and five wide: these are wrapped round the body, and fastened by a girdle, with the hairy-side inwards. The guanico is an animal, that in size, make, and colour, resembles a deer; but it has a hump on its back, and no horns. Some of these people wore a square piece of cloth, made of the hair of the guanico, and a hole being cut to admit the head through, it reached down to the knees. They have also a kind of buskin from the middle of the leg to the instep, which is conveyed under the heel, but the rest of the feet is bare. Their strait and coarse hair is tied back with a cotton string; and their complexion is a dark copper. Both the horses and dogs which we saw, were of a Spanish breed. The horses appeared to be about 14 hands high. Both sexes rode astride; but the men were furnished with wooden spurs. Some of these had their arms painted; the faces of some were variously marked;

marked; and others had the left eye enclosed by a painted circle of a red colour. The eye-lids of all the young women were painted black. They had each a missile weapon of a singular kind tucked into the girdle. It consisted of two round stones covered with leather, each weighing about a pound, and fastened to the two ends of a string about eight feet long. This is used as a sling, one stone being kept in the hand, and the other whirled round the head, till it is supposed to have acquired sufficient power, and then it is discharged at the object, or any mark they wish to hit. They likewise catch guanicoes and ostriches by means of this cord, which is thrown so, that the weight twists round, and hampers the legs of the intended prey. They are so expert at the management of this double-headed shot, as our captain called it, that they will hit a mark, not bigger than a shilling, with both the stones, at the distance of 15 yards. The language of these people is quite unintelligible. They were indeed often heard to repeat the word Ca-pi-ta-ne, on which they were successively addressed in Portuguese, Spanish, Dutch, and French; but they had no knowledge of either of those languages. When they shook hands with any of the crew, they always said chevow; and they were amazingly ready at learning English words, and pronouncing the sentence " Englishmen come on shore," with great facility. During our stay on shore we saw them eat some of their flesh meat raw, particularly the paunch of an ostrich, without any other preparation or cleaning than just turning it inside out, and shaking it. We observed among them several beads, such as we gave them, and two pieces of red baize, which we supposed had been left there, or in the neighbouring country, by Commodore Byron. One man among them had a large pair of such spurs as are worn in Spain, brass stirrups, and a Spanish scimeter, without a scabbard; but notwithstanding these distinctions, he did not appear to have any authority over the rest. The women had no spurs. As above 100 of the natives seemed desirous to visit the ship, Captain Wallis took eight of

No. 30.   6 E.   them

them into the boats. Thefe jumped in with the joy and alacrity of children going to a fair, and having no intention of mifchief againft us, had not the leaft fufpicion that we intended any mifchief againft them. In the boat they fung feveral of their country fongs, expreffive of their joy; but when they came into the fhip, they expreffed no kind of furprize, which the multiplicity of objects, to them equally ftrange and novel, that at once prefented themfelves, might be fuppofed to excite. When introduced into the cabbin, they looked about with a ftupid indifference, till a looking-glafs, which drew their attention, afforded them and us much diverfion: they advanced, retreated, and played a thoufand antic tricks before it, talking with earneftnefs, and laughing immoderately. For their entertainment, we furnifhed a table with beef, pork, bifcuit, and other articles of the fhip's provifions: they eat whatever was fet before them, but would drink nothing but water. When they were conducted to fee the fhip, they looked, with much attention, at the animals we had on board as live ftock: they examined the hogs and fheep, and were delighted exceedingly with the Guinea hens and turkeys. One of them making figns that he fhould be glad of fome cloaths, the captain gave him a pair of fhoes and buckles, and prefented the reft with a little bag each, in which he put new fix-pences and half-pence, with a ribband paffed through a hole in them, to hang round their necks: the remaining contents of the bag were, a looking-glafs, a comb, fome beads, a knife, a pair of fciffars, twine, and a few flips of cloth. We offered them fome leaves of tobacco, rolled up into what are called fegars, and they fmoaked a few moments, but did not feem to like it. The marines being exercifed before them, they feemed terrified at the firing of the mufquets; and one of them, falling down, fhut his eyes, and lay motionlefs, as if to intimate, that he knew the deftructive nature of thofe fire-arms, and their fatal effects. The reft feeing our people merry, and finding themfelves unhurt, foon refumed their cheerfulnefs, and heard the fecond and third volley fired without much

much emotion; but the old man continued proſtrate upon the deck ſome time, and never recovered his ſpirits till the firing was over. It was with much difficulty we got rid of theſe inoffenſive viſitors. At noon, the tide being out, Captain Wallis gave them to underſtand by ſigns, that the ſhip was proceeding farther, and that they muſt return on ſhore: this we ſoon perceived they were unwilling to do; however, all except the old man, and one more, were got into the boat; but theſe ſtopped at the gangway, where the old man turned about, and went aft to the companion ladder: here he ſtood ſome time without ſpeaking a word: he now uttered what we ſuppoſed to be a prayer; for he many times lifted up his hands and eyes to the heavens, and ſpoke in a manner and tone very different from what we had obſerved in the converſation of his countrymen. His oraiſon ſeemed to be rather ſung than ſaid, and we found it impoſſible to diſtinguiſh one word from another. When the captain intimated that it was time for him to go into the boat, he looked up at the ſun, then moved his hand round to the weſtern horizon, pauſed, laughed, and pointed to the ſhore, by which actions, we eaſily underſtood, that he petitioned to ſtay on board till evening: and we took no little pains to convince him, that we could not continue ſo long upon that part of the coaſt. At length, however, we prevailed upon him to go over the ſhip's ſide with his companion, and as ſoon as the boat put off, they all began to ſing, not ceaſing till they reached the ſhore, where many of their companions preſſed eagerly to be taken into the boat, and were highly affronted at being refuſed. Before our departure we found the ſhoal, that runs out from the point, and found it about three miles broad from N to S. and to avoid the ſame it is neceſſary to keep four miles off the Cape, in 13 fathoms water. The ſignal was now made for weighing, and at the ſame time the Swallow received orders to lead, and the Prince Frederick to bring up the rear. The wind being againſt us, and blowing freſh, we turned into the Strait of Magellan, with the flood tide, between Cape Virgin

Mary

Mary and the Sandy Point that refembles Dungenefs. At the diftance of two leagues, weft of Dungenefs, we fell in with a fhoal, upon which, at half flood, we had but feven fathoms water. Between eight and nine o'clock in the evening, we came to an anchor, one league from the fhore, in 20 fathom, with a muddy bottom : Cape Virgin Mary bearing N. E. by E. half E. Point Poffeffion W. half S. diftant five leagues. When abreaft of the Sandy Point, we faw many people on horfeback hunting the guanicoes, which ran up the country with prodigious fwiftnefs. The natives lighted fires oppofite the fhips, and about 400 of them, with their horfes feeding near them, were obferved encamped in a fine green valley. The guanicoes were purfued by the hunters, with flings in their hands ready for the caft; but not one of them was taken while they were within the reach of our fight. This being the fpot where Commodore Byron faw the Patagonians, on the 18th, a party with fome officers were fent towards the fhore, but with orders not to land, as the fhips were too far off to affift them in cafe of neceffity. When they came near the land, many of the natives flocked to fee them, among whom were women and children, and fome of the very men we had feen in the morning of the preceding day. Thefe waded towards the boat, frequently calling out, " Englifhmen come on fhore," and were with difficulty reftrained from getting into the boat, when they found our people would not land. Some bread, tobacco, and toys were diftributed among them, but not an article of provifions could be obtained in return. We had got under fail about fix o'clock, A. M. and at noon there being little wind, and the ebb running with great force, the Swallow, who was a-head, made the fignal and came to an anchor; upon which we did the fame, and fo did the ftore-fhip which was a-ftern.

On Friday the 19th, at fix o'clock, A. M. we weighed, the Swallow being a-head, and at noon we anchored in Poffeffion Bay, having 12 fathoms water, bottom a clean fand. Point Poffeffion bore eaft diftant

three

three leagues: the Aſſes Ears weſt; and the entrance
of the Narrows S. W. half W. Upon the point we ſaw
a great number of Indians, and at night, large fires on
the ſhore of Terra del Fuego. From this day to the
22nd, we made but little way, having ſtrong gales and
heavy ſeas. We now anchored in 18 fathoms, muddy
bottom. The Aſſes Ears bore N. W. by W. half W.
Point Poſſeſſion N. E. by E. and the point of the Narrows, on the ſouth-ſide, S. S. W. diſtant nearly four
leagues. In this ſituation, we found, by obſervation,
our latitude to be 52 deg. 30 min. ſouth, and our longitude 70 deg. 20 min. weſt. On the 23d, we got under
way and made ſail, but the tide was ſo ſtrong, that the
Swallow was ſet one way, the Dolphin another, and the
Prince Frederick a third. We had a freſh breeze,
neverthelefs not one of the veſſels would anſwer her
helm. However we entered the firſt narrow; and at
ſix o'clock in the evening, we anchored on the ſouth-
ſhore, the Swallow on the north, and the ſtore-ſhip not
a cable's length from a ſand-bank, about two miles to
the eaſtward. The ſtrait here is only a league wide,
and, at midnight, the tide being ſlack, we weighed and
towed the ſhip through. On Wedneſday the 24th, we
ſteered from the firſt narrow to the ſecond, S. W. and,
at eight, A. M. we anchored two leagues from the ſhore,
Cape Gregory bearing W. half N. and Sweepſtakes
Foreland S. W. half W. On Thurſday the 25th, we
ſailed through the ſecond narrow. In our run through
this part of the ſtrait we had 12 fathoms within half a
mile of the ſhore. At five o'clock in the evening the
Dolphin ſuddenly ſhoaled from 17 to 5 fathoms, St.
Bartholomew's Iſland then bearing S. half W. diſtant
four miles, and Elizabeth's Iſland, S. S. W. half W.
diſtant ſix miles. The weather being tempeſtuous and
rainy, at eight o'clock in the evening, we caſt anchor
under Elizabeth's iſland; whereon we found great
quantities of wild celery, which being boiled with
portable ſoup and wheat, the crews breakfaſted on it
every morning for ſeveral days. On this iſland we obſerved ſeveral huts, and places where fires had been re-
cently

cently made, but none of the natives. We also saw two dogs, and fresh shells of muscles and limpets scattered about. The wigwams confisted of young trees, which, being sharpened at one end, and thrust into the ground, in such a manner as to form a circle, the other ends were brought to meet, and fastened together at the top. We saw likewise many high mountains, which, though the midst of summer in this part of the world, had their summits covered with snow; but about three parts of their height they were covered with wood, and above with herbage, except where the snow was not yet melted. On Friday the 26th, at two o'clock, A. M. we weighed; and at five, being midway between Elizabeth's ifland, and St. George's, we struck the ground, but the next cast had no bottom with 20 fathoms. The Prince Frederick, who was about half a league to the southward of us, had for a confiderable time not feven fathoms: the Swallow which was two or three miles to the southward had deep water, for fhe kept near St. George's Ifland. We think it is fafeft to run down from the north-end of Elizabeth's Ifland, about two or three miles from the fhore, and fo on all the way to Port Famine. At noon being three miles from the north-fhore, we found by obfervation our latitude to be 53 deg. 12 min. fouth, longitude 71 deg. 20 min. weft, from London. About four o'clock, we anchored in Port Famine Bay, and with all the boats out, towed in the Swallow and Store-fhip. On the 27th, the fick were fent on fhore, where a tent was erected for their reception, as was another for the accommodation of the fail-makers, and thofe who landed to get wood. This day, the weather being fqually, we warped the fhip farther into the harbour, and moored her with a cable each way in nine fathoms. Cape St. Anne now bore N. E. by E. diftant one mile, and Sedger River S. half W. On Sunday the 28th, all the fails were unbent and fent on fhore to be repaired; the empty cafks were alfo landed, with the coopers to trim them, and ten men to wafh and fill them. We alfo hauled the feine, and caught plenty of fifh refembling mullets, but the flefh

was

was very soft; and among others were smelts, some of which weighed a pound and a half, and were 20 inches long. Indeed all the time of our stay at this place, we caught fish enough to furnish one meal a day both for the sick and the healthy: we gathered also great plenty of celery, and pea-tops, which were boiled with the pease and portable soup: besides these we found fruit that resembles cranberries, and the leaves of a shrub somewhat like our thorn, which were remarkably sour. When we arrived here, many of our people had the scurvy to a great degree; but by the plentiful use of vegetables, and bathing in the sea, within a fortnight there was not a scorbutic person in either of the ships. Their recovery also was greatly promoted by the land air, and by being obliged to wash their apparel, and keep their persons clean. All hands were now employed in repairing the ship and making her ready for the sea. To this end the forge was set up on shore; and in the mean time a considerable quantity of wood was cut, and put on board the store-ship; and thousands of young trees were carefully taken up with the mould about them, to be carried to Falkland's Islands, which produce no timber. The Prince Frederick received orders to deliver these to the commanding officer at Port Egmont, and to sail to that place with the first fair wind.

On Wednesday, the 14th of January, the master of the cutter, which was victualed A.D. 1767. for a week, was sent to look out for anchoring places on the north-shore of the strait; and this day we got all our people and tents on board, having taken in 75 tons of water, and 12 months of provisions for ourselves, and ten months for the Swallow, from on board the store-ship. On the 17th, the master of our cutter returned with an account, that he had found anchoring places; and this day the Prince Frederick sailed for Falkland's Islands. The master reported, that between where we lay and Cape Forward, he had been on shore at four places, where was good anchorage, and plenty of wood and water close to the beach, with abundance

of

of cranberries and wild celery: that he had alfo feen a
great number of currant bufhes full of fruit, and a
variety of beautiful fhrubs in full bloffom, befides great
plenty of winter's bark, a grateful fpice, which we have
already particularly defcribed. On Sunday the 18th,
at five o'clock, A. M. we failed; and at noon, obferved
in latitude 54 deg. 3 min. fouth; here we found the
ftrait to be two leagues wide. On the 19th, we came
to an anchor, half a mile from the fhore, near Cape
Holland, oppofite a current of frefh water, that falls
rapidly from the mountains. Cape Holland bore
W. S. W. half W. diftant two miles; Cape Forward
eaft; and by obfervation our latitude was 53 deg.
38 min. fouth. As a more convenient anchoring place,
and better adapted for procuring wood and water, had
been difcovered, we made fail on the 22nd, and at
nine in the evening, being about two miles diftant from
the fhore, Cape Gallant bore W. half N. diftant two
leagues; Cape Holland E. by N. fix leagues; and Rupert's Ifland W. S. W. At this place the ftrait is not
more than five miles over.

On Friday the 23rd, we came to an anchor in a bay
near Cape Gallant, in 10 fathoms water, a muddy bottom. The boats being fent out to found found good
anchorage every where, except within two cables length
S. W. of the fhip, where it was coral, and deepened to
16 fathoms. In this fituation the eaft point of Cape
Gallant bore S. W. by W. one fourth W. the extreme
point of the eaftermoft land E. by S. a point making
the mouth of a river N. by W. and the white patch on
Charles's Ifland S. W. We now examined the bay and
a large lagoon. The laft was the moft commodious
harbour we had yet feen, having five fathom at the
entrance, and four to five in the middle. It is capable
of receiving a great number of veffels, had three large
frefh water rivers, and plenty of wood and celery. We
had here a feine fpoiled, by being entangled with the
wood that lies funk at the mouth of the rivers; but
though we caught not much fifh, we had wild ducks
in fuch numbers as to afford us a very feafonable re-

lief. Near this place are very high mountains, one of which was climbed by the master of our cutter, with the hope of getting a view of the South Seas; but, being disappointed in his expectation, he erected a pyramid, and having written the ship's name, and the date of the year, he left the same, with a shilling, within the structure. On the 24th, in the morning, we examined Cordes Bay, which we found much inferior to that in which the ships lay, the entrance being rocky, and the ground within it foul. It had, it is true, a more spacious lagoon, but the mouth of it was very narrow, and barred by a shoal, whereon was not sufficient depth of water for a ship of burden to float. Here we saw an animal that resembled an ass; as swift as a deer, and had a cloven hoof. This was the first animal we had seen in this strait, except at the entrance, where we found the guanicoes, and two dogs. The circumjacent country has a dreary and forbidding aspect. The mountains on both sides are of a stupendous height; whose lower parts are covered with trees, above which a space is occupied by weathered shrubs; higher up are fragments of broken rocks and heaps of snow; and the tops are totally rude, naked, and desolate. To see their summits towering above the clouds in vast crags, that are piled upon each other, affords to a spectator the idea, that they are the ruins of nature, devoted to everlasting sterility and desolation. This day we sounded about the Royal Islands, but found no bottom ; wherever we came to an opening, we found a rapid tide set through ; and they cannot be approached by shipping without the most imminent danger. And here, for the information of future navigators, we would observe, that in a run through this part of the strait, they should keep the north-shore close on board all the way, and not venture more than a mile from it till the Royal Islands are passed. Through the whole day the current sets easterly, and the indraught should by all means be avoided.

On Tuesday the 27th, we weighed with all expedition, and departed from Cape Gallant Road, which

lies in 53 deg. 50 min. south latitude. At noon on the
28th, the west-point bore W. N. W. half a mile distant. At two o'clock, the west point bore east, distant
three leagues, and York Point W. N. W. distant five
leagues. At five, we opened York Road, the point
bearing N. W. distant half a mile; at which time the
Dolphin was taken a-back, and a strong current with a
heavy squall drove us so far to leeward, that it was with
great difficulty we got into Elizabeth's Bay, and anchored in 12 fathoms water, near a river. The Swallow
being at anchor off the point of the bay, and very near
the rocks, Captain Wallis ordered out all the boats with
anchors and hausers to her assistance, and she was happily warped to windward into good anchorage. At
this time York Point bore W. by N. A shoal with
weeds upon it, at the distance of a cable's length, W. N.
W. Point Passage S. E. half E. distant half a mile;
a rock near Rupert's Isle S. half E. and a rivulet on the
bay N. E. by E. distant about three cables length.
Having this day at sun-set seen a great smoke on the
southern shore, and on Prince Rupert's Island, early in
the morning of the 29th, the boats were sent on shore
for water. Our people had no sooner landed, than
several of the natives came off to them in three canoes;
and having advanced towards the sailors, made signs of
friendship, which being answered to their satisfaction,
they hallooed, and our men shouted in return. When
the Indians drew near they were eating the flesh of
seals raw, and were covered with the skins, which stank
intolerably. They had bows, arrows, and javelins, the
two last of which were pointed with flint. These people were of a middling stature, the tallest of them not
exceeding five feet six inches. Their complexion was
of a deep copper colour. Three of them being admitted on board the Dolphin, they devoured whatever
food was offered them; but like the Patagonians would
only drink water : like them too, they were highly diverted with a looking glass, in which they at first stared
with astonishment; but having become a little more
familiar with it, they smiled at its effect; and finding a
corresponding

corresponding smile from the image in the glass, they burst into immoderate fits of laughter. The captain going on shore with them, presented some trinkets to their wives and children, and received in return some of their weapons, and pieces of mundic, of the kind found in the tin mines of Cornwall. The sails of the canoes belonging to these Indians were made of the seal skin. To kindle a fire they strike a pebble against a piece of mundic, holding under it, to catch the sparks, some moss or down, mixed with a whitish earth, which takes fire like tinder: they then take some dry grass, and putting the lighted moss into it, wave it to and fro, and in a minute it blazes. When they left us, they steered for the southern shore, where we saw many of their huts; and we remarked, that not one of them looked behind, either at us or the ship, so little impression had the curiosities they had seen made upon their minds. As this seems to be the most dreary and inhospitable country in the world, not excepting the worst parts of Sweden and Norway, so the natives seem to be the lowest and most deplorable of all human beings. Their perfect indifference to every thing they saw, which marked the disparity between our state and their own, though it may preserve them from the regret and anguish of unsatisfied desires, seems, notwithstanding, to imply a defect in their nature; for those who are satisfied with the gratifications of a brute, can have little pretension to the prerogatives of men. These Indians when they gave to the gentlemen of our ship several pieces of mundic, intimated, that this substance was found in the mountains, and Captain Wallis is of opinion, that not only mines of tin, but more valuable metals are subsisting there.

On Tuesday, the 3rd of February, we weighed, and, in a sudden squall, were taken a-back, so that both ships were in the most imminent danger of being driven ashore on a reef of rocks; the wind, however, suddenly shifting, we got off without much damage. At five o'clock, P. M. we anchored in York Road, Cape Qued now bore W. half S. distant six leagues; York Point

E. S. E.

E. S. E. diftant one mile ; Bachelor's River N. N. W,
three fourths of a mile ; the entrance of Jerom's Sound
N. W. by W. and a fmall ifland, on the fouth fhore,
W. by S.   In the evening we faw five Indian canoes
come out of Bachelor's River, and go up Jerom's Sound.
Having fent out the boats, in the morning of the 4th,
we were informed on their return, that there was good
anchorage within Jerom's Sound, and all the way thither
from the fhip's ftation ; as likewife at feveral places
under the iflands on the fouth-fhore ; but the force and
uncertainty of the tides, and the heavy gufts of wind
that came off the high lands, rendered thefe fituations
unfafe.   This day Captain Wallis went up Bachelor's
River, and found a bar at the mouth of it, which, at
certain times of the tide muft be dangerous.   We hauled
the feine, but the weeds and ftumps of trees prevented
our catching any fifh.   When afhore, we faw many
wigwams, and feveral dogs, which animals ran away the
moment they were noticed,   We gathered mufcles,
limpets, fea-eggs, celery, and nettles in abundance.   We
alfo faw fome oftriches, but they were beyond the reach
of our pieces.   Three miles up the river, on the weft-fide,
between two mountains of a ftupendous height, one of
which has received the name of Mount Mifery, is a
cataract, which has a very ftriking appearance.   It is
precipitated down an elevation of above 400 yards; half
way over a very fteep declivity, and the other half is a
perpendicular fall : the found of which is not lefs awful
than the fight.   On Saturday the 14th, at ten o'clock,
A. M. we weighed, foon after the current fet the fhip
towards Bachelor's River: we put her in ftays, and while
fhe was coming about, which fhe was fome time in
doing, we drove over a fhoal, where we had little more
than 16 feet water, with rocky ground.   Our danger
was great, for the Dolphin drew 16 feet nine inches aft,
and 15 feet one inch forward ; but when the fhip
gathered way, we fortunately deepened into three
fathoms ; and in a very fhort time, we got into deep
water.   We continued plying to windward till four
o'clock, P. M. when perceiving we had loft ground, we
returned

returned to our laſt ſtation, and again came to an anchor in York Road.

On Tueſday the 17th, at five o'clock, A. M. we ſet ſail, but notwithſtanding we had a fine breeze at weſt, the ſhip was carried by a current with great violence, towards the ſouth ſhore: the boats were all towing a-head, the ſails unfilled, yet we drove ſo cloſe to the rocks, that we were ſeldom farther than a ſhip's length from them, and the oars of the boats were frequently entangled in the weeds. In this manner we were hurried along for near an hour, in momentary expectation of being daſhed to pieces. All our efforts being ineffectual, we reſigned ourſelves to our fate, and waited the event in a ſtate of ſuſpence very little ſhort of deſpair, but Providence interpoſed for our preſervation; for at length we opened St. David's Sound, when, contrary to our expectations, a current ruſhed out of it, and ſet us into mid-channel. The Swallow knew nothing of our unhappy ſituation, being all the time on the north ſhore. We now ſent our boats in ſearch of an anchoring place, and our people returned with the agreeable intelligence, that they had found a convenient one in a ſmall bay, to which the captain gave the name of Butler's Bay, it having been diſcovered by Mr. Butler, one of our mates. We ran in with the tide which ſet faſt to the weſtward, and anchored in 16 fathoms water; but the Swallow caſt anchor in Iſland Bay, at about ſix miles diſtance. Butler's Bay lies to the weſt of Rider's, on the ſouth-ſhore of the ſtrait, which is here about two miles wide. The extreams of the bay from W. by N. to N. half W. are about one fourth of a mile aſunder. A ſmall rivulet bore S. half W. and Cape Quod north, at the diſtance of four miles. We kept this ſtation till Friday the 20th, when we encountered a moſt violent ſtorm, attended with hail and rain, which encreaſed till the evening, the ſea breaking over the fore-caſtle upon the quarterdeck. We made uſe of every expedient in our power to keep the ſhip ſteady, and as the cables did not part, we were again wonderfully preſerved, which, conſidering fidering the narrownefs of the ftrait, and the fmallnefs of the bay in which we were ftationed, might in the judgment of human wifdom be thought impoffible: for had the cables parted, we could not have run out with a fail, and not having room to bring the fhip up with any other anchor, we muft without divine aid have been dafhed to pieces in a few minutes; and under fuch circumftances it is highly probable, that every foul would immediately have perifhed. By eight o'clock in the evening the gale became more moderate, and gradually decreafed during the night. On the 21ft, we had the fatisfaction to find that our cable was found, but our haufers were much rubbed by the rocks. As to the Swallow, the ftorm had little affected her; but two days before fhe had very near been loft by the rapidity of the tide, in pufhing through the iflands. An alteration had been made in her rudder, neverthelefs fhe fteered and worked fo ill, that it was apprehended fhe could not fafely be brought to an anchor again. Her commander was of opinion, that fhe could be of very little fervice to the expedition, and therefore requefted of Captain Wallis to direct what he thought beft for the fervice. The captain returned for anfwer, "That as the Lords of the Admiralty had appointed her to accompany the Dolphin, fhe muft continue to do it as long as it was poffible; that as her condition rendered her a bad failer, he would wait her time, and attend her motions; and that if any difafter fhould happen to either of us, the other fhould be ready to afford fuch affiftance as might be in her power." In this bay we remained eight days, taking in wood and water, and repairing the little damage we had fuftained in the late ftorm. We caught fifh of various kinds, among which were mufcles near fix inches long; alfo a fine firm red fifh, not unlike a gurnet, moft of which were from four to five pounds weight. The mountains in this neighbourhood have a moft rugged and defolate appearance; but their height could not be afcertained, their heads being loft in the cloud; and fome of them, on the fouthern fhore, were fo naked, as not to have

upon

upon them a single blade of grass. Our master having been sent out in search of anchorage, landed upon a large island on the north-side of Snow Sound, and being almost perished with cold, the first thing he did was to make a large fire with some trees which he found upon the spot. He then climbed one of the rocky mountains, with Mr. Pickersgill a midshipman, and one of the seamen, in order to take a view of the strait, and the dismal regions that surround it. He observed the entrance of the sound to be full as broad as several parts of the strait, and to grow but very little narrower on Terra del Fuego side. The country on the south, he said, was more dreary and horrid than any he had yet seen: the mountains hid their heads in the clouds; while the valleys were equally barren, being intirely covered with snow, except where it had been washed away, or converted into ice; and even these bald patches were as destitute of verdure as the rocks between which they lay.

Sunday the 1st of March, at four o'clock, A. M. our companion, the Swallow, was seen under sail, on the north-shore of Cape Quod. At seven we set sail, and stood out of Butler's Bay; and at noon sent the boats to seek for anchorage on the north shore. Cape Notch now bore W. by N. half N. distant four leagues, and Cape Quod E. half N. distant three leagues. At three o'clock, P. M. we anchored in a small bay, which we named Lion's Cove, on account of a steep rocky mountain, the top whereof resembles the head of a lion. On the 2nd, we made sail again, and at five in the evening came to anchor in Good Luck Bay, in 28 fathoms water. A rocky island, at the western extremity of the bay, bore N. W. by W. about a cable's length and a half from the Dolphin; and a low point which forms the eastern extremity of the bay, bore E. S. E. distant one mile. In the interval between this point and the ship are many shoals; and two rocks at the bottom of the bay, the largest of which bore N. E. by N. the smallest N. by E. From these rocks, shoals run out to the S. E. which may be known by the weeds

968 CAPT. WALLIS'S VOYAGE

weeds that are upon them. Cape Notch bore from us W. by S. half W. diftant one league. In the intermediate fpace is a large lagoon, but, the wind blowing hard all the time of our laying here, we could not found it. Having moored, we fent two boats to affift the Swallow, by which fhe was towed into a fmall bay, where, as the wind was foutherly, and blew frefh, fhe was in great danger, for the cove was expofed to S. E. winds, and was alfo full of rocks. On the four following days we encountered fuch terrible weather, that we had no other profpect before us than that of immediate deftruction : and our feamen were fo prepoffeffed with the notion, that the Swallow could not ride out the ftorm, that they even imagined they faw fome of her hands coming over the rocks towards them. The ftorm at length fubfided, and the gale became more moderate on Saturday the 7th ; we therefore at four o'clock, A. M. fent a boat to enquire after the Swallow, who in the afternoon returned with the welcome news that the fhip was fafe ; but the fatigue of the people had been incredible, the whole crew having been upon the deck near three days and three nights. The gufts returned at midnight, though not with equal violence, but attended with hail, fleet, and fnow. On the 8th, Captain Wallis ordered up, the weather being extremely cold, and the crews never dry, 11 bales of the thick woollen ftuff, called fear-nought, and employed all the taylors to make them into jackets, of which every man in the Dolphin had one. Seven bales of the fame cloth were alfo fent on board the Swallow, which made every man on board a jacket of the fame kind. Three bales of finer cloth were cut up for the officers of both fhips, which were very acceptable. On Sunday the 15th, feeing the Swallow under fail, we fent off our launch, whereby fhe was towed into a very good harbour on the fouth-fhore, oppofite to where we lay. The favourable account we received of this harbour determined us to depart from Good Luck Bay, and we thought ourfelves happy when we got fafe out of it. When abreaft of the place where the Swallow lay at anchor, we fired feveral

guns,

guns, as fignals for her boats to affift us, and in a fhort time the mafter came on board, and piloted us to a very commodious ftation, where we caft anchor in 28 fathoms, bottom muddy. This bay, which we called Swallow Harbour, is fheltered from all winds, and excellent in every refpect. There are two narrow channels into it, but neither of them dangerous.

On Monday the 16th, at nine o'clock, A. M. we weighed, and took the Swallow in tow. At five, P. M. being little wind, we caft her off. At nine we had frefh gales, and at midnight Cape Upright bore S. S. W. half W. On the 17th, by the advice of Captain Carteret, we bore away for Upright Bay, and, he being acquainted with the place, the Swallow was ordered to lead. At eleven o'clock we opened a large lagoon, and by means of a current, which fet ftrongly into it, the Swallow was driven among the breakers clofe upon the lee-fhore: fhe made fignals of diftrefs, and notwithftanding the weather was hazy, and the furf ran high, our boats took her in tow, but their utmoft efforts to fave her would have been in vain, had not a breeze from the fhore happily relieved her. At noon a great fwell came on, the waves ran high, and the fog was fo thick, that we narrowly efcaped fhipwreck, in what we conjectured to be, the Bay of Iflands; we therefore endeavoured to haul out, as the only chance of efcaping; this we found no eafy tafk, being obliged to tack continually, to weather fome ifland or rock; but at four o'clock, P. M. the weather clearing up a little, we had a fight of Cape Upright, for which we immediately fteered, and between five and fix came fafely to an anchor in the bay, in 46 fathoms, with a muddy bottom. A high bluff land on the north-fhore bore N. W. half N. diftant five leagues, and a fmall ifland within us S. by E. half E. The Swallow, who was driven to lee-ward, notwithftanding fhe had two anchors a-head, was brought up about a cable's length aftern of us, in 70 fathoms water. To clear her anchors, for which purpofe we fent a confiderable number of our hands, and to warp her into a proper birth, coft us the whole

day, and was not only a work of time, but of the
utmost difficulty and labour. On the 18th, we sent out
boats to sound quite cross the strait, and this day we
moored the ship in 78 fathoms, with the stream anchor.
On the 19th, two canoes, having in them several Indians, came along-side the Dolphin. They were equally
miserable and abject, with those we had before seen.
A seaman gave one of them a fish, which he had just
caught with a line, and it was then alive. The Indian
seized it as a dog would a bone, and instantly killed it
by biting it near the gills; he then began at the head,
and proceeded on to the tail, champing up the bones,
and devouring both the scales and the intrails.
These people would drink no other liquor than water,
but they eagerly tore in pieces and swallowed down
provisions of any kind, whether boiled, roasted, raw,
salt, or fresh. Though the weather was very cold, their
only covering was a seal-skin, and even that they put
off when rowing. We observed that they all had sore
eyes, occasioned probably by the smoke of their fires,
and their filthy way of feeding and living made them
smell as rank as a fox. They had with them some
javelins, rudely pointed with bone, with which they used
to strike seals, fish, and penguins. Their canoes were
about 15 feet in length, three broad, and nearly the
same measurement in depth. They were constructed
with the bark of trees tacked together, either with the
sinews of some beast, or thongs cut out of a hide. A
kind of rush was laid into the seams, and the out-side was
smeared with resin or gum, which prevented the water
from soaking into the bark. To the bottom and sides
were sewed transversely 15 slender branches, bent into
an arch; and some strait pieces were placed cross the
top, from gunwale to gunwale, securely lashed at each
end; but upon the whole the workmanship was very
rough, nor had these people any thing among them,
wherein there was the least appearance of ingenuity.
The Captain presented them a hatchet or two, some
beads, and a few other baubles, with which they departed, seemingly well satisfied, to the southward.
                                                    During

During our stay here, we sent our boats as usual in search of anchoring places. Several small coves were discovered, but most of them dangerous. Twenty-two of the sailors belonging to one of the boats, staying one night on an island, about 30 Indians landed, ran immediately to the boat, and began to make off with every thing they could carry away; the sailors discovered what they were doing, and had but just time to prevent their depredations. When opposed, they went to their canoes, and armed themselves with long poles and pointed javelins. They stood in a threatning attitude, and our people on the defensive; but the latter parting with a few trifles to them, they became friends, and peace and harmony were again restored. From this time to the 30th, we had hard gales, and heavy seas, accompanied with hail, lightning, and rain. Nevertheless, the men were sent frequently ashore for exercise, which contributed not a little to their health, and by them we had almost a constant supply of muscles and vegetables. On Monday the 30th, we improved the first interval of moderate weather, in drying the sails, and airing the spare ones, which last we found much injured by the rats. We also repaired the fire-place of the Swallow in the same manner as we had done our own, and set up a back with lime made of burnt shells. This day we saw several canoes full of Indians, on the east-side of the bay, and the next morning several came on board, and proved to be the same people which the boats crew had seen on shore.

On the 1st of April, several other Indians came off to the ship, and brought with them several of the birds called race-horses, which some of our company purchased for a few trifles. They behaved very peaceably, and the Captain presented them with several hatchets, and dismissed them with a few toys as usual. On the 2nd, eight Indians brought six of their children on board, whom the Captain gratified with bracelets and necklaces. These people were exceedingly tender in the treatment of their children; and a circumstance happened which proves that they are not less delicate in

other

other refpects. A boat was ordered on fhore to get
wood and water ; at which time fome of the Indians
were on board, and others in their canoes along-fide
the fhip : the latter eyed the boat attentively; and, on
her putting off, called aloud to their companions, who,
without fpeaking, inftantly handed down the children,
and jumped into the canoes, which hurried after the
boat, while the poor Indians cried in a moft diftrefsful
tone.   When our boat was near land, fome women
were feen among the rocks, to whom the Indians called
aloud, and they all ran away ; but the boats crew having
remarked their jealous fears, lay on their oars, to convince them that no injury was intended.   The Indians
landed, drew their canoes on fhore, and haftily followed
the objects of their affections.   This day the mafter of
the Swallow, who had been fent out to feek for anchoring places, returned with an account, that he had found
three on the north fhore, moft of which were very good;
one about four miles to the eaftward of Cape Providence,
another under the eaft-fide of Cape Tamar, and a third
about four miles to the eaftward of it ; but it muft be
obferved, that the ground under Cape Providence is
rocky. Our men at this time began to be troubled with
fluxes, on which account, at the requeft of our furgeon,
it was ordered, that no more mufcles (which had been
found continually in abundance) fhould be brought on
board.   On Friday the 10th, we made fail in company
with the Swallow.   At noon, Cape Providence bore
N. N. W. diftant five miles. At four P. M. Cape Tamar
bore N. W. by W. half W. diftant three leagues, and
Cape Pillar W. diftant ten leagues.   Cape Upright
bore E. S. E. half S. diftant three leagues.   On the
11th, having fteered W. half N. all night, we found, at
fix o'clock, A. M. that we had run 38 miles by the log.
At this time, Cape Pillar bearing S. W. diftant half a
mile, the Swallow was about three miles aftern of us,
and being but little wind, we were obliged to croud all
the fail we could, to get without the ftraits mouth.
The Captain, at eleven o'clock, would have fhortened
fail for our confort, but it was not in our power, for it
was

was abfolutely neceffary for us to carry fail, in order to clear the ifles of direction. Soon after we loft fight of the Swallow, and faw her not again during the remainder of our voyage. At noon our latitude by obfervation was 52 deg. 38 min. and our longitude by computation 76 deg. weft from London. The iflands of Direction now bore north 21 weft, diftant three leagues. St. Paul's Cupola, and Cape Victory in one, north, diftant feven leagues, and Cape Pillar eaft, diftant fix leagues. Happy did we now think ourfelves in having cleared the Straits of Magellan, a dreary and inhofpitable region, in which we had contended with innumerable difficulties, and efcaped moft imminent dangers, in a paffage of almoft four months, namely, from December the 17th, 1766, to the 11th of April, 1767.

Our journalift now proceeds to a defcription of the places in which the fhips anchored, during their paffage through the ftraits, from whence we have extracted fuch particulars, as may be of ufe to future navigators, furnifh real improvement to thofe of our fubfcribers who belong to his majefty's navy, and afford an agreeable entertainment to our various and numerous claffes of readers.

(1) Cape Virgin Mary. This is a fteep white cliff, which fomewhat refembles the South Foreland. By obfervation and our reckoning, it lies in latitude 52 deg. 24 min. fouth, and in 68 deg. 22 min. weft longitude from London. Under this cape, when the wind is wefterly, is a good harbour, but we faw no appearance either of wood or water. About a mile from the fhore, you may anchor in ten fathom water with coarfe fandy ground. (2.) Poffeffion Bay. The point of this lies in latitude 52 deg. 23 min. fouth, and in 68 deg. 57 min. weft longitude. Here the foundings are very irregular, but the ground is throughout a fine foft mud and clay. The landing appeared to be good, but we could fee no figns of either wood or water. It is neceffary, in failing into this bay, to give the point a good birth, there being a reef that runs about a mile right off it. (3.) Port Famine. This is an excellent bay, capacious

enough

enough for many ships to moor therein with the utmost safety. Wood and water are to be procured with ease : geese, ducks, teal, &c. are in great plenty, and fish in abundance. It is situated in latitude 53 deg. 42 min. south, and 71 deg. 28 min. west longitude. We moored in nine fathom, having brought Cape St. Anne N. E. by E. and the beautiful river Sedger, (of which we have given a particular description in the history of Commodore Byron's voyage,) S. half W. which perhaps is the most eligible situation, though the whole bay is good ground. In the year 1581, the Spaniards built a town here, which they named Philipville, and left in it a colony of 400 persons. Seventy-six of this number were starved, and of the remainder, 23 proceeded in search of the river Plata, and most probably perished, as no tidings were ever heard of them. When our celebrated navigator Sir William Cavendish arrived at this place in 1587, he found the only one that remained of those unfortunate adventurers, named Hernando, and brought him to England. From their melancholy fate, Sir William named the bay, Port Famine. (4.) Cape Holland Bay. This lies in latitude 53 deg. 57 min. and in 72 deg. 34 min. west longitude. Here is a fine rivulet, and close under the cape a large river, navigable for boats many miles ; and the shore affords plenty of fire-wood. We caught very little fish, but found plenty of muscles and limpets. The adjacent country produces plenty of cranberries and wild celery. We killed some geese, ducks, teal, and race-horses, yet the birds are not numerous. There is no danger in sailing into this bay, and in every part thereof is good anchoring ground. (5.) Cape Gallant Bay. This is situated in 53 deg. 50 min. south latitude, and 73 deg. 9 min. west longitude. The landing is good ; the tide very irregular ; and the best anchoring is on the east-side, where we found from 6 to 10 fathoms. Here are abundance of wood, vegetables, and fish, with good watering from two rivers. In this bay, which may be entered with great safety, there is a spacious lagoon, where a fleet of ships may moor in perfect security. The

lagoon

lagoon abounds with wild fowl, and we found in, and about it, wild celery, muscles, and limpets in plenty. (6.) Elizabeth Bay. Its latitude is 53 deg. 43 min. south, and its longitude 73 deg. 24 min. west. Sufficient quantities of wood may be procured here for the use of ships, and they will find good watering at a small river. We gathered a little celery and a few cranberries, but met with neither fish nor fowl. The best anchorage is at Passage Point, at half a mile distance, bearing S. E. and the river N. E. by E. distant three cables length; in this station, a shoal, which may be known by the weeds, bears W. N. W. distant one cable's length: the ground is coarse sand and shells. At the entrance of this bay are two small reefs, that appear above water. The most dangerous of the two is at the east point of the bay, but this may easily be avoided, by keeping at the distance of about two cables length from the road. (7) York Road. This lies in latitude 53 deg. 39 min. south, and, by our account, 73 deg. 52 min. west longitude. The landing in all parts of this place is very good; and we found celery, cranberries, muscles, limpets, wild fowl, and some fish, but not sufficient to supply our ships company with a single meal. About a mile up Bachelor's River is good watering, and plenty of wood all round the bay. From the Western Point a reef runs off about a cable's length, which, when known, may easily be avoided. To anchor with safety in this bay, bring York Point E. S. E. Bachelor's River N. by W. half W. The reef N. W. half W. and St. Jerom's Sound W. N. W. at the distance of half a mile from the shore. The current here frequently sets in three different directions; the water rises and falls about eight feet; but the tide is irregular. (8.) Butler's Bay. This is situated in latitude 53 deg. 37 min. south, and in 74 deg. 9 min. west longitude. It is not only small, but entirely encircled with rocks, on which account we would caution every navigator against anchoring at this place, if he can possibly avoid it. Here are some rock fish, and a few wild fowl, but

celery

celery and cranberries are very scarce. (9.) Lion's
Cove. The same may be said of this as we have observed of the preceding bay; but though the water
up a small creek is good, here is no wood. The latitude is 53 deg. 26 min. south ; longitude, by our
account, 74 deg. 25 min. west. (10.) Good Luck
Bay. This is situated in latitude 53 deg. 23 min.
and in 74 deg. 33 min. west longitude. Like several
others, it is small, and the rocks with which it is surrounded, render it very difficult of access. We procured here a sufficient quantity of fresh water, but very
little wood. Not any kinds of refreshments are to be
expected at this place ; indeed we caught only a few
rock fish with hook and line. The ground is very
coarse, and the cable of our best bower anchor was so
much rubbed, that we were obliged to condemn it,
and bend a new one. Circumstances may arise under
which it may be thought good luck to get into this
bay, but we thought it very good luck when we got
out of it. (11.) Swallow Bay. This lies in latitude
53 deg. 29 min. south, and in 74 deg. 35 min. west
longitude. The entrance is narrow and rocky, but
when once entered, it is very safe, being sheltered
from all winds. The rocks, by keeping a good look-
out, may be easily avoided. As to the mountains that
surround it they have a most horrid appearance, and
seem to be deserted by every thing that has life ; and
we found no supply of provisions, except a few rock
fish and muscles. The landing is very good, and the
tide rises and falls between four and five feet. (12.)
Upright Bay. This is in latitude 53 deg. 8 min.
south, longitude 75 deg. 35 min. west. The entrance
is very safe, and the water excellent. A sufficiency of
wood may be procured for stock, but provisions are
rather scarce. The landing is not good, the tide very
irregular ; and the water rises and falls above five feet.
Besides these 12 bays, there are three others, a little
beyond Cape Shut-up, which we named River Bay,
Lodging Bay, and Wallis's Bay, the last of which is
the best. Also between Elizabeth Bay and York Road
lies

lies Mufcle Bay, wherein is exceeding good anchorage with a wefterly wind. The ground of Chance Bay is very rocky, and therefore to be avoided. Not far from Cape Quod, to the eaftward, lies Ifland Bay, which is by no means an eligible fituation for fhipping. There is likewife a bay with good anchorage, oppofite to York Road; and another to the eaftward of Cape Crofs-tide, but this latter one will hold only a fingle fhip. Between Cape Crofs and St. David's Head lies St. David's Sound, on the fouth-fide of which we found a bank of coarfe fand and fhells, with a depth of water from 19 to 30 fathom, where a fhip might anchor in cafe of neceffity; and the mafter of the Swallow found a very good fmall bay a little to the eaftward of St. David's Head.

C H A P. II.

The Dolphin proceeds on her Voyage from the Strait to the weftward—Several Iflands difcovered in the South Sea, namely—Whitfun Ifland—Queen Charlotte's—Egmont—Gloucefter—Cumberland—Prince William Henry's—Ofnaburgh—King George the Third's, called by the Natives Otaheite, with a particular, full, and complete Defcription of thofe Iflands—The Cuftoms, Manners, &c. of the Natives—The feveral Incidents which happened on Board the Ship and afhore—Particularly, a very circumftantial Account of the Inhabitants of Otaheite—Their Arts, Trade, domeftic Life, and Character.—An Expedition to difcover the inland Part of the Country—And a variety of Incidents and Tranfactions, till we quitted the Ifland to continue our Voyage.

ON Sunday the 12th of April 1767, after having cleared the ftrait, we held on our courfe to the weftward. Here it may be proper to obferve, that, as all the hard gales by which we fuffered, blew from the weftward, we think it advifeable to ftand about 100

leagues and more to the weftward, after failing out of
the Strait of Magellan, that the fhip may not be endan-
gered on a lee-fhore, which at prefent is wholly unknown. As we continued our courfe a number of
fheerwaters, pintadoes, gannets, and other birds, flew
about the fhip; the upper works of which being open,
and the cloaths and bedding continually wet, the failors
in a few days were attacked with fevers; and having
a continuation of ftrong gales, hazy weather, and heavy
feas, we were frequently brought under our courfes. On
Wednefday the 22nd, we obferved in latitude 42 deg.
24 min. fouth, and in 95 deg. 46 min. weft longitude;
and on Monday the 27th at noon, we found our latitude
to be 36 deg. 54 min. fouth, and our longitude, by account, 100 deg. weft from London. This day being
fair, and the weather moderate, the fick were brought
on deck, to whom were given falop, and portable foup,
in which wheat had been boiled. The violent gales returned, fo that the beds were again wet through, and it
was feared that the fhip would lofe her mafts; we therefore began to think of altering our courfe, in hope of
better weather; and the rather, as the number of our
fick encreafed fo faft, that there was danger of foon
wanting hands to navigate the veffel. On Monday the
4th of May, by obfervation, we found ourfelves in latitude 28 deg. 20 min. fouth; and in 96 deg. 21 min.
weft longitude. On the 8th, we faw feveral fheerwaters and fea-fwallows; and on Tuefday the 12th, we
obferved the fame kind of birds, and fome porpoifes
about the fhip. On the 14th, we faw the appearance
of what we imagined to be high land, towards which a
flock of brown birds were obferved to fly; we therefore
fteered all night for this fuppofed land; but at day-
break could fee no figns of it. As the weather now
became moderate, we found our people recovered very
faft; and the carpenters were bufied in caulking the
upper works of the fhip, and repairing the boats. On
the 15th, our latitude was 24 deg. 50 min. fouth, and
our longitude 106 deg. weft. On Monday the 18th, a
fheep, by the captain's order, was diftributed among our
people

people who were sick and recovering. On Thursday the 21st, we saw a number of flying fish; and on the 22nd some bonettas, dolphins, and flying-fish. About this time, such of the seamen on board as had been recovering from colds and fevers, began to be attacked by the scurvy, upon which, at the surgeon's representation, wine was served to them; wort was also made from malt for their use; and each of the crew had half a pint of pickled cabbage every day, notwithstanding which the men began to look very sickly, and to fall a prey to the scurvy very fast; to repel which they had wine served instead of spirits, with plenty of sweet-wort and salop; portable soup was boiled in their peas and oatmeal; their births and cloaths were kept constantly clean; the hammocks were every day brought upon deck at eight o'clock in the morning, and carried down at four in the afternoon; some or other of the beds and hammocks were washed daily: the ship's water was rendered wholesome by ventilation, and every part between decks was cleansed with vinegar. This day our latitude was 20 deg. 18 min. south, and 111 deg. west longitude. On Tuesday the 26th, we saw two grampuses; and on the 27th, a variety of birds, one of which was taken for a land-bird, and resembled a swallow. On the 31st, we found by observation our latitude to be 29 deg. 38 min. south, longitude 127 deg. 45 min. west.

On Monday the 1st of June, we saw several men of war birds, and, on the 3rd some gannets; and, the weather being at this time very various, we conceived hopes that we drew near to land. On the 4th, a turtle swam close by the ship, and the next day a great variety of birds were seen. On Saturday the 6th, the long wished-for land became visible from the mast-head, the man crying out " Land in the north-west." This in the course of the day proved to be a low island, distant about six leagues. When within five miles of this island, we discovered a second to the W. N. W. The first lieutenant being at this time very ill, Mr. Furneaux, the second lieutenant, was sent with two boats to the first island, the crews of each being well provided with arms. When

the

the boats came near the island, two canoes were observed
to put off to the adjacent one ; and no inhabitants were
seen to remain where our party landed.   Here several
cocoa-nuts, and a large quantity of scurvy-grass were
obtained, which proved a valuable acquisition to the
sick, and a grateful refreshment to those in health.
They returned in the evening to the ship, bringing with
them some fish-hooks, which the islanders had formed
of oyster-shells.   In this excursion they discovered three
huts, supported on posts, and open all round, but
thatched with cocoa-nut and palm leaves.   As no anchorage could be found, and the whole island was encompassed with rocks and breakers, Captain Wallis resolved to steer for the other island, giving the name of
Whitsun Island to this, because it was discovered on
Whitsunday's Eve. Having approached the other island,
Mr. Furneaux was again sent off with the boats, manned and armed.   At this time about 50 of the natives
were seen running about with fire-brands in their hands.
Mr. Furneaux was instructed to steer to that part of
the shore, where the natives had been seen, to avoid
giving offence.   When Mr. Furneaux drew near with
the boats to the shore, the natives put themselves in a
posture of defence, with their pikes ; but the lieutenant
making signs of amity, and exposing to view a few
trinkets, some of the Indians walked into the water :
to whom it was hinted, that some cocoa-nuts and water
would be acceptable ; which was no sooner understood,
than they ventured with a small quantity of each to the
boats ; and received nails and other trifles in exchange.
While bartering with them, one of the Indians stole a
silk handkerchief with its contents, but the thief could
by no means be discovered.

On Monday the 8th, Mr. Furneaux was again dispatched with the boats, and received orders from Captain Wallis to land, if he could do it without offending
the natives.   As this party drew near to the shore, they
observed seven large canoes, each with two masts, lying
ready for the Indians to embark in them. These
having made signs to the crew to proceed higher up,

3   they

they complied, and immediately the Indians embarked
on board the seven large canoes and quitted the spot,
being joined by two canoes at another part of the island.
These latter the Indians steered in a direction of W. S.
W. They were divided, two being brought along-side
of each other, and fastened together, at the distance of
about three feet asunder, by cross beams, passing from
the larboard gunwale of one to the starboard gunwale
of the other, in the middle and near each end. They
appeared to be 30 feet in length, four in breadth, and
three in depth. The people had long black hair hanging over their shoulders, of a dark complexion, of a
middle size, and were dressed in a kind of matting
made fast round the middle. The women are beautiful, and the men justly proportioned. In the afternoon
the second lieutenant being again sent on shore, the
captain commanded him to take possession of the island
in the king's name, and to call it Queen Charlotte's
Island. The boats returned loaded with cocoa-nuts
and scurvy-grass, after having found two wells of
excellent water. Provisions for a week were now
allotted for a mate and 20 men, who were left on shore
to fill water; the sick were landed for the benefit of the
air; and a number of hands were appointed to climb
the cocoa-trees and gather the nuts, which in our situation were very desirable. The water was brought on board
on the 10th, but the cocoa-nuts and vegetables, which the
cutter was bringing off, were lost by the rolling of the
waves, that almost filled her with water. Afterwards
they made an island where were found several tools, resembling adzes, awls, and chissels, which were formed
of shells and stones. The dead bodies were not buried,
but left under a kind of canopy, to decay above ground.
This day the ship sailed again, after taking possession of
the islands for the king; in testimony of which we left
a flag flying, and carved his majesty's name on a piece
of wood, and on the bark of several trees. We left
shillings, sixpences, halfpence, bottles, nails, hatchets,
and other things for the use of the natives. It was
remarkable, that on this island we found the very people

ple who had fled from Queen Charlotte's Island, with
several others, in the whole near 100. It lies in 19 deg.
20 min. south latitude, and 138 deg. 30 min. west longitude, and received the name of Egmont Island.   On
Thursday the 11th, we observed about 16 persons on
an island which was called Gloucester Island; but as it
was surrounded with rocks and breakers, we did not
attempt to land.   This day we likewise discovered another, which was called Cumberland Island; and, on the
day following, a third, which received the name of
Prince William Henry's Island.

On Wednesday the 17th, we again discovered land,
and at ten at night saw a light, which convinced us
that it was inhabited, and remarked, that there were
plenty of cocoa-trees, a certain proof of there being no
want of water.   Mr. Furneaux was sent on shore the
day following with instructions to exchange some toys
for such things as the island produced.   He saw a great
number of the people, but could find no place where
the ship might anchor.   Some of the natives, who had
white sticks in their hands, appeared to have an authority over the rest.   While the lieutenant was trafficking
with them, an Indian diving into the water, seized the
grappling of the boat, while his companions on shore
laid hold of the rope by which she was fastened, and attempted to draw her into the surf, but their endeavours were frustrated by the firing of a musquet, on
which they all let go their hold.   These Indians were
dressed in a kind of cloth, a piece of which was brought
to the ship.   It was concluded from the number of the
people seen, and their having some large double canoes
on the shore, that there were larger islands at no great
distance: the Captain, therefore, having named this
place Osnaburgh Island, made sail and soon discovering
high-land, came to an anchor, because the weather was
very foggy.   The next morning early we saw land,
distant four or five leagues; but, after having sailed towards it some time, thought it prudent again to anchor,
on account of the thickness of the fog; but it no sooner
cleared away, than we found the ship encompassed by a
number

number of canoes, in which were many hundreds of
people. Having approached the ship, they beheld it
with wonder, and talked with great earneftnefs. Some
baubles were now fhewn them, and figns were made for
them to come on board, on which they rowed the
canoes towards each other, and a general confultation
took place; at the conclufion of which they all furrounded the fhip with an appearance of friendfhip, and
one of them delivered an oration, at the conclufion of
which he threw into the fea the branch of a plantain-
tree, which he had held in his hand. This being done,
a young Indian, of more apparent courage than the
reft, ventured on board the fhip. The Captain would
have given him fome baubles, but he refufed the accep-
tance of them till thofe in the canoes came along-fide,
and, having held a confultation, threw on board feveral
branches of the plantain-tree. Others now ventured on
board; but it was remarked, that they all got into the
fhip at fome improper part, not one of them, even by
accident, finding the right place of afcent. A goat belonging to the fhip, having run his horns againft the
back of one of the Indians, he looked round with furprize, and feeing the animal ready to renew the attack
he fprang over the fhip's fide, and was inftantly followed
by all his countrymen. Their terror, however, foon
fubfided, and they returned to the fhip; and the fheep,
hogs, and poultry being fhewn them, they intimated
that they poffeffed the two latter fpecies. The Captain
then gave them nails and other trifles, and made figns
that he wanted hogs, fowls, and fruit; but they could
not comprehend him. They were detected in feveral
attempts to take away any thing they could lay hold
of; but one of them at length jumped overboard with
a laced hat which he had fnatched from one of the
officers.

The interior parts of the ifland abounds in hills,
cloathed with timber-trees, above them are high peaks,
from which large rivers defcend to the fea; the houfes,
when feen at a diftance, refemble barns, having no
fhelter but a roof; the land towards the fea is level, and

produces

produces the cocoa-nut, with a variety of other fruits,
and the face of the whole country is picturesque beyond
description. We now sailed along the shore, while the
canoes, which could not keep pace with us, made towards the land. In the afternoon the ship brought to,
and the boats being sent to found a bay that promised
good anchorage, the Indian canoes flocked round them.
The Captain, apprehensive that their designs were hostile, made a signal for the boats to return to the ship,
and fired a gun over the heads of the Indians. Though
they were frightened at the report, they attempted to
prevent the return of the cutter; but she easily out-
sailed them. This being observed by some canoes in a
different station, they intercepted her, and wounded
some of her people with stones, which occasioned the
firing a musquet, and some shot were lodged in the
shoulder of the man who began the attack; which the
Indians observing, they all made off with the utmost
precipitation. The boats having reached the ship preparations were made for sailing, but a large canoe
making towards her at a great rate, it was resolved to
wait the event of her arrival; on which an Indian,
making a speech, threw a plantain branch on board,
and the captain returned the compliment of peace,
by giving them a branch, which had been left on
board by the other Indians; some toys being likewise
given them, they departed very well satisfied. We now
sailed, and the next morning were off a peak of land
which was almost covered with the natives and their
houses. On the 21st the ship anchored, and several
canoes came along-side of her, bringing a large quantity of fruit, with fowls and hogs, for which they received nails and toys in exchange.

The boats having been sent to found along the coast,
were followed by large double canoes, three of which
ran at the cutter, staved in her quarter, and otherwise
damaged her, the Indians at the same time, armed
with clubs, endeavouring to board her; the crew now
fired, and wounded one man dangerously, and killing
another, they both fell into the sea, whither their companions

panions dived after them, and got them into the canoe. They now tried if they could stand or fit, but as one was quite dead, they laid him at the bottom of the canoe, and the wounded man was supported in a fitting posture. The ships boats kept on their way, while some of the canoes went on shore, and others returned to the ship to renew their merchandise. While the boats continued out in several soundings, the natives swam off to them with water and fruit. The women were particularly urgent for the sailors to land, and, putting off all their cloaths, gave hints, of the most indelicate nature, how acceptable their company would be. The boats being sent on shore with some small casks to get water, the Indians filled two of them, and kept all the rest for their trouble. When the boats came off, the shore was crowded with thousands of men, women, and children. During this time, several canoes remained along-side the ship, but the captain would not permit a single Indian to go on board, as there was no guarding against their artful dispositions.

On Monday the 22nd, the natives brought hogs, poultry, and fruit to the ship, which they bartered for knives and other things, so that the whole crew was supplied with meat for two days, by means of this traffic. The boats having been this day sent for water, every inducement was used by the inhabitants to persuade them to land, and the behaviour of the women was still more lascivious than before. Having procured a small quantity of water, the boats put off: on which the women shouted aloud, pelted them with apples and bananas, and shewed every mark of contempt and detestation. On the 23rd, we made sail, with intention to anchor off the watering-place, but, the man at the mast-head discovering a bay a few miles to the leeward, we immediately stood for it. The boats which were a-head, making a signal for an anchorage, we prepared to bring to; but when the ship had almost reached the place, she suddenly struck, and her head remained immoveable, fixed on a coral rock; in which situation she remained near an hour, when she was happily relieved by a breeze from the shore. During the whole time that she was in danger of being wrecked, she was encompassed by hundreds of Indians in their canoes; but not one of them attempted to board her. The Dolphin was now piloted round a reef, into an harbour, where she was moored. The master was then sent to sound the bay, and found safe anchorage in every part of it. In the mean time some small canoes brought provisions on board; but as the shore was crowded with large canoes, filled with men, the captain loaded and primed his guns, supplied his boats with musqueteers, and kept a number of men under arms.

On Wednesday the 24th, the ship sailed up the harbour, and many canoes followed us, bringing provisions, which were exchanged for nails, knives, &c. A number of very large canoes advanced in the evening, laden with stones, on which the captain ordered the strictest watch to be kept. At length some canoes came off, which had on board a number of women, who being brought almost under the ship, began to practise those arts of indelicacy already mentioned. During this singular exhibition the large canoes came round the ship, some of the Indians playing on a kind of flute, others singing, and the rest blowing a sort of shells. Soon after a large canoe advanced, in which was an awning; and on the top of it sat one of the natives, holding some yellow and red feathers in his hands. The captain having consented to his coming along-side, he delivered the feathers, and while a present was preparing for him, he put back from the ship, and threw the branch of a cocoa-tree in the air. This was, doubtless, the signal for an onset, for there was an instant shout from all the canoes, which, approaching the ship, poured volleys of stones into every part of her. On this two guns, loaded with small shot, were fired, and the people on guard discharged their musquets. The number of Indians round the ship were full 2000, and though they were at first disconcerted, they soon recovered their spirits, and renewed the attack. Thousands of the Indians were now observed on shore, embarking

barking as fast as the canoes could bring them off: orders were therefore given for firing the cannon, some of which were brought to bear upon the shore. This firing put a stop to all hostilities on the part of the Indians, for a small time; but the scattered canoes soon got together again, and, having hoisted white streamers, advanced, and threw stones of two pound weight from flings, by which a number of the seamen were wounded. At this time several canoes approached the bow of the ship, from whence no shot had been yet discharged. In one of these was an Indian, who appeared to have an authority over the rest, a gun was therefore levelled at his canoe, the shot of which split it in two pieces. This put an end to the contest, the canoes rowed off with the utmost speed, and the people on shore ran and concealed themselves behind the hills.

After this skirmish we sailed for our intended anchoring place, and moored the ship within a little distance of a fine river. Some of our people who had been sent to survey the shore, returned the next morning with an account that they had found good fresh water (produced from the river above-mentioned) but that there was not a canoe to be seen. Mr. Furneaux was sent the same day with all the boats, well manned and armed, and a number of marines, having orders to land his men under cover of the ship and boats. This being accordingly effected, he turned a piece of turf, and having hoisted a broad pendant upon a staff, took possession of the isle for his Britannic majesty, naming it King George the Third's Island. Some rum being then mixed with the river-water, the king's health was drank by every person present. During the performance of this ceremony, two old men were seen on the opposite side of the river, who put themselves in a supplicating posture, and appeared to be much terrified. On this, the English made signs to them to cross the river. One of them obeying the signal came over, and crawled on his hands and knees towards the lieutenant, who shewed him some stones that had been thrown at the vessel, but took pains at the same time, to intimate, that no injury

should

should be done to the Indians, if they were not the ag-
greffors. He then caused some hatchets to be produced,
giving the Indian to understand that his people would
be glad to exchange them for various kinds of provisions.
Some trifles were also given to this old man, who expressed his gratitude by his gestures, and by dancing
round the flag-staff, but when they saw the pendant
shaken by the wind, they ran back, with signs of fear
and surprise. When they had recovered themselves
from their fright, they brought two hogs which they
laid down, and began dancing round the pendant as
before. The hogs were afterwards put into a canoe,
which the old Indian rowed towards the ship; and when
he came along-side of her, pronounced a serious oration,
in the course of which he delivered a number of plantain
leaves, (one at a time, somewhat in the manner of the
North Americans, closing their periods with belts of
wampum.) After this he rowed back again, refusing
at that time to accept of any presents. The noise of
drums and other instruments was heard this night, and
the next morning it was observed that the pendant was
taken away, and the natives had quitted the coast.
While the casks were filling with water, the old Indian
already mentioned, crossed the river, and brought the
English some fowls and fruits. At this time the captain was ill, but though he was confined to the vessel,
he had remarked from thence by the help of glasses
what was doing on shore. In the course of his observations, he perceived many of the natives creeping
behind the bushes towards the watering-place, at the
same time that vast numbers advanced through the
woods, and a large party came down the hill in view;
all tending to the same quarter. Two divisions of canoes were besides seen making round the opposite sides
of the bay. As the lieutenant had likewise observed
the threatened danger, he got his people on board the
boats; previous to which he had sent the old Indian to
intimate to his countrymen that the crew wanted
nothing but water, and to prevail on them to keep at a
proper distance whilst it was filling; but so far was this

from

from having the proper effect, that the islanders made a prize of the casks, and those at some distance from the watering-place, went forward with all expedition, in order to keep pace with the canoes, which rowed along very swiftly. At the same time a number of women and children took their station on a hill, which commanded a prospect of the shipping. The canoes drawing near that part of the bay where the vessel was at anchor, took in many from the shore who were laden with bags filled with stones. Then they rowed towards the ship, on which orders were given to fire on the first party that approached in the canoes, which being done, the Indians made off frightened and astonished. Captain Wallis being now resolved that this action should put an end to all disputes, incensed at the behaviour of the natives, commanded his people to fire first into the wood, and afterwards towards the hill, whither the islanders had retreated; when finding at what a distance the guns could reach them, they dispersed and disappeared. After this, the boats were sent out, a strong guard being appointed to attend the carpenters, who, according to orders, destroyed all the Indian canoes which could be met with. At length a small party of the natives came to the beach, stuck up some small branches of trees, as if for tokens, and then retreated to the woods; however they came again, and brought some hogs and dogs with their legs tied, which they left on the shore, together with a quantity of such cloth as they wore, all which they made signs to the sailors to take away. On this, a boat was dispatched which conveyed the hogs on board, but left behind the other articles; hatchets and nails were also deposited on the beach in return for these presents, but the Indians would by no means accept them till the cloth was taken away.

On Saturday the 27th, a party being employed in filling water, the old Indian was seen on the opposite side of the river. After having delivered an oration in his manner, he came over, when the officer referred him to the bags and stones which had been brought down,

I and

and used his endeavours to convince him that the English in the late action had acted only from motives of self defence. The old man, however, seemed to think his countrymen much aggrieved, and with great openness intimated his opinion. However at last he suffered himself to be reconciled, shook hands with the lieutenant, and accepted some presents from him. It was then hinted to him that it would be best for the people of the island to appear only in small parties for the future, with which terms the Indian appeared satisfied, and an advantageous traffic was afterwards established with the natives. Matters being thus settled, the sick were sent on shore, and were lodged, under the care of the surgeon, in tents near the watering place. This gentleman shooting a wild duck, it dropped on the opposite side of the river, in the presence of some Indians, who fled directly; but stopping within a short space, one of them was at last persuaded to bring the duck over, which he laid at the surgeon's feet, but, at the same time, the agitation of his mind was visible in his countenance. Three ducks were killed by a second shot, and the natives were by this time possessed with such a notion of the effects of fire-arms, as whilst it raised their admiration, was supposed to contribute in a great measure to their good behaviour towards the English during their stay in these parts, though there might be another reason assigned for this before their departure, as will be apparent in the sequel. The gunner was now appointed to manage all affairs of trade between the Indians and the sailors, in order to prevent quarrelling and pilfering. This was a judicious choice; the natives sometimes stole certain trifles, but immediate restitution was made on the sight of a gun. Besides, the old Indian made himself very serviceable in recovering any thing that might have been taken away. In particular, an Indian swam one day over the river, and pilfered a hatchet, on which the gunner making preparations, as if he meant to go in search of him, the goods were restored by the old man's means, and the offender was also delivered up to the gunner. Though
he

he had committed other robberies, yet the captain difcharged him; and all his punifhment confifted in his
terrible apprehenfions. Being reftored to his countrymen, he was conducted to the woods in the midft of
their fhouts of applaufe. This man had the gratitude
to bring a roafted hog and fome bread-fruit to the gunner next day, as an acknowledgement for the lenity
fhewn him. The captain, firft lieutenant, and purfer,
were at this time very ill; fo that the charge of the
veffel, and the care of the fick, were committed to Mr.
Furneaux, the fecond lieutenant, who difcharged his
duty with zeal and fidelity; and fruit, fowls, and frefh
pork, were procured in fuch plenty that at the end of
fourteen days almoft every man had perfectly recovered
his health. A piece of falt-petre, of the fize of a fmall
egg, had been found on the 25th on the fhore; but
whether it was brought from the fhip or not, could not
be learned, after the moft diligent enquiry; but however, no other piece was found. On the 2nd of July,
we began to want fruit and frefh meat, owing to the
abfence of the old Indian, but we had ftill a fufficient
fupply for the fick. On the 3rd, the fhip's bottom
was examined, when its condition was found to be
nearly the fame as when fhe left England. This day a
fhark was caught, which proved an acceptable prefent
to the natives. The old Indian, who had vifited the
interior parts of the ifland in queft of provifions, returned on the 5th, and brought with him a roafted hog
as a prefent for the captain, who in return, gave him
a looking-glafs, an iron pot, &c. His return was foon
followed by fome of the natives, who had never yet
vifited the market, and who brought fome hogs that
were larger than any yet purchafed. Another fort of
traffic was now eftablifhed between the Indian girls
and the failors. The price of a female's favours was a
nail or two; but as the feamen could not always get at
the nails, they drew them out of feveral parts of the
fhip; nor could the offenders be difcovered by the
ftricteft enquiry. The damage done to the veffel might
have been eafily repaired; but a worfe confequence

arofe

arose from this traffic; for on the gunner's offering small nails for hogs, the Indians produced large spikes, demanding such as those. Some of the men made use of a particular device to gratify their passions; for when they could procure no more nails, they cut lead into the shape of them, and passed those pieces on their unsuspecting paramours. When the Indians discovered the fraud, they demanded nails for the lead; but this just demand could not be granted, because it would have promoted the stealing of lead, and likewise injured the traffic with iron. In consequence of their connection with the women, the sailors became so impatient of controul, that the articles of war were read, to awe them into obedience; and a corporal of marines was severely punished, for striking the master at arms. The captain's health being nearly restored, he went in his boat to survey the island, which he found extremely delightful, and every where well peopled.

On Wednesday the 8th, the wood-cutters were entertained in a friendly manner by certain Indians, who seemed to be of a rank above those they had yet seen, and some of these visiting the captain, he laid before them a thirty-six-shilling piece, a guinea, a crown-piece, a dollar, some shillings, some new half-pence, and two large nails, intimating that they might take their choice, when they eagerly seized the nails, and then took a few half-pence, but left all the other pieces untouched. The Indians now refused to supply the market, unless they could get large nails in exchange: the captain therefore ordered the ship to be searched, when it was found that almost all the hammock-nails were stolen, and great numbers drawn from different places; on which every man was ordered before the captain, who told them, that not a man should go on shore till the thieves were discovered; but no good consequence arose from his threats, at that time. Three days after, the gunner conducted to the ship a lady of an agreeable face, and portly mein, whose age seemed to be upwards of forty. This lady had but lately arrived in that part of the island, and the gunner

observing

obferving that fhe feemed to have great authority, prefented her with fome toys; on which fhe invited him
to her houfe, and gave him fome fine hogs. She was
afterwards taken on board, at her own defire. Her
whole behaviour fhewed her to be a woman of fine
fenfe and fuperior rank; the captain prefented her
with a looking-glafs and fome toys, and gave her a
handfome blue mantle, which he tied round her with
ribbands. As fhe then intimated that fhe fhould be
glad to fee him on fhore, he fignified his intention of
vifiting her the next day. Accordingly, on Saturday
the 12th, Captain Wallis went on fhore, where fhe met
him, attended by a numerous retinue, fome of whom
fhe directed to carry the captain, and others who had
been ill, over the river, and from thence to her habitation, and the proceffion was clofed by a guard of
marines and feamen. As they advanced, a great number of Indians crowded to fee them; but, on a flight
motion of her hand, they made room for the proceffion to pafs. When they drew near her dwelling, many
perfons of both fexes advanced to meet her, whom
fhe caufed to kifs the captain's hand, while fhe fignified
that they were related to her. Her houfe was 320 feet
in length, and about 40 in breadth. The roof, which
was covered with the leaves of palm-tree, was fupported
by a row of pillars on each fide, and another in the
middle. The higheft part on the thatch on the infide,
was 30 feet from the ground, and the fpace between the
fides of the building and the edge of the roof, which
was about 12 feet, was left open. The captain, lieutenant, and purfer, being feated, the lady helped four
of her female attendants to pull off the gentlemen's
coats, fhoes, and ftockings, which was aukwardly performed; the girls however fmoothed down the fkin,
and rubbed it lightly with their hands for more than
half an hour. The furgeon, being heated with walking, having pulled off his wig, one of the Indians
fcreamed out, and the eyes of the whole company were
inftantly fixed on the wonderful fight, and they remained
for fome time fixed in furprize. After this the queen

ordered several bales of cloth to be brought out, which were the produce of the country, which were now destined for the dress of the captain and his attendants. It was intended that the captain should be carried as he had been before, but as he refused the offer, the queen walked arm and arm with him, and lifted him like an infant over such wet and dirty places as they came to in their way. She gave him a sow pig with young, and took her leave when she had attended him to the beach. The gunner being dispatched to wait on her the next day with a present of bill-hooks, hatchets, &c. found her busied in entertaining some hundreds of the Indians who were regularly seated round her. She ordered a mess to be provided for the gunner, which he found to be very agreeable, and supposed to be fowls and apples cut small, and mixed with salt water. The provisions which were distributed by the queen, were served in cocoa-shells, which her servants brought in a sort of trays. This lady took her seat somewhat above the rest of the company, and when they were supplied, was fed by two women servants, standing on each side of her. It was observed that she received the captain's presents with an air of great satisfaction, and the supply of provisions brought to market was now greater than ever, but the prices were raised, in a great measure owing to the commerce between the English seamen and the women of the Island, of which we have taken notice; for which reason, besides the orders given for restraining the people belonging to the crew from going on shore, it was also thought proper to prohibit any women from passing the river.

On Tuesday the 14th of this month, the gunner being on shore, discovered a woman on the opposite side of the river, who seemed to be weeping in a most piteous manner. Perceiving that he seemed to take notice of her apparent distress, she sent a youth to him, who having made a long oration, laid a branch of plantain at his feet, after which he went to fetch the woman, and also brought two hogs with him. The youth now made a long speech, and, in the end, the gunner was

given

given to underſtand that her huſband and three of her
ſons, had been killed when the Engliſh fired on the
Indians as above related. She fell ſpeechleſs on the
ground after ſhe had told her tale of woe, and two lads
that attended her, ſeemed alſo to be much affected.
The gunner ſeeing her diſtreſſed ſituation endeavoured
to conſole her, and at laſt ſhe became a little calmer,
offered him her hand, and directed the hogs to be given
him, nor would ſhe accept any thing in return for her
preſent. A large party rowed round the iſland in their
boats on the 15th, in order to take a view of it, and to
purchaſe proviſions. Returning, they brought with
them a number of hogs and fowls, and ſome cocoa-nuts,
They found the iſland to be pleaſant, and abounding
with the neceſſaries of life, and ſaw a great number of
canoes, ſeveral of which were not quite finiſhed. The
natives tools were formed of bones, ſtones, and ſhells.
No other four-footed beaſts but dogs and hogs, were
ſeen. The inhabitants ate all their meat either baked
or roaſted, as they neither had any veſſel wherein water
could be boiled, nor ſeemed to entertain an idea that it
could be heated by fire ſo as to anſwer any uſeful pur-
poſe. One morning, when the lady we have mentioned
was at breakfaſt, an Indian that attended her having
obſerved the cock of an urn turned, to fill a tea-pot,
he alſo turned the cock, when the ſcalding water falling
upon his hand, he cried out and jumped about the
cabin, while the Indians were equally ſurpriſed and
terrified at the circumſtance. The captain received
another viſit from the queen on the 17th, and the ſame
day a great quantity of proviſions was purchaſed
of ſome of the natives, whom we had never before
dealt with. The next day the queen repeated her viſit,
and made the captain a preſent of two hogs, and the
maſter attending her home, ſhe cloathed him in the
dreſs of the country, as ſhe had done the captain and
his retinue. Our proviſions received an increaſe on the
19th, by the gunner's ſending on board a number of
hogs and pigs, and abundance of fowls and fruits which
he had purchaſed in the country. At this time an

order

order was made that none of the sailors should be
allowed to go on shore, except those that were appointed
to procure wood, water, or other necessaries.

On Tuesday the 21st, the queen came again to visit
Captain Wallis, and presented him with some hogs.
She likewise invited the captain to her house, who
attended her home with some of his officers. She tied
wreaths of plaited hair round their hats, and on the
captain's she put a tuft of feathers of various colours,
by way of distinction. She came back with them as
far as the water-side on their return, and ordered some
presents to be put into the boat at their departure.
Captain Wallis having intimated before they put off,
that he should leave the island in seven days time, she
made signs that she wished him to stay 20 days ; but he
repeating his resolution, she bursted into a flood of tears.
We were now so well stored with hogs and poultry,
that our decks were covered with them, and as the men
were more inclined to eat fruit than meat, they were
killed faster than had been intended. The captain
presented his friend the old Indian with some cloth and
other articles, and sent a number of things to the queen,
among which were a cat with kitten, turkies, geese,
hens, and several sorts of garden seeds. This compliment was returned by a present of fruit and hogs.
Pease and other European seeds were sowed here, and
the captain staid long enough to to see them come up,
and to observe that they were likely to thrive in the
country.

On the 25th, a party was sent on shore in order to
examine the country, and a tent was erected for the
purpose of observing an eclipse of the sun. When it
was ended, the captain took his telescope to the queen,
who shewed a surprise scarcely to be expressed, on discovering several objects with which she was well acquainted, but which were too distant to be seen without the help of a glass. He afterwards invited her and
her retinue to come on board the ship, where an elegant
dinner was prepared, of which all but the queen ate
heartily ; but she would neither eat nor drink. On
                                                    the

the return of the party from their excursion, the queen was landed with her train. The captain still keeping in the same mind as to the time of his departure, she wept again on being informed of his resolution. Our people who had been sent out this day, reported, that on their first landing they called on the old Indian, and took him into their company, walking some on one side of the river, and some on the other, till the ground rising almost perpendicular, they were all obliged to walk on one side. On the borders of the valley through which the river flowed, the soil was black, and there were several houses with walled gardens, and plenty of fowls and hogs. In many places channels were cut to conduct the water from the hills to the plantations. No underwood was found beneath the trees, but there was good grass; the bread-fruit and apple-trees were set in rows upon the hills, and the cocoa-nut grew upon the level ground. The streams now meandered through various windings, and the crags of mountains hung over the travellers heads. When they had walked about four miles they rested, and began their breakfast under an apple-tree. At this time they were alarmed by a loud shout from a number of the natives. On this they were going to betake themselves to their arms, but the old Indian made signs that they should sit still. He then went to his countrymen, and it was presently observed that they became silent and withdrew. They afterwards returned, bringing with them some refresh-ments, in exchange for which they received buttons and other trifles from the lieutenant. The party then proceeded, looking every where for metals and ores, but found nothing of that sort worth attending to. And now the old Indian being tired, gave his English companions to understand that he was desirous of re-turning, but he did not leave them till he had given directions to the Indians to clear the way over a moun-tain. After his departure his countrymen cut branches from the trees, and laid them in a ceremonious man-ner at the feet of the seamen; they then painted them-selves red with the berries of a tree, and stained their

garments

garments yellow with the bark of another. By the affiftance of thefe people, the moft difficult parts of the
mountains were climbed, and they again refrefhed
themfelves at its fummit, when they faw other mountains fo much above them, that they feemed as in a
valley. Towards the fea, the profpect was inexpreffibly
beautiful, the fides of the hills being covered with
trees, and the valleys with grafs, while the whole country
was interfperfed with villages. They faw but few
houfes on the mountains above them, but as fmoke was
obferved in many places, it was conjectured, that the
higheft were inhabited. Many fprings gufhed from
the fides of the mountains, all of which were covered
with wood on the fides and with fern on the fummit.
The foil even on the high land was rich, and the fugar
cane grew without cultivation; as did likewife tur-
meric and ginger. Having a third time refrefhed
themfelves, they defcended towards the fhip, occafionally deviating from the direct way, tempted by the
pleafant fituation of feveral houfes, the inhabitants of
which entertained them in the moft hofpitable manner.
They faw parrots, parroquets, green doves, and ducks.
The lieutenant planted the ftones of cherries, peaches
and plumbs, feveral kinds of garden feeds, and oranges,
lemons and limes. In the afternoon they refted on a
delightful fpot, where the inhabitants dreffed them two
hogs and feveral fowls. Here they ftaid till evening,
when they rewarded the diligence of their guides, and
repaired to the fhip.

On the 26th, the captain was vifited by the queen
with her ufual prefents, and this day we difcontinued
taking in wood and water, and prepared for failing. A
greater number of Indians now came to the fea-fhore,
than we had ever yet feen; and of thefe feveral appeared
to be perfons of confequence. In the afternoon the
queen vifited Captain Wallis, and folicited him to
remain ten days longer; but being informed that he
fhould certainly fail on the following day, fhe burft into
tears. She now demanded when he would come again,
and was told in 50 days; fhe remained on board till
evening,

ndon; Published as the Act directs, by Alex.ᵗ Hogg, at the Kings Arms, N.ᵒ 16, Paternoster Row.

evening, when being informed that the boat waited for her, she wept with more violence than she had yet done. At length this affectionate woman went over the ship's side, as did the old Indian who had been so serviceable to the crew. This man had signified that his son should sail with the captain ; but when the time came the youth was not to be found, from whence it was concluded that parental affection had caused the old man to forfeit his word. The next morning early two boats were sent to fill a few casks of water ; but the officer, alarmed at finding the shore crowed with the natives, prepared to return. This occasioned the queen to come forward, who ordered the Indians to retire to the other side of the river, after which she made signs for the boats to come on shore. While they were filling the water she ordered some presents to be put into the boat, and earnestly desired to go once more to the ship, but the officer being ordered not to bring off a single native, she ordered her double canoe out, and was followed by many others. When she had been on board for an hour, weeping and lamenting, we took advantage of a fresh breeze, and got under sail. She now embraced the captain and officers, and left the ship ; but as the wind fell, the canoes put back, and reached the ship again, to which the queen's was made fast, and advancing to the bow of it she there renewed her lamentations. Captain Wallis presented her with several articles of use and ornament, all which she received in mournful silence. The breeze springing up again, the queen and her attendants took their final leave, and tears were shed on both sides.

The place where the ship had lain at anchor, was called Port Royal Harbour, and is situate in 17 deg. 30 min. of south lat. and 150 deg. of west long.

The following are the particulars we have selected of the customs, manners, &c. of the people of Otaheite. With regard to their stature, the men are from five feet seven to five feet ten inches high, the standard of the women, in general, near three inches shorter, the tallest among them being about five feet seven inches, they

were

were mostly handsome, and some of them are described as being really beautiful. The complexion of such of the men as are much employed on the water is reddish, but their natural colour is what is called tawny. The colour of their hair is not like that of the East Indians and Americans, black, but is diversified like that of the Europeans, having among them black, brown, red, and flaxen; most of the children having the latter: when loose, it has a strong natural curl, but it is usually worn tied in two bunches, one on each side the head, or in a single bunch in the middle. They anoint the head with the oil of the cocoa-nut, mixed with a root of a fragrant smell. The women, as we have before observed, do not consider chastity as a virtue, for they not only readily and openly trafficked with our people for personal favours, but were brought down by their fathers and brothers for the purpose of prostitution: they were, however, conscious of the value of beauty; and the size of the nail that was demanded for the enjoyment of the lady, was always in proportion to her charms. When a man offered a girl to the caresses of a sailor, he shewed a stick of the size of the nail that was to purchase her company; and if our people agreed, she was sent over to them, for our seamen were not permitted to cross the river.

Their cloaths are formed of two pieces of cloth, made of the bark of a shrub, and not unlike coarse china paper. In one of them a hole is made for the head to pass through, and this hangs down to the middle of the leg, from the shoulders both before and behind; the other piece which is between four and five yards long, and nearly one broad, they wrap round the body, and the whole forms an easy, decent, and graceful dress. They adorn themselves with flowers, feathers, shells, and pearls. The last are worn chiefly by the women; the captain purchased two dozen of a small size and good colour, but they were all spoiled by boring. Mr. Furneaux saw several, in his excursion to the west, but he could purchase none with any thing he had to offer. It is a universal custom with both sexes, to mark the

1   hinder

hinder part of their thighs and loins with black lines in various forms. This is done by ftriking the teeth of an inftrument, fomewhat like a comb, juft through the fkin, and rubbing into the punctures a kind of pafte made of foot and oil, which leaves an indelible ftain. The boys and girls under twelve years of age are not marked, but we faw a few men whofe legs were punctuated, and thefe appeared to be perfons of diftinction.

One of the principal attendants on the queen, was much more difpofed to imitate our manners than the reft; and our people, with whom he foon became a favourite, diftinguifhed him by the name of Jonathan. This man Mr. Furneaux clothed completely in an Englifh drefs, and it became him extremely well. As it was fhoal water at the landing place, our officers were carried by the Indians on fhore, and Jonathan, affuming ftate with his new finery, would be carried by fome of his people in the fame manner. In attempting to ufe a knife and fork at meals, at firft his hand always came to his mouth, and the victuals, on the end of the fork, went away to his ear. Befides the articles already mentioned, thefe people eat the fiefh of dogs. Rats abound in the ifland, but, as far as we could difcover, they make no part of their food. In their rivers are good tafted mullets, but they are neither large nor in plenty. On the reef are cray-fifh, conchs, mufcles, and other fhell-fifh, which they gather at low water, and eat raw with bread-fruit before they come on fhore. At a fmall diftance from hence, they catch with lines, and hooks of mother of pearl, parrot-fifh, groopers, and many other forts, of which they are fo fond, that we could feldom prevail upon them to fell us a few at any price. Their nets are of an enormous fize, with very fmall mefhes, with which they catch abundance of the fmall fry; but while they were ufing both nets and lines with great fuccefs, we could not catch a fingle fifh with either; not even with their hooks and lines, fome of which we had procured.

The manner in which they drefs their food is fomewhat

fingular. They firft kindle a fire by rubbing the end of one piece of dry wood together, in the fame manner as our carpenters whet a chiffel. Having alfo dug a pit about half a foot deep, and two or three yards in cir-cumference, they pave the bottom with large pebble ftones, laid down fmooth and even, and then kindle a fire in it with dry wood, leaves, and the hufks of the cocoa-nut. When the ftones are fufficiently heated, they take out the embers, and rake up the afhes on every fide; then they cover the ftones with a layer of green cocoa-nut tree leaves, and wrap up the animal that is to be dreffed in the leaves of the plantain : if a fmall hog they wrap it up whole, if a large one they fplit it. When it is placed in the pit, they cover it with the hot embers, and lay upon them bread-fruit and yams, which are alfo wrapped up in the leaves of the plantain: over thefe they fpread the remainder of the embers, mixing among them fome of the hot ftones, with more leaves upon them, and laftly, to keep the heat in, they clofe all up with earth. After a time proportioned to the fize of what is dreffing, the oven is opened, and the meat taken out, which is tender, full of gravy, and, in the opinion of Captain Wallis, better in every refpect than that which is dreffed in the European manner. Their only fauces are fruit and falt water; and their knives are made of fhells, with which they carve very dexteroufly, always cutting from them. They were greatly afto-nifhed when they faw meat boiled in a pot by our gun-ner, who, while he prefided over the market, ufed to dine on fhore ; but from the time that the old man was in poffeffion of an iron pot, he, and his friends, had boiled meat every day. The iron pots which the cap-tain gave to the queen, were alfo conftantly in ufe. The only liquor thefe people have for drinking, is water ; and they are ignorant of the art of fermenting the juice of any vegetable, fo as to give it an intoxicating qua-lity. It is true they occafionally pluck and chew pieces of the fugar cane, but have no idea of extracting any fpirit from it.

By the fcars, with which many of thefe people are
marked,

marked, it feems evident, that they fometimes engaged
in war with each other. The remains of wounds that
were vifible appeared to be made with ftones, blud-
geons, or other blunt weapons. That they have fkill
in furgery, the following inftance afforded us fufficient
proof. One of our failors, when on fhore, had a large
fplinter run into his foot, and his meffmate tried in vain
to extract it with a pen-knife. The old Indian, who happened to be prefent, called over one of his countrymen,
who was ftanding on the oppofite fide of the river, who,
having examined the feaman's foot, went immediately
down to the beach, and taking up a fhell, broke it to a
point with his teeth ; with this inftrument he laid open
the place, and drew out the fplinter. In the mean time
the old man repaired to a wood, and returned with fome
gum of the apple-tree, and, having fpread it upon a
piece of cloth, applied it to the wound, which, in two
days time, was perfectly healed. Our furgeon afterwards ufed this vulnerary balfam with great fuccefs.
In this ifland are feveral fheds enclofed within a wall,
and the area is generally paved with large round ftones ;
but it appeared not to be much trodden, for the grafs
grew every where between them. On the outfide
of the wall were feveral rude figures refembling men,
women, hogs and dogs, carved on pofts, that were
fixed in the ground. We do not think thefe places are
fet apart for religious worfhip, of which we could not
difcover the leaft traces among thefe people ; but we
conjecture they may be repofitories of the dead, for we
faw many of the natives enter them, with a flow pace
and dejected countenance.

They have three kinds of canoes. One are formed
out of fingle trees, ufed chiefly for fifhing, and carry
from two to fix men. We faw many of thefe upon the
reef. A fecond fort are made of planks fewed neatly
together, and large enough to hold forty men. Two of
them are generally lafhed together, having two mafts
fet up between them ; but, if fingle, they have an out-
rigger on one fide, and only one maft in the middle.
They fail in thefe beyond the fight of land, probably to

other

other iflands, and bring home plantains, bananas, and other fruits.   A third kind, not unlike the gondolas of Venice, are intended principally for fhew, and ufed by parties of pleafure.   Thefe are very large, but have not any fails.   The middle is covered with a large awning, and fome of the people fit upon it and fome under it. On the firft and fecond day after our arrival, fome of thefe veffels came near the fhip ; but afterwards we only faw, three or four times a week, a proceffion of eight or ten of them paffing at a diftance, with ftreamers fly-ing, and a great number of fmall canoes attending them. They frequently rowed to the outward point of a reef, that lay about four miles to the weftward of us, where they continued about an hour and then returned. Thefe proceffions are made only in fine weather, and on fuch occafions the people on board are dreffed ; though in the other canoes, they have nothing but a piece of cloth wrapped round the middle. Thofe in the large ca-noes, who rowed and fteered, were dreffed in white ; thofe who fat upon the awning and under it, in white and red ; and two men, who were mounted on the prow of each veffel, in red only. The plank of thefe veffels is made by fplitting a tree, with the grain, into as many thin pieces as they can. The tree is firft felled with a kind of hatchet, or adze, made of a hard greenifh ftone, fitted very completely into a handle : it is then cut into fuch lengths, as are required for the plank, one end of which is heated till it begins to crack, and then with wedges of hard wood they fplit it down : fome of thefe planks are two feet broad, and from 15 to 20 feet long. They fmooth them with adzes of the fame materials and conftruction, but of a fmaller fize. We faw fix or eight men fometimes at work upon the fame plank, and, as their tools foon lofe their edge, every man has by him a cocoa-nut fhell filled with water, and a flat ftone, whereon he fharpens his adze almoft every minute. The planks are generally brought to the thicknefs of about an inch, and are afterwards fitted to the boat with the fame exactnefs as would be expected from an expert joiner. To faften thefe planks together, holes are bored,

through

through which a kind of plaited cordage is paffed, but our nails anfwered the purpofe of faftening them together much better. The feams are caulked with dried rufhes, and the whole outfide of the canoe is paid with a gummy fubftance, produced from their trees, and which is fubftituted in the room of pitch. The wood which they ufe for their large canoes, is that of the apple tree; which grows very large and ftrait. Many of thefe meafured near eight feet in the girth, and from twenty to forty in the branches, with very little diminution in the fize. Their fmall canoes are nothing more than the hollowed trunks of the bread-fruit-tree, which is ftill more light and fpongy. The trunk of this tree is fix feet in girth.

In the opinion of Captain Wallis, this ifland of Otaheite is one of the moft healthy as well as delightful fpots in the world. The climate appears to be very good, and we faw no appearance of difeafe among the natives. The hills are covered with wood, and the valleys with herbage. The air in general is fo pure, that, notwithftanding the heat, our flefh meat kept very well two days, and our fifh one. We met with no frog, toad, fcorpion, centipied, or ferpent, of any kind; and the only troublefome infects that we faw were ants, of which there were but few. The fouth-eaft part of the ifland feems to be better cultivated and inhabited than where we lay, for we faw every day boats come round from thence laden with plantains and other fruits. While we lay off this ifland, the benefit we received, with refpect to the fhip's company, was beyond our moft fanguine expectations, for we had not now an invalid aboard, except the two lieutenants, and the captain, and they were recovering, though ftill in a feeble condition.

Many affertions have been advanced with refpect to the firft introducers of the venereal difeafe into this ifland. "It is certain, (obferves Captain Wallis) that none of our people contracted the venereal difeafe here, and therefore, as they had free commerce with great numbers of the women, there is the greateft probability that it was not then known in the country. It was,
however,

however, found here by Captain Cook in the Endeavour, and as no European veſſel is known to have viſited this iſland before Captain Cook's arrival, but the
Dolphin, and the Boudeuſe and Etoil, commanded by
M. Bongainville, the reproach of having contaminated
with that dreadful peſt, a race of happy people, to whom
its miſeries had till then been unknown, muſt be due
either to him or to me, to England or to France; and
I think myſelf happy to be able to exculpate myſelf
and my country beyond a poſſibility of a doubt. It is
well known, that the ſurgeon on board his majeſty's
ſhips keeps a liſt of the perſons who are ſick on board,
ſpecifying their diſeaſes, and the times when they came
under his care, and when they were diſcharged. It
happened that I was once at the pay-table on board a
ſhip, when ſeveral ſailors objected to the payment of
the ſurgeon, alledging, that although he had diſcharged
them from the liſt, and reported them to be cured, yet
their cure was incomplete. From this time it has been
my conſtant practice when the ſurgeon reported a man
to be cured, who had been upon the ſick liſt, to call the
man before me, and aſk him whether the report was
true: if he alledged that any ſymptoms of his complaint remained, I continued him upon the liſt; if not,
I required him, as a confirmation of the ſurgeon's report,
to ſign the book, which was always done in my pre-
ſence. A copy of the ſick liſt on board the Dolphin,
during this voyage, ſigned by every man in my pre-
ſence, when he was diſcharged well, in confirmation of
the ſurgeon's report, written in my own hand, and confirmed by my affidavit, I have depoſited in the admiralty; by which it appears, that the laſt man on board
the ſhip, in her voyage outward, who was upon the ſick
liſt for the venereal diſeaſe, except one who was ſent to
England in the ſtore ſhip, was diſcharged cured, and
ſigned the book on the 27th of December 1766, near ſix
months before our arrival at Otaheite, which was on the
19th of June 1767; and that the firſt man who was upon
the liſt for that diſeaſe, in our return home, was entered
on the 26th of February 1768, ſix months after we left
the

the ifland, which was on the 26th of July 1767 ; fo that the fhip's company was intirely free fourteen months within one day, the very middle of which time we fpent at Otaheite ; and the man who was firft entered as a venereal patient, in our return home, was known to have contracted the difeafe at the Cape of Good Hope, where we then lay."

The old Indian, who had been fo ufeful in carrying on an intercourfe with the natives, had often intimated, that his fon, a boy about fourteen years of age, fhould embark on board the fhip ; and the lad feemed well inclined to quit his country, and undertake the voyage ; however, when the fhip was about to fail, the youth thought fit to conceal himfelf, from a change of mind either in him or his father. A few months after the Dolphin left this ifland, M. de Bougainville touched here, and with him one of the natives embarked ; but from the difparity in their ages, it could not be the fame perfon who had engaged to accompany Captain Wallis. The name of this adventurer was Aotourou. He left his country with great fatisfaction and cheerfulnefs. His hiftory is fhort, and as follows. The firft European fettlement that M. de Bougainville touched at, after leaving Otaheite, was Boero, in the Moluccas. The furprize of Aotourou was extravagant, at feeing men dreffed in the European manner ; houfes, gardens. and various domeftic animals, in great variety and abundance. Above all, he is faid to have valued that hofpitality that was there exercifed, with an air of fincerity and freedom. As he faw no exchanges made, he apprehended the people gave every thing without receiving any return. He prefently took occafion to let the Dutch underftand, that in his country he was a chief, and that he had undertaken this voyage with his friends for his own pleafure. In vifits, at table, and in walking, he endeavoured to imitate the manners and cuftoms of the Europeans. When M. de Bougainville left Aotourou on board, on his firft vifit to the governor, he imagined the omiffion was owing to his knees being bent inwards, and with greater fimplicity than good

fenfe,

senfe, he applied to some of the seamen to get upon them, suppofing they would, by that means, be forced into a ftraight direction. He was very earneft to know if Paris was as fine as the Dutch factory where he then was. At Batavia, the delight which he felt on his firft arrival, from the fight of the objects that prefented themfelves might operate, in fome degree, as an antidote to the poifon of the place; but during the latter part of their ftay here, he fell fick, and continued ill a confider able time through the remainder of the voyage; but his readinefs in taking physic, was equal to a man born at Paris. Whenever he fpoke of Batavia afterwards, he always called it enoue mate " the land that kills." This Indian, during a refidence of two years in France, does not appear to have done much credit to himfelf or his country. At the end of that time he could only utter a few words of the language; which indocile difpofition M. de Bougainville excufes with great ingenuity and apparent reafon, by obferving, that, " he was at leaft thirty years of age: that his memory had never been exercifed before in any kind of ftudy, nor had his mind ever been employed at all. He was totally different from an Italian, a German, or an Englifhman, who can, in a twelvemonth's time, fpeak a French jargon tolerably well; but then thefe have a fimilar grammar; their moral, phyfical, political, and focial ideas are much the fame, and all expreffed by certain words in their language as they are in the French tongue; they have therefore little more than a tranflation to fix in their memories, which retentive faculties have been exercifed from their infancy. The Otaheitean man, on the contrary, having only a fmall number of ideas, relative on the one hand, to the moft fimple and limited fociety, and, on the other, to wants which are reduced to the fmalleft number poffible, he would have, firft of all, as it were, to create a world of new ideas, in a mind as indolent as his body; and this previous work muft be done before he can come fo far as to adapt to them the words of an European language, by which they are to be expreffed." But Aotourou feems to have kept very much below the
ftandard,

standard, which the French apologift pleads he was not required to furpafs ; for he really was not able, after two years inftruction, to tranflate his Otaheitean ideas, few and fimple as they were, into French. This itinerant embarked at Rochelle A. D. 1770, on board the Briffon, which was to carry him to the ifle of France, from whence, by order of the French miniftry, he was to be fent by the intendant to his native country : and for this purpofe, M. de Bougainville informs us that he gave fifteen hundred pounds fterling, (a third part of his whole fortune) towards the equipment of the fhip intended for this navigation. But notwithftanding thefe endeavours to reftore the adventurous Aotourou to his country and connections, he had not reached them when Capt. Cook was at Otaheite in 1774 : and Mr. Forfter fays he died of the fmall pox.

C H A P. III.

The Dolphin fails from King George the Third's Ifland— Her Paffage from thence to Tinian—Sir Charles Saunders's—Lord Howe's—Scilly—Bofcawen's—Keppel's— And Captain Wallis's Iflands difcovered—The prefent State of Tinian defcribed—Run from that Ifland to Batavia—Incidents and Tranfactions at this laft Place .. The Dolphin continues her Voyage to the Cape of Good Hope —Returns to England, and anchors in the Downs on Friday the 20th of May, 1768; having circumnavigated the Globe, from the Time of weighing Anchor in Plymouth Sound, in juft 637 Days ; and accomplifhed her Voyage a Month and a Day fooner than fhe had done when under the Command of Commodore Byron.

ON Sunday the 26th of July, 1767, we took our departure from the ifland of Otaheite; and on the 27th, paffed the Duke of York's Ifland, the middle and weft end whereof is very mountainous, but the eaft end is lower, and the coaft juft within the beach abounds with plantain-trees, cocoa-nuts, bread-fruit, and apple-trees. On the 28th, we difcovered land, which was called Sir Charles Saunders's Ifland. It is about fix miles long from E. to W. and lies in latitude 17 deg. 28 min. fouth, and in 151 deg. 4 min. weft longitude. On the weather fide are many great breakers, and the lee-fide is rocky, neverthelefs, in many places there appears to be good anchorage. In the center is a mountain, which feems to be fertile. The few inhabitants we faw appeared to live in a wretched manner, in fmall huts, very different from the ingenious natives of King George's Ifland. Cocoa-nut and other trees grew on the fhore, but all of them had their tops blown away. On the 30th, we again made land, at day-break, bearing N. by E. to N. W. We ftood for it but could find no anchorage, the whole ifland being encircled by dangerous breakers. It is about ten miles in length, and four in breadth, and lies in latitude 16 deg. 46 min. fouth, and in 154 deg. 13 min. weft longitude. On the lee part a few cocoa-nuts were growing, and we perceived fmoke, but no inhabitants. The captain named this new difcovered land Lord Howe's Ifland. In the afternoon we difcovered in latitude 16 deg. 28 min. fouth, longitude 155 deg. 30 min. weft, a group of iflands or fhoals, exceeding dangerous; for in the night, however clear the weather, and by day, if it is hazy, a fhip may run upon them without feeing land. At five o'clock we defcried the breakers, running a great way to the fouthward; and foon after low land to the S. W. We turned to windward all night, and at nine o'clock, of the 31ft, got round the fhoals and named them Scilly Iflands.

On Thurfday the 13th of Auguft, having continued our courfe weftward, two fmall iflands came in view. The firft, at noon, bore W. half S. diftant five leagues, and had the appearance of a fugar loaf. The center of the fecond rofe in the form of a peak, and bore W. S. W. diftant fix leagues. To one, which is nearly a circle, in diameter three miles, we gave the name of Bofcawen's Ifland; and this we believe to be the only inftance which occurs, of an ifland receiving the name of a deceafed

ceafed great man. Admiral Bofcawen died in the year
1761. The other ifland, which is three miles and a
half in length, we called Keppel's Ifle. Port Royal at
this time bore eaft 4 deg. fouth, diftant 478 leagues.
At two o'clock, P. M. we faw feveral inhabitants upon
Bofcawen's Ifland; but Keppel's being to windward, and
appearing more likely to afford us good anchorage,
we hauled up for it. At fix, being diftant therefrom
nearly two miles, we obferved, by the help of our glaffes,
many of the natives upon the beach; but we did not
attempt to anchor, on account of fome breakers at a
confiderable diftance from the ifland. However, on
the 14th, early in the morning, the boats were difpatched to found and vifit the ifland. At noon they
returned, without having found any ground, within a
cable's length of it; but feeing a reef of rocks, they had
hauled round the fame, and got into a large deep bay
full of rocks: without this was anchorage from 14 to
20 fathoms, bottom fand and coral; and within a
rivulet of good water; but the fhore being rocky, they
went in fearch of a better landing place, which they
found about half a mile farther, and went afhore. Our
people reported, that the inhabitants were not unlike
thofe of Otaheite; they were cloathed in a kind of
matting, and were remarkable for having the firft joint
of their little fingers cut off. They feemed to be peaceably inclined, and three of them from their canoes came
into the boats when they put off, but fuddenly jumped
overboard, and fwam back to the ifland, where about
50 of their countrymen ftood on the fhore ready to
receive them, but who would not advance nearer than
about 100 yards to our people. Thefe brought on
board two fowls, and fome fruit, but they faw not any
hogs. Till this day, Captain Willis had entertained a
defign of returning to England by the way of the Magellanic Straits; but as no convenient watering place
was to be found at this ifland, and as the fhip had received fome damages, that had rendered her unfit to
encounter a rough fea, he determined to fail for Tinian,
from thence to Batavia, and fo home by the Cape of

Good Hope. By this route, as far as we could judge,
we expected to be fooner at home, and fuppofing the
ship might not be in a condition to make the whole
voyage, we fhould ftill have a greater probability of
faving our lives, as from this place to Batavia, we fhould
have a calm fea, and be not far from port. We think
it rather extraordinary that a thought fhould be entertained by Captain Wallis, of returning by the way we
came; as, independent of the prodigious unneceffary
rifk that would be run, the honour of having gone over
the entire circumference of the globe would have been
loft: for a voyage into the South Sea would have had
nothing attractive in its found; but a voyage round the
world, was calculated to draw general attention. In
confequence of the above refolution, we paffed Bofcawen's Ifland, which is well inhabited, and abounds
with timber; but Keppel's is by far the largeft and
beft Ifland of the two. The former lies in latitude
15 deg. 50 min. fouth, longitude 175 deg. weft;
and the latter in latitude 15 deg. 55 min. longitude
175 deg. 3 min. weft from London. We continued
our courfe W. N. W. and,

On Sunday the 16th, at ten o'clock, A. M. we difcovered land bearing N. by E. and at noon were within
three leagues of it. Within fhore the land appeared
to be high, but at the water-fide it was low; and feemed
to be furrounded with reefs that extended two or three
miles into the fea. The coaft is rocky, and the trees
grow almoft to the edge of the water. We hauled
without a reef of rocks, to get round the lee-fide of the
ifland, and at the fame time fent off the boats to found
and examine the coaft. Our people found the trees to
be of different forts, many of them very large, but
all without fruit: on the lee-fide indeed were a few
cocoa-nuts, but not a fingle habitation was to be feen;
nor any kind of animals, either birds or beafts, except
fea fowl. Soon after they had got near the fhore,
feveral canoes came up to them, each having fix or
eight men on board. They appeared to be a robuft,
active people, and were clothed with only a kind of

mat

mat that was wrapped round their waifts. They were armed with large maces or clubs, fuch as Hercules is reprefented with, two of which they fold to our mafter for a few nails and trinkets. Thefe people attempting to fteal the cutter, by hauling her upon the rocks, a gun was fired clofe to one of their faces, the report of which fo terrified them, that they decamped with the utmoft fpeed. When the boats, on their return to the fhip, came near to deep water, they were impeded by points of rocks ftanding up, the whole reef, except in one part, being now dry, and a great fea broke over it. The Indians obferving this followed our boats in their canoes, all along the reef till they got to the breach, and then they rowed back. We fhall here remark, as an extraordinary circumftance, that although no fort of metal was feen on any of the lately difcovered iflands, yet the natives were no fooner poffeffed of a piece of iron than they began to fharpen it, but did not treat copper or brafs in the fame manner. When the boats returned, which was about fix in the evening, the mafter reported, that all within the reef was rocky, but that at two or three places without it there was good anchorage in 18, 14 and 12 fathoms, upon fand and coral. The opening in the reef is 60 fathoms broad, where, if preffed by neceffity, a fhip may anchor, or moor, in eight fathoms; but it will not be fafe to moor with a greater length than half a cable. This ifland the officers called after the name of our commander, Wallis's Ifland. It is fituated in latitude 13 deg. 18 min. fouth, and in 177 deg. weft longitude. Having hoifted in our boats we ran down four miles to leeward, where we lay till the morning; and then, finding that the current had fet us out of fight of the ifland, we made fail to the N. W.

On Friday the 28th, we croffed the line into northern latitude, our longitude being, by obfervation, 187 deg. 24 min. weft from London. During this courfe many birds were feen about the fhip, one of which was caught, and refembled exactly a dove in fize, fhape, and colour. On the 29th, in latitude 2 deg. 50 min. north,

and

and in 188 deg. weft longitude, we croffed a great rippling, which ftretched from the N. E. to the S. W. as far as the eye could reach from the maft-head. We founded, but found no bottom, with a line of 200 fathoms.

On the 3rd of September, being Thurfday, we faw land, which was thought to be two of the Pifcadone Iflands. The latitude of one of them is 11 deg. north, longitude 192 deg. 30 min. weft, and that of the other 11 deg. 20 min. north, longitude 192 deg. 58 min. At five o'clock, A. M. we faw more land in the N. W. and at fix, in the N. E. obferved an Indian prow, fuch as is defcribed in the account of Lord Anfon's voyage. Perceiving fhe made towards us, we hoifted Spanifh colours: but fhe came no nearer than within two miles, at which diftance fhe tacked, ftood to the N. N. W. and was out of fight in a fhort time. On the 7th, we faw a curlew, and on the 9th, we caught a land bird, very much refembling a ftarling. On Thurfday the 17th, we obferved in latitude 15 deg. north, longitude 212 deg. 30 min. W. On the 18th, at fix o'clock, A. M. we defcried the ifland of Saypan, bearing W. by N. diftant ten leagues. In the afternoon we came in fight of Tinian, made fail for the road; and on Saturday the 19th, we came to an anchor in 22 fathoms, fandy ground, at about a mile diftant from the fhore, and half a mile from the reef. We loft no time, after the fhip was fecured, in fending the boats on fhore, to erect tents, and procure fome re-frefhments. In a few hours they returned with oranges, limes, and cocoa-nuts. The furgeon, with all the in-valids, were landed with the utmoft expedition; alfo the fmith's forge, and a cheft of carpenters tools. The Captain and firft lieutenant, both being in a very fickly condition, went likewife afhore, taking with them a mate and 12 men to hunt for cattle in the country. On the 20th, the mafter informed us, that there was a better fituation to the fouthward: we therefore warped the fhip a little way up, and moored with a cable each way. At fix o'clock in the evening, our hunters brought in a fine young bull, of near 500 weight, part of which

we

we kept on shore, and sent the remainder on board, with a good supply of fruit. The amount of the people now on shore, sick and well, was 53. On the 21st, we began the necessary repairs of the ship. The carpenters were set at work to caulk her: all the sails were got on shore, and the sail-makers were employed to mend them: while the armourers were busy on the iron work, and making new chains for the rudder. The sick recovered very fast from the day they first breathed the land air: this, however, was so different from what we found it in Otaheite, that flesh meat, which there kept sweet two days, could here be scarcely kept sweet one. Near the landing-place we saw the remains of many cocoa-nut trees, which had all been wantonly cut down for the fruit; and we were obliged to go three miles into the country to procure a single nut. The hunters also suffered incredible fatigue, going frequently 10 or 12 miles, through one continued thicket, and the cattle were so wild, that it was very difficult to come near them. On this account one party was ordered to relieve another; and Mr. Gore with 14 men were stationed at the north part of the island, where cattle were in much greater plenty. At day-break every morning, a boat went off to bring in what they caught, or killed, and in this island we procured beef, poultry, papaw apples, and all the other refreshments, of which an account is given in Lord Anson's voyage; but which differs in some particulars from the report made of this place by Commodore Byron. During our stay at this place, the ship was laid down by the stern, to get at some of the sheathing which had been much torn; and in repairing the copper, the carpenter discovered and stopped a leak under the lining of the knee of the head, by which we had reason to hope most of the water, that the vessel had lately admitted in foul weather, came in.

On Thursday the 15th of October, all the sick being recovered, our wood and water completed, and the Dolphin made fit for sea, every thing was ordered on board from the shore; and all our men were embarked

3   from

from the watering-place, each having, at leaft, 500 limes; and we had feveral tubs full of the fame fruit on the quarter deck, for every one of the crew to fqueeze into his water what he fhould think fit. On the 16th at day break, we weighed, and failed out of the bay, fending the boats at the fame time to the north end of the ifland, to bring off Mr. Gore and his hunters. At noon they came on board with a fine large bull which they had juft killed. On Wednefday the 21ft, we held on a wefterly courfe; and on the 22nd, Tinian being diftant 277 leagues, we faw feveral birds, particularly three refembling gannets, of the fame kind that we had feen when within about 30 leagues of Tinian. On the 23rd, and the two following days it blew a violent ftorm, and we had much thunder, lightning, rain, and a great fea. The fhip laboured very much: the rudder became again loofe, and fhook the ftern, a defect which we had before experienced, and which we thought had been remedied at Tinian. The gales increafing fplit our gib and main-top-maft ftay-fail: the fore-fail, and mizen fail were torn to pieces; and, having bent others, we wore, and ftood under a reefed fore-fail, and balanced mizen. The effects of the ftorm were more dreaded, as the Dolphin admitted more water than fhe had done at any time during the voyage. Soon after we had got the top-gallant-mafts down upon the deck, and took in the gib-boom, a fea ftruck the fhip upon her bow, and wafhed away the round-houfes, with all the rails of the head, and every thing upon the fore-caftle: neverthelefs, we were forced to carry as much fail as the fhip would bear, being by Lord Anfon's account near the Bafhee Iflands; and by Commodore Byron's, not more than 30 leagues, with a lee-fhore. The inceffant and heavy rain had kept every man on board wet to the fkin for more than two days and two nights, and the fea was breaking continually over the fhip. A mountainous one, on Tuefday the 27th, ftaved all the half ports to pieces on the ftarboard-fide, broke all the iron ftanchions on the gunwale, wafhed the boat off the fkids, and carried many things overboard. We
were,

were, however, this day favoured with a gleam of fun-
fhine; and on the 28th, the weather became more moderate. At none we altered our courfe, fteering S. by
W. and paft one o'clock, we faw the Bafhee Iflands
bearing from S. by E. to S. S. E. diftant fix leagues.
Thefe are all high, but the northernmoft is higher than
the reft. Grafton Ifland, one of them is laid down by
Captain Wallis in the latitude of 21 deg. 4 min. north,
and in 239 deg. weft longitude; but Captain King, in
his relation of the conclufion of the laft voyage of difcovery, afferts that this is erroneous, as the Refolution
and Difcovery fought for them in vain in that pofition;
and Mr. Dalrymple in his maps has laid them down
in 118 deg. 14 min. eaft longitude. At midnight of
this day, the weather being very dark, with fudden
gufts of wind, we miffed one Edmund Morgan, a marine
taylor. It was fuppofed he had fallen overboard, when
under the influence of intoxication, he having found
means to indulge himfelf with more than his allowance.

On Tuefday the 3rd of November, at feven o'clock,
A. M. we difcovered a ledge of breakers, in latitude 11
deg. 8 min. north, diftant three miles. At eleven we
faw another fhoal in latitude 10 deg. 46 min. N. diftant
five miles. At noon we hauled off, being diftant from
them not more than one fourth of a mile. At one
o'clock P. M. we faw fhoal water on our larboard bow,
and, ftanding from it, paffed another ledge of breakers
at two. At three o'clock we had in fight a low fandy
point, in latitude 10 deg. 40 min. N. and in 247 deg.
12 min. weft longitude, to which the name was given
of Sandy Ifle. At five, in 10 deg. 37 min. N. latitude,
and in 247 deg. 16 min. W. long. we faw a fmall ifland,
which was named Small Key. Soon after, in latitude
10 deg. 20 min. N. longitude 247 deg. 24 min. another
larger was feen, and called Long Ifland. On Wednefday, the 4th, we fell in with a fourth ifland, in latitude
10 deg. 10 min. N. and in 247 deg. 40 min. W. longitude. This we named New Ifland. On Saturday, the
7th, having continued our courfe, we paffed through

several ripplings of a current: and this day we saw great quantities of drift wood, cocoa-nut leaves, things like cones of firs, and weeds, which swam in a stream N. E. and S. W.   At noon we observed in latitude 8 deg. 36 min. N. longitude 253 deg. W.   At two o'clock, P. M. we descried from the mast head the island of Condone, which lies in latitude 8 deg. 40 min. N. and in 254 deg. 15 min. west longitude by our reckoning.   On the 8th, we altered our course, and on the 9th, the captain took from the petty officers and fore-mast men all their log and journal books relative to the voyage.   On Friday the 13th, we came in sight of the islands Timoun, Aros, and Pesang.   On Monday the 16th, we again crossed the line into south latitude, in the longitude of 255 deg. W. and soon after we saw two islands, distant seven leagues.   On the 17th, we had tempestuous weather with heavy rain.   The two islands proved to be Pulo Tote, and Pulo Weste; and having made sail till one o'clock P. M. we saw at that time the seven islands. On the 18th, at two o'clock, A. M. a singular incident happened.   At this time the weather was so tempestuous and dark, that we could not see from one part of the ship to the other, we had also heavy squalls and much rain.   During the full violence of the wind, a flash of lightning suddenly discovered a large vessel close aboard of us.   The steersman instantly put the helm a lee, and the Dolphin answering her rudder, just cleared the other ship, and thus escaped the impending destruction, which threatened to bury for ever in the vast deep every circumstance of the voyage.   This was the first ship that had been seen since our parting with the Swallow in April; and it blew so hard, that, not being able to understand any thing that was said, we could not learn to what nation she belonged.   The weather having cleared up at six o'clock, A. M. we saw a sail at anchor in the E. S. E. and at noon came in sight of Pulo Taya, near which we anchored at six in the evening in 15 fathoms, sandy ground.   On the 19th we sailed again, and saw two vessels a-head of us, but, finding we lost much ground, came to an anchor again in 15 fathoms.   On

Friday

Friday the 20th, our small bower anchor parted, and could not be recovered. We immediately took in the cable, and perceived that it had been cut through with the rocks. On the 22nd, at half an hour after six A. M. we saw the coast of Sumatra; and cast anchor in Batavia road on Monday, the 30th.

On Tuesday, the 1st of December, we saluted the governor with 13 guns, which, contrary to the usual custom, he returned with one more, instead of one less, from the fort ; and permission having been obtained to purchase provisions, we were soon supplied with beef, and plenty of vegetables, which the captain ordered to be served immediately : at the same time he told the ship's company, that he would not suffer any liquor to be brought on board, and would severely punish those who made such an attempt, observing, in order to reconcile them to this regulation, that intemperance, particularly in a too free use of arrack, would inevitably destroy them. As a further preservative, the captain would not suffer a man to go on shore, except upon duty, nor were even these permitted to go into the town. At this time 14 sail of Dutch East Indiamen, and a great number of small vessels were laying in this road. Here also we saw the Falmouth, an English man of war, of 50 guns, lying upon the mud in a rotten condition. She touched at this inhospitable place, on her return from Manila, in the year 1762, and was condemned. On examining the stores and ship, every thing was found in so decayed a state, as to be totally useless. The officers and crew of this ship were in a miserable condition. The boatswain through vexation and distress had lost his senses, and was at this time in a Dutch hospital : the carpenter was dying ; and the cook a wounded cripple. The warrant officers belonging to this wreck presented a petition to Captain Wallis, requesting that he would take them on board the Dolphin. They stated, that nothing now remained for them to look after; that they had ten years pay due, which they would gladly relinquish, to be relieved from their present sufferings, as the treatment they received from the Dutch was most in-

human.

human. They were not permitted to spend a single night on shore, and in sickness no one visited them on board: they were besides robbed by the Malays, and in continual dread of being murdered by them. Captain Wallis told them, with the utmost regret and compassion, that the relief they prayed for, it was not in his power to render; that as they had received charge of stores, they must wait for orders from home; but he assured them he would do all in his power to relieve them; and with this remote consolation only, the poor neglected, forgotten, unassisted suffering Englishmen took their leave with tears in their eyes. About six months before Captain Cook touched at Batavia, on board the Endeavour, in 1770, the Dutch thought fit to sell the Falmouth, and all her damaged stores, by public auction, and sent the officers home in their own ships.

The exorbitant prices which were demanded for cordage, and every other article which the Dolphin stood in need of, obliged Captain Wallis to leave the place without procuring any thing of that kind, although his need of them was very great. During our stay at this place, which was eight days, the most salutary regulations were established, in order, if possible, to preserve the crew from the malignity of the climate; and the most beneficial consequences ensued. The ship's company continued sober and healthful the whole time; for, except a sailor who had been afflicted with rheumatic pains ever since we had left the Straits of Magellan, only one man was on the sick list.

On Wednesday the 2nd, our boatswain and carpenter were sent to examine such of the stores, belonging to the Falmouth, as had been landed at Onrust, with orders, that if any were fit for our use they should be purchased. On their return they reported, that all the stores they had surveyed were rotten, except one pair of tacks, which they brought with them: the masts, yards, and cables, were all dropping to pieces; and even the iron work was so rusty that it was worth nothing. They also examined her hulk, and found her in a most
shattered

shattered condition. Many of her ports were washed into one; the stern post was quite decayed; and there was no place in her where a man could be sheltered from the weather. The few unhappy sufferers who remained in her, were in as wretched a state as the ship, being quite broken and wore down, and expecting to be drowned as soon as the monsoon should set in. Among other necessaries, we were in want of an anchor, and of three inch rope for rounding the cables; but the officers, whom the captain sent to procure these articles from the Dutch, as he could not be supplied with them from the Falmouth, reported, that the price which had been demanded for them was so unreasonable, that they had not agreed to give it. On Saturday the 5th, therefore, the captain himself went on shore, for the first time, but found it impossible, after having visited the various store-houses and arsenals, to make a better bargain than his officers would have done. We now suspected that the Dutch thought to take advantage of our apparent necessity, and, supposing we could not depart without what we had offered to purchase, were determined to extort from us more than four times its value. But the captain resolved to make any shift, rather than submit to what he knew to be a shameful imposition, and therefore told them, that he would give them till next Tuesday to come to his terms, at which time, if they did not, he would certainly, if it were possible, set sail without taking the things he had treated for. Accordingly, on the 8th, having heard nothing more about the anchor and rope, we sailed from the road of Batavia, at six o'clock, A. M. On Friday the 11th, at noon, we were between the coasts of Sumatra and Sava, when several of the crew began to be affected with colds and fluxes. On the 12th, a Dutch boat came along side, and some turtles were purchased for the use of our company. At night, being at the distance of two miles from the Java shore, we saw an amazing number of lights on the beach, intended, as we imagined, to draw the fish near thereto. On the 14th, we anchored off Prince's Island, at which place

we

we took in wood and water; and the next morning, the natives came down with turtle, poultry, and hog-deer, which they parted with at moderate rates. Here we lay till the 19th, during which time one of the seamen fell from the main-yard into the barge, which lay along-fide the ship, by which accident he was dreadfully bruised, and many of his bones were broken. In his fall he struck two other men, one of whom was so much hurt, that he continued speechless for a few days, and then died; but the other had only one of his toes broken. While at this island, we buried three more of our hands, among whom was George Lewis, our quarter-master, a diligent, sober man, and exceeding useful, as he spoke both the Spanish and Portuguese languages. On Sunday the 20th, at six o'clock, A. M. we made sail, and from this time to the 24th, many of our people began to complain of an intermitting disorder something like an ague.

A.D. 1768. On Friday the 1st of January, not less than 40 of our crew were down upon the sick list, laid up with fluxes and fevers of the putrid kind, diseases especially fatal on board a ship. The surgeon's mate was of this number; and even those who were appointed to attend the sick, were always taken ill in a day or two after they had been upon that service. The attention which our commander paid to the sick does him honour. He caused a commodious birth to be made for them, which he ordered to be hung with painted canvas, keeping it always clean, and directing it to be washed with vinegar, and fumigated once or twice a day: the water, though well tasted, was constantly ventilated: a large piece of iron was also heated red hot, and quenched in it, before it was given out to be drank: the sick had also wine instead of grog, and salop, or sago, every morning for breakfast: two days in a week they had mutton broth: sometimes a fowl or two on the intermediate days: besides all which restoratives and nourishment, they had plenty of rice and sugar, and frequently malt mashed for them. We believe people in a sickly ship had never so many refreshments

freſhments before. Nor was the ſurgeon leſs aſſiduous in diſcharging, with unremitted attention, the duties of his office; yet, notwithſtanding all theſe advantages, ſickneſs gained ground from the malignant and contagious nature of the fevers with which the men were ſeized. To augment theſe our afflictions, the ſhip grew very leaky, her upper works were looſe, and ſhe made more than three feet water in a watch. However, through the divine bleſſing upon human means, by the 10th, the ſickneſs began to abate, but more than half the crew were ſo feeble, that they could ſcarcely crawl about. This day we ſaw many tropic birds about the ſhip, and on the 17th, we obſerved ſeveral albatroſſes, and caught ſome bonettas. On the 24th, in latitude 33 deg. 40 min. ſouth, longitude 328 deg. 17 min. weſt, we encountered a violent ſtorm, which tore the main-top-ſail to pieces. A dreadful ſea broke over the ſhip, by which the ſtarboard rudder-chain was demoliſhed, and ſeveral of the booms were waſhed overboard; yet during the ſtorm we obſerved a number of birds; and after it ſubſided all hands were employed in drying the bedding, and in repairing our ſhattered ſails. On the 27th, we were by obſervation in latitude 34 deg. 16 min. and in longitude 323 deg. 30 min. weſt, and on the 30th, at ſix o'clock in the evening, we ſaw land.

February the 4th, being Thurſday, we arrived at the Cape of Good Hope, and came to an anchor in Table Bay: in the run to which place from Prince's Iſland, the Dolphin had got 3 deg. to the eaſtward of her reckoning. We found riding in the bay a Dutch commodore, with 16 ſail of Dutch Eaſt Indiamen, a French Eaſt India ſhip, and the Admiral Watſon, Captain Griffin, an Eaſt India packet-boat for Bengal. The captain having ſent the uſual compliments to the governor, he received our officer with great civility, aſſuring him, that we were welcome to all ſuch refreſhments and aſſiſtance that the cape afforded, and that he would return our ſalute with the ſame number of guns. We therefore ſaluted the governor with 13

guns,

guns, and he returned the full complement. Admiral Watfon faluted us with eleven guns, and we returned nine: the Frenchman faluted us with nine guns, and we returned feven. We now loft no time in procuring frefh meat and vegetables for the ufe of the fick. The furgeon was fent on fhore to hire lodgings for them; but as the rate demanded was two fhillings a day, and as the fmall-pox, (which many of our crew had not had) raged furioufly in almoft every houfe in Cape Town, Captain Wallis obtained permiffion of the governor, to erect tents on a fpacious plain called Green Point, about two miles diftant from the town, where the invalids were fent during the day, and every evening returned to the fhip. At the fame time pofitive orders were given, that no liquors fhould be fent to the fhip, or the tents; that no one fhould be permitted to go into the town; and that extra provifions fhould be procured for thofe who were moft reduced by ficknefs. Much relief was found the very firft day of their be-ing on fhore; on their return in the evening, at fix o'clock, they feemed to be greatly refrefhed; and a general recovery rapidly took place. Captain Wallis being himfelf extremely ill, was put on fhore, and car-ried eight miles up the country, where he continued the whole time that the fhip remained here, and when fhe was ready for fea, he returned on board, but without having received the leaft benefit. Every man who was able to do any kind of duty, was now employed in the neceffary repairs of the fhip; the fails were all un-bent, the yards and top-mafts ftruck, the forge was fet up, the carpenters were engaged in caulking, the fail-makers in mending the fails, the cooper in repairing the cafks, the people in overhauling the rigging, and the boats in filling the water. The heavy work being nearly done by Wednefday the 10th, feveral of the men, who had been feized with the fmall-pox, were permitted to vifit the town; and thofe who had not been touched with that malignant diftemper, were allowed to take daily walks in the country; and as they did not abufe this liberty, it was continued to them as long as

                                                              the

the ship remained at the cape. At this place, the neceffaries that could not be bought of the Dutch at Batavia, were purchafed reafonably; and frefh water was
procured by diftillation, with a view of convincing the
Dutch, how eafily water might be procured at fea.
Nothing can be more ftrongly contrafted, than the
conduct of the Dutch at Batavia, and at the Cape.
The Afiatic Dutch can fcarcely be induced to render
the common offices of humanity to fuch of their
fpecies who refort to them to be faved from the jaws
of death, and their rapacity knows no bounds: the
African Dutch are difpofed to adminifter every comfort to thofe who want relief, and in doing this no ex-
tortion is practifed. The principle upon which the
people at each fettlement act is eafily to be traced: at
the firft place, they fufpect every foreign European fhip
which enters their port as endangering a fecure poffeffion of the moft valuable branch of their commerce;
in the latter, the wealth of the inhabitants, as well as
the emoluments of government, are derived from the
offices of humanity which they difcharge. This day,
at five o'clock, A. M. we put 56 gallons of falt-water
into the ftill; at feven it began to run, and, in little
more than five hours, afforded us 42 gallons of frefh
water, at an expence of nine pounds of wood, and 69
pounds of coals. What we drew off had no ill tafte,
nor, as we had often experienced, any hurtful quality.
Captain Wallis never once put the fhip's company to an
allowance of water, during the whole voyage, always
ufing the ftill, when we were reduced to 45 tons, and
preferving the rain water with the utmoft diligence;
nor would he permit water to be fetched away at pleafure; but the officer of the watch had orders to ferve
out a fufficient quantity to thofe who might want it
for tea, coffee, grog, and provifions of any kind. On
Thurfday the 26th, we had nearly got on board all our
wood and water; all our hands, and the tents were
brought off from the fhore; and, upon a general mufter,
we had the happinefs to find, that in our whole company, three only were incapable of doing duty, and that
we had loft only the fame number, fince our departure

from Batavia, by ficknefs. This day the captain came on board; and on the 27th and 28th, after having ftowed all our bread, a confiderable quantity of ftraw, and above 30 fheep for fea ftores, we unmoored, and lay waiting for a favourable wind.

On Thurfday, the 3rd of March, we got under fail. From many obfervations we had an opportunity of making at Green point, we determined Table Bay to lie in latitude 34 deg. 2 min. fouth, and in 18 deg. 8 min. eaft longitude from Greenwich. On the 7th, we were in latitude 29 deg. 33 min. fouth, longitude 347 deg. 38 min. from London. Oa Saturday the 13th, we found a day had been loft by having failed weftward 360 deg. from the meridian of London; we therefore called the latter part of this day, Monday the 14th of March. On Wednefday the 16th, at fix o'clock, P. M. we came in fight of the ifland of St. Helena, diftant 14 leagues; and on the 17th, at nine o'clock, A. M. we caft anchor in the bay. We found riding here the Northumberland Indiaman, Captain Milford, who faluted us with 11 guns, and we returned nine. All our boats being hoifted ont as foon as poflible, we fent one party to fill our empty cafks with water, and others to gather purflain, of which there is great plenty. The captain going on fhore was faluted with 13 guns from the fort, which compliment we returned. The governor and principal gentlemen of the ifland met him upon landing; and having conducted him to the fort, requefted that he would make that place his refidence, during his ftay; but our water being completed, and the fhip made ready for fea, on the 18th, Captain Wallis returned on board; upon which we unmoored, at five o'clock, P. M. got under way, and fet fail for our native country, happy old England. On Wednefday the 23rd, at five o'clock, A. M. we had in view the ifland of Afcenfion; and at eight a fail was feen to the eaftward, which brought to, and hoifted a jack at her main-top-maft head; but we had no fooner fhewed our colours than fhe went about, and ftood in for the land again. Paffing by the N. E. fide of the ifland, we
looked

looked into the bay, but feeing no veffel there, and it blowing a ftiff gale, we held on our courfe. On Monday the 28th, we croffed, for the fourth time, the equinoxial line, getting again into north latitude.

On Wednefday the 13th of April, we paffed a great quantity of gulph weed, and on Tuefday the 19th, perceiving the water to be difcoloured, we founded, but could find no bottom. On the 24th, at five o'clock, A. M. we came in fight of Cape Pico, bearing N. N. E. diftant 18 leagues; and at noon, by obfervation, we found Fyal to lie in latitude 38 deg. 20 min. north, and in 28 deg. 30 min. weft longitude from London.

On Wednefday the 11th of May, we faw the Savage Sloop of war Captain Hammond, in chace of a floop, at which he fired feveral guns. On this we alfo fired, and brought her to. She belonged to Liverpool, was called the Jenny, and commanded by Robert Chriftian. Captain Hammond informed us, that when he firft faw her, fhe was in company with an Irifh wherry, and that as foon as they difcovered him, they took different ways: the wherry hauled the wind, and the Jenny bore away. At firft he ftood after the wherry, but finding he gained no ground, he bore away after the Jenny, who probably would likewife have outfailed him, and efcaped, had we not brought her to. She was laden with tea, brandy and other goods from Rofcoe in France. Her brandy and tea were in fmall kegs and bags. Captain Wallis detained her, in order to her being fent to England, as from all appearances, which were ftrongly againft her, we judged Mifs Jenny to be a fmuggler; for though failing a S. W. courfe, fhe pretended to be bound to Bergen in Norway. On the 13th, at five o'clock, A. M. the iflands of Scilly appeared; and on Thurfday the 19th, Captain Wallis landed at Haftings in Suffex. On the following day this voyage was happily completed, and the circumnavigation of the globe fuccefsfully accomplifhed; for on Friday the 20th, the Dolphin came to an anchor in the Downs, having been 637 days from the time that fhe took her departure from Plymouth Sound. As the main end propofed by this

6 O 2 arduous

arduous and hazardous undertaking was to make difcoveries, Captain Wallis, when navigating thofe parts
of the South Sea, which were imperfectly known, that
nothing might efcape him, conftantly laid to every
night, and made fail only in the day; notwithftanding
which confiderable delay in failing, he accomplifhed his
voyage a month and a day fooner than his predeceffor
had done in the fame circumnavigation. The ill health
which the captain complains of almoft through the
voyage, may ferve as a fufficient apology for the want
of a more copious information in his narrative, concerning the places which he vifited, particularly Otaheite, the Indian name of which he does not mention.
In the relations of this commander, we fee little of that
watchful attention, curiofity, and ardent defire, to
" catch the manners living as they rife," which were
poffeffed by Captain Carteret, and which appear fo
eminently confpicuous in Captain Cook, wherever he is,
and in whatever manner he is engaged; yet in juftice to
the refpectable character of Captain Wallis, we muft
obferve, that he conftantly and indefatigably purfued
the grand object of his voyage; and if we confider his
nautical abilities, his amiable philanthropy, apparent in
his conduct and behaviour to thofe under his command,
together with his judicious obfervations as a mariner,
at the feveral ports, and the various fituations of the
Dolphin at fea, we cannot but think he is defervedly
worthy of being placed in the firft rank of our able and
fkilful circumnavigators.

A NEW

A NEW, AUTHENTIC, REMARKABLE, and ENTERTAINING

HISTORY and NARRATIVE, of

A VOYAGE Round the WORLD;

UNDERTAKEN and PERFORMED,

By that NEGLECTED and GALLANT OFFICER,

Capt. PHILIP CARTERET, Efq.

In his Majefty's Sloop the SWALLOW;

During the Years 1766, 1767, 1768, and 1769.

CONTAINING,

A lively Defcription of the generous Nature of Captain Carteret; the Inattention which was fhewn to his fitting out; and his fcanty Supply of Neceffaries; together with an affecting and complete Account of the perilous Situation of the Swallow, on the weftern Extremity of the Magellanic Straits; who, notwithftanding her bad Sailing, dangerous Situations, and fhattered Condition, without any Marks of Defpondency from her Company, continued her Voyage, after her Separation from the Dolphin, and accomplifhed the Circumnavigation of the Globe; having fet fail from Plymouth Sound Auguft the 22nd, 1766—Parted from her Confort, the Dolphin, on the 11th of April, 1767—and anchored at Spithead on the 20th of March 1769—The whole being drawn up from authentic Journals and private Papers, and illuftrated with a rich Variety of Communications from Captain JOHN HOGG, late of the Royal Navy.

INTRO-

INTRODUCTION.

CAPTAIN Philip Carteret, the history of whose voyage round the world we are about writing, had sailed with Commodore Byron on his expedition, and soon after his return, was appointed to the command of the Swallow Sloop, destined to accompany the Dolphin, and Prince Frederick Store-ship. The Captain having received his commission, bearing date July the 1st, 1766, was ordered to fit out the Swallow, which then lay at Chatham, with all possible expedition. This gallant officer describes emphatically, and in a most feeling manner, like his predecessor, Commodore Anson, the inattention which was shewn to his fitting out. It had been hinted to him, that he was to go out in the Dolphin, but the amazing disparity of the two ships, and the distinguished superiority in the equipment of one to the other, induced him to conclude, that they could not be intended for the same duty; for whilst the Dolphin was furnished with every thing requisite for a long and dangerous navigation, the neglected Swallow Sloop had only a scanty supply of necessaries. Besides, she was an old vessel, having been built 30 years, and was by no means fit for a long voyage. Upon her bottom was only a slight thin sheathing, which was not even filled with nails to supply the want of a covering, that would more effectually keep out the worm. Captain Carteret observing the Swallow to be totally unprovided with many things, which particular situations might render absolutely necessary for her preservation, applied for a forge, some iron, a small skiff, and several other things; not one of which articles he could obtain; but was told, that the vessel and her equipment were very fit for the service she was to perform; though, at the same time, she had not a single trinket or toy put on board her, to enable her commander to procure refreshments from the Indians of the Southern Hemisphere. Add to all this, there was a deficiency of junk on board, an article essentially necessary in every voyage;

and

and when application was made for this at Plymouth, the captain was told, that a sufficient quantity was put on board the Dolphin. Thus circumstanced, it cannot be even supposed, that a commander of Captain Carteret's discernment, would think of being a consort with the Dolphin in her hazardous expedition; and we cannot but credit the declaration of this brave officer, when he tells us, he was therefore confirmed in his opinion, that if the Dolphin was to go round the world, it could never be intended that the Swallow should go farther than Falkland's Islands, where the Jason, a fine frigate, which was, like the Dolphin sheathed with copper, and amply equipped, would, in the captain's opinion, supply her place. Nothing can place a commander of seamen in a more respectable point of view, than his appearing to possess equanimity and fortitude under the most disheartening circumstances. Numerous and great as these were, Captain Carteret resolved to serve his country in the line of his profession; and therefore proceeded to Plymouth Sound with the Swallow, in company with the Dolphin, under the command of Captain Wallis, and the Prince Frederick Store-ship, commanded by Lieutenant James Brine. While the Swallow lay at this place, not being yet acquainted with his destination, Captain Carteret represented to Captain Wallis his being in want of junk, who sent him 500 weight, a quantity so small and insufficient, that we were soon reduced to the disagreeable necessity of cutting off some of the cables to save our rigging.

CHAP. I.

The Swallow sails in Company with the Dolphin, and Frederick Store-ship, from Plymouth Sound, Friday the 22nd of August, 1766—Passage from thence to the Island of Madeira—Proceeds on her Voyage to the Straits of Magellan—And anchors off Cape Virgin Mary—The bad Condition

*Condition of the Swallow in her Navigation through the
Straits—With great Difficulty reaches Port Famine—
Is obliged to continue her Voyage, after her Commander
had requested of Captain Wallis to alter her Destination
—On the 11th of April, 1767, is separated from her
Consort, the Dolphin, without the least Hope of seeing
her during the Remainder of the Voyage—The gallant
Behaviour of Captain Carteret in this alarming Situa-
tion—The Run of the Swallow from the western Entrance
of the Strait of Magellan to the Island of Masafuero—
Incidents and Transactions whilst the Ship lay off this
Island—Observations—She departs from Masafuero and
makes Queen Charlotte's Island—A Description of these
and their Inhabitants—An obstinate Skirmish with the
Natives of Egmont Island described, with an Account of
their Country, Canoes, and Weapons.*

A. D. 1766.   ON Thursday the 21st of August, our
ship's company on board the Swal-
low received two months pay; and the next day,
Friday the 22nd, we weighed and made sail, with the
Dolphin and Frederick Store-ship. We proceeded together without any material occurrence, till the 7th of
September, when we came to an anchor in the road of
Madeira. On Tuesday the 9th, nine of our prime seamen left the ship secretly, and swam on shore naked.
They left behind them all their clothes; and took only
their money, which they had secured in handkerchiefs
that were tied round their waists. They proceeded together till they came very near the surf, when one of
them, somewhat terrified at the dashing waves, which
here break very high on the shore, returned to the
Swallow, and was taken on board, but the rest bolily
pushed through. While Captain Carteret was writing
to the consul, entreating his assistance to recover those
brave but imprudent fellows, whose loss would have
been severely felt, he received a message, by which he
was informed, that they had been found by the natives
naked on shore; that they had been taken into custody,
but would be delivered up to his order. A boat was
instantly

3

inftantly difpatched to bring them on board, where they cut a moft ridiculous figure, and feemed heartily afhamed at what they had done. When our noble captain came upon deck, he appeared pleafed at feeing the marks of contrition in their countenances, and afked in the mild tone of humanity, what could be their reafons and motives for quitting the fhip, and deferting the fervice of their country, at the rifk of being devoured by fharks, or dafhed to pieces by the furf againft the fhore. To this they replied, that though they had indeed, at fuch rifks, ventured to fwim on fhore, yet they had never entertained a thought of deferting the fhip, which they were determined to ftand by as long as fhe could fwim; but that being well affured they were going a long voyage, and none being able to tell who might live or who might die, they thought it hard to be deprived of an opportunity of fpending their own money, and therefore refolved once more to get a fkinful of liquor, and then to have fwam back to the fhip, which they expected to have done before they were miffed. The captain having determined fecretly not to inflict the punifhment by which they feemed moft heartily willing to expiate their fault, did not fcrutinize feverely their apology, obferving only, that with a fkinful of liquor they would have been in a very unfit condition to fwim through the furf to the fhip; and, hoping they would expofe their lives only upon more important occafions, and that he fhould in future have no caufe to complain of their conduct, upon thefe conditions, he would for this time be fatisfied with that fhame and regret, which he perceived plainly imprinted on their countenances, and which indicated a proper fenfe of their mifbehaviour; at the fame time, he advifed them to put on their clothes and turn in, being confident they wanted reft; adding, that as good fwimmers might probably be wanted in the courfe of our voyage, he was very glad that he knew to whom he might apply. Captain Carteret endeared himfelf very much to thefe men by this act of tendernefs, and he had fcarcely difmiffed them when he was infinitely gratified by the murmur of fatisfaction which inftantly ran through the fhip's company; and the future conduct of the offenders amply repaid his well timed lenity, there being no fervice, during all the toils and dangers of the voyage, which they did not perform, with a zeal and alacrity that were much to their honour, and our advantage, as an example to the reft.

Friday the 12th of September, we failed out of the road of Madeira; and were now convinced, we were fent upon a fervice, to which the Swallow and her equipment were by no means equal; for this day our commander received from Captain Wallis a copy of his inftructions, who alfo appointed, in cafe of a feparation, Port Famine, in the Strait of Magellan, to be the place of rendezvous. We continued our voyage, without any material incident, till we reached Cape Virgin Mary, where we faw the Patagonians, a full account of whom has been given in our hiftory of the two expeditions performed by Commodore Byron and Captain Wallis, in their circuit round the world; and as the particulars in the narrative before us are the fame, it will be needlefs to recite them. With much labour, and at no inconfiderable rifk, (for we could but feldom make the Swallow tack, without a boat to tow her round) we anchored in Port Famine, on the 28th of December; where we unhung our rudder, and having made it fomewhat broader, we hoped to obtain an advantage in working the fhip, but in this particular we were entirely difappointed.

A.D. 1767. On Tuefday the 17th of February, after having encountered many difficulties and dangers, we fteered into Ifland Bay; and at this place our commander, in a letter to Captain Wallis, fet forth in affecting language, the ill condition of the Swallow, requefting of him to confider what was beft for the king's fervice, whether fhe fhould be difmiffed, or continue the voyage; to which Captain Wallis returned for anfwer, that as the Lords of the Admiralty had ordered the Swallow on this fervice, in conjunction with

the

3

the Dolphin, he did not think himself at liberty to alter the deftination of the former. In confequence of this reply, founded only on the fingle opinion of Captain Wallis, we continued to navigate the ftrait in company with the Dolphin; and as our captain had paffed it before, we were ordered to keep a-head and to lead the way, with liberty to anchor and weigh when and where we thought proper; " but (to ufe Captain Carteret's own words) perceiving, fays he, that the bad failing of the Swallow would fo much retard the Dolphin, as probably to make her lofe the feafon for getting into high fouthern latitudes, and defeat the intention of the voyage, I propofed to Captain Wallis, that he fhould lay the Swallow up in fome cove or bay, and that I fhould attend and affift him with her boats till the ftrait fhould be paffed, which would probably be in much lefs time than if he continued to be retarded by my fhip; and I urged as an additional advantage that he might complete not only his ftock of provifions and ftores, but his company out of her, and then fend her back to England, with fuch of his crew as ficknefs had rendered unfit for the voyage; propofing alfo, that in my way home, I would examine the eaftern coaft of Patagonia, or attempt fuch difcoveries as he fhould think proper. If this was not approved, and my knowledge of the South Seas was thought neceffary to the fuccefs of the voyage, I offered to go with him on board the Dolphin, and give up the Swallow to be commanded by his firft lieutenant, whofe duty I would perform during the reft of the voyage, or to make the voyage myfelf in the Dolphin, if he would take the Swallow back to England:" but Captain Wallis was ftill of opinion, " that the voyage fhould be profecuted by the two fhips jointly, purfuant to the orders that had been given;" but he affured Captain Carteret, at the fame time, that, " in confideration of the very dangerous condition of the Swallow, the Dolphin fhould continue to keep company with her as long as it was poffible, waiting her time, and attending her motions." The generous nature of Captain Carteret our readers will infer, from his not

availing

availing himſelf of this aſſurance, when ſtating the conduct of his ſuperior officer in ſo trying an inſtance. By
this time the Swallow was become ſo foul, that with all
the ſails ſhe could ſet, it was not in her power to make
ſo much way as the Dolphin, not even when the latter
had only her top-ſails and a reef in them: however,
under theſe trying circumſtances, we continued with
our companion till the 10th of April, on which day the
weſtern entrance of the ſtrait was open, and the great
South Sea in ſight. We had hitherto, agreeable to
orders, kept a-head, but now, the Dolphin being nearly
abreaſt of us, ſhe ſet her fore-ſail, which ſoon carried
her a-head of us, and by nine o'clock in the evening ſhe
was out of ſight, for when the day cloſed ſhe ſhewed no
lights. A fine eaſtern breeze blew at this time, of
which, during the night, we made every poſſible uſe,
by carrying all our ſmall ſails, even to the top-gallant
ſtudding-ſails, by which we were expoſed to great
danger.

On Saturday the 11th, notwithſtanding every means
had been uſed to come up with the fugitive, yet ſuch
was the diſparity of ſailing between the two ſhips, that,
at day-break, the top-ſails of the Dolphin could only be
ſeen above the horizon; but we could perceive ſhe had
ſtudded-ſails ſets; and at nine o'clock we entirely loſt
ſight of her, judging ſhe might be then clear of the
ſtrait's mouth. The Swallow was now under the land;
and in this bad ſailing, ill provided ſhip, having neither
a forge, nor a ſingle trinket on board, was our neglected,
but gallant officer, deſtined to proceed over the vaſt
expanſe of the great Southern Ocean; yet amidſt all
theſe diſcouraging circumſtances, no ſigns of deſpon-
dency were viſible among our people, whom the captain encouraged by telling them, that though the Dolphin was the beſt ſhip, he did not doubt but he ſhould
find more than equivalent advantages in their courage,
ability, and good conduct. Such an aſcendency over
his ſeamen, is a plain proof, how much they revered,
confided in, and loved him. From this day, we gave
up all hope of ſeeing our conſort again till we ſhould
arrive

arrived in England, no plan of operation having been settled, nor any place of rendezvous appointed, as had been done from England to the strait. At noon, when abreast of Cape Pillar, a strong gale from S. W. obliged us to take down our small sails, and haul close to the wind; soon after which we had the mortification to find, that when we had made two boards, we could not weather the land on either tack. The gale increased, driving before it a hollow swell, and a fog came on, with violent rain, which compelled us to get close under the south-shore. We now sent out our boat in search of Tuesday's Bay, which is said by Sir John Narborough to lie about four leagues within the strait, or to find out any other good anchorage. At five o'clock, P. M. we could not see the land, notwithstanding its mountainous height, though within half a mile of it; and, at six, it was so dark that we could not see half the ship's length. Being concerned for the safety of our boat, we put out lights, made false fires, and fired a gun every half hour; and at last she reached the ship, but had made no discovery either of Tuesday's Bay, or any other anchoring place. During the remainder of the night we made sail, endeavouring to keep near the south shore. The next day, being the 12th, as soon as it was light, the boat was sent out again to explore the south shore for an anchoring place; and at five o'clock, P. M. when we almost despaired of her returning in time, saw her sounding a bay, and stood in after her. The master said, that we might here safely cast anchor, which we did about six o'clock, and then the captain retired to take some rest. In a few minutes after, he was disturbed by an universal shout and tumult among the people upon deck, and the noise of those below running to join them. When Captain Carteret came upon deck, the general cry was, the Dolphin! the Dolphin! in a transport of surprize and joy: but this delusive appearance soon vanished, and proved to be only water forced up, and whirled in the air by a gust of wind. The people were for a few minutes dejected by their disappointment, but before the captain went

down,

down, he had the pleasure to see a return of their usual fortitude and cheerfulness. The little bay where we now lay, is about three leagues E. by S. from Cape Pillar, and bears S. by E. four leagues from the island which Sir John Narborough called Westminster Hall. The western point of this bay has a resemblance to a perpendicular oblong square, like the wall of a house; within its entrance are three islands, and within these a very good harbour, with anchorage in between 25 and 30 fathoms, bottom soft mud. We anchored without the islands, the passage on each side of them being not more than a cable's length wide. Our small cove is about two cables length broad; and in the inner part is from 16 to 18 fathoms, but where we lay it is deeper. The landing is every where good, with plenty of wood, water, muscles, and wild geese. As a current sets continually into it, our captain is of opinion, that it has another communication with the sea to the south of Cape Defeada. Our master reported, that he went up it four miles in a boat, and could not then be above four miles from the western ocean, yet he still saw a wide entrance to the S. W. Here we rode out a very hard gale of wind, and, the ground being very uneven, we expected our cables to be cut in two every minute, yet when we weighed, to our great surprize, they did not appear to have been rubbed in any part, though we found it very difficult to heave them clear of the rocks. From the north shore of the western end of the Strait of Magellan, the land, which is the western coast of Patagonia, runs nearly N. and S. being a group of broken islands, among which are those laid down by Sharp, by the name of the Duke of York's Islands. They are indeed placed by him at a considerable distance from the coast, but if there had been many islands in that situation, the Dolphin, the Tamar, or the Swallow must have seen them. Till we came into this latitude, we had tolerable weather, and little or no current in any direction, but when northward of 48 deg. we had a current setting strongly to the north, so that probably we then opened the great bay, which is said to be 90 leagues deep.

deep. Here we found a prodigious swell from the N. W. and the winds generally blew from the same quarter.

On Wednesday the 15th, we once more got again abreast of Cape Pillar; but between five and six o'clock, A. M. just as we opened Cape Deseada, the wind suddenly shifting, and its excessive violence, produced a sea so dreadfully hollow, that we were in the utmost danger of sinking; yet we could not shorten sail, it being necessary to carry all we could spread, for fear of running foul of some rocky islands, which, in Narborough's voyage, are called the islands of Direction; nor could we now go back into the strait, without the danger of running foul of a lee-shore, towards which the ship settled very fast, notwithstanding our utmost efforts. Thus circumstanced, we were obliged to stave the water-casks on and between the decks, in order that she might carry better sail, and by this expedient we escaped the threatened destruction. We now got into the open sea, after a very providential deliverance, for had the wind again shifted, the Swallow must have been unavoidably lost. Having got clear of the Strait of Magellan, we steered to the northward along the coast of Chili, intending to make the island of Juan Fernandes, or Masafuero, that we might increase our stock of water, which at this time amounted only to between four and five and twenty tons, a quantity not sufficient for so long a voyage as was probably before us. On the 16th, the wind, which had hitherto been favourable, on a sudden shifted, and continued contrary till Saturturday the 18th. We had now sailed nearly 100 leagues from the straits mouth when our latitude was 48 deg. 39 min. south, and our longitude, by account, 4 deg. 33 min. west from Cape Pillar. From this time to the 8th of May, the wind continued unfavourable, and blew an incessant storm, with sudden gusts still more violent, accompanied at intervals, with dreadful thunder, lightning, rain, and hail. In our passage along this coast we saw abundance of sea birds; among which were two sorts, one like a pigeon, of a dark brown colour,

colour, called by feamen the Cape of Good Hope hen, and fometimes the black gull; the other pintado birds, which are prettily fpotted with black and white, and conftantly on the wing; but they appear frequently as if walking on the water, like the peterels; and thefe our failors call Mother Carey's Chickens. During nine days we experienced an uninterrupted courfe of dangers, fatigues and misfortunes. The Swallow worked and failed very ill, the weather was dark and tempeftuous; and the boats, which the exigencies of the fhip kept conftantly employed, were in continual danger of being loft, as well by the gales which blew conftantly, as by the fudden gufts which rufhed frequently upon us, with a violence that can fcarcely be conceived: thofe off the land were fo boifterous, that not daring to fhew any canvafs, the fhip lay to under her bare poles, and the water at times was torn up, and whirled round in the air, much higher than the mafts heads. This diftrefs was the more fevere, by its being unexpected; for Captain Carteret had experienced very different weather in thofe parts, when he accompanied Commodore Byron: it was then the latter end of April when he was near this coaft, fo that this change of climate could not be owing to a change of feafon. On Friday the 1ft of May, the wind fhifted from the N. W. to the S. W. and brought the fhip up with her head right againft the vaft fea, which the N. W. wind had raifed; for about an hour it blew, if poffible, ftronger than ever; and at every pitch the Swallow made, the end of her bowfprit was under water, and the furge broke over the forecaftle as far aft as the main maft, in the fame manner as it would have broke over a rock, fo that there was the greateft reafon to apprehend fhe would founder. With all her defects we muft acknowledge fhe was a good fea boat: if fhe had not been fo, it would have been impoffible for her to have outlived this ftorm, in which, as on feveral other occafions, we experienced the benefit of the bulk-heads, which we had fixed on the fore-part of the half deck, and to the after part of the fore-caftle. On the 3rd, at day-break

we

London: Published as the Act directs, by Alex.ʳ Hogg, on the Kings Arms, N.º 16, Paternoster Row.

A BRANCH *of the* BREAD FRUIT TREE,
with the FRUIT.

we found the rudder chain broken, which made us, as we had often done, moft feelingly regret the want of a forge. However we made beft fhift we could; and on the 4th, the weather being more moderate, we mended the fails that had been fplit, and repaired our rigging. On the 5th, a hurricane from the N. by W. and N. N. W. brought us again under our courfes, and the fhip was toffed about with fuch violence that we had no command of her. In this ftorm two of our chain-plates were broken, and we continued toiling in a confufed hollow fea till midnight. On the 6th, at two o'clock, A. M. we were taken right a-head by a furious fquall at weft, which was very near carrying all by the board, before we could get the fhip round. With this gale we ftood north, and the carpenters, in the forenoon, fixed new chain-plates in the place of thofe which had been broken; and on this occafion we could not refrain from again lamenting the want of a forge and iron. We held on our courfe till the 7th, when, at eight o'clock, A. M. the wind returned to its old quarter, the N. W. attended with unfettled weather.

On Friday the 8th, the wind having come to the fouth, we were favoured with a fine day, being the firft we had feen fince we took our departure from the Straits of Magellan. At noon we obferved in latitude 38 deg. 39 min. fouth, and were about 5 deg. to the weftward of Cape Pillar. On the 9th, we were in fight of the ifland of Mafafuero; and on the 10th, made that of Juan Fernandes. In the afternoon, we failed round the north end of it, and opened Cumberland Bay. We were furprized, not knowing that the Spaniards had fortified this ifland, to fee a confiderable number of men about the beach, alfo a houfe and four pieces of cannon near the water fide; and upon the fide of the hill, about 300 yards farther from the fea, a fort with Spanifh colours flying. We faw fcattered round it, and on different parts of the ifland, more than 20 houfes, and much cattle feeding on the brow of the hills, which feemed to be cultivated, many fpots being divided by enclofures from the reft. We faw alfo two large

No. 33.   6 Q   boats

boats lying on the beach. The fort, which is faced
with stone, has 18 or 20 embrasures, and within it a
long house, which we supposed to be barracks for the
garrison. The wind blew in such violent gusts out of
the bay, as to prevent our getting very near it; and, in
the captain's opinion, it is impossible to work a ship
into this bay, when the wind blows hard from the south.
We now stood to the westward, and were followed by
one of the boats, which put off from the shore, and
rowed towards us; but she soon returned, on observing
that the heavy squalls made us lie at a considerable distance from the land. Having opened west-bay, we observed on the east part, what we took for a guard-
house, and two pieces of cannon on carriages near it.
We now wore, and stood again for Cumberland Bay,
and the boat again put off towards us, but night coming
on, we lost sight of her. As we had only English
colours on board we hoisted none, as we could not suppose the Spaniards well disposed to receive English
visitants. Thus disappointed of the refreshments, of
which we stood in the most pressing need, our captain
thought it more adviseable to proceed to the neighbouring island of Masafuero, where we arrived on Tuesday the 12th, and on Friday the 15th, chose our station
on the eastern-side, anchoring in the same place where
Commodore Byron lay in the Dolphin, about two years
before. On the 16th, we were driven from our moorings and kept out at sea all night. In the morning the
cutter was sent for water, and the ship got near the
shore, where she soon received several casks, and dispatched the cutter back for more. The long boat was
likewise appointed to this service, as well as to carry
provisions to those on shore. In the afternoon the boats
being observed running along the shore, the ship followed and took them in, but not without their sustain-
ing so much damage by the violence of the sea, that
the carpenters were obliged to work all night in repairing them.

On Sunday the 17th, the lieutenant, Mr. Erasmus
Gower, was sent again with the cutter to procure water,

I   and

and the furf being very great, three of the feamen fwam
on fhore with the empty cafks, in order to fill them,
and bring them back to the boat; but the furf foon
after rofe fo high, and broke with fuch fury on the
fhore, as rendered it utterly impracticable for them to
return. A very dark and tempeftuous night fucceeded; the poor fellows were ftark naked, and cut off from
all means of procuring affiftance from the boat, which,
to efcape the fury of a gathering ftorm, was obliged to
return to the fhip, into which it was fafely received but
the minute before the impending ftorm rufhed forth,
by which, had fhe been upon the water, fhe muft have
been inevitably funk, and every foul on board perifhed.
The three naked, defencelefs mariners on fhore, during
the night, were doomed to " bide the pelting of the
pitilefs ftorm," without clothes, without fhelter, without
food, and without fire. To augment their diftrefs, a
party was then on fhore, and had erected a tent; but
the darknefs of the night, and the impenetrable thicknefs of the woods, cut off all poffibility of receiving
fuccour from them. Being thus reduced to an entire
ftate of nature, without the habits which render that
ftate fupportable, in order to preferve a living portion
of animal heat, they lay one upon another, each man
alternately placing himfelf between the other two. At
the firft dawn of light, they made their way along the
fhore, in fearch of the tent; an attempt to penetrate
through the country being confidered as fruitlefs. In
this circuit they were frequently ftopped by high, fteep,
bluff points, which they were obliged to fwim round
at a confiderable diftance; for, if they had not taken a
fufficient compafs, they would have been dafhed to
pieces againft the rocks, in avoiding which they were
every moment in danger of being devoured by fharks.
About ten o'clock in the morning they joined their
comrades, being almoft perifhed with hunger and cold.
They were received with the moft cordial welcome,
their fhipmates fharing with them their cloaths and
provifions; and it is hard to fay of which they ftood
moft in need. On the 18th, they were brought on

board the ship, where the captain gave orders, that they should have all proper refreshments, and remain in their hammocks the whole night; and the next day we had the pleasure to find they were perfectly hearty, nor did they suffer any future inconvenience from the extreme hardships they had gone through. These men were three of the nine honest fellows, who had swam naked from the ship, when she lay in the road of Madeira, to get a skinful of liquor. Than which nothing could paint more strongly the general character of English sailors, which may perhaps be defined to consist in a contempt of danger, a love of strong liquor, and a girl, and an aversion to be possessed of any coin, when embarked on a long voyage. This day the weather was moderate, and in the evening we were within half a mile of the anchoring ground from whence we had been driven; but the wind suddenly failing, and a current making against us, we could not reach it. During the whole night we had a perfect calm, so that in the morning of the 19th, we found the current and the swell had driven us no less than nine miles from the land; but a breeze springing up, we kept off and on near the shore, and in the interim sent the cutter for water, who as she rowed along shore caught as much fish with hook and line as served all the ship's company, which was some alleviation of our disappointment.

On Wednesday the 20th, we happily regained our station, and came again to an anchor, at two cables length from the beach, in 18 fathoms water, and moored with a small anchor in shore. We now sent out the long boat, who in a short time procured fish enough to supply all our company on board. The two following days we had exceeding bad weather. In the morning of the 21st, the wind blew with such violence along shore, that we frequently drove, though we had not less than 200 fathoms of cable out: however we rode out the storm without damage, but the rain was so violent, and the sea ran so high, that nothing could be done with the boats, which was the more mortifying, as it was for the sake of completing our water, that we

had

had endured almost inceffant labour, for five days and
nights, to regain the fituation in which we now lay.
At a fhort interval, when the wind became more moderate, we fent three men afhore, abreaft of the fhip, to
kill feals, and to make oil of their fat, for burning in the
lamps, and other ufes. On the 22nd, in the morning,
the wind blew very hard, as it had done all night,
but, being off the land, we fent the boats away at day-
break, and about ten o'clock they returned with each
of them a load of water, and a great number of pintado
birds, or peterels. Thefe were obtained from the people on fhore, who told them, that when a gale of wind
happened in the night, thefe birds flew fafter into the
fire than they could well take them out; and that,
during the gale of laft ni*ht, they got no lefs than 700
of them. Throughout this day the boats were all employed in bringing water on board; but the furf was fo
great that feveral of the cafks were ftaved and loft;
however by the 23rd, a few only were wanted to complete our ftock. The weather now grew fo bad that
the captain was impatient to fail: he therefore gave
orders for all our people on fhore to come on board.
At this time the Swallow again drove from her moor
ings, dragging the anchor after her, till fhe got into
deep water. We now brought the anchor up, and lay
under bare poles, waiting for the boats. In the evening
the long boat with ten men were taken on board; but
there yet remained the cutter with the lieutenant and
18 men; which brings to our recollection a very
fimilar fituation, in which thofe on board the Centurion,
under Commodore Anfon, were thrown off the ifland
of Tinian. The weather becoming more moderate
about midnight, the Swallow ftood in for land; and on
the 24th, at ten o'clock, A. M. we were very near the
fhore, but the cutter was not to be feen; about noon,
however, fhe was happily difcovered clofe under land,
and in three hours time we took her crew on board.
The Lieutenant reported, that the night before he had
attempted to come off, but that he had fcarcely cleared
the fhore, when a fudden guft of wind almoft filled the
boat

boat with water, which narrowly efcaped filling: that, all hands bailing with the utmoft activity, they fortunately cleared her; that he then made for the land again, which with great difficulty he regained, and having left a fufficient number of men with the boat, to watch, and keep her free from water, he, with the reft of the people went on fhore. That, having paffed the night in a ftate of inexpreffible anxiety and diftrefs, they looked out for the fhip with the firft dawn of day, and feeing nothing of her, concluded that fhe had foundered in the ftorm, which they had never feen exceeded. They did not however give way to gloomy reflections, nor fit down in torpid defpair, but began immediately to clear the ground near the beach of bufhes and weeds, and to cut down feveral trees, of which they made rollers to affift them in hauling up the boat on land, in order to fecure her, intending, as they had no hope of the fhip's return, to wait till the fummer feafon, and then attempt to make the ifland of Juan Fernandes: but thefe thoughts were loft in their happy deliverance. Having thus once more got our people and boats fafe on board, we made fail from this turbulent climate; and thought ourfelves fortunate not to have left any thing behind except the wood, which had been cut for firing.

It is a common opinion, that upon this coaft the winds are conftantly from the fouth to the S. W. though Frazier mentions his having had ftrong gales and high feas from the N. N. W. and N. W. quarter, which was unhappily our cafe. The ifland of Mafa-fuero, which lies in latitude 33 deg. 45 min. fouth, longitude 80 deg. 46 min. weft from the meridian of London, is of a triangular form, about 23 miles in circumference; being weft of Juan Fernandes; both of the iflands are nearly in the fame latitude. At a diftance it has the appearance of a high, mountainous rock. The fouth part is much the higheft, and on the north end are feveral clear fpots, which perhaps might admit of cultivation. On the coaft in many places is good anchorage, particularly on the weft-fide, at about

a mile

a mile from the shore, in 20 fathoms, and at nearly three miles, in 40 and 45 fathoms, with a fine black sand at the bottom. The author of the account of Lord Anson's voyage mentions a reef of rocks, which he says, " runs off the eastern point of the island, about two miles in length, which may be seen by the sea's breaking over them," but in this he is mistaken; though indeed there is a reef of rocks or shoal running off the western-side, near the south-end thereof. He is not less mistaken with respect to the distance of this island from Juan Fernandes, and its direction, for he makes the former 22 leagues, and the latter W. by S. but we found the distance one third more, and the direction is due west; for, as we have before observed, the latitude of both islands is nearly the same. On the S. W. part of the island there is a remarkable perforated rock, which is a good mark to come to an anchor on the western-side, and here is the best bank of any about the place. To the northward of the hole in the rock, distant about a mile and a half, is a low point of land; and from hence runs the above-mentioned reef, in the direction of W. by S. to the distance of about three quarters of a mile, where the sea continually breaks upon it. To come to anchor, you must run in till the hole in the rock is shut in, about a cable's length upon this low point of land, then bearing S. by E. half E. and you may anchor in 20 and 22 fathoms, fine black sand and shells. Anchorage may likewise be found on the other sides of the island, particularly off the north point, in 14 and 15 fathoms, with fine sand. Plenty of wood and water may be procured all round the island, but not without much labour and difficulty, by reason of a great quantity of stones, and large fragments of rocks, which have fallen down from the high land, and upon these such a violent surf breaks that a boat cannot approach safely within a cable's length of the shore, so that there is no landing here but by swimming from the boat, and then mooring her without the rocks; nor is there any method of getting off the wood and water, but by hauling them to the boat with ropes: but Captain

tain Carteret obferves, there are many places where it
would be very eafy to make a commodious landing by
building a temporary wharf, which it would be worth
while even for a fingle fhip to do, if fhe was to continue any time at the ifland. Here we found the feals
fo numerous, that, fays the captain, I verily think, if
many thoufands of them were killed in the night, they
would not be miffed in the morning. Thefe animals
yielded excellent train oil, and their hearts and plucks
are very good eating, being in tafte fomething like thofe
of a hog; and their fkins are covered with the fineft
fur of the kind. In this ifland are many birds, among
others vaft numbers of pintadoes, and fome very large
hawks. While the tent was erected on fhore, a king-
fifher was caught, which weighed 87 pounds, and was
five feet and a half long. Goats are to be found in
great abundance, and may be eafily caught. We had
not an opportunity to botanize, or fearch after vegetable productions, but we faw feveral leaves of the mountain cabbage, which is a proof that the tree is a native
of this place. The ifland is furrounded with abundance
of fifh, in fuch plenty, that a boat's crew, with three
hooks and lines, may obtain as much in a fhort time
as will ferve 100 people: among others we caught
cray-fifh, cod, hallibut, cavallies, and excellent coal-fifh.
The fharks were fo ravenous, that when we were founding one of them fwallowed the lead, by which we hauled
him above water, but as he then difgorged it, we loft
him. So much for this ifland of Mafafuero, of which
we have given feveral particular and full accounts in
former parts of this work.

When we departed from hence, on Sunday the 24th
of May, we failed to the north, hoping to fall in with
the S. E. trade wind; but having run farther to the
northward than was at firft propofed, we looked out
for the iflands of St. Ambrofe, and St. Felix, or St.
Paul, which are laid down in Green's charts, publifhed
in the year 1753; but, as was fuppofed, we miffed
them by attending to the erroneous pofition which is
afcribed to them in Robinfon's navigation, who has laid
down

down the ifland of St. Ambrofe in 25 deg. 30 min.
fouth latitude, and in 82 deg. 20 min. weft longitude;
but we might perhaps go too far to the northward, for
we faw great numbers of birds and fifh, which are indications of land not far diftant. We continued fteering between the latitude of 25 deg. 50 min. and 30 fec.
in fearch of thofe iflands, till we had proceeded 5 deg.
to the weftward of our departure; we then directed our
courfe more to the fouthward, and found ourfelves in the
latitude of 27 deg. 20 min. In this parallel we had light
airs and foul winds, with a ftrong northerly current,
which led Captain Carteret to conjecture, that he was
near the land which Roggewein vifited in the year
1722, and called Eaftern Land, and which fome have
fuppofed to be the fame as a difcovery before made by
Davis, which in the charts is called Davis's Land; and
in this conjecture concerning Eaftern Land our commander has been found to be perfectly right, as Captain
Cook happened to fall in with this fpot in the year
1774; and by the pofition he affigns it, our navigator
appears to have been not more than a degree to the
fouthward of it. It was now, being June the 17th, the
depth of winter, and we had hard gales with heavy feas
that frequently brought us under our courfes; and
though we were near the tropic of capricorn, the weather
was dark, hazy, and cold, with frequent thunder, lightning, fleet, and rain. The fun was above the horizon
about ten hours in the four and twenty, but many days
were frequently paffed without feeing his face; and the
weather was fo thick, that when he was below it, the
darknefs was inexpreffibly horrible; and this dreadful
gloom in the day deprived us for a confiderable time of
an opportunity to make an obfervation; notwithftanding
which dangerous circumftance we were obliged to carry
all the fail we could fpread both day and night, as the
fhip making way fo flowly, and the voyage being fo
long, we were expofed to the danger of perifhing by
famine.

On Thurfday the 2nd of July, in the evening, we difcovered land to the northward of us; which appeared

No. 33.   6 R   like

like a great rock rifing out of the fea.   It is fituated in latitude 25 deg. 2 min. fouth, and in 133 deg. 21 min. weft longitude.   It is an ifland well covered with trees, and down the fide of it runs a ftream of frefh water. The height of it is fo immenfe, that we faw it at the dif-tance of more than 15 leagues. We judged it to be not more than five miles in circumference, and we could perceive no figns of its being inhabited.   The captain was defirous of fending out a boat to attempt a landing, but the furf, which, at this feafon, broke upon it with great violence, rendered it impracticable.   We faw a great number of fea birds at fomewhat lefs than a mile from the fhore, and the fea here feemed not deftitute of fifh.   Having been difcovered by a fon of Major Pit-cairn, we called it Pitcairn's Ifland.   This young gen-tleman was afterwards loft in the Aurora, in her paffage to the Eaft Indies ; and his father, major of the ma-rines, fell in the action of Bunker's Hill, and died in the arms of another of his fons.   While in the neigh-bourhood of this ifland, we feldom had a gale to the eaftward, fo that we were prevented from keeping in a high fouth latitude, and were continually driving to the northward.   The winds chiefly blew from the S. S. W. and W. N. W. and the weather was extremely tempeftuous, with long rolling billows from the fouth-ward, larger and higher than any we had feen before. On the 4th, the fhip admitted a great quantity of water, and was otherwife in a very crazy condition, from the rough feas fhe had encountered.   Our fails alfo, being much worn, were continually fplitting ; and our com-pany who had hitherto enjoyed good health, began to be afflicted with the fcurvy.   When the fhip lay in the Straits of Magellan, Captain Carteret had caufed a fmall awning to be made, and covered it with a clean painted canvafs, which he had for a floor-cloth in his cabin ; and in this he caught fo much rain water, at a very little expence of trouble and attendance, that the crew were never put to fhort allowance of this neceffary article during the voyage.   This method of obtaining rain water we have already particularly defcribed, and is

constantly

conftantly practiced by the Spanifh fhips, which annually crofs the South Sea from the Manilas to Acapulco, and in their return. The awning alfo afforded
fhelter from the inclemency of the weather. The furgeon likewife mixed a fmall quantity of fpirits of vitriol
with the water, which was thus preferved ; and to thefe
precautions the captain imputes the efcape which our
men had fo long had from the fcurvy. On Saturday the
11th, in latitude 22 deg. fouth, and longitude 141 deg.
weft, another fmall, low, flat ifland was difcovered, which
we called the Bifhop of Ofnaburgh's Ifland, in honour
of his prefent majefty's fecond fon ; and as Captain
Wallis had given the fame name to another ifland, that
prince holds two honorary fiefs in the South Sea. This
low piece of land, which appeared to be almoft level
with the waters edge, is well cloathed with verdure ;
but being to the fouth, and directly to the windward
of us, we could not fetch it.

On Sunday the 12th, we faw two more fmall iflands,
on one of which a boat's crew landed, and found birds
fo tame, as to be taken by the hand. They were both
covered with green trees, but appeared to be uninhabited. The fouthermoft, with which we were clofe in,
is a flip of land in the form of a half moon, low, flat,
and fandy. From the fouth end thereof a reef runs out
to the diftance of about half a mile, whereon the fea
breaks with great fury. Notwithftanding its pleafant
afpect it affords neither vegetables nor water ; and the
fame may be faid of the other ifland, which is diftant
from it about five leagues. One of them lies in latitude
20 deg. 38 min. fouth, longitude 146 deg. weft ; the
other in 20 deg. 34 min. fouth, longitude 146 deg.
15 min. weft, and we called them the Duke of Gloucefter's Iflands. They may be the land feen by Quiros,
as the fituation is nearly the fame ; but however this be,
we went to the fouthward of it, and the long billows
we had here, convinced us that no land was near us in
that direction. Captain Carteret was peculiarly unfortunate in having feen four iflands, not one of
which was capable of yielding the leaft refrefhment

to the ship's company, in the important articles of fruit and water; in consequence of which the men became very sickly, and the scurvy made swift progress among them. The wind here being to the eastward, we hauled to the southward again; and on the 13th, in the evening, as we were steering W. S. W. we lost the long rolling billows in latitude 21 deg. 7 min. south, and got them again on the 14th, at seven o'clock, A. M. in latitude 21 deg. 43 min. south, longitude 149 deg. 48 min. west; from whence our captain conjectured, that there was then some land, not far off, to the southward. From this day to Tuesday the 16th, the winds were variable, and blew very hard, with violent gusts, one of which was very near being fatal to us. These were accompanied with thick hazy weather, and heavy rain. We were then in latitude 22 deg. south, and in 70 deg. 30 min. west, of our departure. After some time the wind settled in the W. S. W. which drove us again to the northward, so that on Monday the 20th, we were in latitude 19 deg. south, and in 75 deg. 30 min. west of our departure. On the 22nd, we were in latitude 18 deg. south, longitude 161 deg. west of London, and 1800 leagues westward of the continent of America; yet in all this run not any signs of a continent were discovered. As the scurvy was now daily increasing among our people, and finding all our endeavours, from the badness of the weather, and the defects of the Swallow, to keep in a high southern latitude, were ineffectual, Captain Carteret thought it absolutely necessary to fix upon such a course as might most probably tend to the preservation of the vessel and her crew. In consequence of this resolution, instead of attempting a S. E. course, in which, considering our condition, and the advanced season of the year, it was scarcely possible to succeed, we bore away to the northward, with a view of getting a trade wind; but at the same time keeping such a track, as, if the charts were to be trusted, was most likely to bring us to some island, where refreshments, of which we stood so much in need, might be obtained; we proposed then, if the

ship

ſhip could be put into a proper condition, to have proceeded at the proper ſeaſon to the ſouthward, and to have attempted farther diſcoveries; and ſhould a continent have been diſcovered, and a ſupply of proviſions procured, we, in this caſe, intended to keep along the coaſt to the ſouthward till the ſun had croſſed the equinoxial line; and then, after having got into a high ſouthern latitude, to have ſteered either weſt about to the Cape of Good Hope, or returned to the eaſtward, and in our way to England, to have touched, if neceſſary, at Falkland's Iſlands. Wedneſday the 22nd, in latitude 16 deg. ſouth, and not before, we found the true trade wind; and to Saturday the 25th, we had foul weather, hard gales, and a great ſea to the eaſtward. We were now in latitude 12 deg. 15 min. ſouth, and ſeeing great flocks of birds, we were inclined to think, that we were near ſome land, particularly ſeveral iſlands, one of which was called by Commodore Byron, the iſland of Danger; none of which, however, could we ſee. On the 26th, in the morning, we were in latitude 10 deg. ſouth, and in 167 deg. weſt longitude. We kept nearly in the ſame parallel, hoping to fall in with Solomon's Iſlands, this being the latitude in which the ſouthermoſt of them is laid down. At this time we had a ſtrong trade wind, with violent ſqualls, and much rain.

On Monday the 3rd of Auguſt, we were 5 deg. to the weſtward of the ſituation of thoſe iſlands in the charts; and about 2100 leagues diſtant from the continent of America. We were this day in latitude 10 deg. 18 min. ſouth, and in 177 deg. 30 min. eaſt longitude by account; yet it was not our good fortune to fall in with any land; but probably we might paſs near ſome, which the hazineſs of the weather prevented our ſeeing; for in this run great numbers of ſea-birds were frequently hovering about the ſhip: however, obſerves Captain Carteret, "as Commodore Byron, in his laſt voyage ſailed over the northern limits of that part of the ocean in which the iſlands of Solomon are ſaid to lie, and as I ſailed over the ſouthern limits without

without feeing them, there is great reason to conclude, that, if there are any such islands, their situation, in all our charts, is erroneously laid down." This day the current was observed to set strongly to the southward, though it had hitherto, from the Straits of Magellan, ran in a contrary direction; whence we concluded, that the passage between New Zealand and New Holland opened here in this latitude. The difficulties which our able navigator had to contend with, will appear to have been as great as the best seamen and the firmest minds were capable of making head against, from the following description which he gives of his perplexity at this time. " Our stock of log-lines, observes the captain, was now nearly exhausted, though he had already converted all our fishing lines to the same use. I was for some time in perplexity how to supply this defect; but upon a very diligent enquiry found that we had, by chance, a very few fathoms of thick untarred rope. This, which in our situation, was an inestimable treasure, I ordered to be untwisted; but as the yarns were found to be too thick for our purpose, it became necessary to pick them into oakham; and when this was done, the most difficult part of the work remained; for this oakham could not be spun into yarn, till by combing, it was brought into hemp, its original state. This was not seamens work, and if it had, we should have been at a loss how to perform it for want of combs, and it was necessary to make these before we could try our skill in making hemp. Upon this trying occasion we were again sensible of the danger to which we were exposed by the want of a forge: necessity, however, the fruitful mother of invention, suggested an expedient. The armourer was set to work to file nails down to a smooth point, with which was produced a tolerable succedaneum for a comb; and one of the quarter masters was found sufficiently skilled in the use of this instrument to render the oakham so smooth and even, that we contrived to spin it into yarn, as fine as our coarse implements would admit; and thus we made tolerable log-lines, although we found it much more difficult than

to

untry being covered

. That no vegetables for the reſtoration of
the

3

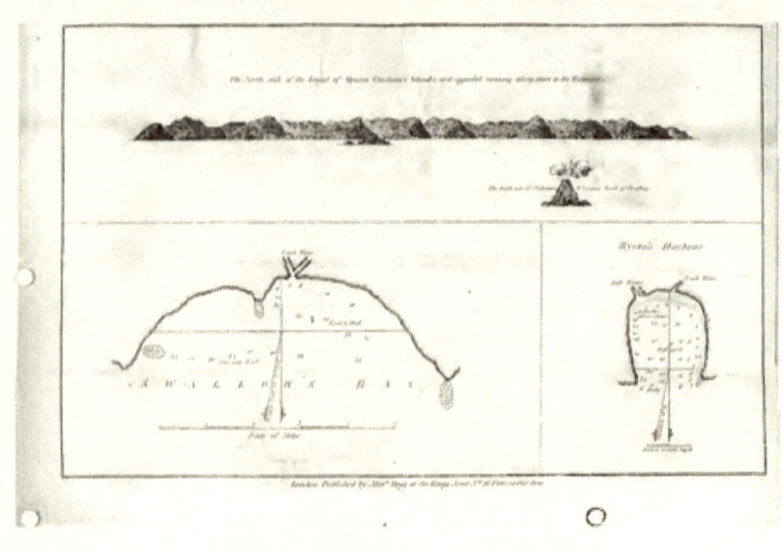

The North side of the Island of Queen Charlotte's Islands and appended running along shore to the Eastward.

The South east of Volcano 2 Leagues North of Brabby

Hvvaa's Harbour

S W A L L O W S B A Y

Scale of Miles

London Published by Alex.r Hogg at the Kings Arms N.o 16 Paternoster Row

to make cordage of our old cables, after they had been converted into junk, which was an expedient we had been obliged to practice long before. We also had long before used all our sowing sail-twine; and if (knowing the quantity with which I had been supplied was altogether inadequate to the wants of such a voyage) I had not taken the whole quantity that had been put on board to repair the seine into my own custody, this deficiency might have been fatal to us all."

We had now sailed over upwards of 110 deg. of longitude, in a dull shattered vessel, that, on account of her bad condition would scarcely answer the helm, nor had we met with any spot of earth which would afford us effectual relief. The scurvy continued to make great progress; insomuch, that those hands which were not rendered useless by disease, were worn down by excessive labour; and, to render our situation completely distressful, on the 10th of August, the Swallow sprung a leak in her bows, which being under water, it was impossible to come at while we were at sea. Our situation was now in the highest degree perilous; but on Wednesday the 12th, at break of day, land was discovered, which gave fresh spirits to our almost desponding crew, and the transport of joy which this prospect occasioned, may be compared to that which a criminal feels who hears the cry of a reprieve at the place of execution. The captain counted seven islands, and we made sail towards two of them which were right a-head, and lay very near together. In the evening we came to an anchor on the north-east side of the largest and highest of them, whereon we saw two of the natives, who were negroes, with woolly heads, and who were not covered with any kind of cloathing. A boat having been sent on shore, the two negroes fled, and an account was brought back by our people, that there was a fine run of fresh water opposite to the ship, but that it would be difficult to procure the water, the whole country being covered with wood quite to the sea-shore. That no vegetables for the restoration of
the

3

the fick could be found, nor any habitations, as far as the country had been examined, which appeared wild, forlorn, and mountainous. Thefe circumflances, added to the danger there might be of the natives attacking us from the woods, determined the captain to look for a more convenient landing-place. On the 13th, there-fore, at day-break, the mafter, with 15 feamen, well armed, and provided, were fent off in the cutter to the weftward, in fearch of a watering-place, refrefhments for the fick, and a convenient fituation, where the fhip might be laid down in order to examine and ftop her leak. He received ftrict orders to be upon his guard againft the natives, but at the fame time to conciliate their good will, to procure which he took with him a few beads and other trifles, which by chance happened to be among the fhip's company : he was alfo enjoined particularly by the captain, to return to the fhip if any occurrence happened that might occafion hoftilities : he was likewife charged on no account to leave the boat, nor to fuffer more than two men to go on fhore at a time, while the reft ftood ready for their defence ; and the captain recommended to him, in the ftrongeft terms, a diligent difcharge of his duty, in finding out a proper place for the fhip ; which fervice, of the utmoft impor-tance to us all, when performed, he was to return with all poffible fpeed. At the time the cutter was difpatch-ed on this expedition, the long-boat was likewife fent off, with ten men on board well armed, which foon returned laden with water. She was difpatched a fecond time, but upon our obferving fome of the natives ad-vancing to the landing-place, a fignal was made for her to return ; for we knew not to what number they might be expofed, and we had no boat to fend off with affif-tance, in cafe they fhould have been attacked. After our men had returned on board, we faw three of the Indians, who fat down on the fhore, looking ftedfaftly on the fhip for feveral hours. The lieutenant was fent to them in the long boat, with a few trinkets, to en-deavour to eftablifh fome kind of intercourfe, by their means, with the reft of the natives ; but when the three

men

men faw the boat approaching, they quitted their ftation, and moved along the coaft, where they were joined by three others. When they had conferred together, the former went on, while the latter advanced haftily towards the boat. This being obferved from the fhip, a fignal was made for the lieutenant to act with caution, who, feeing only three men of the natives, backed the boat into fhore, and offered them fome prefents as tokens of friendfhip, at the fame time concealing carefully their arms. The Indians regardlefs of the beads and ribbands, advanced refolutely, and then difcharged their arrows, which went over the boat without doing any mifchief; upon which they ran away inftantly into the woods, and our people fired in their turn, without doing any execution, not one of them being wounded by the fhot. In a fhort time after this the cutter came under the fhip's fide, the mafter who commanded her having three arrows fticking in his body. We needed no other proof to convince us he had acted contrary to the captain's orders, as appeared fully from his own report, which was, in fubftance, as follows: He faid, that having feen fome Indian houfes, but only a few of the natives, at a place about 14 miles to the weftward of the fhip, he came to a grappling, and veered the boat to the beach, where he landed with four men, armed with mufquets and piftols: that the Indians, at firft, were afraid of him, and retired, but that foon after they came down to him, and he gave them a few trifles, with which they feemed to be much pleafed: that in return they brought him a broiled fifh, and fome broiled yams: that, encouraged by thefe appearances of hofpitality, he proceeded with his party to the houfes, which were not more than 20 yards from the water-fide, and foon after faw a great number of canoes coming round the weftern point of the bay, and many Indians among the trees: that being fomewhat alarmed at their motions, he left haftily the houfe where he had been entertained, and made the beft of his way towards the boat; but that before he could embark, a general attack was made, with bows

and arrows, as well on thofe in the boat, as on thofe
upon the fhore. Their number, according to his account, was between three and four hundred: their
weapons were bows and arrows; the bows were fix feet
five inches long, and the arrows four feet four, which,
he faid, they difcharged in platoons, as regularly as the
beft difciplined troops in England: that, being thus attacked, his party found it neceffary to fire upon the
Indians, which they did repeatedly, killing fome, and
wounding many more: ftill however they were not dif-
couraged; but maintained the fight, preffing forward,
and difcharging their arrows in almoft one continued
flight: that when our people arrived at the boat, a
delay was occafioned in hauling her off, by the grappling being foul; during which time, he, and half of
his crew were defperately wounded: that at laft they
cut the rope, and ran off under their fore-fail, ftill keeping up their fire with blunderbuffes loaded with eight
or ten balls, which the enemy returned with a fhower
of arrows, and waded after them breaft-high into the
fea: when they got clear of thefe affailants, the canoes
purfued them with great vigour, nor would they retreat
till one of them was funk, and many of the people in
the others were killed. This is the account of the
mafter, which it is reafonable to fuppofe, was as favourable to himfelf as he could make it. This rafh
man, with three of our beft hands, died fome time
afterwards of the wounds they had received. It appeared from the evidence of the furvivors, that the
Indians behaved with the greateft confidence and
friendfhip, until the mafter arrogantly ordered the people who were with him, and who had been generoufly
entertained, to cut down a cocoa-tree; and even per-
fifted in that order, notwithftanding the natives difcovered ftrong marks of difpleafure. The Indians
hereupon withdrew, and muftering their whole force,
proved by their manner of attack, that their courage
was equal to their hofpitality. After this difafter,
Captain Carteret dropped all thoughts of removing to
a more eligible harbour, but he determined to try
                                                    what

what could be done towards putting the ship in a better condition, while we continued in our prefent ftation.

Accordingly, Friday the 14th, she was brought down by the ftern, and means were found by our carpenter, the only one of the whole crew in tolerable health, to reduce the leak, though he could not quite ftop it. In the afternoon the Swallow rode with her ftern very near the fhore; and we obferved feveral of the natives fculking among the trees upon the beach, watching our motions. On the 15th, in the morning, the weather being fine, the ship was veered clofe in fhore, upon which, having a fpring upon our cable, we brought her broadfide to bear. It was now become abfolutely ne-ceffary, for the prefervation of all on board, that water fhould be procured; but the only fpring that had been feen on the ifland was fkirted with a thick impenetra-ble wood, from whence the Indians could difcharge their arrows unperceived; the captain was therefore reduced to the painful neceffity of driving them from that lurking-place, by difcharging the fhip's guns, which caufed the lives of many of the natives to be facri-ficed; for at the time the people were at the watering-place, their ears were affailed by dreadful groans from different parts of the wood, like thofe of dying men.

Captain Carteret had long been ill of an inflammatory and bilious diforder, of a nature fimilar to that which had feized Captain Wallis; yet, hitherto, he had been able to keep the deck; but this day the fymptoms be-came fo violent as to compel him to take to his bed, to which he was confined for fome time afterwards. To aggravate our misfortunes, the mafter of the Swallow was dying of his wounds; Mr. Gower, our lieutenant, was very ill; the gunner and 30 of our feamen were unfit for duty; among which laft were feven of the moft healthy, who had been wounded with the mafter, three of them mortally; the recovery of the captain and lieutenant was very doubtful; and, except thefe two, there was no one on board capable of navigating the fhip home. It has already been obferved, that we were

unprovided

unprovided with any toys, iron tools, or cutlery ware, which might have given us a chance for recovering the good-will of the natives, and establishing a traffic with them for those refreshments we most needed, and which they could have furnished us with. Under these circumstances, whereby our people were greatly dispirited, our commander was obliged to lay aside all thoughts of prosecuting the voyage farther to the southward, which the captain intended, as soon as the proper season should return. On Monday the 17th, therefore, we weighed, having called this place Egmont's Island, in honour of a noble earl of that name; but Captain Carteret, in his chart, has called this island New Guernsey, of which he was a native. In his opinion it is the same as that to which the Spaniards gave the name of Santa Cruz. The place in which we lay was called Swallow Bay; the eastermost point thereof Swallow Point; the westermost, Hanway's Point. The N. E. promontory of the island was named Cape Byron. From Swallow Point to Cape Byron is about 7 miles E. and from Hanway's Point to the same cape is about 10 miles. Between Swallow Point and Hanway's Point, in the bottom of the bay is a third point, a little to the westward of which we found the best anchoring-place, but it is necessary to give it birth, the ground near it being shoally. When we lay at anchor in this bay, Swallow Point bore E. by N. and Hanway's Point W. N. W. From hence a reef runs, whereon the sea breaks very high: the outer part of this reef bears N. W. by W; and an island which has the appearance of a volcano, was seen just over the breakers. A little beyond Hanway's Point is a small village, which stands upon the beach, surrounded with cocoa-nut trees. It lies in a bay between Hanway's Point and another, which we called Howe's Point; the distance from the former to the latter is about five miles. We found close to the shore 30 fathoms water, but in crossing the bay, at the distance of two miles, we had no bottom. Beyond Howe's Point, another harbour opens, which had the appearance of a deep lagoon, this we called Carlisle Harbour.

Harbour. Over againſt its entrance, and north of the coaſt, a ſmall iſland was diſcovered, which we named Portland's Iſland. A reef of rocks runs on the weſt ſide of this to the main; and the paſſage into the harbour is on the eaſt-ſide of it, running in and out E. N. E. and W. S. W. its width is two cables length, and it has eight fathoms water. The harbour may be a commodious one, but a ſhip muſt be warped both in and out, and would be in danger if attacked by the natives, who are bold even to temerity, and have a perſeverance, not common among rude ſavages. Weſt of Portland's Iſland, is a fine ſmall round harbour, juſt big enough to receive three veſſels, which was named Byron's Harbour. Our boat having entered it, found two runs of water, one freſh and the other ſalt; from obſerving the latter we judged it had a communication with Carliſle Harbour. Having proceeded about three leagues from where the Swallow lay at anchor, we opened the bay where our cutter had been attacked by the Indians, which we called for that reaſon Bloody Bay. Here is a rivulet of freſh water, and many houſes regularly built. Near the water-ſide ſtood one neatly built and thatched; it ſeemed to be a kind of council-room, or ſtate-houſe, and was much longer than any of the reſt. In this the maſter and his party had been courteouſly received by the natives, before the wanton cutting down of the cocoa-nut tree. We were informed by thoſe of our people who had been received here, that a large number of arrows were hung in bundles round the room, the floor and ſides of which were covered with matting. In the neighbourhood of this place, they ſaid, were many plantations encloſed by ſtone-walls, and planted with fruit trees; the cocoa-nut trees we could diſcern from the ſhip, in great numbers, among the houſes of the village. Three miles weſtward of this, we ſaw another village of conſiderable extent, in the front whereof, towards the ſea, was an angular kind of breaſt-work, of ſtone, and near five feet high. Three miles from hence, as we proceeded weſtward, a bay was diſcovered, into which a river empties itſelf.

4

itfelf. It appeared, when viewed from the maft head, to run very far into the country, and we called it Granville's River. Weftward of it is a point, which we named Ferrer's Point; from whence the land forms a large bay, near which is a town of great extent that feemed to fwarm like a bee-hive. While the fhip failed by, an incredible number of the inhabitants came forth from their houfes, holding fomething like a wifp of grafs in their hands, with which they appeared to ftroke each other, at the fame time dancing, or running in rings. Sailing on about feven miles to the weftward, we faw another point, on which was a large canoe, with an awning over it. To this we gave the name of Cape Carteret. From this a reef of rocks, that appears above water, runs out to the diftance of about a cable's length. At a fmall diftance was another village, fortified as that before mentioned. The inhabitants of this place likewife danced as the others had done; after which many of them launched their canoes, and made towards the fhip: upon which we lay to, that they might have time to come up; but when they approached near enough to have a diftinct view of the Swallow, they lay upon their paddles, gazed at us, but would advance no farther. Being thus difappointed in our hopes of prevailing upon them to come on board, we made fail, and left them behind us. From Carteret Point the land trends away W. S. W. and S. W. forming a deep lagoon, at the mouth of which lies an ifland, which was named Trevanion's Ifland. There are two entrances into the lagoon, which, if it affords good anchorage, is certainly a fine harbour for fhipping. Having croffed the firft entrance, and being off the N. W. part of Trevanion's Ifland, which was named Cape Trevanion, we faw a great ripling, caufed by the meeting of the tides. Having hauled round this cape, we perceived the land trend to the fouthward, and we continued to ftand along the fhore, till we opened the weftern paffage into the lagoon between Trevanion's Ifland and the main; both of which, at this place, appeared to be one continued town, and the inhabitants
were

were innumerable. We found in this entrance a bottom of coral rock, with very irregular foundings. The natives no sooner observed that the boat had left the ship, than they sent off several armed canoes, who advanced to attack her. The first that came within bow-shot discharged her arrows at our people, who, being prepared, fired a volley, by which one of the Indians was killed, and another wounded. We fired at the same time from the ship, a great gun loaded with grape shot, on which all the canoes pulled hard for the shore, except the one with the wounded man, who being brought to the ship, the surgeon was ordered to examine his wounds, one shot had gone through his head, and one of his arms was broke by another. The surgeon was of opinion, that the former wound was mortal, in consequence of this he was put again into his canoe, and, notwithstanding his condition, he with one hand paddled away towards the shore. He was a young fellow, almost as black as a negro of Guinea, with a woolly head; of a common stature, well featured, and, like the rest of the people we had seen upon this island, quite naked. His canoe had an out-rigger, without a sail, but in workmanship it was very rude, being nothing more than part of the trunk of a tree made hollow. We were now at the western extremity of the island; and the distance between that and the eastern extremity is 50 miles due E. and W. A strong current sets westward along the shore. The natives of Egmont Island are extremely nimble, active, and vigorous; and seem to be almost equally qualified to live in the water as upon land, for they were in and out of their canoes every minute. Their common canoes are capable of carrying about a dozen men, though three or four manage them with amazing dexterity. The men have a daring fortitude, which proves them to be descended from the same stock as those who now inhabit the Philippine Isles, lying about 45 degrees more to the westward, whose contempt of death was really astonishing when the city of Manilla was defended against the English, under the command of Sir William Draper.

As

As we failed along fhore, to raife our mortification to the higheft pitch, hogs and poultry were feen in great abundance, with cocoa-nut trees, plantains, bananas, and a variety of vegetable productions, which would foon have reftored to us the health and vigour we had loft, by the hardfhips of a long voyage: but no friendly intercourfe with the natives could now be expected, and we were not in a fituation to obtain what we wanted by force: befides, great part of the crew were difabled by ficknefs, and the reft were much depreffed in their fpirits, by a continual fucceffion of difappointments and vexations; and if the men had been in health, we had no officers to lead them on, or direct them in any enterprize, nor even to fuperintend the duties that were to be performed on board the fhip; for even the Captain himfelf was ftill confined to his bed, dangeroufly ill. Thus fituated, unable to proceed farther to the fouth, and in danger of being too late for the monfoon, he gave immediate orders for fteering north-weftward, with a view to fall in with the land which Dampier has diftinguifhed by the name of Nova Britannia, and which was now diftant about 12 deg. of longitude. In our diftrefsful fituation, it could not be expected, that Captain Carteret fhould examine all the iflands we touched at; curiofity muft yield to the inftinctive principle of felf-prefervation; but we gave particular names to feveral of thofe we approached; and to the whole clufter we gave the general name of Queen Charlotte's Iflands. To the fout:hermoft of the two, which when we firft difcovered land were right a-head, the name was given of Lord Howe's Ifland, and the other was Egmont Ifland, of which we have already gizen a particular account. The latitude of Lord Howe's Ifland is 11 deg. 10 min. fouth; longitude 164 deg. 43 min. eaft. The latitude of Cape Byron, the N. E. point of Egmont Ifland, is 10 deg. 40 min. fouth; longitude 164 deg. 49 min. eaft. Thefe two iflands lie exactly in a line with each other, about N. by W. and S. by E. and including the paffage between them, extend 11 leagues; the paffage is very broad. Both of them appear to be

fertile,

fertile, have a pleasant appearance, and are covered with tall trees of a beautiful verdure. Lord Howe's Island, which is more upon a level than the other, is neverthelefs high land. From Cape Byron, distant 13 leagues W. N. W. half N. by compafs, is an island of a stupendous height, and in the figure of a cone. Its top is shaped like a funnel, from whence smoke issues, but we saw no flame; we thought it, however, to be a volcano, and therefore called it Volcano Island. To a long flat island, that, when Howe's and Egmont's Islands were right a-head, bore N. W. we gave the name of Keppel's Island. It is situated in latitude 10 deg. 15 min. south; longitude, by our account, 165 deg. 4 min. east. We discovered two others to the S. E. The largest we named Lord Edgecumb's Island, and the smaller Ourry's Island. The former, which has a fine appearance, lies in latitude 11 deg. 10 min. south; longitude 165 deg. 14 min. east, the latter is in latitude 11 deg. 10 min. south; longitude 165 deg. 19 min. east. Egmont Island, in general, is woody and mountainous, intermixed with many beautiful valleys. Several small rivers flow from the interior parts of the country into the sea, and we have mentioned many harbours upon the coast. The inhabitants, whom we have particularly described, do execution at an incredible distance with their arrows. One of them went through the boat's wash-board, and dangerously wounded a midshipman in the thigh. They were pointed with flint, and we saw among them no signs of any metal.

C H A P. II.

The Swallow departs from Queen Charlotte's Islands — Her run to Nova Britannia — Other Islands discovered, with a Description of them, and their Inhabitants — Nova Britannia found to be two Islands; with a Strait between them — Several small Islands discovered in the Strait, with an Account of the Land and Natives on each Side —

The Swallow enters St. George's Channel—Paſſage from thence to the Iſland of Mindanao—A Deſcription of many Iſlands that were ſeen, and Incidents in this Courſe—A Geographical Account of the Coaſt of Mindanao and the Iſlands near it—Errors of other Navigators corrected—The Swallow continues her Voyage from Mindanao to the Iſland of Celebes—A particular Deſcription of the Strait of Macaſſar—Tranſactions while the Swallow lay off the Town.

TUESDAY the 18th of Auguſt, we took our departure from Egmont iſland, one of the cluſter of iſlands which the Captain named Queen Charlotte's, with a freſh trade wind from the eaſtward. On the 20th, a ſmall flat iſland was diſcovered, and named after Mr. Gower, our lieutenant. It lies in latitude 7 deg. 56 min. ſouth; longitude 158 deg. 56 min. eaſt. The natives did not differ in any thing material, from thoſe of the iſlands we had lately left; but ſome cocoa-nuts were here procured in exchange for nails; and the inhabitants had intimated, that they would furniſh a freſh ſupply the next morning, being Friday the 21ſt, but, at day break, we found that a current had ſet the ſhip conſiderably to the ſouthward of the iſland, and brought us in ſight of two other iſlands. They are ſituated nearly E. and W. of each other, at the diſtance of about two miles. The ſmalleſt, which lies to the eaſtward, we called Simpſon's Iſland; and to the other, which has a lofty appearance, we gave the name of Carteret's Iſland. From Gower's, the eaſt end bears ſouth, and the diſtance between them is nearly 11 leagues. Carteret's Iſland is in latitude 8 deg. 26 min. ſouth; longitude 159 deg. 14 min. eaſt, and its length from E. to W. is 18 miles. As both theſe iſlands were to the windward of us, we ſailed again to Gower's Iſland, which abounds with fine trees, many of them of the cocoa-nut kind. Here a canoe was ſeized, the natives having attempted to cut off the ſhip's boat; in it we found about 100 cocoa-nuts, which were very acceptable. The canoe was large enough to carry 40 men,

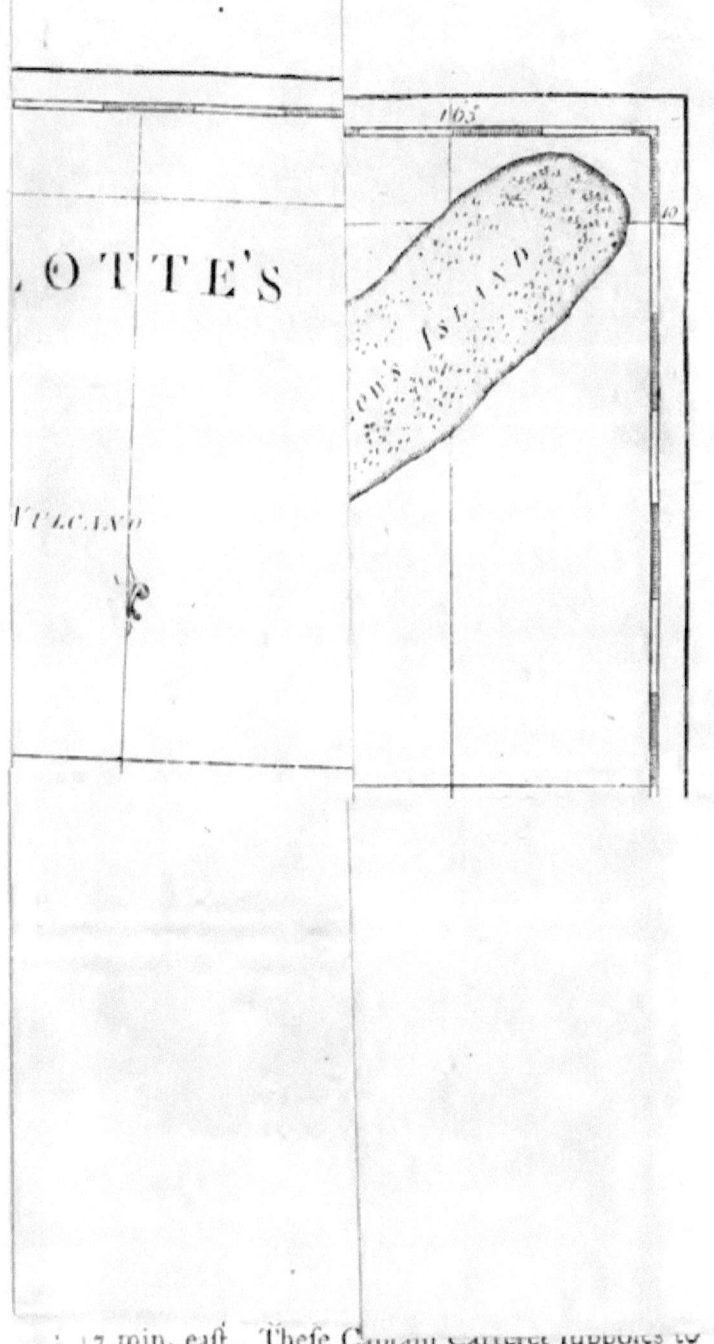

OTTE'S

105

ISLAND

VULCANO

; 17 min. east. These Captain Carteret supposes to
the same which were seen by Tasman, and called by
6 T 2   him

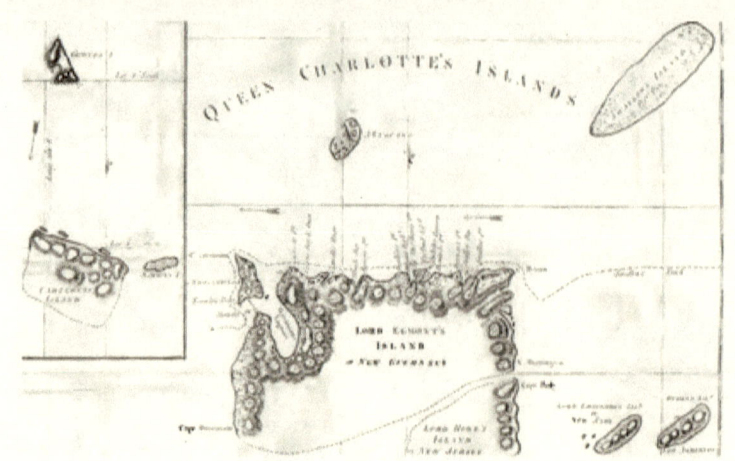

10 men, and was very neatly built, with planks well joined. It was adorned with shell-work, and figures rudely painted, and the seams were covered with a substance somewhat like our black putty. With respect to its size, it was much larger than any one we had seen at Egmont Island. The appearance of these Indians, and their arms, were much the same as those that had been seen more to the eastward, only spears made an addition to their weapons. By some signs which they made, pointing to our musquets, we concluded they were not wholly unacquainted with fire-arms. We saw some turtle near the beach, but were not fortunate enough to take any of them; but the cocoa-nuts we got here, and at Egmont Island, were of inexpressible service to the sick. As from the time of our leaving Egmont Island we had a current setting strongly to the southward, and finding, in the neighbourhood of these islands, its force greatly increased, we now steered a north-westerly course, fearing we might otherwise fall in with the main land too far to the southward; and the bad condition of the ship, and sickness of the crew, would have rendered it impossible for us ever to have got to sea again, if we had been driven into any gulph or deep bay. On the 22d, as we were continuing our course with a fresh gale, Patrick Dwyer, a marine, who was doing something over the ship's quarter, by some accident fell into the sea: we immediately threw overboard the canoe we had made a prize of at Gower's Island, brought the ship to, and hoisted out the cutter, but the unfortunate man, though strong and healthy, sunk at once, and was drowned, notwithstanding all our efforts to save him. The canoe we were obliged to cut up, she having received much damage by striking against one of the guns as our people were hoisting her overboard.

On Monday the 24th, we fell in with nine islands, stretching N. W. and S. E. about 15 leagues, and lying in latitude 4 deg. 36 min. south; longitude 154 deg. 17 min. east. These Captain Carteret supposes to be the same which were seen by Tasman, and called by

him Ohang Java: the other iſlands he believes had
never been viſited by any European before; and he is
of opinion, that there is much land not yet known in
this part of the ocean.   One of theſe iſlands is of conſiderable extent; the other eight are little better than
large rocks; but, though low and flat, they are covered
with wood, and abound with inhabitants.   We ſteered
to the northward of theſe iſlands, W. by S. having a
ſtrong ſouth-weſterly current.   In the night we fell
in with another pleaſant iſland of conſiderable extent.
By the many fires we ſaw, it appeared to be inhabited,
but we ſaw none of the natives.   We called this flat,
green iſle, Sir Charles Hardy's Iſland.   It is ſituated
in latitude 4 deg. 50 min. ſouth; and bore weſt 15
leagues from the northermoſt of the nine iſlands.   On
the 25th, at day break we diſcovered another large
high iſland, which received the name of Winchelſea's
Iſland; and is diſtant from Sir Charles Hardy's Iſland
ten leagues, in the direction of S. by E.   On Wedneſday the 26th, an iſland was diſcovered to the northward, which the Captain ſuppoſed to be the ſame that
was ſeen by Schouten, and called the iſland of St. John.
Not many hours after, Nova Britannia appeared, and
the Swallow entered what was thought to be a deep bay,
or gulph, which Dampier had diſtinguiſhed by the name
of St. George's Bay.   It lies in latitude 5 deg. ſouth;
longitude 152 deg. 19 min. eaſt.   Here we caſt anchor,
while the boats went to ſearch for a good harbour;
which, when they returned and reported to have found,
the united ſtrength of the whole ſhip's company was not
ſufficient to weigh the anchor; an inſtance of debility
ſomewhat ſimilar to that related in Commodore Anſon's
voyage, when the Centurion arrived at Tinian.   It was
not until the next day, when our ſtrength was ſomewhat
recruited, that the anchor was brought up, and it was
then found to have been ſo much injured, as to be
totally unſerviceable. No fiſh could be caught, either by
the ſeine, or hook and line: ſome rock oyſters and
cockles were, however, obtained, and in the country
ſome cocoa nuts, with wood and water. The upper part

I   of

3 | 3

Ant Coves

Volcano | I.Man

St. Johns I. | St. Ct Hardys I.

C. St Mary | Capts Carterets Tract

4 | Callister | 4

Butler | The 9 Isles

C. St George

C. Orford | Shoal Ansons I.

5 | 5

Tract | N E A
00

6 | P | 6

7 | A | 7

P CHART of

...eret's Discoveries at

Partaken from Old Charts. | BRITAIN,

8 | ...pt. Cook's Passage thro | 8

...UR STREIGHTS.

...pier's Tract & Discoveries

9 | ...699, & 1700, at | 9

...EA & NEW BRITAIN

10 | 10

143 | 144 | 152 | 153 | 154

Hogg, at the Kings Arm

of the tree which bears the cocoa-nut, is called the cabbage, which is a white, crisp, juicy substance; if eaten raw it tastes somewhat like a chesnut, but when boiled is superior to the best parsnip. This was cut small into the broth, which was made of the portable soup, and being thickened with some oatmeal, made a most comfortable mess; for each of these cabbages we were forced to cut down a tree, which was done with great regret, but the depredation on the parent stock was unavoidable. This regimen, with the milk of the nut, relieved the sick presently, and recovered them very fast. Here we found nutmeg-trees in great plenty: they did not appear to be the best sort, which may be owing partly to their growing wild, and partly to their being too much in the shade of taller trees: all the different sorts of palm were also found. We likewise received great refreshment from the fruit of a tall tree, that resembles a plumb, and particularly that which in the West Indies is called the Jamaica plumb. Here we saw many trees, shrubs, and plants, altogether unknown; but no esculent vegetables of any kind. In the woods, a large bird with black plumage was seen, which made a noise like the barking of a dog. The only quadrupeds some of our people saw, were two of a small size, which were supposed to be dogs: they were very wild, and ran with great swiftness. None of the human race appeared, but we found several deserted habitations. By the shells scattered about them, with some sticks half burnt, and the embers of a fire, it appeared, that the natives had but just left the place when the Swallow arrived, or more probably they fled at her approach. If the people may be judged of from the appearance of their dwellings, they must stand low even in the scale of savage life, for they were the most miserable hovels we had ever seen. A small island in this bay we called Wallis's Island. The harbour, in which our ship lay, received the name of English Cove; and here Captain Carteret took possession of the country, with all its islands, bays, ports, and harbours, for the king his master; nailing upon a high tree a piece of board, faced

with

with lead, on which was engraved an English union, the name of the ship, and her commander; the name given to the cove; and the time of coming in and sailing out of it.

On the 7th of September, being Monday, we left this cove, and anchored on the same day almost close to a grove of cocoa-nut trees, where we plentifully supplied ourselves with fruit and the cabbage. We called this place Carteret's Harbour, which being formed by the main and two islands, one of them was named Leigh's, and the other Cocoa-nut Island. The Captain now resolved to sail for Batavia, while the monsoon continued favourable: on the 9th, therefore, we weighed anchor, and when about four leagues from land, the wind and current being both against us, we steered round the coast into a channel between two islands, which channel was divided by another island, to which Captain Carteret gave the name of the Duke of York's Island, near which are several smaller islands. To the south of the largest of them are three hills of singular form, which were called the Mother and Daughters, one of which we supposed to be a volcano from the large clouds of smoke that were seen issuing from it. A point we called Cape Palliser, lies to the east of these hills, and Cape Stephens to the west; north of which last, lies an island, which took the name of the Isle of Man. The country in general is mountainous and woody, and was supposed to be inhabited, from the numbers of fires seen on it in the night. On the Duke of York's Island, the houses were situated among groves of cocoa-nut trees, and thus formed a most beautiful prospect. We brought to, for the night, and sailed again in the morning, when some of the Indians put off in canoes towards the ship; but the wind being fair and blowing fresh, it was not thought prudent to wait for them. We now steered N. W. by W. and lost sight of New Britain on the 11th, when it was found that what had been taken for a bay, was a strait, and it was called St. George's Channel, whilst the island on the north of it received the name of New Ireland. In the evening we discovered a large

island,

NOVA HIBERNIA

ifland, well clothed with verdure, which was denomi-
nated Sandwich Ifland : off this ifland the fhip lay great
part of the night, during which time a perpetual noife
refembling the found of a drum was heard from the
fhore. When we had almoft cleared the ftrait, the
weather falling calm, a number of canoes approached
the fhip, and though their crews could not be prevailed
on to go on board, they exchanged fome trifles with us
for nails and bits of iron, which they preferred to every
thing elfe that was offered them. Though the canoes
of thefe people were formed out of fingle trees, they
were between 80 and 100 feet in length. The natives
were negroes, and their hair was of the woolly kind;
but they had neither thick lips nor flat nofes. They
wore fhell-work on their legs and arms, but were otherwife naked. Their hair and beards were powdered
with white powder, and a feather was ftuck into the
head of each, above the ear. Their weapons confifted
of a long ftick and a fpear; and it was obferved, that
they had fifhing-nets and cordage.

Sailing from hence weftward, we came in fight of the
S. W. point of the ifland; it was called Cape Byron;
near which is an ifland of confiderable extent, which
received the name of New Hanover. The ftrait we
had now paffed was called Byron's Strait; one of the
largeft iflands we had feen, Byron's Ifland; and the
S. W. point of New Hanover, Queen Charlotte's Foreland. On the following day, we faw feveral fmall iflands,
which received the name of the Duke of Portland's
Iflands. Having completely navigated St. George's
Channel, the whole length of which is about 100 leagues,
we held on a weftward courfe, and on Monday the
14th, difcovered feveral iflands. The next morning
fome hundreds of the natives came off in canoes towards the fhip, and were invited on board by every
token of friendfhip and good will; notwithftanding
which, when they came within reach, they threw feveral
lances at the feamen on the deck. A great gun and
feveral mufquets were then fired at them, by which
fome were killed or wounded; on which they rowed
towards

towards fhore ; and after they had got to a diftance, a fhot was fired, fo as to fall beyond them, to convince them that they were not out of the reach of the guns. Soon after, fome other canoes advanced from a diftant part of the ifland, and one of them coming nearer than the reft, the people in it were invited on board the fhip: inftead of complying, they threw in a number of darts and lances. This affault was returned by the firing of feveral mufquets, by which one of the Indians was killed; on which his companions jumped over-board, and fwam to the other canoes, all of whom rowed to the fhore. The canoe being taken on board, was found to contain turtle, and fome other fifh, alfo a fruit of a fpecies between an apple and a plumb, hitherto un-known to Europeans. Thefe people were moftly negroes, with woolly hair, which they powdered, and went naked, except the ornaments of fhells round their arms and legs. We now coafted along the iflands, to which we gave the general name of the Admiralty Iflands. They have a beautiful appearance, being covered with woods, groves of cocoa-nut trees and the houfes of the natives. The largeft we computed to be about 50 miles in length ; and they produce many valuable arti-cles, particularly fpices. We difcovered two fmall ver-dant iflands, on Saturday the 19th, which were called Durour's Ifland and Matty's Ifland, the inhabitants of which laft ran along the coaft with lights during the night. We had fight of other two fmall iflands on the 24th, which were called Stephens's Iflands, and which abounded with beautiful trees. We faw alfo three iflands on Friday the 25th, in the evening, when the natives came off in canoes, and went on board the fhip. They bartered cocoa-nuts for fome bits of iron, with which metal they did not feem unacquainted, and ap-peared extravagantly fond of it. They called it parram, and hinted that a fhip fometimes touched at their iflands. Thefe people were of the copper colour, and had fine black hair; but their beards were very fmall, as they were continually plucking the hair from their faces. Their teeth were even and white, and
their

their countenances very agreeable. They were so extremely active that they ran up to the mast-head quicker than the sailors. Every thing that was given them they ate and drank with freedom, and seemed to have no sort of reserve in their behaviour. A piece of fine matting wrapped round their waists, constituted the whole of their dress, and good nature appeared to be the only rule of their actions. The current carrying the ship swiftly along, the captain had not the opportunity of landing; and was therefore obliged to refuse gratifying these friendly people in that particular, though they very readily offered that some of their people should remain as hostages for the safe return of any of the officers or ship's company who should chuse to go on shore. Finding that their offer was not accepted, one of the Indians absolutely refused to quit the ship: he was carried in consequence, as far as the island of Celebes, where he died. This man was named Joseph Freewill, and we called the largest of the isles, Freewill Island, (by the natives called Pagan.) The names of the two other islands were Onata and Onello.

An island was discovered from the mast-head as we held on our course, on Monday the 28th, in the evening, but we neither landed there nor gave it a name. Monday the 12th of October, we saw a small isle which we named Current Island, from the great strength of the southerly current in those parts; and the next day two islands were discovered, to which we gave the name of St. Andrew's Island. The next land appeared to be Mindanao, along the S. E. part of which we coasted, seeking for a bay which Dampier had described; but this we could not find. The boat, however, found a little creek at the southern extremity of the isle, near which a town and a fort were seen. The people having descried the boat from the shore, a gun was fired, and several canoes came off after it. The lieutenant therefore retreated towards the ship, which when the canoes discovered, they retired and made towards the shore. We now stood to the eastward, and on Monday the 2d of November, anchored in a bay near the shore, whither the boats were dispatched to take in water. No signs appeared of that part of the island being inhabited; a canoe however came round a point, seemingly with a view of observing us, which rowed back again, after having taken a survey of the vessel. In the night, a great noise was heard on the shore, somewhat like the war-song of the Americans. The captain therefore made proper preparations to defend himself in case hostilities should be commenced on the part of the islanders. One of the boats was sent on shore for water the next morning, and the other was ordered to hold herself in readiness, in case her assistance should be necessary. The crew had no sooner landed than several armed men came forward from the woods, and one of them held up something white, which being construed as a sign of amity, the captain having no white flag on board, determined to send the lieutenant with a table cloth in order to answer the token of peace. For the present this had the desired effect. Two Indians, who spoke bad Dutch and Spanish, having at last made themselves understood by the officer, in the latter language, made several enquiries which chiefly turned upon desiring to be informed whether the ships belonged to the states of Holland, and whether she was bound to Batavia or elsewhere. He also wanted to know whether she was a ship of war and what number of guns she carried. Having been resolved as to these particulars, he said they might proceed to the town; some armed Indians were ordered to retreat, and the lieutenant presented a silk handkerchief to the person he conversed with, receiving a neckcloth in return. When the captain heard this, he was highly pleased, thinking that all matters were now in a proper train, especially as he had received a supply of water; but while he was enjoying this prospect, he perceived some hundreds of armed Indians on the shore, who held up their targets, and brandished their swords, by way of defiance, and at the same time discharged their lances and arrows towards the vessel. Notwithstanding this

hostile

hostile appearance, the captain was still willing, if possible, to avoid coming to extremities with the islanders,
and for that purpose, sent the lieutenant on shore to
display again the former sign of peace. As the boat
approached the shore, but without landing her men,
one of the natives beckoned them to come where he
stood, but the lieutenant did not chuse to obey this
summons, lest he should come within reach of the
arrows of the islanders. He now concluded that there
were Dutchmen or people in the Dutch interest on
shore, to whose interference this apparent alteration in
the disposition of the natives was owing, and who had
irritated the natives against the Swallow's crew, on being informed that she was an English vessel. Captain
Carteret however sailed from this place, which he called
Deceitful Bay, with a full intention to visit the town ;
but soon after the wind blowing violently in shore, he
altered his resolution, and steered directly for Batavia,
which was probably the best course he could have taken
in such a critical situation.

On Saturday the 14th of November, we reached the
strait of Macassar, which strait lies between the islands
of Celebes and Borneo. To a point of the former, we
at this time gave the name of Hummock Point ; and to
the westward of this point we discovered a great many
boats fishing upon the shoals. On the 21st, we were in
sight of two very small islands, which were covered
with verdure, and Captain Carteret supposed them to
be the Taba Isles, mentioned in the French charts. We
crossed the equinoctial line, and came into southern
latitude, on Sunday the 29th ; the tornadoes becoming
violent, and the current setting against us. Death had
now diminished the crew, and sickness was daily weaken-
ing the remainder. We had sight of the Little Pater-
Nosters (islands so called) which are situate something
more than two degrees to the southward of the equinoctial line, but the winds and currents would not suffer
us at that time to land for any refreshment. At this
time the whole crew were alike afflicted with the scurvy ;
and what was very distressing we were attacked soon

after in the night by a piratical veffel, which had been feen the evening before. She engaged us with fwivel guns and fmall arms; but though we could not fee the enemy, we returned her fire fo warmly that we fent her to the bottom, and all her crew perifhed. As to the Swallow fhe received fome fmall damage, and had two perfons wounded on board. The veffel that fhe funk belonged to a pirate who had no lefs than thirty of them engaged in the bufinefs of plunder, which conftantly infefted thefe feas.

The difeafes of our men now daily increafed. By the 12th, we had loft 13 of our crew, and 30 others were almoft on the point of death. The wefterly monfoon being fet in we could have no hopes of reaching Batavia, and our fituation was fuch that we muft perifh if we could not fpeedily make land. On this account, it was refolved to fteer for Macaffar, a Dutch fettlement on the ifland of Celebes; and happily we accomplifhed our defign, coming to anchor off that ifland, at the diftance of more than a league from Macaffar, on Tuefday the 15th of December.

The governor fent a Dutchman on board the Swallow late that night, who feemed much alarmed on finding that fhe was an Englifh fhip of war, and would not truft himfelf in the cabin. Early the next morning, the captain difpatched a letter to the governor, requefting leave to buy provifions, and to fhelter his fhip till the feafon for failing weftward came on. The boat arriving at the fhore, none of the crew were fuffered to land; and, the lieutenant having refufed to deliver the letter to any but the governor himfelf, two officers, called the Shebandar and the Fifcal, came to him with a meffage, importing that the governor was fick and had commanded them to come for the letter. The lieutenant, though he thought this was only a mere pretence, at length delivered the letter, which they took away with them. After the boat's crew had waited without any refrefhments for feveral hours in the heat of the fun, they were told that the governor had ordered two gentlemen to wait on their captain with an anfwer. As the

boat

boat lay off the wharf, our people on board observed a great hurry on shore, and concluded that all hands were busy in fitting out armed vessels, a circumstance which could not much contribute to our satisfaction. But according to the promise given, soon after the boat's return, two gentlemen of the names of De Cerf and Douglas, came with dispatches, desiring, that the ship might instantly depart from the port, without coming any nearer to the town; insisting that she should not anchor on any part of the coast, and that the captain should not permit any of the people to land on any place under the governor's jurisdiction.

The captain could not but sensibly feel the cruelty of this proceeding. As the strongest argument that could be used in answer to the letter, he shewed his dying men to the gentlemen, and urged the necessity of the case; nor could they but feel the propriety of granting refreshments to the subjects of a power at peace with their country, and who were in such a deplorable situation; but they observed that their orders were absolute and must be obeyed. Incensed at this treatment, Captain Carteret, at last, declared, that he would come to an anchor close to the town, and then, if they persisted in refusing him necessary refreshments, that he would run the ship aground, when his crew would sell their lives as dear as possible. Being alarmed at this declaration, they intreated the captain to remain in his present situation till further orders should arrive. This he promised, on condition that an answer should be sent before the setting in of the sea-breeze the next day.

In the morning early, it was observed that a sloop of war, and another vessel with soldiers on board, anchored under the ship's bow. They refused to speak with Captain Carteret, and as he weighed and set sail with the sea-breeze, they did the same, and closely followed him. As he proceeded, a vessel from the town approached him, wherein were several gentlemen, and Mr. Douglas among them; but, till the Swallow dropped anchor they could not come on board. They expressed some surprize at the English vessel having advanced so far; but the captain alledged that he had only acted according to his former declaration, which his present situation would sufficiently justify to every candid person.

These gentlemen brought with them two sheep, some fowls, fruit, and other provisions, which were extremely welcome to the English; but, after they had made several proposals, with which he could not comply, he shewed them the dead body of a man who had expired but a few hours before, and whose life might probably have been saved, had the Dutch sent them a timely supply of refreshments, and again declared his resolution of executing what he had threatened, if they would not comply with his requisition. His guests now enquired whether the ship had touched at the spice islands, and were answered in the negative. At last it was agreed, that the Swallow should sail for a bay at a little distance, where an hospital for the sick might be provided, and where provisions were generally plentiful, and, if there was a want of any article, they might be supplied occasionally from the town. It will be imagined that a proposal of this kind was readily agreed to by captain Carteret; all he insisted upon was, that it should be ratified by the governor and council, which was afterwards done in the proper manner. He could not forbear asking, however, for what reason the two vessels had anchored under his ship's bows. He received for answer, that this was only done in a friendly manner, to protect her from any insult that might be offered by the natives of the country. While this treaty was going forward, the English Captain had nothing to give his guests but rotten biscuit and bad salt meat; however, they had ordered an elegant dinner to be dressed on board their own vessel, which was afterwards served up at his table, and they parted in friendship.

The next day an officer from the town came on board, to whom the captain applied to get money for his bills on the English government. He promised to endeavour to do this, and for that purpose went on shore, but when he returned in the evening, he said that there

was

was no person in the town that had any cash to remit to Europe, and that the company's chest was quite empty. This was a great difficulty; however it was surmounted at last by an order being sent to the Resident at Bonthain, who had money to remit, and who, in consequence, received the bills in question.

CHAP. III.

The Swallow sails from Macassar to Bonthain—Transactions during her Stay at this Place—A Description of the Town of Macassar and circumjacent Country—She proceeds from the Bay of Bonthain, in the Island of Celebes, to Batavia, in the Island of Java—Remarkable Incidents and Transactions—The Swallow anchors at Onrust, in order to have her Defects repaired—An Account of the Dutch Governor, and the courteous Behaviour of Admiral Houting to Captain Carteret—The Swallow being refitted departs from Onrust—Loses many of her Hands by Sickness—Arrives at Prince's Island in the Strait of Sunda—Run from thence to the Cape of Good Hope—Anchors in Table Bay—Makes the Island of St. Helena—Proceeds to the Island of Ascension, and comes to an Anchor in Cross Hill Bay—Continues her Voyage—Is hailed by a French Ship, commanded by M. Bougainville—Enters the English Channel—And, after a fine Passage, and fair Wind, from the Cape of Good Hope, anchors at Spithead, on Saturday the 20th of March, 1769, having been absent two Years and seven Months.

ON Tuesday the 15th, we anchored, as we have observed, at the distance of four miles from the town of Macassar, which, by our reckoning, lies in latitude 5 deg. 10 min. S. and in 117 deg. 28 min. E. longitude, having been in our run from the Strait of Magellan not less than 35 weeks. On Sunday the 20th, we sailed, at day-break, and in the afternoon of the ensuing day, anchored in the road of Bonthain. The

guard

guard boats were immediately moored close to the shore, to prevent all communication between our boats and those of the country. Captain Carteret having waited upon the resident, to settle the price, and mode of procuring provisions, a house was allotted to his use, situated near the sea-side, and close to a small fort of eight guns, the only one in this place. The house being fitted up as an hospital, the sick were landed, and as soon as our people were on shore, a guard of 36 privates, two sergeants, and two corporals, under the command of Le Cerf, was set over them, who were not permitted to above 30 yards from the hospital, nor were any of the natives suffered to come near enough to sell them any thing; so that the profits of the traffic fell into the hands of the Dutch soldiers, whose gains were immoderate; so great indeed, that some of them sold various articles at a profit of more than a thousand per cent. after having extorted the provisions at what price they pleased from the natives; and if a countryman ventured to express any signs of discontent, a broad sword was immediately flourished over his head; this was always sufficient to silence complaint, and send the sufferer quietly away. The captain having remonstrated with Mr. Swellingrable on the injustice of this procedure, he reprimanded the soldiers with becoming spirit; but this produced no good effect; and after this, Le Cerf's wife sold provisions at more than double the prime cost, while it was suspected, that he sold arrack to the seamen. It was the duty of one of the soldiers, by rotation, to procure the day's provision for the whole guard, which service he performed by going into the country with his musquet and bag; nor was this honest provider satisfied with what his bag would hold, for one of them, without any ceremony, drove down a young buffalo, and his comrades supplied themselves with wood to dress it from the pallisadoes of the fort. The captain thought the report of this fact so extraordinary, that he went on shore to see the breach, and found the poor blacks repairing it. On the 26th and 27th, three vessels arrived here, one of which had

1   troops

troops on board, deftined for the Banda Iflands, but their boats not being allowed to fpeak with any of our people, the captain prevailed on the refident, to pur-chafe for his ufe four cafks of very good falt provifions, two being pork, and two beef. On Monday the 28th, above 100 country veffels, called proas, anchored in the bay of Bonthain. Thefe veffels fifh round the ifland of Celebes, going out at one monfoon, and coming back with the other: they carry Dutch colours, and fend the produce of their labours to China for fale.

On Monday the 18th of January, a let-ter from Macaffar was brought to the A. D. 1768. captain, by which he was informed, that the Dolphin, our old confort, had been at Batavia. On Thurfday the 28th, the fecretary of the council, who accompanied Le Cerf hither, received orders to return to Macaffar. Our carpenter by this time having greatly recovered his health, began to examine into the condition of the Swallow, and fhe was found to have feveral leaks; and as little could be done to thefe, we were reduced to an entire dependance on our pumps. Her main-maft was alfo fprung, and appeared to be rotten. As no wood could be procured here to make a new one, we patched it up, without either iron or forge, as well as we could. On the 19th of February, Le Cerf, the military officer was recalled, in order, as was reported, to make preparations for an expedition to the ifland of Bally; and on Monday the 7th of March, the largeft of the guard boats, a floop of 40 tons, was likewife ordered to return to Macaffar, with part of the foldiers. On the 9th, the refident received a letter from the governor, enquiring when Captain Carteret would fail for Batavia, though he muft have known this would not be before the eaftern monfoon fet in, which would not be till May. Thefe were fufpicious circumftances, which gained ftrength toward the conclufion of the month, at which time a canoe was obferved to paddle round the fhip, feveral times in the night, and to retire as foon as fhe was feen. It is proper to obferve here, that the town of Macaffar is in a diftrict called Macaffar, or Bony, the

king

king whereof is an ally of the Dutch, who have frequently been repulsed in their attempts to reduce other parts of the island, one of which is inhabited by a people called Bugguesses, and another Waggs, or Tosora. The last place is fortified with cannon ; for the natives were acquainted with the use of fire-arms, and were supplied with them from Europe, before the Dutch settled themselves at Macassar in the room of the Portuguese.

On Tuesday the 29th, a black man delivered a letter to our lieutenant, directed to "The commander of the English ship at Bonthain," the purport of which was to acquaint the captain, that the king of Bony, in conjunction with the Dutch, had formed a design to cut us off; they were not to appear in the business, but the son of the king of Bony was appointed the principal agent. Besides the plunder of the Swallow, he was to receive a gratuity from his employers. The letter intimated that he was now at Bonthain, with 800 men, ready to execute the project, which was formed from a jealousy of our being connected with the enemies of the Dutch, with a view of expelling them out of the island ; or at least they suspected, that by our intelligence, a scheme of that kind might be planned, on our return to England. This letter became a new subject of speculation, and though ill written, with respect to style and manner, yet it did not therefore deserve the less notice ; especially when we recollected the recall of Le Cerf, and other remarkable circumstances, which have been already related. However, whether the intelligence, and our conjectures, were true or false, it was our duty to take proper measures for our security. Accordingly all hands were immediately set to work. We rigged the ship, bent the sails, unmoored, got springs upon our cables, loaded all our guns, and barricadoed the deck. Every one slept under arms during the night ; and the next day being the 30th, we fixed four swivel guns on the fore part of the quarter deck ; and warped the ship farther off from the bottom of the bay, towards the eastern shore, that, in case of necessity, we might have
more

more room for action.   At this time the resident was
up the country, transacting business for the company,
and, before his departure, he told the captain, he should
certainly return by the 1st of April.   It was now the
4th, and we had neither seen him, nor received any
answer to a letter the captain had wrote him; but on
Tuesday the 5th, he came on board, and a few minutes
convinced us, he was not in any respect privy to the
supposed design against us.   He acknowledged, that a
minister of the king of Bony, had lately paid him a
visit, and had not well accounted for his being in this
part of the country; and, at the captain's request, very
readily undertook to make farther enquiries concerning
Bony and his people; and a few days after he sent us
word, that having made a very strict enquiry, whether
any persons belonging to the king of Bony had been
at Bonthain, he had been informed, that one of the
princes of that kingdom had been there in disguise;
but that of the 800 men, who were said, according to
our intelligence, to be with him, he could find no
traces.   At this visit, while aboard, Mr. Swellingrabel
took notice of the ship, observing, that it was put in a
state of defence, and seeing every thing ready for immediate action, he said, that the people on shore had
informed him of our vigilance and activity, and in
particular, of our having exercised our men at small
arms every day.   In return, the captain told him,
we should continue on our guard, which he seemed to
approve, and we parted with mutual promises of
friendship and good faith.

On Saturday the 16th, the resident, M. Le Cerf, with
another officer, who was likewise an ensign, came on
board and dined with us.   After dinner, the captain
asked Le Cerf, what was become of his expedition to
Bally, to which he answered drily, that it was laid aside,
without saying any thing more on the subject.   On
the 23rd, he returned to Macassar, and the other ensign
took upon him the command of the soldiers that still
remained at this place.   The season now advanced
apace, when navigation to the westward would again

be practicable, which gave us all great pleasure, especially as putrid fevers began to make their appearance among us, by which several were attacked, and one was carried off. On the 7th of May, Captain Carteret received a long letter, written in Dutch, from the governor of Macassar, the general purport of which was, to exculpate himself from the charge of having, in conjunction with the king of Bony, formed a design to cut us off. He denied, in the most solemn manner, his having the least knowledge of such a project, and required the letter to be put into his hands, that the writer might be brought to such punishment as he deserved ; but the captain would not deliver up the letter, knowing that the writer would certainly have been punished with equal severity, whether the contents were true or false ; and it must be confessed, we had the greatest reason to believe that there was not sufficient ground for the main charge contained therein, though it is not equally probable that the writer believed it to be false. By the 22nd, we were ready to sail from this place, but before we take our departure, we shall make a few observations ; and also give a particular account of the situation, trade, and produce of the Sunda Islands, the manners and customs of the inhabitants, &c. as these places are generally mentioned, and some of them touched at, by all our circumnavigators.

I, *Of the Celebes, or the Island of Macassar.*

. Southward of the Philippines (of which we have given a full description) lies the island of Celebes, or Macassar, extending from 1 deg. 30 min. N. latitude, to 5 deg. 30 min. S. having the great island of Borneo on the west, and the Mollucca's on the east. The length of it from the S. W. point to the N. E. is about 500 miles, and in the broadest part of it, it is near 200 miles over. The south part of the island is divided by a bay seven or eight leagues wide, which runs forty or fifty leagues up into the country, and on the east side of the island are several bays and harbours, and abundance of

small

small islands and shoals: towards the north there is some high land: but on the east the country is low and flat, and watered with many little rivulets. This island is divided into six petty kingdoms or provinces, the principal whereof are Celebes, on the N. W. lying under the equinoctial; and Macassar, which takes in all the south part of the island: the rest of the provinces were usually under the dominion of one of these; whereupon the island sometimes receives its name from one, and sometimes from the other.

The air is hot and moist, the whole country lying under or very near the line, subject to great rains. It is most healthful during the northern monsoons: if they fail of blowing at their accustomed time, the island grows sickly, and great numbers of people are swept away. They have mines of copper, tin, and gold, but we do not find they are much wrought; the gold they have is found chiefly in the sands of their rivers, and at the bottom of hills, washed down by torrents. In their woods they have ebony, calambac and sanders, and several sorts of wood proper for dying; and no place, it is said, affords larger bamboos, some of them being four or five fathoms long, and above two foot diameter, which they make use of in building their houses and boats. Their fruits and flowers are much the same with those in the Philippines, and therefore we shall not tire the reader with a repetition of them, only mention some of the principal. They have pepper and sugar of their own growth, as well as betel and arek, in great plenty; but no nutmegs, mace or cloves; however, of these they used formerly to import such quantities from the spice islands that they had sufficient for their own use, and sold great quantities to foreigners. Their rice is said to be better than in any other parts of India, it not being overflowed annually as in other countries, but watered from time to time by the husbandman as occasion requires; and from the goodness of their rice, the natives are of a stronger constitution than those of Siam or other parts of India. Their fruits are also held to be of a more delicious taste than the

fruits

fruits of other countries which are expofed to floods : the plains here are covered with the cotton fhrub which bears a red flower, and when the flower falls, it leaves a head about as big as a walnut, from whence the cotton is drawn ; and that which comes from Macaffar is accounted the fineft in India. Of all their plants, opium is what they moft admire; it is a fhrub which grows at the bottom of mountains, or in ftony ground : the branches afford a liquor which is drawn out much after the fame manner as palm wine, and being ftopped up clofe in a pot, comes to a confiftency, when they make it up in little pills : they often diffolve one of thefe pills in water and fprinkle their tobacco with it ; and thofe who are ufed to take it can never leave it off : they are lulled into a pleafing dream, and intoxicated as with ftrong liquor ; but it infenfibly preys upon their fpirits and fhortens their lives : they will take the quantity of two pins heads in a pipe of tobacco, when they enter into a battle, and become almoft infenfible of wounds or danger till the effect of it is worn off.

The natives of this ifland are famous for the poifons they compound of the venomous drugs and herbs their country produces ; of which, it is faid, the very touch or fmell occafions prefent death : their young gentlemen are inftructed how to blow their little poifoned darts through a tube or hollow cane, about fix feet in length ; with thefe they engage their enemies ; and if they make the leaft wound with thefe darts, it is faid to be mortal. Though thefe weapons would not be much dreaded among people that are well cloathed, yet as the natives engage naked, their fkins are eafily penetrated, and the poifon operates fo fpeedily, that it is not eafy to cure them : they will ftrike a man with thefe darts at near an hundred yards diftance.

Macaffar, the chief city here, is fituated on the banks of the river of the fame name, near the S. W. corner of the ifland. Here the Dutch have a very ftrong fort, mounted with a great number of cannon ; and the garrifon confifts of 800 men. The ftreets of the town are wide and neat, but not paved, and trees are planted on

each

each fide of them. The palaces, mofque, and great
houfes are of ftone, but the houfes of the meaner fort
of wood of various colours, which make them look very
beautiful, but are built on pillars like thofe of Siam, and
the roofs like theirs alfo are covered with palm or cocoa
leaves. Here are fhops along the ftreets, and large
market places, where a market is held twice in 24
hours, viz. in the morning before fun-rife, and an
hour before fun-fet, where only women are feen ; a man
would be laughed at to be found amongft them ; from
all the villages you fee the young wenches crowding to
market with flefh, fifh, rice and fowls; they abftain only
from pork, which their religion forbids. Upon a computation of the number of inhabitants, in this city and
the neighbouring villages, fome years ago, they amounted to 160,000 men able to bear arms ; but now are not
half that number, many of them having forfaken their
country fince the Dutch deprived them of their trade.
The reft of the towns and villages were once equally
populous, but are now many of them deferted. The
people of Macaffar have excellent memories, and are
quick of apprehenfion ; they will imitate any thing they
fee, and would probably become good proficients in all
arts and fciences, if they did not want good mafters
to improve their talents.

They have alfo ftrong robuft bodies, are extremely
induftrious, and as ready to undergo fatigues as any
people whatever : nor are any people more addicted to
arms and hardy enterprifes, infomuch that they may
be looked upon as almoft the only foldiers on the other
fide the bay of Bengal ; and accordingly are hired
into the fervice of other princes and ftates on that fide,
as the Swifs are in this part of the world : even the
Europeans frequently employ them in their fervice,
but have fometimes fuffered by trufting them too far ;
or rather, our people being two apt to ufe them like
flaves, as they do the poor Portuguefe and Muftees in
their fervice ; this is a treatment which the Macaffarians
will not bear, and never fail to revenge whenever it is
attempted by our European governors.

I   The

The people of Macassar are of a moderate stature, their complexions swarthy, their cheek-bones stand high, and their noses are generally flat ; the last is esteemed a beauty, and almost as much pains taken to make them so in their infancy, as to make the Chinese ladies have little feet.

They have shining black hair, which is tied up and covered with a turban, or cloth wound about their heads when they are dressed, but at other times they wear a kind of hat or cap with little brims.

They continually rub and supple the limbs of their infants with oil, to render them nimble and active ; and this is thought to be one reason there is hardly ever seen a lame or crooked person among them.

Their male children of the better sort, it is said, are always taken from their mothers at six or seven years of age, and committed to the care of some remote relation, that they may not be too much indulged and effeminated by the caresses of the mother : they are sent to school to their priests, who teach them to write and read and cast accounts, and the precepts of the koran : their characters very much resemble the Arabic, which is not strange, since their ancestors, many of them, were Arabians.

Besides their books, every child is bred up to some handicraft trade ; they are also taught several sports and martial exercises, if they are of quality ; but the meaner sort are employed in husbandry, fishing, and ordinary trades, as in other places.

This people seem to be inspired with just notions of honour and friendship, and there are instances of many of them who have exposed their lives even in defence of foreigners and Christians ; and of others who have generously relieved and maintained people in distress, and even suffered them to share their estates. They retained that love of liberty, that they were the last of the Indian nations that were enslaved by the Dutch, which did not happen neither till after a long and very expensive war, wherein almost the whole force of the Hollanders in India was employed. The people in

general

general are very much subject to passion ; and they
will condemn their own rashness if they are in the
wrong.

The women are remarkable chaste and reserved, at
least they cannot help appearing so ; for the least smile
or glance on any but their husbands, is held a sufficient
reason for a divorce : nor dare they admit of a visit even
from a brother, but in the presence of the husband :
and the law indemnifies him for killing any man he
shall find alone with his wife, or on whom she has conferred any mark of her favour. But the inhabitants of
this country are in general so little addicted to infamous
practices, or litigious disputes, that they have neither
attornies or bailiffs among them. If any differences
arise, the parties apply personally to the judge, who
determines the matter with expedition and equity. In
some criminal cases, such as murder, robbery, &c. he
has a right to execute justice himself, by destroying the
offender. On the other hand, the man keeps as many
wives and concubines as he pleases, and nothing can be
more ignominious than the want of children, and the
having but one wife : the love of women, and the desire of children is universal ; and according to the number of women and children the man possesses his happiness is rated.

To proceed ; though the women of fashion generally
keep close, yet upon certain festivals they are suffered
to come abroad and spend their time in public company, in dancing and other diversions used in the country ; but the men do not mix with them as in this part of
the world, only they have the happiness to see and be
seen, which makes them wait for this happy time with
impatience.

Their princes and great men wear a garment made
of scarlet cloth or brocaded silk, with large buttons of
gold ; they have likewise a very handsome embroidered
sash made of silk, in which their dagger and purse are
placed, with their knife, crice, and other little trinkets.
People of figures dye the nail of the little finger of the
left-hand red, and let it grow as long as the finger.

No. 35.   6 Y   The

The women wear a muslin shift, or rather waistcoat, close to their bodies, and a pair of breeches, which reaches down to the middle of the leg, made of silk or cotton, and have no other head dress than their hair tied up in a roll, with some curls hanging down their necks; they throw a loose piece of linen or muslin over all when they go abroad; nor have they any ornaments but a gold chain about their necks. They are fond of a fine equipage and a great number of servants to attend them, and if they have not so many of their own as their quality requires, they will not stir out, till they have got the usual number, by hiring or borrowing them. The furniture of their houses consist chiefly of carpets and cushions, and the couches they sleep on. They sit crofs-legged on mats and carpets, as most Asiatics do.

This island produces most animals except sheep. There are monkeys and baboons in abundance, that will set upon travellers; some of them are quite black, some of a straw colour, and others white, the latter of which are generally as big as mastiffs, and much more mischievous than the others. Some have long tails, and walk on all-fours; others are without tails, and walk upright, using their fore-feet as hands, and in their actions greatly resemble the human species. Their going in large companies secures them from the more powerful beasts of the forests; but they are sometimes conquered by the large serpents, which pursue them to the tops of trees, and destroy them.

The natives do not scruple eating any flesh but pork, this no Mahometan will touch; but their food is chiefly rice, fish, herbs, fruit and roots; flesh they eat but little of. They have but two meals a day, one in the morning, and the other about sun-set; but their chief meal is in the evening; they chew betel and areka, or smoke tobacco mixed with opium most part of the day. Their liquor is tea, coffee, sherbet, or chocolate, and they have palm wine, arrac, or spirits, which they sometimes indulge in, though it is prohibited by their religion. They loll upon carpets at their meals, and

eat

eat off of diſhes made of China, wood, ſilver or copper, which are ſet on little low lacquered tables; and take up the rice with their hands inſtead of ſpoons, which they ſeem not to know the uſe of. In the celebration of marriage the huſband receives no other portion with his wife than the preſents ſhe received before marriage. As ſoon as the prieſt has performed the ceremony, the new-married couple are confined in an apartment by themſelves for three ſucceſſive days, having only a ſervant to bring them ſuch neceſſaries as they may have occaſion for, during which time their friends and acquaintances are entertained, and great rejoicings made at the houſe of the bride's father. At the expiration of the three days the parties are ſet at liberty, and receive the congratulations of their friends; after which, the bridegroom conducts his wife home, and both apply themſelves to buſineſs, he to his accuſtomed profeſſion, and ſhe to the duties belonging to houſewifery, and the management of a family. When a man has reaſon to ſuſpect his wife of infidelity, he applies to a prieſt for a divorce; and if the complaint appears juſt, there is no difficulty in obtaining it. In this caſe the ſecular judge pronounces the accuſed party guilty, declares her to be divorced, and ſettles the terms; both parties, after this judgment, have liberty to marry again.

The Macaſſarians had originally ſtrange notions of religion: they believed there were no other gods but the ſun and moon; and to them they ſacrificed in the public ſquares, not having materials which they thought ſufficiently valuable to be employed in erecting temples. According to their creed, the ſun and moon were eternal, as well as the heavens, whoſe empire they divided between them. Theſe abſurdities, however, had not ſo laſting an influence either over the nobles or people, as is found from the religious doctrines of other nations; for the Turks and apoſtles of the koran arriving in the country, the ſovereign and his people embraced Mahometaniſm, and the other parts of the iſland ſoon followed their example. They are great pretenders to magic; and carry charms about them, ſup-

poſing

posing these will secure them from every danger. When any one is so ill as to be given over by the physician, the priests are sent for, who, attributing the violence of their disease to the influence of some evil spirit, first pray to them, and then write the names of God and Mahomet on small pieces of paper, which are carefully hung about their necks; and if the patient does not soon recover, his death is considered as inevitable, and every preparation is made for his expected departure. These people perform their funeral ceremonies with great decency; to secure which, the meanest person makes provision while in health, by assigning a certain sum to defray the necessary expences attending it. As soon as a person is dead, the dead body is washed, and, being cloathed in a white robe, is placed in a room hung with white, which is scented with the strongest perfumes. Here it continues for three days, and on the fourth it is carried on a palanquin to the grave, preceded by the friends and relations, and followed by the priests, who have attendants that carry incense and perfumes, which are burnt all the way from the house to the grave. The body is interred without a coffin, there being only a plank, at the bottom of the grave for it to lie on, and another to cover it: and when this last is placed, the earth is thrown in, and the grave filled up. If the person is of any distinguished quality, a handsome tomb is immediately placed over the grave, adorned with flowers, and the relations burn incense and other perfumes for 40 days successively.

This island was formerly under a monarchial government; and in order to prevent the crown falling to an infant, the eldest brother succeeded after the death of the king. All places of trust in the civil government were disposed of by the prime ministers; but the officers of the revenue and of the houshold were appointed by the sovereign. The king's forces, when out of actual service, were not allowed any pay, but only their cloaths, arms, and ammunition. It is said, that in former wars he has brought 12,000 horse, and 80,000 foot

foot into the field ; but the laft war with the Dutch, proved the total deftruction of both king and country ; fince which, this ifland has been under the government of three different princes, who are conftantly at variance with each other ; which is a favourable circumftance for the Dutch, who might otherwife meet with a powerful oppofition, and be deprived of thofe advantages they have fo long poffeffed on this fide the globe. Thefe princes hold affemblies at particular times on affairs that concern the general intereft ; and the refult of their determinations becomes a law to each ftate. When any conteft arifes, it is decided by the governor of the Dutch colony, who prefides at the above diet. He keeps a watchful eye over thefe different fovereigns, and holds them in perfect equality with each other, to prevent any of them from aggrandizing themfelves to the prejudice of the company. The Dutch have dif-armed them all, under pretence of hindering them from injuring each other, but in reality only to keep them in a ftate of fubjection.

Jampadan is another port-town about 15 miles fouth of Macaffar River, one of the beft harbours in India, and the firft town the Dutch took from the natives; here they funk or feized all the Portuguefe fleet when they were in full peace with that nation. The reft of the towns and villages lying in the flat country near the fea or the mouths of rivers, are for the moft part built with wood or cane, and ftand upon high pillars on ac-count of the annual flood, when they have a communi-cation with one another only by boats.

About the Celebes are feveral iflands that go by the fame name, the principal of which is fituated about five leagues from the S. E. corner. This ifland is about 80 miles long, and 30 broad : on the eaft-fide of it is a large town and harbour called Callacaffong, the ftreets of which are fpacious, and enclofed on each fide with cocoa trees. The inhabitants are governed by an ab-folute prince, fpeak the Malayan tongue, and are Ma-hometans. The Straits of Patience are on the other fide of this ifland ; they are fo called from the great

I   difficulty

difficulty in passing them, which arises from the violence of the currents, and the contrariety of the winds.

II. *Of the Situation, Trade, and Produce of Borneo, Sumatra, and Java, commonly called the Sunda Islands; and of the Manners and Customs of the Inhabitants, &c.*

THE most considerable of the Sunda Islands, called so from the straits near which they lie, are Borneo, Sumatra and Java.

Borneo extends from 7 deg. 30 min. N. latitude, to 4 deg. S. latitude, and from 107 to 117 degrees of longitude, being about 700 miles in length and 500 in breadth, and is computed to be 2500 miles in circumference. The figure of this island being almost round, it probably contains a greater number of acres than any island hitherto discovered. To the eastward of it lies the island of Celebes or Macassar, to the south the island of Java, to the west the island of Sumatra, and to the N. E. the Philippine Islands.

The air of this country is not excessive hot, considering it is situated under the equinoctial, being refreshed almost every day with showers and cool breezes, as all other countries that are under the line; but as those parts of the island which border on the sea-coast lie upon a flat for several hundred miles, and are annually flooded; upon the retiring of the waters, the whole surface of the ground is covered with mud or soft ouze, which the sun darting its rays perpendicularly upon, raises thick noisome fogs, which are not dispersed till nine or ten in the morning, and render those parts of the island very unwholesome. The multitude of frogs and insects that the waters leave behind, and are soon killed by the heat of the sun, cause an intolerable stench also at that time of the year, and corrupt the air: add to this the cold chilling winds and damps which succeed the hottest days; from all which, we may conclude it must be very unhealthful, at least to European constitutions: and the loss of our countrymen, who yearly travel thither, sufficiently convinces us of this truth. As to their monsoons, or periodical winds, they are wester-

ly

ly from September to April, or thereabouts; during which time is their wet feafon, when heavy rains continually pour down, intermixed with violent ftorms of thunder and lightning; and at this time it is very rare to have two hours fair weather together on the fouth coaft of the ifland, whither the Europeans principally refort.   The dry feafon begins ufually in April and continues till September; and in this part of the year too, they feldom fail of a fhower every day, when the fea breeze comes in.

The harbours of greateft note, and to which the Europeans ufually refort, are Banjar Maffeen, Succadanea and Borneo, but much more to Banjar Maffeen than either of the other; the greateft quantities of pepper growing towards the fource of that river, which falls into the fea 3 deg. 18 min. S. latitude.   The town of Banjar formerly ftood about 12 miles up the river, and was built partly on wooden pillars, and partly on floats of timber in the river; but there is now no fign of a town there, the inhabitants being removed to Tatas, about fix miles higher.

The city of Borneo, formerly the refidence of the principal fultan or king of the ifland, lies on the N. W. part of the ifland, in 4 deg. 55 min. N. latitude, and is a very commodious harbour.   This city is very large, the ftreets fpacious, and the houfes well built; they are in general three ftories high, covered with flat roofs, and the fultan's palace is a very elegant and extenfive building.   It is the chief feat of commerce in the ifland, and the port is continually crowded with fhips from China, Cambodia, Siam, Malacca, &c. · The Englifh and Portuguefe have fome trade here, though no fettled factory. The port of Succadanea lies on the weft-fide of the ifland, in 15 min. S. latitude, and was heretofore more reforted to by the Europeans than any other.   Over againft this, on the eaft-fide of the ifland, ftands another fea-port town, called Paffeir, in 15 min. S. latitude; but is not a place of any great trade.

One of the moft confiderable inland towns is Caytonge, the fultan whereof is now the moft potent prince
in

in the island: this city lies about 100 miles up the river Banjar; and about 200 miles higher stands the town of Negaree, the residence of another sultan. The names of the other principal towns are Tanjongbuoro, Sedang, Tanjongdatoo, Sambas, Landa, Pisagadan, Cotapanjang Sampit, Tanjong, Selatan, Gonwarengen and Pomanoocan.

Their chief rivers are, 1. Banjar. 2. Tatas. 3. Java. 4. Succadanea; and, 5. Borneo.

Banjar is a fine river, rising in the mountains in the middle of the island, and, running south, discharges itself into a bay on the S. E. part of the island, being navigable for several hundred miles; the banks are planted with tall ever-green trees. The river Tatas falls into the mouth of Banjar River, and is frequently called the China River, because the China junks lie in the mouth of it. The rivers Java and Succadanea run from the N. E. to the S. W. and fall into the bay of Succadanea in the S. W. part of the island.

The river Borneo falls into the bay of Borneo, in the N. W. part of the island. The tides in the river Banjar flow but once in 24 hours, and that in the day-time; they never rise more than half a foot in the night (unless in a very dry season) which is occasioned by the rapid torrents, and the land winds blowing very strong in the night-time. There lie three islands within the entrance of the river, the first of which is covered with tall trees, that may be seen at sea, and are a good mark for sailing over the bar. If a ship be aground, the ebb is so very strong, occasioned by the land floods, that she will run the hazard of being broke to pieces; and the trees continually driving down the river, render the navigation still more dangerous. The best anchoring place is a mile or two within the river; it is best to sail up with the flood, the tide of ebb runs so strong. There are a great many fine bays and harbours on the coast, but that most resorted to is at the mouth of the river Banjar.

The natives of Borneo consist of two different people,

ple, that are of different religions; those upon the sea coast are usually called Banjareens, from the town of Banjar, to which most nations resort, to trade with them. The Banjareens are of a low stature, very swarthy, their features bad, resembling much the negroes of Guinea, though their complexion are not so dark; they are well proportioned, their hair is black, and shines with the oil with which they perpetually grease it. The women are of a low stature and small limbs, as the men are, but their features and complexion much better, and they move with a good grace. The lower class of people go almost naked; they have only a little bit of cloth before, and a piece of linen tied about their heads. Their betters, when they are dressed on days of ceremony, wear a vest of red or blue silk, and a loose piece of silk or fine linen tied about their loins, and thrown over their left shoulder. They wear a pair of drawers, but no shirt, and their legs and feet are bare; their hair is bound up in a roll, and a piece of muslin or callico tied over it; they always carry a crice or dagger in their sash when they go abroad. The Byaios or mountaineers are much taller and larger bodied men than the Banjareens, and a braver people, which their situation and manner of life may account for, being inured to labour, and to follow the chace for their daily food; whereas the Banjareens use very little exercise, travelling chiefly by water. The Byaios have scarce any cloathing, but, not admiring their tawny skins, paint their bodies blue, and, like all other people that live in hot climates, anoint themselves with oil, which smells very strong; and the better sort, it is said, pull out their fore-teeth, and place artificial ones, made of gold, in their stead; but their greatest ornament consists of a number of tygers teeth, which are strung together, and worn about the neck. Some of them are very fond of having large ears; to obtain which, they make holes in the soft parts of them when young; to these holes are fastened weights about the breadth of a crown piece, which is continually pressing on the ears, and expand them to such a length, as to cause them to rest upon the shoulders.

The Banjareens are an hospitable friendly people, where they are not abused, or apprehend foreigners have a design upon their liberties; they seem to be men of good sense, but not being acquainted with the world, are frequently imposed upon in their traffic with the crafty Chinese. The chief part of their food here is rice, as it is in other hot countries, but with it they eat venison, fish, or fowl, and almost all kind of meat, except hogs flesh; and men of figure are served in gold or silver plate; the common people are content with brass or earthen dishes, and all sit cross-legged upon mats or carpets at their meals, and indeed almost all day long, chewing betel and arek, or smoaking tobacco, which both sexes are very fond of when it is mixed with opium. The whole company usually smoke out of one pipe; the master of the feast having smoked first, passes it round the company, and they will sometimes sit smoaking so long, that they grow stupid. At other times they divert themselves with comedies, and the Chinese have taught them to game; their rural sports are hunting, shooting, and fishing. They have such plenty of fish, that they may take as many as will serve them a day at one cast, from their houses, which are built upon floats in their rivers. Their usual salute is the salam, lifting up their hands to their heads, and bowing their bodies a little; and before their princes, they throw themselves prostrate on the ground: no one presumes to speak to a great man, till he is first spoken to, and required to tell his business: they usually travel in covered boats upon their rivers: but the great men who live in the inland country ride on elephants or horses. Besides rice, already mentioned, the produce of this country is cocoa-nuts, oranges, citrons, plantains, melons, bananas, pine-apples, mangoes, and all manner of tropical fruits; cotton, canes, rattans, and plenty of very fine timber; gold, precious stones, camphire, bezoar, and pepper. There are three sorts of black pepper; the first and best is the Molucca, or lout pepper; the second is called Caytonge pepper, and the worst sort is the Negaree pepper, of which there is the greatest

3   plenty.

plenty. This is small, hollow and light; and commonly full of duft, and the buyer will be imposed on if he
buys it by meafure, and does not weigh it. He muft
take care alfo, that the pepper be not mixed with little
black ftones, which are not eafily feen. The white
pepper grows on the fame tree as the black pepper does,
and bears twice the price: it is conjectured to be the
beft of the fruit that drops off itfelf, and is gathered up
by the poor people in fmall quantities, before it turns
black, and the fcarcity of it occafions it to be fo dear;
but we feem to want a more fatisfactory account of this
matter.

The animals here are the fame as on the continent of
India, viz. bears, tygers, elephants, buffaloes, deer, &c.
but the moft remarkable animal, and which is almoft
peculiar to this ifland, is that monftrous monkey called
the oran-outang, or man of the woods, near fix feet high,
and walks upon his hinder legs. He has a face like a
man, and is not fo ugly as fome of the human fpecies,
particularly the Hottentots; he has no tail, or any hair
on his body, but where a man has hair. Mr. Beeck-
man, captain of an Indiaman, purchafed one of them,
who would drink punch, and open his cafe of brandy to
get a dram, if he was left alone with it, drink a quantity,
and then return the bottle to the cafe. He would lay
himfelf down to fleep as a man does: if the captain appeared angry with him, he would whine and figh till he
was reconciled. He would wreftle with the feamen,
and was ftronger than any of them, though he was not
a year old when he died; for the captain loft him as foon
as he came into cold weather, having been bred in the
hotteft climates.

Among their minerals is gold, which the mountaineers get out of the fands of their rivulets in the dry
feafon, and difpofe of it to the Banjareens, from whom
the Europeans receive it: there are alfo iron mines,
and the load-ftone is found here.

The principal articles of merchandize imported from
Borneo by the Europeans, are pepper, gold, diamonds,
camphire, bezoar, aloes, maftick and other gums;

and the goods proper to be carried thither, besides bullion and treasure, are small cannon from 100 to 200 weight, lead, callimancoes, cutlery wares, iron bars, small steel bars, hangers, the smallest sort of spike nails, twenty-penny nails, graplings of 40 pounds weight, red leather boots, spectacles, clock-work, small arms with brass mountings, horse pistols, blunderbusses, gunpowder and looking-glasses. The purchasing gold is a profitable article, and diamonds may be had reasonably, though they are generally small ones : they usually purchase gold with dollars, giving a certain number of silver dollars for the weight of one dollar in gold. The current money is dollars, half and quarter dollars; and for small change they have a sort of money made of lead in the form of rings, which are strung on a kind of dry leaf.

The language of the inhabitants on the coast is the Malayan ; but the islanders have a language peculiar to themselves, and both retain the superstitious customs of the Chinese. They are intirely ignorant of astronomy ; and when an eclipse happens, they think the world is going to be destroyed. Arithmetic they know but little of ; and their only method of calculating, is, by parallel lines and moveable buttons on a board. They have likewise little knowledge of physic ; and the letting of blood, how desperate soever the case of the patient may be, is to them a circumstance of a very alarming nature, as they suppose, by the operation, we let out our very souls and lives. It is their opinion, that most of their distempers are caused through the malice of some evil demon ; and when a person is sick, instead of applying to medicine, they make an entertainment of various kinds of provisions, which they hold under some conspicuous tree in a field ; these provisions, which consist of rice, fowl, fish, &c. they offer for the relief of the person afflicted ; and if he recover, they repeat the offering, by way of returning thanks, for the blessing received ; but if the patient dies, they express their resentment against the spirit by whom he is supposed to have been afflicted. Both Pagans and
Mahometans

Mahometans allow a plurality of wives and concubines; and the marriage ceremonies of both are the same as in other Mahometan countries. The girls are generally married at the age of ten, and leave child-bearing before they are twenty-five. The women are very constant after marriage; but are apt to bestow favours with great freedom when single; and however indiscreet they may have been in this point, they are not considered the worse for it by their husbands, nor dare any one reproach them for what they have committed previous to their marriage. They in general live to an advanced age, which is attributed to their frequent use of the water; for both men and women bathe in the rivers once in the day; and from this practice they are very expert swimmers. In burying their dead, they always place the head to the north, and they throw into the grave several kinds of provisions, from an absurd and superstitious notion that these may be useful to them in the other world. They fix the place of interment out of the reach of the floods; and the mourners, as in Japan and China, are dressed in white, and carry lighted torches in their hands.

In the inland part of this country, are several petty kingdoms, each of which is governed by a rajah, or king. All the rajahs were formerly subject to the rajah of Borneo, who was esteemed the supreme king over the whole island; but his authority has been of late years greatly diminished; and there are other kings equal, if not more powerful than himself; particularly the king of Caytonge. The town where this prince resides is situated about 80 miles up the Banjar River. His palace is a very elegant building erected on pillars, and is open on all sides. Before the palace is a large building, consisting only of one room, which is set apart for holding councils, and entertaining foreigners. In the centre of the room is the throne, covered with a rich canopy of gold and silver brocade. About the palace are planted several cannon, which are so old, and mounted on such wretched carriages, that they are neither ornamental nor useful. This prince is esteemed

the

the greateſt, on account of the cuſtoms he receives at the port of Banjar Maſſeen, which are eſtimated at 8000 pieces of eight per annum. The king or Sultan of Negaree is the moſt conſiderable prince, next to the above : his palace is ſituated at a place called Metapoora, about 10 miles from Caytonge. There is a handſome armoury before the gates of his palace, which contains a great number of fire-arms, and ſeveral cannon. He is always on good terms with his neighbour the prince of Caytonge, and the reſt are ſubordinate to theſe two princes; great homage is paid them by the natives, and it is difficult for a ſtranger to get acceſs to them : the only means to effect this, is, by complimenting them with ſome valuable preſent, for avarice is their darling paſſion; and the ſtranger will be treated with reſpect in proportion to the preſent he makes.

Sumatra is one of the Sunda Iſlands, ſituate in the Indian ocean, between 93 and 104 deg. of eaſtern longitude, and between 5 deg. 30 min. N. latitude, and 5 deg. 30 min. S. latitude, the equinoctial line running croſs the middle of it; having Malacca on the N. Borneo on the E. Java on the S. E. and the Indian ocean on the weſt, and is 800 miles long, and about 150 broad. The air is generally unhealthful near the coaſt, the country being very hot, and very moiſt, and changing ſuddenly from ſultry heat in the day-time, to cold chilling winds in the night. It is the firſt of the remarkable iſlands that form the great Archipelago of the eaſt, the entrance of which is, as it were, blocked up by this iſland and Java, which form a barrier ſeparating the Indian from the Chineſe ocean; except that in the center between the two iſlands there is an opening, which appears as if purpoſely deſigned to admit a free paſſage for the advantages of commerce. This opening is called the Strait of Sunda, the ſouth part of which is the north of Java, and called Java Head; and the north point is the ſouth of Sumatra, called Flat Point. Theſe two are about ſix leagues aſunder, between which ſhips paſs from Europe directly to Batavia or China, without touching at the Indies; they ſtretch away eaſt from the Cape of Good Hope, and

and make no land till having traverfed the whole Indian fea they arrive at Java Head.

In Sumatra are no phyficians, but they rely upon the fkill and experience of fome good old women, who are acquainted with the nature of their fimples. The flux is the diftemper that ufually carries off foreigners, againft which the fruit guava and the pomegranate are certain remedies, if taken before the diftemper becomes violent; but moft other fruits promote the difeafe. Bathing in cold water is efteemed another remedy for the flux. Their water, unboiled, as well as fherbet, is very unwholefome; full meals of flefh ought to be avoided, occafioning a diftemper called the Mort Duchin, which is attended with a violent vomiting and purging, and ufually carries off the patient in 24 hours. Thofe gentlemen that drink ftrong liquors to excefs, ufually avoid the flux, but are carried off by fevers. The cholic and fmall-pox are often fatal to the natives, as well as foreigners; but they are feldom troubled with dropfies, gout, or ftone. People who are careful of their health, eat and drink moderately, and boil their water; nor do they avoid wine or arrack punch altogether, for thefe drank moderately in this moift air preferve, rather than deftroy health.

There is a chain of mountains which runs the whole length of the ifland, from the N. W. to the S. E. and here the air is fomething better than on the coaft; but the European factories are generally fituated at the mouths of rivers near the fea, for conveniency of trade, and here three years may be reckoned a long life, the falt ftinking oufe fends up fuch unwholefome vapours as perfectly poifon foreigners that are fent thither. The monfoons, or periodical winds, fhift here at the equinoxes, as they do in other parts of the Indian feas, blowing fix months in one direction, and fix months in the oppofite direction; and near the coaft there are other periodical winds, which blow the greateft part of the day from the fea, and in the night-time and part of the morning from the land; but thefe fcarce extend feven miles from the coaft. Here is alfo a mountain called

Single-

Single-demond, about 40 miles S. E. of Bencoolen, which is a mile in height perpendicular; the rocks near the weft coaft are generally barren, producing little befides fhrubs; but towards the bottom of them grows fome good timber. The country has a great many fmall rivers, but none of them navigable much above their mouths, falling from high mountains, and difcharging themfelves precipitately into the fea, either on the E. or W. after a very fhort courfe; the rains continuing here, as they do in moft places near the equinoctial, fix months and upwards, every year, and no where with more violence. The waters of the river Indapoora, during rains, look red for two miles beyond the mouth out at fea, occafioned, it is faid, by the great number of oaks that grow in their boggy grounds, and are almoft covered when the floods are higheft. The waters of all their rivers, which overflow the low countries, are very unwholefome, foul, and not fit to be drank till they are fettled, nor indeed till they have been boiled, and tea or fome other wholefome herbs infufed into them; and this, no doubt, is one caufe of the unwholefomenefs of the air, it being a very juft obfervation, that wherever the water is bad, the air is fo too.

The ifland of Sumatra was antiently, and is at prefent, divided into a great many kingdoms and ftates, of which Achen is the moft confiderable, whofe king is the moft powerful monarch in the ifland, the north part of it being in a manner fubject to him. Befides this prince, there are feveral orancayas, or great lords, in this kingdom, who exercife fovereign authority in their refpective territories; but they all acknowledge the king of Achen their fuperior, and accept of the great officers in his court. In former times the kings have exercifed fuch defpotic power as to difplace fome of thefe, and depofe others; and, on the other hand, inftances have been known where thefe princes have depofed the king, and placed another on the throne. There have been frequent ftruggles between the king of Achen and thefe princes for fovereign power; and if the former has in

some

some reigns been absolute, he has in others had a very limited authority. The king has the power of disposing of the crown, during his life, to such of his children as he thinks proper, whether born of a wife or a concubine: but if the king does not dispose of it in his life time, there are sometimes several competitors for it; and he who is most favoured by the orancayas, or vassal princes, usually carries his point; so that the crown is elective in these cases.

Achen, the metropolis of the kingdom of the same name, is situated at the N. W. end of Sumatra, in 93 deg. 30 min. E. longitude, and in 5 deg. 30 min. N. latitude, and is much the most considerable port in the island. It stands in a plain, surrounded with woods and marshes, about five miles distant from the sea, near a pleasant rivulet: it is an open town, without wall or moat, and the king's palace stands in the middle of it, being of an oval figure, about half a league in circumference, surrounded by a moat 25 feet broad, and as many deep: and about the palace there are cast up great banks of earth instead of a wall, well planted with reeds and canes, that grow to a prodigious height and thickness, insomuch that they cover the palace, and render it almost inaccessible; these reeds also are continually green, and not easily set on fire. There is no ditch or draw-bridge before the gates, but on each side a wall of stone about ten feet high that supports a terrace, on which some guns are planted; and a small stream runs through the middle of the palace, which is lined with stone, and has steps down to the bottom of it, for the conveniency of bathing. There are four gates, and as many courts, to be passed before we come to the royal apartments; and in some of these outward courts are the king's magazines, and the standings of his elephants: as for the inward courts of the palace, foreigners, or even the natives, hardly ever approach them; and therefore a just description of these is not to be expected. But notwithstanding the fortifications of this palace or castle, as it is sometimes called, are very mean and inconsiderable, yet the avenues to it are natu-

No. 35.   7 A   rally

rally well defended; for the country round about Achen is full of rivulets, marshes, and thick woods of cane or bamboo, which are almost impenetrable, and very hard to cut: there are several little forts erected also at proper distances in the marshes, where guards are planted to prevent any surprize. In the king's magazines, some authors tell us, are found a numerous artillery, and a good quantity of fire-arms, and that his guards consist of many thousand men; but that his greatest strength is in his elephants, who are trained up to trample upon fire, and stand unmoved at the report of a cannon; but this we shall examine more particularly when we come to speak of the maintenance of the prince, both with respect to domestic and military supplies, for later travellers do not seem to admire his power or grandeur. This city consists of 7 or 8000 houses, which take up the more ground because they are not contiguous, every person surrounding his dwelling with a pallisado pale that stands some yards distant from it; except in two or three of the principal streets where the markets are kept, and where foreigners inhabit, who chuse to live near one another, to defend themselves from thieves, robberies being very common here. The harbour, which is so large as to be capable of containing any number of the largest ships, is commanded by a spacious fortress encompassed with a ditch well fortified according to the Italian manner, and mounted with cannon. The English, Dutch, Danes, Portuguese, Guzarats, and Chinese, are the chief traders in this city. The king has a great number of horses, which, as well as the elephants, have rich and magnificent trappings. He is at no expence in times of war, for all his subjects are obliged to march at their own expence, and carry with them provisions for three months: he only furnishes them with arms, powder, lead, and rice, which is very trifling. In peace, it does not cost him any thing, even for the maintenance of his family, for his subjects supply him with all kinds of provisions: they also provide him and his concubines with cloaths. He is heir to all his subjects who die without issue male, and to all

forcigners

foreigners who die within his territories; and succeeds to the estates of all those who are put to death. From all which it appears, that the revenue of this prince, though not paid in money, is very considerable.

The inhabitants of Achen are more vicious than in other places on the coast: they are proud, envious, and treacherous; despise their neighbours, and yet pretend to have more humanity than the inhabitants of any other nation. Some of them are good machanics, especially in the building of gallies; and they are very dexterous in doing all kinds of smiths work: they also work well in wood and copper, and some of them are skilled in making artillery. They live very abstemiously, their chief food being rice, to which some of the better sort add a small quantity of fish, and their usual drink is water. They are very fond of tobacco, though they have but little of their own raising; and for want of pipes, they smoke in a bunco, in the same manner as the inhabitants on the coast of Coromandel. The buncho is the leaf of a tree, rolled up with a little tobacco in it, which they light at one end, and draw the smoke through the other till it is nearly burnt to the lips. These rolls are very curiously formed, and sold in the public markets in great quantities.

They hold a court of justice five times a week, for determining all matters of controversy, in which one of the chief orancayas presides as judge. There is also a criminal court, where cognizance is taken of all quarrels, robberies, murders, &c. committed in the city: and there is a third court, in which the cadi, or chief priest, presides, who judges concerning all infringements of an ecclesiastical nature. Besides these, there is a court for determining disputes between merchants, whether foreigners or natives. An exact account is kept here of all the customs, gifts, fines, and commodities, belonging to the king, with a list of all the persons who buy of his majesty, pay the duty, or make presents to him. Offenders are brought to a speedy trial, and the punishment is inflicted immediately after their conviction. If the offence be of a trifling nature, the punishment for

the

the first time is the loss only of a hand or foot, and the same for the second; but for the third, or if they rob to a considerable amount, they are impaled alive. When the hand or foot is to be cut off, the limb is laid on the edge of a broad hatchet, and the executioner strikes it with a large mallet till the amputation is perfected; and then they put the stump into a hollow bamboo stuffed with rags or moss, to prevent the criminal from dying by loss of blood. After he has thus suffered whether by the king's command, or by the sentence of the judge, all the ignominy of his crime is wiped off; and if any one upbraids him with it, he may kill him with impunity. Murder and adultery are punished with death; and, in this case the criminal has many executioners, he being placed amidst a number of people, who stab him with their daggers; but female offenders\are put to death by strangling. The king is frequently a spectator of these punishments, and sometimes even acts as executioner: and though such a spectacle must to a feeling mind, appear extremely shocking, yet so little does he seem affected by it, that instances have been known of his executing a criminal, and immediately after entertaining himself with cock-fighting; a diversion which in this country is more universally esteemed than any other.

Having given the situation of the most considerable places on the east-side of Sumatra, we proceed through the straits of Sunda to the west coast; and advancing from thence towards the north, the first English settlement we meet with is Sillabar, which lies in a bay at the mouth of a large river of the same name, in 4 deg. S. latitude. Here the English have a residence, or a small detachment from Marlborough fort, (erected soon after the destruction of York Fort at Bencoolen) to receive the pepper the natives bring hither. Ten miles to the northward of Sillabar stands the town of Bencoolen, where was the principal settlement the English had upon the island of Sumatra, from the year 1685 to the year 1719, when there happened a general insurrection

furrection of the natives, who cut off part of the garrifon ; the reft efcaping in their boats to fea.

Bencoolen is known at fea by a high flender mountain
that rifes 20 miles beyond it in the country, called the
Sugar-loaf. Before the town of Bencoolen there lies an
ifland, within which the fhipping ufually ride ; and the
point of Sillabar extending two or three leagues to the
fouthward of it, makes a large bay ; befides thefe
marks the old Englifh fort, which fronted towards the
fea, might have been difcerned when a fhip came
within feven or eight miles of the place. The town is
almoft two miles in compafs, and was inhabited chiefly
by the natives, who built their houfes upon bamboo
pillars, as in other parts of the ifland. The Portuguefe,
Chinefe, and Englifh had each a feparate quarter. The
Chinefe people built all upon a floor, after the cuftom
of their country. The Englifh houfes were after their
own model ; but they found themfelves under a neceffity of building with timber, (though there was no want
of brick or ftone), upon account of the frequent earthquakes. The adjacent country is mountainous and
woody, and in fome parts are volcanoes that frequently
vomit fire. The air is very unwholefome, and the
mountains are generally covered with thick clouds that
burft in ftorms of thunder, rain, &c. The foil is a
fertile clay, and the chief produce is grafs ; but near
the fea it is all a morafs. There is a fmall river on the
N. W. fide of the town, by which the pepper is brought
here from the inland part of the country ; but there is
a great inconvenience in fhipping it, on account of a
dangerous bar at the mouth of the river. The road is
alfo dangerous for fhips, as it has no other defence from
the violence of the fea during the S. W. monfoons,
than a fmall place called Rat Ifland, which, with the
land point of Sillabar, makes the haven.

The pepper brought here comes from the territories
of the two neighbouring rajahs, one of whom refides at
Sindle-'demond, at the bottom of a bay 10 or 12 miles
to the north ; and the other of Bafar, 10 miles to the eaft.
There two rajahs have houfes in the town, whither they
come

come when they have any bufinefs to tranfact with the English, who pay them half a dollar duty for every 560 pounds weight of pepper; and they alfo pay to the owner for every fuch quantity 10 Spanifh dollars, weighing each 17 penny weights and 12 grains.

The Englifh have alfo other fettlements to the N. W. of the above, particularly at Cattoun, fituated about 40 miles from Bencoolen; Ippo, about 30 miles farther to the north; Bantall, which is upwards of 100 miles north of Bencoolen; and Mocho, fituated a little to the fouth of Indrapour. There are likewife feveral good Dutch fettlements on this ifland, the moft confiderable of which is Pullambam, or Pullamban, fituate about 120 miles N. E. of Bencoolen. The chief article of trade here is pepper, of which the Dutch have prodigious quantities, being under contract with the king of Pullamban, and other Indian princes, to take it at a certain price, one half of which they pay in money, and the other in cloth. All other nations are prohibited from trading except the Chinefe, by means of whom the Englifh get a fhare of their pepper, as our fhips pafs through the Straits of Banca. The Dutch formerly carried on a great trade here in opium; but as that was found to impoverifh the country, by drawing away its ready cafh, the king, in 1708, ordered only three chefts of about 160 pounds each, to be imported; and that if any fhould be detected in acting contrary to this order, they fhould forfeit not only their goods, but their lives alfo.

Pullambam is a very large town, and pleafantly fituated on the banks of a fine river, which divides itfelf into feveral branches that run by four channels into the fea. It continued to be a confiderable city till the year 1659, when it was deftroyed by the Dutch, in revenge for fome injuries they pretended to have received from the natives. About this time the Dutch reduced the chief of the kingdoms in the fouth part of this ifland; but feveral of them were afterwards recovered by the natives, who have ever fince remained independant. The Dutch have feveral other factories here; namely, (1.) Bancalis, fituated nearly oppofite to

I   Malacca,

Malacca, on the banks of a fpacious river of its own name. The chief articles fold by the company here are, cloth and opium; in return for which, they receive gold-duft. The country is very fertile, and in the woods and mountains are prodigious numbers of wild-hogs, whofe flefh is exceeding fweet and fat. They have likewife fome good poultry, and there are various kinds of fifh in the river. (2.) Siack, fituate on the river Andraghima: this is a very inconfiderable place, on account of the unwholefomenefs of the air, which is attributed to the great number of fhads caught in the river at a particular feafon of the year, for the fake of the roes; and the reft of the fifh being thrown in heaps, corrupt, and exhale peftilential vapours. Thefe roes the natives pickle, and then dry in fmoke; after which they put them in large leaves of trees, and then fend them to different countries between Achen and Siam. They call it Turbow, and reckon it a great delicacy. (3.) Pedang, which is fituated about 60 miles fouth of the equator, and has a fine river, where large fhips may come up, and ride in fafety; but it is the moft infig-nificant fettlement the Dutch have on this ifland: it produces but a fmall quantity of pepper; and the trade in gold is fo trifling, as hardly to defray the natural expences attending it. Many other places on this ifland are independant of the Englifh and Dutch; the chief of which are the following.

Priaman, it lies nearly oppofite to Pedang, about 100 miles N. W. of Indrapour. It is very populous, and plentifully fupplied with moft kinds of provifions. The natives carry on a confiderable trade with the in-habitants of Manimcabo. The Dutch had a factory here for many years, but were at length driven from it by the king of Achen.

Ticow, another very confiderable place, which is fituated about feven leagues from Daffaman, in 20 deg. S. latitude. The inland part of the country is very high; but that next the fea is low, covered with woods, and watered with feveral fmall rivers, which render it marfhy. There are, however, many pleafant meadows
well

well stocked with buffaloes and other horned cattle, which are purchased at a very easy price. It likewise affords plenty of rice, poultry, and several forts of fruits, as durians, ananas, oranges, citrons, pomegranates, melons, mangoes, cucumbers, and potatoes: but its most valuable produce is pepper, with which it abounds, and is in quality esteemed superior to that of any other place on the island. The pepper chiefly grows at the bottom of the mountains; for which reason these parts are exceedingly populous. The city stands about two miles from the sea, opposite to a small island. It is but a little mean place, for the city and suburbs do not contain 800 houses, which are chiefly built with reeds, and are neither strong or commodious. The king is subject to the kings of Achen, who appoints a new governor every three years, and without him the king of Ticow cannot execute any business of importance. The governor, therefore, is the person applied to by foreigners in the transacting of business, and even the natives pay him the most distinguished respect. The inhabitants of the city are Malayans, but the inland parts are possessed by the natives, who disown the king of Achen's authority, and have a peculiar language and king of their own. This part of the country produces great quantities of gold, which the natives exchange with the Dutch, or the inhabitants near the coast, for pepper, salt, iron, cotton, red-cloth, and Surat pearls. The air here is very unhealthy, particularly from July to October, and the people are very subject to fevers, which are so violent in their nature, as seldom to admit of a cure; so that were it not for the pepper, no stranger would venture to go near them. Every person who trades to this place, must have a licence for that purpose from the king of Achen; and when that is obtained, they cannot be interrupted either by the king or governor of Ticow. They sell their pepper by bahars of 116 pounds avoirdupois: and the king of Achen has 15 per cent. out of all that is sold, that is, seven and a half for the export of the pepper, and seven and a half for the

import

import of the merchandize given in exchange for that commodity.

Barras, which belongs to the king of Achen, is one of the moſt conſiderable places on the weſt coaſt; it is ſituated on a fine river near the center between Ticow and Achen, and, like the former, no perſon muſt trade here without permiſſion from the king. This place produces great plenty of gold, camphire, and benjamin, the latter of which ſerves the natives inſtead of money. The country is very pleaſant, and abounds with rice, and ſeveral ſorts of the moſt delicious fruits. The Dutch and Engliſh, as alſo the inhabitants of the coaſt, buy up the camphire here, in order to carry it for Surat, and the Straits of Sunda.

The province of Andzigzi is ſmall, but remarkable for producing great quantities of pepper: and gold is cheaper here than in any other part of the iſland.

Jamly is ſituated on a river on the eaſt-ſide of the iſland, about 50 miles from the ſea, in 2 deg. S. latitude. Great quantities of pepper are produced in it, which is ſaid to be much ſuperior in quality to that of Andrigri. The Dutch had a factory here, the moſt conſiderable of all their ſettlements on the coaſt, but they withdrew from it in 1710. The Engliſh had likewiſe a factory near it, which they alſo quitted on account of the obſtructions they met with from the Dutch in their trade.

Pedir is ſituated about 30 miles eaſt of Achen, and is a large territory: it has the advantage of an excellent river. The ſoil is very fertile, and the country produces ſuch quantities of rice, that it is called the granary of Achen. It alſo produces a large quantity of ſilk, part of which is wove by the natives into ſtuffs, that are valued in moſt parts throughout the iſland, and the reſt is ſold to the inhabitants of the coaſt of Coromandel.

Paſſaiman, almoſt under the equinoctial, is a large place, ſituated at the foot of a very high mountain, but is remarkable only for producing pepper, which is both large and excellent in its quality.

No. 36.   7 B   Cinquele

Cinquele produces annually a large quantity of cam-phire, which the inhabitants of Surat, on the coast of Coromandel, purchase for 15 or 16 rials the coff, or 28 ounces. Daya abounds in rice and cattle.

In the island of Sumatra, they have a small breed of horses; they have also buffaloes, deer, goats, hogs, tygers, hog-deers, monkies, squirrels, guanoes, porcu-pines, alligators, serpents, scorpions, muskatoes, and other insects: from the hog-deer is obtained a species of the bezoar-stone, which is of a dark brown colour, and has two coats; a small quantity of this stone, dis-solved in any liquor, will remove an oppression of the stomach, rectifies foul bood, and restores the appetite: it is also very efficacious in other disorders incident to human nature. Here are also hens, ducks, and other poultry; pigeons, doves, parrots, parroquets, maccaws and small birds; sea and river fish also are very plenti-ful, and turtle or sea tortoise. They have elephants, but they are supposed not to be natives. Rice is much the greatest part of their food in all their meals: strong soup, made of flesh or fish, and a very little meat high seasoned, serves to eat with their rice. The Mahome-tans that inhabit the coast, abstain from swines flesh, and from strong liquors, as they do in all countries of the same faith. The mountaineers will eat any flesh, except beef, the bull being one of the objects of their worship, and if we could give any credit to their neigh-bours, the people of Achen, they eat human flesh; but the world is pretty well satisfied by this time that there are no nations of cannibals. Their common drink is tea, or plain water; but they sometimes use the liquor of young cocoa-nuts, which is very cooling and pleasant. They always sit cross-legged on the floor at their meals. Their salutations are much the same as in other Asiatic countries.

Learning is not to be expected here. The common language is the Malayan tongue, and the koran and re-ligious books of the Mahometans are written in Arabic, which is now a dead language. They have indeed the use of letters here, as they have almost in every other
eastern

eaftern nation except China ; but thofe gentlemen were fo felf-fufficient, fo much above being taught by people they look upon as their inferiors, that they have now the leaft pretence to learning of any nation on the face of the earth. The Mahometans of Sumatra fpeak and write the Malayan language. The Pagan mountaineers have a language peculiar to themfelves. As the Malayans write from the right-hand to the left, the mountaineers write as we do, from the left-hand to the right; and inftead of pen, ink, and paper, they write, or rather engrave, with a ftile on the outfide of a bamboo cane; the Malays, indeed, ufe ink and a coarfe brown paper. Both nations are poor accomptants, and are forced to make ufe of the Banians that refide amongft them as their clerks, when they have any confiderable accounts to make up, the Banians being faid to be poffeffed of great abilities in this particular, and are alfo fome of the fharpeft traders in the world.

The inhabitants of this ifland are in general of a moderate ftature, and a very fwarthy complexion : they have black eyes, flat faces, and high cheek bones : their hair is long and black, and they take great pains to dye their teeth black : they likewife befmear themfelves with oil, as in other hot countries, to prevent being ftung by the infects ; and let their nails grow exceeding long, fcraping them till they are tranfparent, and dying them with vermillion : the poorer fort go almoft naked, having only a fmall piece of cloth faftened round the waift ; and about their heads they wear a piece of linen, or a cap made of leaves, refembling the crown of a hat ; but they have no fhoes or ftockings. The better fort wear drawers or breeches, and a piece of callico or filk wrapped about their loins, and thrown over the left fhoulder, and they wear fandals on their feet, when in towns. They are very proud and revengeful in their difpofitions ; and are fo indolent, that they will neither endeavour to improve themfelves in arts and fciences, or in hufbandry, but fuffer their manufactures to be neglected, and their lands to lie without cultiva-

7 B 2   tion.

tion. If foreigners, therefore, were not to supply their defects, they would in all probability suffer themselves to be reduced to a savage state, and only preserve their existence, like the beasts of the country, with what the earth spontaneously produces. The king has no other standing forces than his guards, but depends on his militia, which, as we hinted above, are as numerous as the people in his kingdom, all who are able to bear arms, are obliged to appear under arms whenever they are summoned. They have scarce any fortified towns and castles, but what are natural; and the country seems to be so inaccessible, that the natives boast it has never been conquered by any foreign power; but this must be a mistake, for the present generation, who are masters of the north part of the island and the sea-coast, are not the original inhabitants, but came from Egypt and Arabia, and having driven the Pagans up into the mountains, succeeded them on the sea-coasts. The religion of Mahomet is professed at Achen, and upon all the coasts of Sumatra; but they are not such bigotted zealots as they are in some other Mahometan countries. Their temples or mosques are but meanly built, some of them no better than cottages. The chief priest resides at Achen, and has a great influence on affairs of state. Their marriage contracts are made before their priests, who are judges in cases of divorce, as well as in civil causes. Their priests also assist at the celebration of their funeral rites, as in other Mahometan states.

This, as well as the rest of the Indian islands, was, no doubt, first peopled from the neighbouring continent. The Phœnicians, Egyptians, and Arabians afterwards trafficed with them; and we find Solomon desiring Hiram, king of Tyre, to send him skilful mariners to pilot his fleet into these seas; and the Ophir mentioned in scripture, is supposed to be this very island, from whence he fetched his gold. The Arabians and other nations bordering on the red-sea, afterwards planted colonies here, and became so potent, that they drove the former inhabitants up into the mountains,

mountains, and poffeffed the coaft. The Portuguefe
found the defcendants of thofe nations fixed on the
fhores of the Indian continent as well as the iflands
when they arrived there. The Portuguefe enjoyed the
fole traffic with this and the adjacent iflands for near
100 years, viz. from the year 1500 almoft to the year
of our Lord 1600, when other nations followed them
round the Cape of Good Hope, and put in for a fhare
of the Indian trade. Some writers affure us, that this
kingdom has been ever governed by queens; others
affirm that there never was a queen regent here; we
may, however, take the middle way, and allow that
it has been fubject both to kings and queens: certain
it is, a king was upon the throne when we firft vifited
this ifland, becaufe we have his letter which he wrote
to queen Elizabeth, and kings have of late years filled
that throne.

The inhabitants of the mountains are governed by
the chiefs of their refpective tribes, who are under a
neceffity of maintaining a good correfpondence among
themfelves, in order to defend their country againft their
powerful neighbours; for as they are poffeffed of all
the gold the ifland produces, there is no doubt but the
Mahometan princes that lie round them, would make
an effort to fubdue thofe golden mountains, if their
princes were at variance: or if they did not, the Dutch
would find a way to their gold, if they fhould find their
chiefs divided: for the Dutch are poffeffed of feveral
ftrong places and countries in the ifland, which would be
fupported in fuch an enterprife by fleets and forces from
Batavia and Malacca, that lie but a very little diftance
from them.

The coins of the country are, firft cafh, or pieces of
lead, 1500 of which make one mas, valued at 15 pence,
which is a gold coin. A pollum or copang is a quarter
of a mas, 16 mas is one tael, which is an imaginary
coin, and equivalent to 20 fhillings fterling; dollars and
other Spanifh coins alfo are current here. With refpect to their weights, five tael, make a buncal, 20
buncals one catty, and 100 catty one pecul, being 132
                                                    pounds

pounds English; three peculs are a China bahar of 396 pounds China weight; and of Malay weight, at Achen 422 pounds 15 ounces, and at Bencoolen, and the rest of the western coast, a bahar is 500 pounds great weight, or 560 pounds English. They make their payments at Achen oftener in gold pieces than in coin.

Several other islands belong to Sumatra, among which is one called by the inhabitants Pulo Lanchakay, and, by the natives of Achen, Pulo Lada, or the island of Pepper. This is a large island, situated in 6 deg. 15 min. N. latitude. In the centre of it are two high mountains separated from each other by a very narrow valley; and at the foot of these mountains is a plain at least 12 miles in length. Pepper is produced in it; but the island is very thinly inhabited. The soil of the plain is well calculated for all kinds of drugs, fruit, rice, and cattle; and, as it has several good springs and rivers, it might produce excellent pasturage; but the inhabitants only attend to the cultivation of pepper, that being the article which turns out most to their advantage. The other parts of the island are covered with thick woods, in which are some remarkable strait and lofty trees. The winds are westerly from the beginning of July to the end of October, during which time they have very heavy rains; and the climate, as in other parts of the same latitude, is very unwholesome. The island at present produces 500,000 pounds weight of pepper annually, which is said to be preferable to that of any other place in the Indies. The inhabitants are Malayans, but are naturally better disposed than those of Achen; their habits are much the same in make, but not so elegant: they are very zealous Mahometans, and in their customs and ways of living differ little from the inhabitants of Achen.

The island of Lingen is situated about 60 miles N. E. of Jamby, and about the same distance to the S. E. of Johore. It is 50 miles in length, and 10 in breadth: the interior part of it is very mountainous, but that next the sea lies low, and is very fertile. It produces

pepper

pepper and canes, and in fome parts of it are great numbers of porcupines. That of Banca is very large, being at leaft 150 miles in length, and about 20 in breadth. The natives, like moft of the Malayans, are treacherous, and very unhofpitable to fuch ftrangers as unfortunately happen to be fhipwrecked on the coaft. At the mouth of the ftraits of Banca is Lucipara, a fmall ifland but fo barren, that it has but few inhabitants, and only produces a fmall quantity of pepper. There are feveral other fmall iflands, belonging to Sumatra, moft of which are either uninhabited, or fo infignificant as not to merit a particular defcription.

Java, one of the Sunda Iflands, is fituate in the Indian ocean, between 102 and 113 degrees of eaft longitude, and between 5 and 8 degrees of fouth latitude, being 700 miles long, and upwards of 100 broad, having the Ifland of Borneo on the north, the Straits of Bally on the eaft, the Indian ocean on the fouth, and the Straits of Sunda (from whence it is called one of the Sunda Iflands) on the N. W.

The air of Java, near the fea, is generally unhealthful, unlefs where the bogs have been drained, and the lands cultivated; there it is much better, and in the middle of the ifland much more fo. The worft weather upon the north coaft of Java is during the wefterly monfoon, which begins the firft week in November, when they have fome rain. In December the rains increafe, and it blows frefh, and in January it blows ftill harder, and the rains continue very heavy till the middle of February, when both the wind and rains become more moderate and decreafe, till the end of March. Their fair feafon commences in April, the winds are then variable, and it is fometimes calm, only at the change of the moon there are fudden gufts of wind from the weft. In the beginning of May the eaftern monfoon becomes conftant, and in June and July there is a little rain; but in this monfoon they have generally clear, wholefome weather, until the end of September. In October the eafterly wind blows faintly, and in November the wefterly monfoon fets in again : when the wefterly wind
and

and currents are ftrongeft here, namely, in December, January and February, there is no failing againft them. The eafterly winds and currents are more moderate; fhips may fail againft this monfoon, and a fhip may come from the weftward through the Straits of Sunda to Batavia almoft at any time. There is good anchorage on the Java fide, in 20 or 30 fathoms water: near the coaft of Java and Borneo, from April to November, they have land and fea breezes from different points; the wind blows from the land between one and four in the morning, and continues till noon; at one or two in the afternoon it blows frefh from the fea for five or fix hours.

A chain of mountains runs through the middle of the ifland from E. to W. which are covered with fine woods. It is faid thefe mountains produce great quan-tities of gold; but the natives conceal it from the Eu-ropeans. The moft diftinguifhed of thefe mountains is called the Blue Mountain. The low lands are flooded in the time of the rains. Along the north coaft of Java are fine groves of cocoa-nut trees, and wherever we fee one of thefe groves, we do not fail to meet with a vil-lage of the natives.

The ifland was antiently divided into abundance of petty kingdoms and ftates, and when Admiral Drake vifited this ifland in his voyage round the globe, in the year 1579, he relates there were five kingdoms in it. We may now divide it into two parts, 1. The north coaft, which is under the dominion of the Dutch; and, 2. The fouth coaft, fubject to the kings of Palamboan and Mataram. Bantam was, till lately, the moft con-fiderable kingdom of Java, but this king is now a vaffal to the Dutch. We fhall here give fome account of that city.

Bantam, once the metropolis of a great kingdom (till the Dutch deftroyed it, and depofed the king,) is feated in a plain at the foot of a mountain, out of which iffues three rivers, or rather one river dividing itfelf into three branches, two whereof furround the town, and the other runs through the middle of it.

The

The circumference of this city, when in its glory, was not lefs than 12 miles, and very populous. It lay open towards the land; but had a very good wall to the fea, fortified with baftions, and defended by a numerous artillery; and the palace, or rather caftle, where the king refided, was no mean fortification; befides which there were feveral public buildings and palaces of the great men, which made no ordinary figure in this country. It was alfo one of the greateft ports in the eaftern feas, to which all nations reforted, but is now become a wretched poor place, and has neither trade or any thing to render it defirable. The principal inhabitants are removed, and the buildings ruined, their king deprived of his fovereignty, and become a vaffal to the Dutch.

Batavia, by the Indians named Jacatra, and by the natives and Chinefe Calacka, or Calappa, as they call the fruit of the cocoa-trees, (which are very common here, and faid to be fuperior to any in the Indies) lies in 6 deg. S. latitude, longitude from London 106, and ftands about 40 miles to the eaftward of Bantam; it is fituated at the bottom of a fine bay, in which there are 17 or 18 fmall iflands, which break the violence of the winds and waves; infomuch that 1000 fail may ride here very fecurely. Two large piers runs out half a mile into the fea, between which 100 flaves are conftantly employed, in taking up the mud and foil which is wafhed out of the town, or the mouth of the river would be foon choaked up. The city of the fame name ftands in a flat country, and is almoft fquare, and about the bignefs of Briftol, regularly built like the towns in Holland, but with white ftone. Their ftreets are wide and ftrait, and in 12 or 15 of the principal are canals, faced with ftone, and planted with ever-greens: the fides of the ftreets alfo are paved, and over their canals are reckoned no lefs than 56 ftone bridges; after which defcription there cannot be much occafion to tell the reader that the place is extremely pleafant, and that travellers are furprized with its beauty. It is furrounded with a good wall, and 22 baftions well furnifhed with

No. 36.   7 C   cannon,

cannon, and so contrived as to be of equal service against
an insurrection in the city, as against a foreign enemy ;
the guns being easily brought to point down the principal streets.

The houses are plain, but very neat, and behind them
are large gardens well stocked with herbs and vegetables, and most kinds of fruit.   They have several handsome public buildings, such as the great church : the
stadt-house, the hospitals, the spin-house or house of
correction, the pest-house, Chinese hospital, the house of
artisans, &c.   And there are two churches built for the
reformed Portuguese, and another for the Malays ; but
they do not allow either the Papists or Lutherans the
public exercise of their religion.   The fort stands upon
the west side of the city, and commands both the town
and road : it is very large, and has four royal bastions
faced with stone, but has no moat, except the canals,
which lie at some distance from the rampart, may have
been mistaken for moats : they are about 25 feet broad,
and fordable in most places ; the inside of the fort is
crowded with buildings, there being the general's house,
as well as the houses of most of the principal officers,
and company's servants : in the middle of the city there
is a large square, which serves as a parade for the garrison, on the west-side of which stands the great church,
on the south the stadt-house, on the north a fine range
of buildings, and on the east is one of their great canals :
there are also several spacious market-places in the city.
The suburbs reach almost half a league into the country,
and form a town larger than the former, but not so com-
pact : being intermixed with kitchen gardens and or-
chards.   Here the Chinese chiefly live, and here they
have their temples and burying places, and the free exercise of their religion, which is denied the Lutheran
protestants.   In this part of the town also live the Malays, and native Javans, and other nations, which the
Dutch have transplanted from Banda, Amboyna, &c.
There are small forts erected every way, at two or three
leagues distance from the town, to defend the avenues ;
the Dutch being conscious that the king of Mataran

I   and

and the natives would lay hold of any opportunity of re-
poffeffing themfelves of their country, and driving the
Hollanders from their coafts, however they may feem
to acquiefce and tacitly confent, according to the modern phrafe, to be infulted and tyrannized over by the
Dutch, there is not a nation in India but would gladly
throw off the yoke, and declare in behalf of liberty, and
for any prince who fhould come to their relief.

The people who inhabit the city and fuburbs of Batavia being formed of various nations, who all preferve the dreffes, modes, and cuftoms of their refpective countries, they confequently exhibit a very ftrange
appearance ; we fhall therefore, for the information of
our readers, give a particular defcription of them.

The Chinefe do not only drive the greateft retail
trade here, but are many of them good mechanics ; they
alfo generally farm the fifhery, excife and cuftoms, and
apply themfelves to hufbandry and gardening ; to ma-
nure and cultivate the rice, cotton, and fugars which
grow in the fields, about Batavia and other great towns;
and exceeding the Dutch, it is faid, in their thriftinefs,
as well as in cozening and over-reaching thofe they deal
with.   They drefs in a veft and gown of filk or callico,
after the fafhion of their country, and wear their hair
wound up in a roll, on the hinder part of the head, and
faftened with bodkins ; for which every one pays a certain tribute to the Dutch.   The Dutch company allow
fome privileges to the Chinefe ; for they have not only a
governor of their own nation, who manages their affairs,
but are alfo allowed a reprefentative in the council.
They bring tea and porcelane hither from China ; but
they who are employed for this purpofe, muft not continue on the ifland longer than fix months.   They have
fingular maxims in the interment of their dead ; for
they will never open the fame grave where any one has
been buried ; their burial grounds, therefore, in the
neighbourhood of Batavia, cover a prodigious fpace of
ground, for which the Dutch make them pay large
fums.   In order to preferve the body they make the
coffin of very thick wood, not with planks faftened to-

gether, but cut out of a folid piece like a canoe; the
coffin, being covered and put into the grave, is furrounded with a kind of mortar about eight inches
thick, which in time becomes as hard as ftone. A
great number of weeping women, hired on puipofe, attend the funeral, befides the relations of the deceafed.
In Batavia, the law requires that every man fhould be
buried according to his rank; fo that if the deceafed
has not left money fuflicient to pay his funeral expences,
an oflicer takes an inventory of his goods, which are
fold, and out of the produce he buries him in the manner prefcribed.

The greateft merchants here are the Dutch, who are
alfo very good mechanics; they keep the chief inns and
moft places of public entertainment. They pay two
reals a month for their licence, and 70 for every pipe
they fell of Spanifh wine: but thefe inn-keepers are far
from being obliging to their guefts, and particularly to
foreigners. Here are alfo great numbers of Portuguefe; and in order to diftingufh them from other
Europeans, they are called by the natives Oran-ferante,
or Nazarene men. They in general fpeak the Malayan language, but fome of them a corrupt dialect of
the Portuguefe; and they have all renounced their
religion, by profefling the principles of Luther. They
are chiefly employed in the moft fervile oflices: fome
of them are handicraftfmen, others get their living by
hunting, and the greateft number by wafhing linen.
They have fo clofely followed the cuftoms and manners
of the Indians, that they are only diftinguifhed from
them by their features and complexion, their fkin being
confiderably lighter, and their nofes not fo flat; and
the manners of adjufting their hair conftitutes the only
difference in their drefs. Moft of the inhabitants have
very tawny complexions. The Malays wear a fhort
coat with ftrait fleeves, and a cloth about their loins,
binding their temples with a piece of linen, in which
they enclofe part of their hair, the reft hanging down.
The women wear a waiftcoat and a cloth about their
waift, which reaches half-way down their legs, and
ferves

ferves inftead of a petticoat ; they wear nothing but their hair on their heads, and go bare-foot. The men get their living by fifhing, and have fome retail trade, though not comparable to the Chinefe. They profefs the Mahometan religion ; but are naturally very profligate, and will not fcruple to commit crimes of the moft infamous nature.

The Amboynefe wear vefts, and wrap a piece of callico feveral times about their heads, the ends whereof hang down. Their women only wrap a piece of callico about their loins, throwing part of it over their breafts and fhoulders, their legs and arms bare ; the men are moft of them carpenters, and fome of thefe, as well as of the other nations, the Dutch inlift in their troops, being efteemed brave bold fellows, but given to mutiny, as the Dutch relate, by which they probably mean, they are not yet reconciled to flavery. Their houfes are made of wood, and covered with branches of trees ; they are pretty lofty, and the floors are divided into feparate apartments, fo that one houfe will contain feveral families. The native Javanefe wear a kind of fcull cap, but their bodies are naked to the middle, wrapping a piece of filk or callico about their loins, which reaches below the middle of their legs, which are bare. The women cover their bodies with a piece of filk or callico, and have another piece wrapped about their loins, and drefs in their hair. The men are employed in hufbandry and fifhing, or in building country boats. There is likewife a mixed breed, called Topaffes or Mandikers, confifting of feveral nations, incorporated with the Dutch, and have greater privileges than the reft. Many of thefe are merchants, and differ but little in their habits, or way of life from the Dutch, only the men wear large breeches or trowfers, which reach down to their ancles. The women tie up their hair in a roll on their heads, wear a waift-coat, and a petticoat of filk or callico, which reaches down to their feet. Thefe live both in city and fuburbs, their houfes are feveral ftories high, built of brick or ftone, and very neatly furnifhed within. The Macaffars, whofe anceftors poffeffed the ifland of Celebes,

and

and were enslaved by the Dutch, though they went almost naked in their mother country, wear cloathing here. Several of the Timoreans, inhabitants of an island of East China, having been brought hither by the Dutch, now constitute part of the people of Batavia. The habits and customs of these and of the Macassars, are nearly the same: their chief employment is husbandry and gardening. As many of them profess Christianity, and are conformable to the Dutch in their religion and customs, it is to be presumed they clothe themselves as the Hollanders do. Some of the negroes here are pedlars, and hawk about the streets glass-beads and coral; others follow mechanical trades; but the most considerable of them deal in free-stone, which they bring from the neighbouring islands. These people are chiefly Mahometans. All the inhabitants enjoy liberty of conscience; but they are not allowed to exercise their different modes of worship. Priests and monks are permitted to live here, but they are prohibited from being publickly seen in the respective habits of their priestly orders.

As the women of Java are remarkable for their amorous disposition and constancy to the man they espouse, and expect that the man should be equally constant, if her lover goes astray, she makes no scruple to prepare a dose for him. An old traveller, who seems much enamoured with the javanese ladies, gives this description of them; he observes that they are much fairer than the men, have good features, little swelling breasts, a soft air, sprightly eyes, a most agreeable laugh, and a bewitching mein, especially in dancing: that they express the greatest submission to their husband, prostrating themselves before him when he enters the house. Polygamy prevails here; the Javanese have several wives besides female slaves, of whom they make concubines when they see fit. There being a scarcity of European women, the Dutch are allowed to marry a native, provided she will profess Christianity, which she is seldom averse to, as it gratifies her pride; a Christian and the wife of a Dutchman taking place of a native

Javanese,

Javanese, and being allowed a great many privileges, which the natives cannot enjoy ; and her husband is obliged to confine himself to her bed, and bring no rivals into the family.

Rice is the principal grain that grows here. They have also plantations of sugar, tobacco, and coffee: their kitchen gardens are well replenished with cabbages, purslain, lettuce, parsley, fennel, melons, pompions, potatoes, cucumbers, and radishes. Here are also all manner of Indian fruits, such as plantains, bananas, cocoas, ananas, mangoes, mangosteens, durions, oranges of several sorts; limes, lemons, the betel and arek nut ; gums of several kinds, particularly benjamin : in March they plant rice, and their harvest is in July. In October they have the greatest plenty of fruit, but they have some all the year. They have good timber, cotton, and other trees proper to the climate, besides oak, cedar, and several kinds of red wood. The cocoa-tree is very common, which is of universal use, affording them meat, drink, oil and vinegar ; and of the fibres of the bark they make them cordage ; the branches cover their houses, and they write on the leaves with a steel stile, and with the tree, and the great bamboo cane, they build their houses, boats and other vessels. Here are buffaloes and some oxen, and a small breed of horses. The few sheep we find here have hair, rather than wool, and their flesh is dry. Their hogs, wild and tame, are the best meat we find there, or in any other countries between the tropics ; and their venison is good: here are also tygers and other wild beasts, crocodiles, porcupines, serpents, scorpions, locusts, and a multitude of insects. Monkies of various kinds are found here, also flying squirrels; and a remarkable animal called jackoa ; it is almost like a lizard, is very malicious, and darts its urine at every thing which offends it : the urine is of such a quality, that it will canker the flesh, and if the part is not immediately cut out, the object on which it falls must immediately perish. Few accidents, however, happen from this creature, as it always gives notice of its situation from

the

the fingularity of its voice, fo that the natives, as well as animals, have an opportunity of efcaping it. The food, falutations, and diverfions of the Indians in this ifland, are the fame as in Borneo and Sumatra, and therefore need not to be repeated here. The Dutch travel in couches, and on horfeback, and fometimes in pelanquins, or covered couches, carried on men's fhoulders, as the Indians do, with a grand retinue. Not any of the nations of Europe are fuffered to trade to Java, but from China 14 or 15 junks of 200 or 300 ton, ufed to come every year in November or December, and return home in June; which furnifhed the Dutch with the merchandize of China upon eafier terms than they could purchafe it in that country: and this is the reafon the Dutch fo feldom vifit that kingdom, and permit other nations to trade thither, which they could prevent if they pleafed, by fhutting up the Straits of Sunda and Malacca, which the fquadrons of men of war they always keep in India, enable them to do. Befides the goods imported to Batavia by the Chinefe, the Dutch themfelves import the produce of Japan, the Spice Iflands, Perfia, Surat, Bengal, the coaft of Coromandel and Malabar, and all the merchandize of Europe and Africa. Never were fuch magazines of goods laid up in any city, as are to be found in Batavia, except in Amfterdam itfelf; and as they barter the goods of one country for another, the Indian trade is fo far from diminifhing their treafure, that it brings them in more gold and filver than any other traffic.

The Dutch governor of Batavia takes great ftate upon him, and has in reality the power of a fovereign prince. A troop of horfe-guards precede his coach when he goes out, halberdiers furround the coach, and a company of foot-guards march after it, cloathed in yellow fattin, enriched with filver lace and fringe; and the governor's lady has her guards, and is attended in all refpects, both within and in public, with a dignity equal to that of a queen. The moft confiderable officer next to him is the director-general whofe bufinefs is to purchafe fuch commodities as are brought to the port, and to
difpofe

difpofe of fuch as are taken from it.   He is fole mafter of all the magazines, and has the fupreme direction of every thing that relates to the commercial intereft of the company.

Batavia being a place of the greateft trade in India, the cuftoms muft be very confiderable; more efpecially as the inhabitants are in general wealthy, and almoft every article is fubject to a duty.   The taxes are paid monthly; and to fave the charge and trouble of gathering them, on the day they become due a flag is difplayed on the top of a houfe in the center of the town, and all parties are obliged immediately to pay their money to the proper officers appointed to receive the fame.   The money current here confifts of feveral forts; as ducats, which are valued at 132 ftivers; ducatoons, at 80 ftivers; imperial rix-dollars, at 60; rupees of Batavia, at 30; fchellings, at fix; double cheys, at two ftivers and a half; and doits, at one-fourth of a ftiver. Some of thefe coins are of two forts, though of the fame denomination, namely, milled and unmilled, the former of which is of moft value; a milled ducatoon is worth 80 ftivers, but an unmilled one is not worth more than 72.   All accounts are kept in rix-dollars and ftivers which are here merely nominal coins, like our pounds fterling.   The Dutch, befides their land forces, which are very numerous, have men of war fufficient to engage any fleets they are likely to meet with on the Indian feas: and from their great ftrength and importance in this part of the globe, they affume the title of " Sovereigns of all the feas, from the Cape of Good Hope caftward, to Cape Horn in America."

Cherebon is fituate about 80 miles eaft of Batavia: it is a place of confiderable extent, and where the Dutch have a factory.   The country is very fertile, and produces moft kinds of provifions, particularly rice.   The inhabitants are under the dominion of four great lords, called fultans, one of whom is particularly attached to the Dutch, and for that reafon is diftinguifhed from the reft by the name of the company's fultan.   The reft, indeed, may not be undeferving of the like epithet, as

No. 36.   7 D   they

they are in alliance with the Dutch, whose frendship
they endeavour to preserve, and whom they consider as
their sole protectors; for had it not been for them,
these petty princes would have been reduced to the subjection of the king of Bantam, who made inroads on
their district, but was repulsed by the interposition of
the Dutch. Since this circumstance, the sultans have
testified their gratitude by granting many distinguished
privileges to their protectors in these dominions. The
chief person belonging to the Dutch factory here is called
the resident, who corresponds with the governor-general
of Batavia, but is solely independant of any other officer.
Here is a good fort, where the Dutch have a garrison
consisting of 80 men; about a mile and a half from
which is a large temple containing the tombs of several
of the princes of Cherebon. It is a lofty building of
variegated stones, and very elegantly ornamented within.
The generality of their priests reside near this temple,
the whole order of whom are treated with the most distinguished respect by the inhabitants. We shall now
proceed to the description of Palamboan and Mataram,
the latter of which is subject to the Dutch.

Palamboan, the capital of the kingdom of that name,
is situate in 114 deg. of E. long. and in 7 deg. 30 min. S.
lat. on the Straits of Bally, through which the East India ships sometimes pass, when they are homeward bound
from Borneo; such ships touch at the town of Balamboan
for fresh water and provisions; but the surf often beats
with such violence on the shore, that makes it difficult
watering there. This kingdom, which is independant of
the Dutch, lies at the S. E. end of Java, in a pleasant
country, watered with several rivulets, which fall on each
side of the town into the neighbouring straits. The
rajah, or king of this country, generally resides either
at Palamboan, or at a fort 15 miles from the sea. His
dominions reach from the east end of Java, 80 miles
along the south coast, and about 60 miles from N. to S.
but its extent up the country is not known. This kingdom is said to produce gold, pepper and cotton, also
rice, India corn, roots, and garden stuff. Their animals
are

are horfes, buffaloes, oxen, deer, and goats, and they have great plenty of ducks, geefe, and other forts of poultry. The fovereign and his fubjects are Pagans, but there are fome Mahometans among them, and a few Chinefe.

Mataram, when in its moft flourifhing ftate, extended its dominion over the whole ifland, and even now takes up a confiderable part of it : this kingdom was the laft in the ifland which the Dutch reduced under their government ; having continued its ftruggles for independency till the year 1704, when the Dutch took the advantage of an opportunity that offered in a difpute relative to the fucceffion of the crown, between the fon and brother of the deceafed fovereign. Thefe two rivals produced an univerfal divifion in the nation. He who was intitled to the crown by order of fucceffion had fo much the advantage over his antagonift, that had it not been for the Dutch, who declared in favour of his rival, he would certainly have poffeffed himfelf of the fupreme power. After a feries of contefts, the party efpoufed by the Dutch at length prevailed : the young prince was deprived of his fucceffion, and his uncle, who was unworthy of the character, affumed the fovereignty. After the death of this prince the company placed the legal heir on the throne, and dictated fuch laws to him as they thought beft calculated to anfwer their finifter purpofes. They chofe the place where his court was to be fixed, and fecured his attachment by erecting a caftle, in which a guard was kept with no other apparent view than to protect the prince. They employed every artifice to lull his attention by pleafures, made him valuable prefents, and foothed him by pompous embaffies. From this time the prince and his fucceffors have become mere tools of the company. The neceffary protection allowed them by the company confifts of 500 horfe and 400 foot ; but the expences the company are at on this account are amply repaid by the advantages that accrue to them.

The harbours afford docks for building all the fmall veffels employed in the fervice ; and they are fupplied

from

from hence with the chief part of the timber that is
ufed in their refpective fettlements. Befides thefe advantages they are furnifhed with various productions of
the country at ftipulated prices, which are fo low as to
be extremely profitable to them.

This country is in general very fertile, and produces
great quantities of rice, as alfo plenty of fruit. There
are alfo various forts of animals, particularly horfes,
fheep, goats, and remarkable large oxen. The rivers
abound with fifh, and the woods produce great plenty
of game; but the moft valuable articles in this kingdom
are, rice, pepper, cadiang, cotton, yarn, cardamum and
indigo; the latter of which is efteemed to be as good in
quality as any found in this part of the world. The
refidence of the king is ufually at Mataram, the capital
of the kingdom. His palace is a very handfome fpacious
building, adjoining to which are many good houfes
belonging to his nobles, who continually wait on
him, and the greateft homage is paid him by his fubjects in general; for though thefe princes are vaffals,
yet they are permitted to live in as great ftate as
when they were independant monarchs; and the orders of the Dutch are always executed in their names.
They therefore affume a dignity not inferior to that
of the moft defpotic prince, and when they go abroad,
a very diftinguifhed mark of loyalty is beftowed on
them.

Japara is the laft place of importance that remains to
be mentioned in this ifland; it is fituated at the bottom
of an eminence called the Invincible Mountain, on the
top of which is a fort built of wood. It is a very confiderable town, and has a good road fecured by two
fmall iflands. The Englifh had once a factory here,
but they were driven from it by the Portuguefe, who at
that time were mafters of the place. This country produces almoft every neceffary of life, efpecially cattle,
hogs, and poultry: they have alfo great plenty of rice,
with various forts of the moft delicious fruits; and their
waters abound with the beft of fifh. But the moft valuable commodities here are pepper, ginger, cinnamon,

and

and indigo. In the woods and mountains are several kinds of wild beasts, as buffaloes, stags, tygers, and rhinoceros's : the latter of these the natives hunt for the sake of their horns, which are much admired, because they will not contain poison; for they will immediately break to pieces if any such composition is put into them. As to the natives of this country, they very much resemble those of other Indian nations, and have the same kind of customs and ceremonies. They are fond of public diversions, particularly the representation of comedies, which principally consist in singing and dancing; and they are slaves to cock-fighting, that by the large sums they bet, they are frequently reduced to the most abject distress and poverty. They are chiefly of the Mahometan religion, as is also the king, who generally resides at a place called Kattafura, where the Dutch have a fort and garrison. This prince reigns absolute among his subjects, who are very faithful to him, and pay him the greatest homage. Like most eastern monarchs, he is constantly attended by women, and takes as many wives and concubines as he thinks proper. When his courtiers obtain an audience, they approach him with the profoundest humility; and even his priests so much revere him, that some of them go in pilgrimage to Mecca, to make vows, and pray for his prosperity, and that of his family and government.

The island of Balla, or lesser Java, is only divided from the larger by the Straits of Bally, and eastward of this are the islands Lambock, Combava, Flores, Solor, Timor, and several more, upon which the Dutch have forts and settlements, and take the liberty of governing and even transplanting the natives whenever they please, from hence they frequently recruit their troops, and thus make one nation of Indians contribute to keep another in subjection.

Timor is the largest of these islands, being about 200 miles in length, and 50 in breadth, and is divided into several petty states, which the Dutch oppose against one another, and by that means govern the whole. It has not any navigable rivers or harbours, but there are

several commodious bays. The Portuguese had formerly colonies here, whose descendants are now so intermixed with the original natives, that they are scarce to
be distinguished from them, especially as they profess
the same religion. The principal kingdoms in this
island are Namquimal, Lortriby, Pobumby, and Am-
aby; each of which has an independant and absolute
sovereign: these have several rajahs, and other distinguished officers under them; all of whom, with their
subjects in general, pay them the greatest homage.
Each kingdom has a language peculiar to itself, but
the manners and customs of the inhabitants differ
but little. There are some Pagans and Mahometans
still remaining, and the Chinese come hither to trade
once a year: the inhabitants are so very swarthy, that
they are sometimes taken for blacks, and those that are
not under the government of the Portuguese or Dutch
are represented as savages; they wear no clothing but
a little piece of cloth about their loins, and the better
sort wear a kind of coronet about their temples, adorned
with thin plates of gold or silver; the rest have caps
made with palmetto leaves. Their arms are swords,
darts, and lances or spears, and with these they run
down and kill their game. Their animals are the same
as in the island of Java, as well as their forest and fruit
trees. The Dutch do not seem to make any great profit of these islands; the principal design of their building forts here, is to defend the avenues to the spice
islands, which lie in their neighbourhood. On this last
mentioned island there is a Portuguese settlement, called
Laphao: it is situated by the sea-side, about three
leagues to the east of the Dutch fort, called Concordia.
It is a very small place, containing only a few mean
houses, and a church made of boards, covered with
palmetto leaves. There is a kind of platform here, on
which are six iron guns; but the whole are so much
decayed, as to be rendered almost useless. The people,
in general, speak the Portuguese language; and the
natives have been so intermixed with the Portuguese by
marriages, that it is difficult to know one from the
                                                    other.

............y, nor is there any danger coming
in ;

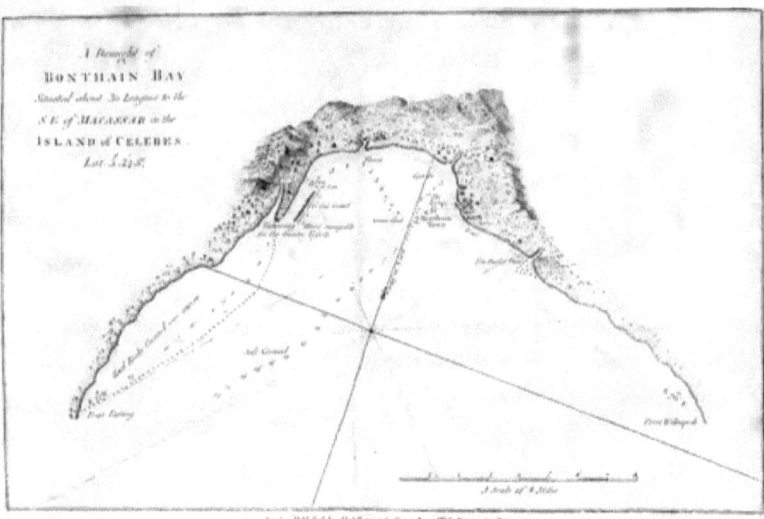

A Draught of
BONTHAIN BAY
Situated about 30 Leagues to the
S.E. of MACASSAR in the
ISLAND of CELEBES
Lat. 5. 34. S.

Scale of 4 Miles

London Published by Abel Roper at the Ship, Amen Wet Paternoster Row

other. Moft of them profefs the Roman catholic faith; but in the other parts of the ifland they are either Mahometans or Pagans.   The chief trade is carried on at Porta Nova, fituated at the eaft end of the ifland, and where the Portuguefe governor ufually refides.   Some years ago a pirate attacked, plundered, and then deftroyed feveral of the buildings in this town, with that of Concordia belonging to the Dutch.

Mandura is an ifland oppofite the eafternmoft point of Java, the moft valuable produce of which, for foreign markets, are deer fkins.   Its principal town is Arabia, fituated near a deep bay, about eight leagues from the weftermoft land of Java.   The foil of this ifland is very fertile, and produces feveral forts of grain, particularly rice; alfo feveral kinds of the moft delicious fruits. The chief animals are buffaloes, horfes, fheep, and oxen, the latter are remarkably large, and the flefh little inferior to thofe of Europe.   Their buildings, maxims, cuftoms, &c. refemble thofe of other Indian nations: fome of them are Mahometans, and others Pagans. The men are in general very robuft and courageous, for which reafon, when there is any deficiency in the fixed number of the Dutch troops, they recruit from them their forces at Batavia and other fettlements.

We now proceed to the continuation of the hiftory of our voyage.   By our account the town of Macaffar lies in latitude 5 deg. 10 min. and in 117 deg. 28 min. Eaft longitude from London.   It is built upon a point, or neck of land, and is watered by a river or two which either run through, or very near it.   It feemed to us to be large, and there is water for a fhip to come within half a cannon fhot of the walls.   The country about it is level, and has a moft béautiful appearance; it abounds with plantations, and groves of cocoa-nut trees, with a great number of houfes interfperfed.   At a diftance inland, the country rifes into hills of a great height, and becomes rude and mountainous.

The Bay of Bonthain is large, with good foundings, and a foft bottom of mud; wherein fhips may moor with perfect fecurity; nor is there any danger coming

in;

in ; for the rocks at the entrance are above water, and a good mark for anchoring. The higheft land in fight here is Bonthain hill ; and a fhip in the offing, at the diftance of two or three miles from the land, fhould bring this hill N. or N. half W. and then run in and anchor. We lay right under the hill, at the diftance of about a mile from the fhore. In this bay are many fmall towns: Bonthain lies in the N. E. part of it ; and the fort which we have mentioned, is intended for no other purpofe than to keep the country people in fub- jection. The Dutch refident has the command of the place, and of Bullocomba, which lies about twenty miles farther to the eaftward. There are feveral fmall rivers from whence water may be got upon occafion : indeed wood and water are here in great plenty : we cut our wood near the river, under Bonthain hill : our wa- ter was procured partly from that river, and partly from another ; when from the latter, our boat went above the fort with the cafks that were to be filled, where there is a good rolling way ; but as the river is fmall, and has a bar, the boat, after it is loaded, can come out only at high-water. Frefh provifions were purchafed here, at reafonable rates : the beef is excel- lent, but not in plenty ; but rice may be had in any quantity, as may fowls and fruit. In the woods are abundance of wild hogs, and as the natives, who are Mahometans, never eat them, they may be purchafed at a low price. The natives at times, fupplied us with turtle ; for this, like pork, is a dainty which they never touch. The bullocks here are the breed that have a bunch on their backs. The arrack and fugar that are confumed are brought from Batavia. Celebes is the key of the Molucca or fpice iflands, which, whoever is in poffeffion of it, muft neceffarily command : moft of the fhips that are bound to them, or to Banda, touch here, and always go between this ifland and that of Solayer. The latitude of Bonthain Hill is 5 deg. 30 min. S. longitude 117 deg. 53 min. E.

On Sunday the 22nd of May, at day break, we failed from Bonthain Bay, keeping along fhore till the

3   evening,

evening, when we anchored in the paffage between the two iflands of Celebes and Tonikaky; the latter of which, according to our account, lies in latitude 5 deg. 31 min. S. longitude 117 deg. 17 min. E. On the 23d, we weighed, fteered to the fouthward of Tonikaky, and ftood to the weftward. At three o'clock P. M. we were abreaft of the eaftermoft of three iflands, called by the Dutch Tonyn's Iflands. Thefe make a right angle triangle with each other; the diftance between the eaftermoft and weftermoft is eleven miles, and their relative bearings are nearly eaft and weft. At fix o'clock, after we had founded and got no ground, we fuddenly found ourfelves upon a fhoal, having not three fathoms water, which, being fmooth and clear, afforded us the fight of great crags of coral rocks under our bottom. We immediately threw all our fails aback, and providentially got off without damage. This is a very dangerous fhoal, and feemed to extend itfelf to the fouthward and weftward, all round the two weftermoft of thefe three iflands, for near fix miles, but about the eaftermoft ifland there feemed to be no danger; we obferved alfo a clear paffage between this ifland and the other two. The latitude of the eaftermoft and weftermoft of thefe iflands is 5 deg. 31 min. S. The eaftermoft is diftant 34 miles due W. from Tonikaky, and the weftermoft lies ten miles farther. On the 25th P. M. we found the water much difcoloured; foon after we went over the northermoft part of a fhoal. Here we found the water very foul when to the fouthward, but to the northward of us it appeared to be clear. At 11 o'clock we faw to the northward of us, the foutherrmoft iflands of Salombo, in latitude 5 deg. 33 min. S. at the diftance of eighty-two leagues weft of Tonikaky. We muft here remark, that off the ifland of Madura, the winds of the monfoons are commonly a month later in fettling than at Celebes. On Thurfday the 26th P. M. we faw from the maft head the ifland of Luback, which is in latitude 5 deg. 43 min. S. and in longitude 5 deg. 36 min. W. of Tonikaky, and diftant from thence 112 leagues. To the northward of this ifland we found a

No. 37.   7 E   current

current setting W. N. W.   On the 29th we saw the
cluster of small islands, called Carimon Java, distant
from Luback 45 leagues.   The eastermost island is the
largest, and is in latitude 5 deg. 48 min. S. longitude
7 deg. 52 min. W. of Tonikaky, from which it is distant about 158 leagues.

Thursday, the 2nd of June, we made that part of
the island of Java which makes the eastermost point of
the bay of Batavia, called Carawawang.   When we first
got sight of the land we decreased gradually our soundings, and, having steered along the shore for Batavia,
we had thirteen fathoms, in which depth, night coming
on, we anchored, in sight of Batavia, near the two
small islands called Leyden and Alkmar.   On the 3d
we came to an anchor in the road, which is so good
that it may be considered as a harbour.   We thought
ourselves happy in having attained our present situation;
for with great difficulty we had prevented the Swallow
from sinking by the constant working of the pumps,
during her whole passage from Celebes.   In this road of
Batavia we found laying eleven large Dutch ships, besides several that were less, one Spanish ship, a Portuguese snow, and several Chinese junks.   On the 4th
we saluted with 11 guns, which number was returned;
and this being his Majesty's birth day, we afterwards
fired 21 guns more on that occasion.   In the afternoon
Captain Carteret waited upon the governor, requesting
permission to repair the defects of the ship; but he was
directed to petition the council.   Accordingly on Monday the 6th when the council met, the captain sent a
letter, stating to them the defects of the ship, and requesting permission to repair her; adding that he *hoped*
they would allow him the use of such wharfs and store-
houses as should be necessary.   On the 7th in the afternoon, the shebander, Mr. Garrison, a merchant, as interpreter, and another person, came to the captain,
saying, that he was sent by the governor and council
for a letter, which they had heard he had received
when at Bonthain, that the author of it, who had injured both him and their nation, might be punished.
Captain

Captain Carteret acknowledged he had received information of a defign to cut off the fhip, but faid, he had never told any one it was by means of a letter. The fhebander then defired to know if the captain would take an oath, of his not having received the letter in queftion; to which the captain returned, that if the council had any fuch extraordinary requifition to make of him, he defired it might be in writing, and then he would give fuch a reply, as, upon mature confideration, he fhould think proper. He then afked the fhebander, what anfwer he had been inftructed to give to his letter, concerning the refitting of the fhip; to which the fhebander replied, that the council had taken offence, at his having ufed the word *hoped*, all merchants having, upon a like occafion, ufed the ftile of *requeft*; Captain Carteret in return faid, that no offence had been intended on his part, and that he had ufed the firft words that occurred, which he thought moft expreffive of his meaning. On the 9th the fame gentlemen vifited the captain a fecond time, when the fhebander required a writing under his hand, importing, that he believed the report, of an intention formed at the ifland of Celebes to cut off the Swallow, was falfe and malicious, obferving at the fame time, that he hoped the captain had a better opinion of the Dutch nation, than to fuppofe them capable of fuffering fo execrable a deed to be perpetrated under their government. After this altercation Mr. Garrifon read a certificate, which, he faid, had been drawn up, by order of the council, for Captain Carteret to fign. This the captain refufed to do, becaufe it appeared to be made a condition of complying with his requeft refpecting the fhip. During this converfation, the captain defired to fee by what authority the fhebander made his requifition: he replied, he had no teftimony of authority, but that of the notoriety of his being a public officer, and the evidence of the gentlemen who were prefent, who would confirm his declaration, that he acted in this particular by the exprefs order of council. The captain now repeated his requeft of having the requifition of the council in

writing;

writing; the shebander said, he could not do this without an order from his superiors; the captain upon this absolutely refused to sign the paper, and they parted not in very good humour with each other.

On Wednesday, the 15th, the same three gentlemen paid Captain Carteret a third visit, informing him, that the council had protested against his behaviour at Macassar, and his refusing to sign the certificate, as an insult upon them, and an act of injustice to their nation. The captain said, he was not conscious of having, in any instance, acted contrary to the treaties subsisting between the two kingdoms, unworthy of his character as an officer, honoured with a commission from his Britannic Majesty, or unsuitable to the trust reposed in him; nor did he think he had been used by the governor of Macassar as the subject of a friend and ally; he then requested, that if they had any thing to alledge against him, it might be reduced to writing, and laid before the king his master, to whom alone he thought himself to be responsible. With this answer they departed; and, the next day, the captain wrote a second letter to the governor and council, in which he represented, that the leaks of the Swallow were every day increasing, and urged, in more pressing terms, his request, that she might be repaired. In consequence of this application, on Saturday the 18th the shebander informed us, that the council had given orders for the repair of the ship at Onrust, and, as there was no storehouse empty, they had appointed one of the company's vessels to receive our stores. The captain enquired of the shebander whether he had not an answer to his letter; he said he had not; nor was this the usual mode with the council, a message by him, or some other officer, being always thought sufficient. All disputes being now terminated, without any improper compliances on the part of this intrepid commander, he was, after this, supplied for his money with every thing he could desire from the company's stores, and a pilot was ordered to attend us to Onrust, where we came to anchor on Wednesday the 22nd. We immediately began

to

to clear the ship, and put her stores on board the company's vessel. On examination we found the poor weather-beaten Swallow in a very decayed state. Her bowsprit and cap, as well as her main yard, were rotten, and altogether unserviceable, her sheathing was every where eaten off by the worms, and the main planks were so much damaged, that it was absolutely necessary to heave her down, before she could be sufficiently repaired; but the wharfs being at this time pre-engaged by other ships, her repairs did not commence till the 24th of July. When the Dutch carpenters came to examine her bottom, they were all of one opinion, that the whole should be shifted. This the captain strenuously opposed, being afraid, as the Swallow was an old ship, that should her bottom be opened, and found worse than was imagined, she might undergo the fate of the Falmouth, and be condemned: he therefore desired, that a good sheathing only might be put over all; but the bawse, or master carpenter, would not undertake the required repairs, unless the captain would certify under his hand, that what should be done was in consequence of his own express orders, judgement, and direction; which the Dutchman thought was necessary for his own justification; for, said he, should the Swallow never reach England, the blame, if I go according to your directions, will nevertheless consequently fall upon me. This being thought a reasonable proposition, the captain readily assented to it; but being by this act become responsible for the fate of the ship, he thought proper to have her surveyed carefully by our own carpenter and mate, he himself with his officers always attending. Among others defects, seven chain-plates were useless; the iron work was in a very decayed state; several of the knees were loose, others were broken, and the butt-ends of the planks that joined the stern were so open, that a man's hand might be thrust in between.

During our stay at this port, we found, among other private ships from India, the Dudley, from Bengal; and application having been made to the council, leave had
been

been granted to careen her, but as the wharfs had been kept in continual use, she had been put off above four months. The captain apprehending, that if he suffered a delay much longer, the worms would eat through the bottom of his vessel, applied to our commander to intercede for him with Admiral Houting, which he did with such success, that a wharf was immediately allotted her. "Admiral Houting," says Captain Carteret, "is an old man, in the service of the states, with the rank of commander in chief of their marine, and the ships belonging to the company in India. He received his first maritime knowledge on board an English man of war, speaks English and French extremely well, and does honour to the service both by his abilities and politeness: he was so obliging as to give me a general invitation to his table, in consequence of which I was often with him, and it is with pleasure that I take this opportunity of making a public acknowledgement of the favours I received from him, and bearing this testimony to his public and private merit: he was, indeed, the only officer from whom I received any civility, or with whom I had the least communication; for I found them, in general, a reserved and supercilious set of people." The spirited behaviour of Captain Carteret to the governor at this Dutch settlement, in refusing to pay him an extravagant homage, which is exacted of the captains of all merchant ships which touch here, deserves also particular notice. The governor of Batavia, although a servant of the republic, assumes the state of a sovereign prince. When he goes abroad, he is escorted by a party of horse-guards, and two black footmen run before his coach, each having a large cane in his hand, with which they take the liberty of chastising those who do not make the obeisance that is expected from persons of all ranks, whether belonging to the country or strangers. In this settlement almost every one keeps a carriage, which is drawn by two horses, and driven by a man upon a box, like our chariots, but is open in front. When any one of these coaches meets that of the gover-

nor's, either in the town, or upon the road, it is drawn
on one side, and the persons in it must get out to pay
their respects, while his excellency's coach goes by; nor,
if a coach is behind, must it drive past that of the governor's, however pressing necessity may require speed.
A similar homage is likewise required by the members
of the council, called Edele Heeren, only that the person does not quit his carriage, but standing up in it,
pays them a respectful homage. One black man, with
a stick in his hand, runs likewise before the coach of
every member of the council, nor must any one presume to pass it any more than that of the governor's.
It was hinted to Captain Carteret by the landlord of the
hotel where he lodged, that his carriage must stop, if
he should meet the governor, or any one of the Edele
Heeren; this ceremony being generally complied with
by the captains of Indiamen, and other trading ships;
and he intimated, that the shebander had ordered him
to give the captain this information: but our commander disdaining to pay a degree of servile homage to
the servants of the States of Holland, which is not paid
to the king of Great Britain, would not consent to perform any such ceremony; and when the landlord mentioned the black men with their sticks, he pointed to
his pistols, which then happened to lie upon the table,
and told him, that he would be upon his guard; and
should any insult be offered to his person, he knew well
how to defend himself: upon this he went out, and in
a few hours after told the captain, he had orders from
the governor, to let him know, that he might do as he
pleased. We had now been at Batavia between three
and four months, and during that time, says Captain
Carteret, " I had the honour to see the governor but
twice: the first time was at my arrival, when I waited
upon him at one of his houses, a little way in the country; the next was in town, as he was walking before his
house there, when I addressed him upon a particular
occasion. Soon after the news of the Prince of Orange's
marriage arrived at Batavia, he gave a public entertainment, to which I had the honour of being invited;
but

but having heard, that Commodore Tinker, upon a like occasion, finding that he was to be placed below the gentlemen of the Dutch council, had abruptly left the room, and was followed by all the captains of his squadron; and being willing to avoid the disagreeable dilemma, of either fitting below the council, or following the commodore's example, I applied to the governor to know what station would be allotted me, before I accepted his invitation, and finding I could not be permitted to take place of the council, I declined it. On both these occasions I spoke to his excellency by an English merchant, who acted as an interpreter. The first time he had not the civility to offer me the least refreshment, nor did he the last time so much as ask me to go into his house." The ship was now repaired to our satisfaction, though the Dutch carpenters thought she was not in a condition to proceed to Europe; and Admiral Houting intimated, that if we went to sea before the proper time, we should meet with such weather off the Cape of Good Hope, as would make us repent our haste; but the captain being ill, and the people very sickly; and especially as the west monsoon was setting in, during which the mortality is yet greater at Batavia than at other times, we thought it better to run the risk of a few hard gales off the cape, than to remain longer in this unhealthy place.

We therefore, on Wednesday the 15th of September, sailed from Onrust, without returning, as is usual, into Batavia Road, and the captain, on account of his illness, sent his lieutenant, Mr. Gower, to take leave of the governor, and to offer him his service, if he had any dispatches for Europe. When we left this port 24 of our seamen, which were brought from Europe, had died, and the same number were now very ill, seven of whom died on our passage to the cape; but we were so happy as to procure a number of English seamen at Batavia before our departure, which recruited the strength that had been wasted in the voyage, and without these recruits, in the captain's opinion, we should not at last have been able to bring the ship home. On
Monday

Monday, the 20th, we anchored on the S. E. fide of Prince's Iſland, in the Strait of Sunda, at which time we had the wind freſh from the S. E. We have juſt given a deſcriptive, hiſtorical, and geographical account, of the iſlands of Sunda, and Java, and in a former voyage of the Philippine Iſles, to render which full and complete, we ſhall here deſcribe ſome other noted iſlands and places in the Indian ſeas, to which, at leaſt, references are made in the inſtructive and entertaining voyages which compoſe this work.

(1.) The Nicobar Iſlands, which are ſituated in the Indian ſea, between 7 and 10 degrees of north latitude, and between 92 and 94 degrees eaſt longitude, near the entrance of the bay of Bengal, a little north of the iſland of Sumatra. Theſe iſles form three cluſters; the middle, called Sombrero, are well inhabited, except one; the northern cluſter, called Carnicubars, are not ſo populous. The ſouthern cluſter of the Nicobars, are very mountainous, and the people much more ſavage than thoſe of the middle and northern cluſters. The prieſts of Sombrero, are dreſſed much in the ſame manner as we paint the devil, by which appearance they keep the inhabitants in awe. The largeſt of theſe iſlands, which lies moſt to the ſouth, is 40 miles long, and 15 broad: the ſouth end is mountainous, and there are ſome ſteep rocks near the ſea; the reſt of the iſland is covered with woods, but has no high land. It is a rich ſoil, that would produce almoſt any grain, if it was cultivated. The groves of cocoa-nut trees that grow in the flat country near the ſea, are exceeding pleaſant; but we do not find an account of any towns; only, as we ſail by ſea, we can perceive groups, containing each five or ſix houſes in every creek and bay, which are built on bamboo pillars, eight or nine feet above the ſurface of the ground, the roof being neatly arched with bended cane, and covered with palm branches.

Theſe iſlanders are of the middle ſtature, their complexion a deep olive, their long hair and eyes black. The men wear no cloaths, but a piece of linen cloth about their loins; that of the women reaches below the

knees. Their women might be esteemed handsome, if
it was not the custom to pull the hair off their eye-brows
by the roots. They neglect to clear the country, and
cultivate the ground, which is over-run with wood;
and they live chiefly on fish, and such fruits as the
country produces spontaneously. They have little trade
or commerce with any other people; but as ships fail
in their way to and from the Straits of Malacca, they
bring off hogs, poultry, and such fruits as the country
affords, taking tobacco, linen, and other necessaries in
return.

(2.) The Andoman, and Cocoa Islands. The former
are situated in the bay of Bengal, north of the Nicobar
Islands, in between 10 and 15 degrees of north latitude,
longitude 92 degrees east. These islands do not seem
to differ much from those of Nicobar, except in producing rice, which is cultivated and eaten by the natives
as well as fish and fruit. The Cocoa Islands lie 35
leagues W. S. W. of Cape Negrais; they produce great
abundance of cocoa-trees, but are uninhabited.

(3.) The famous island of Ceylon; which lies between
5 deg. 30 min. and 10 deg. 16 min. N. latitude; and
between 79 deg. 40 min. and 82 deg. 45 min. E. longitude; at the distance of about 190 miles from Cape
Comorin. Ptolemy described this island under the
name of Taprobane. It is 900 miles in circumference,
300 in length, and 140 in breadth. It is for the most
part a mountainous country, covered with wood; but
there are several fruitful plains and valleys, well watered
by rivulets. A very remarkable mountain, which stands
on the south-side of Condula, the name of the northern
division, is, by the natives, called Hamalel; but by the
Europeans, Adam's Peak, being of a pyramidal form,
only on the top is a little rocky plain, with a print of a
man's foot on it, near two feet long, to which the natives
go in pilgrimage once a year, to worship the impression, having a tradition, according to some, that their
god Buddow ascended to heaven from hence, leaving
this print of his foot, which the Portuguese, when they
possessed this island, called Adam's Foot, and the mountain

tain Pico de Adam ; but others affirm, that it received
its name from a tradition of the natives, that Adam
was created and buried here. In this mountain rife
the principal rivers, which run into the fea in different
directions.   The largeft of thefe is the Mavillagonga,
which runs N. E. of the cities of Candy and Alatneur,
difcharging itfelf into the ocean at Trincomale. Thefe
rivers run with fuch rapidity. and are fo full of rocks,
that none of them are navigable : the rains, which happen when the fun is vertical, increafe their waters, and
create abundance of torrents, which are not vifible in
the dry feafon. The air is for the moft part healthful,
except near the fea, and the north part of the ifland,
where they have no fprings, or rivers ; and if the rain
fails them, they are fure to be afflicted with famine or
ficknefs. The chief towns are, 1. Candy, the capital
of the ifland, and fituate near the center of it, in latitude 8 deg. N. and 79 deg. E. longitude. This is an
open town with fortifications, and yet almoft inacceffible, being furrounded by rocks and thick woods that
are impaffable, except through fome lanes, which are
fenced with gates of ftrong thorns : and yet it appears
that the Portuguefe made themfelves mafters of Candy,
and almoft demolifhed it, obliging the king to retire to
Digligyneur, five miles S. E. of Candy. 2. Columbo,
the capital of the Dutch fettlements, is a great port
town in the S. W. part of the ifland, in 7 deg. N. latitude, and in 78 deg. E. longitude. It has a good
harbour, defended by a caftle, and feveral batteries of
guns. In this caftle refides the governor, merchants,
officers and foldiers, belonging to the Eaft India Company; and 4000 flaves have their huts between the
caftle and the fea. The Dutch have two hofpitals
here : one for the fick and wounded, and another for
the orphans. As the boys grow up, they are entered
into the fea and land fervice; and the girls are married
at 12 or 13 years of age; and they have a Malabarian
fchool for teaching the Indian language. 3. Negumbo,
which is alfo a port town, lies about 25 miles north of
Columbo. 4. Jaffnapatan, the capital of the province

of

of the fame name, and the northern divifion of this
ifland.   There is no cinnamon in this part of the ifland,
neverthelefs the Dutch have fortified it all round, to
prevent any other nations fending colonies thither. 5.
Trincomale is fituate on the eaft-fide of the ifland, about
80 miles fouth of Punta Pedra, the moft northerly promontory of the ifland. 6. Battadalio is another fortrefs,
50 miles fouth of the former: befides which places,
there are the feven little iflands Ourature, Xho, De-
ferba, Analativa, Caradiva, Pongardiva, and Nainan-
diva.

With regard to the hiftory of this ifland, the country
villages of the natives are very irregular, being not laid
out in ftreets, but every man inclofes a fpot of ground,
with a bank or pale fuitable to his circumftances, and
there are frequently 20 or 30 of thofe inclofures pretty
near together.   The buildings are mean, the houfes of
the generality of the people, low thatched cottages,
confifting of one or two ground rooms, the fides
whereof are fplintered with rattans or cane, which they
do not always cover with clay, and if they do, it feems
they are not permitted to white-wafh them, this being
a royal privilege.   The better fort of people have a
fquare in the middle of their houfes, and as many
rooms on the fides of it as the number of the family
requires, with banks of earth raifed a yard high above
this fquare court, whereon they fit crofs-legged, and eat
or converfe with their friends.   Their meat is dreffed
in their yards, or a corner of the room.   Their furniture confifts of a mat, a ftool or two, a few china plates,
with fome earthen and brazen veffels for water, and to
drefs their meat in, except one bedftead, which is allotted
to the mafter of the houfe to fit or fleep on, and this is
corded, if we may ufe the expreffion, with rattans or
fmall canes; and has a mat or two and a ftraw pillow
upon it, but no tefter and curtains.   The women and
children lie on mats by the fire-fide, covering themfelves only with the cloth they wear in the day time;
but they will have a fire burning at their feet, all night,
the pooreft among them never wanting fuel, wood being

ing fo plentiful that no one thinks it worth while to claim any property in it. Their Pagodas or Temples, which are of any antiquity, are built of hewn ftone, with numbers of images both on the infide and out, but no windows in them, and in all other refpects like thofe on the neighbouring continent of India; but their temples of a modern date are little low buildings with clay walls, almoft in the form of a dove-houfe; and befides their public temples, they have fmall chapels in their yards, fometimes not more than two feet fquare, which they fet upon a pillar four feet high, and having placed in it the image they reverence moft, they light candles and lamps before it, and every morning ftrew flowers while performing their devotions.

The natives are efteemed men of good parts and addrefs, grave, yet of an eafy temper. They eat and fleep moderately, but are lazy and indolent, which is the cafe in moft hot climates. It is faid, that they are not given to thieving, but are much addicted to lying, which feems to be a parodox; for a man who will lye and deceive, would not make much fcruple to cheat. They are far from being jealous, or reftraining of their women from taking innocent freedoms. The men are of a moderate ftature, and well proportioned, wear long beards, and have good features; their hair and eyes are black; they have dark complexions, but not black as the natives upon the neighbouring continent of India are. They fit on mats and carpets on the floor, but have a ftool or two for perfons of diftinction; but the vulgar are prohibited the ufe of ftools. Young men of figure wear their hair long and combed back; but, in a more advanced age, caps in the form of a mitre are worn. Their drefs is a waiftcoat of callico, and a piece of the fame wrapped round their waifts, in which they put their knives and trinkets, and they have a hanger by their fide, in a filver fcabbard; befides which they walk with a cane or tuck, and a boy carries a box with betel and areca after them. The betel is a leaf of the fhape of a laurel leaf, and the areca-nut about the bignefs

nefs of a nutmeg, which they cut in thin flices, with an inftrument made on purpofe for it, and this, with a pafte made of lime, they chew together almoft all day long, as moft other Indians do : this mixture feems to be a kind of opiate, and renders them perfectly eafy while they ufe it. They have a perfon to carry a covered filver pot, or one made of fome other metal, to fpit in : for this compofition has a naufeous fmell, and it would be the greateft affront imaginable to fpit on the carpets or floors in a friend's houfe, and thofe that chew it fpit perpetually. It makes their lips very red, of which they are proud, and this may be one reafon for their taking it ; but there is nothing inviting in the tafte of this luxurious dainty, though univerfally chewed, and is the firft thing offered a ftranger when he makes a vifit. The women wear their hair long without any covering, and make it fhine with cocoa-nut oil, which has a very rancid fmell, though the natives efteem it a perfume, for cuftom will bring people to like almoft any thing. The women are dreffed in a callico waiftcoat, which difcovers their fhape, and they wrap a piece of callico about them, which falls below their knees, and does the fervice of a petticoat ; thefe are longer, or fhorter, according to the quality of the perfon who wears them. They bore holes in their ears, in which they hang fuch a weight of jewels, or fomething that refembles them, that you may put a half crown through the hole of their ears: they load their necks alfo with weighty necklaces, which fall upon their breafts, containing a great many ftrings or rounds of beads : their arms are adorned with bracelets ; and they have a number of rings on their fingers and toes; and a girdle of filver wire furrounds their waifts. When they go abroad, they throw a piece of ftriped filk over their heads, which fometimes refembles a hood. The people are obliged to go bare-footed, becaufe none but the king is allowed to wear fhoes and ftockings. The ufual falutation among thefe people, is the fame as in other parts of India, namely, the carrying one or both hands to their heads, according to the quality of the

perfon

person they falute. Talkative people are in no repute; for the nearest relations, or most particular friends, do not talk much when they visit, but sit silent a great part of the time. A man before marriage, sends a friend to purchase the woman's cloaths, which she freely sells for a stipulated sum. In the evening he carries them to her, sleeps with her all night, and in the morning appoints the day of marriage; on which he provides an entertainment of two courses for the friends of both parties. The feast is held at the bride's house, when the young couple eat out of the same dish, sleep together that night, and on the ensuing morning depart for the bridegroom's habitation. The meaning of making a purchase of the bride's cloaths is, that she and her friends may be satisfied with respect to the man's circumstances. They are permitted to part with each other whenever they please; but if there should be any children, the man is obliged to maintain the boys, and the woman the girls; and they are so inclined to avail themselves of this liberty, that some of them have been known to change a dozen times. The profession of a midwife is unknown, as the women, in general, are both willing and qualified on that occasion to assist each other.

This island produces rice, of which they have several kinds: one of them will be seven months before it comes to maturity, some six, and others five, between the seed time and harvest: that which grows fastest is the best tasted, but yields the least increase; and as all sorts of rice grow in water, the inhabitants are at great labour and expence in levelling the ground they design for tillage, and making channels from their wells and repositories of water, to convey to these fields: they cut out the sides of their hills from the top to the bottom, into little level plains, one above another, that the water may stand in them till the corn is ripe; and these levels not being more than six or eight feet wide, many of them look like stairs to ascend the mountain, at a little distance. In the north part of the island where there are few springs, they save the rain water

in

in great ponds, or tanques, of a mile in compafs, in the time of the monfoons, and when their feeds are fown, let it down into them gradually, fo that it may hold out till harveft. They do not thrafh, but tread out their corn with oxen and buffaloes, frequently in the field where it grows. When it is reaped, they lay out a round fpot of ground for this purpofe, about 25 feet over, which they dig a foot and a half deep, and the women, whofe bufinefs it is, bring the corn in bundles on their heads, after which the cattle are driven round the pit till they have trampled it out of the ftraw: then a new floor is laid; and with half a dozen oxen they will trample out 40 or 50 bufhels a day. Before they begin to tread out the corn, they always perform a religious ceremony, and apply to their idols for a blefling on their labours. They have feveral other kinds of grain, which they eat at the latter end of the year, when rice begins to be fcarce, particularly coracan, which is as fmall as a muftard feed. Having beat this, and ground it into flour, they make cakes of it. This grain grows in dry ground, and is ripe within three or four months after it is fown. They have alfo a feed, called tolla, of which they make oil, and anoint themfelves with it.

In this ifland are a great variety of fruits, but the natives feldom eat them ripe, or cultivate any but thofe which ferve to make pickles for their foup or curree, and for fauces, when they are green, to eat with their rice. Of the betel they have great abundance, which they formerly exported to the coaft of Coromandel, to great advantage, before the Dutch excluded them from all trade with foreigners. The fruit called jacka, is part of their food. They grow upon large trees, are round in their fhape, and as big as a peck loaf. They are covered with a green prickly rind; have feeds and kernels in them as big as a chefnut; and are in colour and tafte like them. They gather thefe jackas before they are ripe; and, when boiled, they eat much like cabbage; if fuffered to grow till ripe, they are very good to eat raw. The natives roaft the kernel in the embers,

3

embers, and carry with them when they take a journey, for their provision. There is another kind of fruit called jumbo, which is very juicy, and tastes like an apple; it is white, streaked with red, and looks very beautiful. They have also some fruits that resemble our plumbs and cherries; nor do they want any of the common Indian fruits, such as mangoes, cocoas, pineapples, melons, pomegranates, oranges of several forts, citrons, limes, &c. They frequently dedicate their fruit to some dæmon, to prevent their being stolen; after which their neighbours dare not touch them, left the dæmon, to which they are devoted, should punish them for the theft; and before the owner eats of it himself, he offers part of it to the idol. Their kitchen gardens are well stored with roots, plants, and herbs, for the Portuguese and Dutch have introduced all manner of European plants that grow in our kitchen gardens. They also abound in medicinal herbs, which they know very well how to apply, and with which they perform many notable cures.

Nor are they in want of flowers of various colours, and a delicious scent, which grow spontaneously; but are never cultivated; with these, the young people of both sexes adorn their hair. With a variety of others, they have white and red roses, as sweet and beautiful as those in Europe, and a white flower resembling jessamine, which the king reserves for his own use, no subject being allowed to wear it. There is another flower, which is observed to open about four every evening, and close again at four in the morning.

Among their trees the talipot, which grows very tall and strait, is in high repute. A single leaf of this will cover 15 or 20 men, and will fold up like a fan: they wear a piece of it on their heads, when travelling, to skreen them from the sun. They also serve the soldiers for tents to lie under in the fields; and their leaves are so tough, that they make their way with them through the thickets without tearing them. There is likewise a tree called kettule, a kind of palm, as high as a cocoa-tree, from whence they draw a pleasant liquor; an ordinary tree yielding three or four gallons a day; and when boiled, it makes a kind of brown sugar, called jaggory. The wood of this tree is black, hard, and very heavy. But that of most value to the Dutch, as it was formerly to the Arabs, and the Portuguese, is the cinnamon-tree, which grows commonly in the woods, on the S. W. part of the island. The tree is of a middle size, and has a leaf of the form of a laurel leaf. When the leaves first appear, they are as red as scarlet, and being rubbed between the fingers, smell like cloves. It bears a fruit like an acorn, which neither smells nor tastes like the bark; but if boiled in water, an oil swims on the top, which smells sweetly, and is used as an ointment in several distempers: but as they have great plenty of it, they frequently burn it in their lamps. The tree having two barks, they strip off the outside bark, which is good for little, and then cut the inner bark round the tree with a pruning knife; after which they cut it long ways in little slips, and after they have stripped these pieces off, lay them in the sun to dry, when they roll up in the manner we see them brought over. The body of the tree is white, and serves for building, and other uses, but has neither the smell nor taste of the bark. When the wind sets off the island, the cinnamon groves perfume the air for many miles out at sea, of which we have incontestible evidence; and most likely it is at that time of the year, when the cinnamon trees are in blossom.

Of the animals that abound in this island, are elephants of a very large size; also oxen, buffaloes, deer, hogs, goats, monkeys, and some wild beasts; but they had neither horses, asses, or sheep, till they were imported by the Europeans; nor have they any lions or wolves. The elephants feed upon the tender twigs of trees, corn, and grass, as it is growing, and do the husbandmen a great deal of mischief, by trampling down their corn, as well as eating it, and spoiling their trees. The monkeys have black faces and white beards, much resembling old men. Alligators and crocodiles abound, as do also serpents of a monstrous size; and here is an animal in all respects like a deer, but not bigger than a hare. Vermin and insects are very numerous, particularly ants, which eat every thing they come at, except iron, and such hard substances. Their houses are pestered with them. When full grown they have wings, and fly up in such clouds, that they intercept the light of the sun; soon after which they fall down dead, and are eaten by fowls, who devour them also at other times. The common sort of bees build in hollow trees, or in holes of the rocks; but there are much larger bees, of a more lively colour, which form their combs upon the high boughs of trees, and, at the proper season, the country people go out into the woods and take their honey. In the season when the rains begin to fall, they are troubled with small red leeches, which are not at first much bigger than a hair; these run up the bare legs of travellers, and fixing themselves there, are not easily removed, till the blood runs about their heels. The remedy used against their bite is, to rub the legs with a composition of ashes, lemon-juice, and salt. The bite of these creatures is so far from being attended with any ill consequences, that the bleeding, which is the effect of it, is esteemed very wholesome. Their fowls are geese, ducks, turkeys, hens, woodcocks, partridges, snipes, wild peacocks, parroquets, and a beautiful sparrow as white as snow, all but its head, which is black, with a plume of feathers standing upright upon it. The tail of these birds is a foot in length.

In this island the inhabitants make savoury soups of flesh or fish, which they eat with their rice: people of condition will have several dishes at their tables, but they consist chiefly of rice, soups, herbs, garden-roots, and vegetables. Of flesh and fish they eat but little. Their meat is cut into small square pieces, and two or three ounces of it laid on the side of the dish by their rice, and, being seasoned very high, gives a relish to that insipid food. They use no knives or forks, but have ladles and spoons made of the cocoa-nut shell;

Their

Their plates are of brass or china-ware; but the poor have a broad leaf instead of a plate, and sometimes several leaves sewed together with bents, where broad ones are not to be had. Water is their usual drink, which they pour out of a cruce or bottle, holding it more than a foot above their heads; and some of them will swallow near a quart of water in this manner without gulping once. Neither wine nor beer is made in this country, but arrack and spirits are drawn from rice. They never eat beef, the bull and cow being objects of adoration. Neither the people in a high or low station eat with their wives: the man sits by himself, and the women and children eat after he has dined. In this woody and mountainous country are no wheel carriages, unless what belong to the Dutch near the sea coast. The baggage is carried usually upon the backs of their slaves. The chief manufactures here are callico and cotton cloths: they make also brass, copper, and earthen vessels, swords, knives, and working tools: they also now make pretty good fire-arms; and goldsmith's work, painting, and carving, are performed tolerably well. We may trace their foreign trade up to the earliest ages. They supplied Persia, Arabia, Egypt, and Ethiopia, with their spices, before Jacob went down into Egypt, which is above 3000 years since, as appears by the history of Joseph's being sold to Ishmaelite merchants, who were travelling with a caravan across Arabia to Egypt with the spices of India, of which the cinnamon of Ceylon, that lies near the coast of hither India, was no doubt the chief; and so profitable was this branch of trade, that all the nations above mentioned sent colonies hither, whose descendants were planted here when the Portuguese first visited this coast.

Here the Portuguese language is spoken; however, the natives have a language of their own, which comes nearest to that spoken on the Malabar coast: the Bramins or priests speak a dead language, in which the books relating to their religion are written. They write upon the leaves of the talipot cut into pieces

of

of three fingers broad, and two foot long, with a fteel
ftyle or bodkin. They have long ftudied aftronomy,
which they learnt from the Arabians, and foretel eclipfes
tolerably well: they are great pretenders alfo to aftro-
logy, and by the planets calculate nativities, and direct
people when will be the moft lucky days to enter upon
any affair of moment, or to begin a journey; and they
find thofe who are weak enough to be impofed upon,
though they may have been many times difappointed.
Their year is divided into 365 days, and every day into
30 pays or parts, and their night into as many; and
they have a little copper difh, with a hole in the bottom
of it, which being put into a tub of water, is filled
during one of their pays, when it finks, and then it
is put into the water again to meafure another pay;
for they have neither fun-dials nor clocks.

In Ceylon, the criminals are frequently impaled
alive; others have ftakes driven through their bodies;
fome are hung upon trees; and many are worried by
dogs, who are fo accuftomed to the horrid butchery,
that, on the days appointed for the death of criminals,
they, by certain tokens, run to the place of execution.
But the moft remarkable punifhment is inflicted by the
king himfelf, who rides an elephant trained up on purpofe. The beaft tramples the unhappy wretch to
death, and tears him limb from limb. Some are punifhed by fines and imprifonment, at the difcretion of
the judges. When the fine is decreed, the officers
feize the culprit, wherever they meet him, ftrip him
naked, his cloaths going as part of payment, and oblige
him to carry a large ftone, the weight being increafed
daily, by the addition of others that are fmaller, till the
remainder of the mulct is either paid or remitted. Any
of the male cingloffes may indifferently charge another
within hearing (as we do the conftables) to aid and
affift them in the execution of their duty, or upon any
emergency; but the women are not permitted to mention the king's name, upon the fevere penalty of having
their tongues cut out for the offence. A creditor
fometimes will go to the houfe of the debtor, and very
                                              gravely

gravely affirm, that if he does not difcharge the debt he owes him immediately, he will deftroy himfelf: this fo terrifies the other, that he inftantly collects all the money he can, even felling his wife and children rather than be deficient in his payment of the fum demanded. This is owing to a law, which fpecifies, that, if any man deftroys himfelf on account of a debt not being difcharged, the debtor fhall immediately pay the money to the furviving relations, and forfeit his own life, un- lefs he is able to redeem it by a large fine to the king. They have two modes of deciding controverfies; the one is by imprecating curfes to fall upon them if they do not fpeak the truth; and by the other, both perfons are obliged to put their fingers into boiling oil, when the perfon who can bear the pain the longeft, and with the leaft appearance of being affected, is deemed in- nocent. They have, however, methods of evading both thefe laws; the firft, by ufing ambiguous expref- fions; and the latter, by certain preparations, which prevent the oil from doing them any injury. It is not lawful to beat a woman without permiffion from the king; fo that the females may thank his majefty for all the blows they get. But they may be made to carry heavy bafkets of fand upon their heads as long as the man pleafes, which is much more dreadful to them than a hearty drubbing. The circumftances of the children depend upon thofe of the mother; for if the mother is a free woman, they are free, but if fhe is a flave, they are always vaffals.

They have neither phyficians nor furgeons among them; yet, as to phyfic, every one almoft underftands the common remedies, applying herbs or roots, ac- cording to the nature of the complaint; and they have au herb which cures the bite of a fnake. As they abound in poifonous herbs and plants, fo they have others that are antidotes againft them. Their difeafes are chiefly fevers, fluxes, and the fmall-pox. They are never let blood, except by the leaches, already mention- ed, from which they acknowledge they have fometimes received great benefit.

With

With regard to the religion of thefe people, they worfhip God, but make no image of him; however, they have idols, the reprefentatives of fome great men, who formerly lived upon the earth, and are now, they imagine, mediators for them to the fupreme God of heaven. The chief of thofe demi-gods is Buddow, who according to their tradition originally came from heaven to procure the happinefs of men, and afcended thither again from Adam's Mountain, leaving the impreffion of his foot upon the rock. They are faid, likewife, to worfhip the devil, that he fhould do them no mifchief; and another of their objects of worfhip is the tooth of a monkey. They worfhip alfo the fun, moon, and other planets. Every town has its tutelar dæmon, and every family their penates, or houfhold gods, to whom they build chapels in their courts, paying their devotions, and facrificing to them every morning; but to the fupreme deity they erect no temples or altars. There are three claffes of idols, and as many orders of priefts, who have their feveral temples, to which eftates in land are appropriated. Buddow is the chief of thefe fubordinate deities, and his priefts in the greateft efteem, being all of the higheft caft or tribe in the nation. They wear a yellow veft and mantle, have their heads fhaved, and their beards grow to a great length. Their difciples fall down on their faces before them; and they have a ftool to fit on wherever they vifit, which is an honour only fhewn to their princes and great men. Thefe priefts have no commerce with women, drink no ftrong liquor, and eat only one meal a day; but they are not debarred from flefh, except beef. They are ftiled fons of the god Buddow, and cannot be called to account by the civil power, whatever crimes they commit. There is a fecond order of priefts, that officiate in the temples of other idols; thefe are allowed to follow any fecular employment, and are not diftinguifhed from the laity by their habits, but have, however, a certain revenue. Every morning and evening they attend the fervice of their temples; and when the people facrifice rice and

I   fruits,

fruits, the prieſt preſents them before the idol, and then delivers them to the ſinging men and women, and other ſervants that belong to the temple, and to the poor devotees, who eat the proviſions: no fleſh is ever ſacrificed to the idols of this claſs. The third order of prieſts have no revenues, but build temples for themſelves, without any election or conſecration, and beg money to maintain themſelves. Theſe mendicants are mountebanks in their way, ſhewing a variety of whimſical tricks for their bread. They are prohibited by law, from touching the waters in wells or ſprings, nor muſt they uſe any but what is procured from rivers and ditches. They are conſidered in ſo deſpicable a light, that it is held diſgraceful to have any connections with them. Wedneſdays and Saturdays are the days they reſort to their temples ; and at the new and full moon they offer ſacrifices to the god Buddow ; and on New Year's-day, in the month of March, they offer a ſolemn ſacrifice to him, on a high mountain, or under a ſpreading tree that is deemed ſacred. The principal feſtival of the Chingulays is obſerved in the month of July, in honour of the moon, when a prieſt goes in ſolemn proceſſion with a garland of flowers, to which the people preſent their offerings. The ridiculous pageantry attending this feſtival, was attempted to be aboliſhed in 1664; but the attempt occaſioned an inſurrection, ſo that the kings of Ceylon are obliged to let them continue the pompous mummery. They have alſo idols of monſtrous ſhapes and forms, made of ſilver, braſs, and other metals, and ſometimes of clay ; but thoſe in Buddow's temples are the figures of men ſitting croſs-legged, in yellow habits, like his prieſts, repreſenting ſome holy men, who, they ſay, were teachers of virtue, and benefactors to mankind.

The iſland of Ceylon was formerly divided into nine monarchies, but, at preſent it is under the dominion of one king, whoſe court is kept in the center of the iſland, at a place called Digligy-Neur: the palace is but newly built, the gates large, ſtately, and finely carved : the
window-

window-frames are made of ebony, and inlaid with silver: the kings elephants, troops, and concubines, are numerous. The guards are commanded by Dutch and Portuguese renegado officers. This monarch assumes great dignity, and demands much respect, which his subjects readily pay him, as they imagine, that all their kings immediately on their demise, are turned into gods. He expects that Christians should salute him kneeling, and uncovered, but requires nothing more of them. His title is, Emperor of Ceylon, king of Candy, prince of Onva, and the four Corles, great duke of the seven Corles, marquis of Duranura, lord of the sea-ports, and fisheries of pearls, and precious stones, lord of the golden sun, &c. His revenue consists in the gifts and offerings of his subjects; his palaces are built upon almost inaccessible places, for the greater security: no bridges are permitted to be erected over rivers or streams, nor any good roads to be made, to render the country as impassable as possible. None are suffered to approach his palace without a passport stamped in clay. The troops are hereditary, and their weapons are swords, guns, pikes, bows and arrows. They are subtle, but not courageous, and will not engage an enemy but by surprise, or when there is some manifest advantage in their favour. It is so difficult to penetrate into the inland parts, and all the passes are so well guarded, that even the Dutch themselves are unacquainted with the greatest part of the island. In the year 1505 the Portuguese landed in Ceylon, and about twelve years after they established factories there, the reigning king permitting them to build forts; and, upon his demise, he declared the king of Portugal his heir; but in process of time the Portuguese behaving with great insolence and cruelty, the young king of Candy invited in the Dutch, in 1639, who after a tedious war, at length, in the year 1655, subdued the Portuguese, and became masters of the trade and coast: upon which they drove the king, their ally, into the mountains, and, with their wonted gratitude, made him their tributary. The Dutch have in subsequent years committed many cruelties, and the natives frequently retaliate by making excursions among them, or murdering all they meet with at a distance from the forts, and in the interior part of the island.

(4.) The Maldives. The Maldivia islands, so called from Male, the chief of them, which is the residence of their king, lie about four hundred miles south west of Ceylon and Cape Comorin. They extend from 4 deg. S. to 8 deg. N. latitude; and are about 600 miles in length, and upwards of 100 in the broadest part. They are said to be 1000 in number, but many of them are only large hillocks of sand, and from the barrenness of the soil, are uninhabited. The whole country is divided into 13 provinces, called Attolons, each of which contains many small islands, and is of a circular form, about 100 miles in circumference. These provinces all lie in a line, and are separated from each other by channels, four of which are navigable for large ships; but are very dangerous, on account of the amazing rocks that break the force of the sea, and raise prodigious surges. At the bottom of these channels is found a substance like white coral, which, when boiled in cocoa-water, greatly resembles sugar. The currents generally run east and west alternately six months, but the time of the change is uncertain; and sometimes they change from N. to S. The climate is exceeding sultry, this country lying near the equinoxial line on both sides: the nights, however, are tolerably cool, and produce heavy dews that are refreshing to the trees and vegetables. Their winter commences in April, and continues till October, during which they have perpetual rains, with strong easterly winds, but never any frost. The summer begins in October, and continues six months, during which time the winds are easterly, and the heat is so excessive as scarce to be borne, there not being any rain throughout that season.

In general these islands are very fertile, and produce great quantities of millet, and another grain much like it, of both which they have two harvests every year.

Here

Here are also several kind of roots that serve for food, particularly a sort of bread-fruit, called nell-pou, which grows wild and in great plenty. The woods produce excellent fruits, as cocoas, citrons, pomegranates, and India figs. Their only animals for use are sheep and buffaloes, except a few cows and bulls that belong to the king, and are imported from the continent; but these are only used at particular festivals. The natives have not much poultry, but they are supplied with prodigious quantities of wild fowl that are caught in the woods, and sold at a very low price. They have also plenty of wild pigeons, ducks, rails, and birds resembling sparrow-hawks. The sea produces most kinds of fish, great quantities of which are exported from hence to Sumatra. Among the fish is one called a cowrie, the shells of which (called in England blackmoor's teeth) are used in most part of the Indies instead of coin.

The only poisonous animals here are snakes; a dangerous sort of them infest the borders of the sea. The inhabitants also are much troubled with rats, dormice, pismires, and other species of vermin, which are very destructive to their provisions, fruit, and other perishable commodities; for which reason they build their granaries on piles in the sea, at some distance from the shore; and in this manner most of the king's granaries are built.

In these islands the natives are very robust, of an olive complexion, and well featured. They are naturally ingenious, and apply themselves with great industry to various manufactures, particularly the making of silk and cotton. They are cautious, and sharp in trading, courageous, and well skilled in arms. The common people go almost naked, having only a piece of cotton fastened round the waist, except on festival days, when they wear cotton or silk jerkins, with waistcoats, the sleeves of which reach only to their elbows. The wealthier sort tie a piece of cloth between their legs, and round the waist, next to which they have a piece of blue, or red cotton, that reaches to the knees, and to that is joined a large piece of cotton and silk, reaching to their ancles, and girded with a square handkerchief embroidered with gold or silver; and the whole is secured by a large silk girdle fringed, the ends of which hang down before; and within this girdle, on the left side, they keep their money and betel, and on the right side a knife. They set great value on this instrument, from its being their only weapon; for none but the king's officers and soldiers are permitted to wear any other. The rich have silk turbans on their heads, richly adorned, but those of the poor are made of cotton, and only ornamented with ribbons of various colours. The women are fairer than the men, and, in general, of a very agreeable disposition. They wear a coat of cotton, or silk, that reaches down to the ancles, over which they have a long robe of taffety, or fine cotton, that extends from the shoulders to the feet, and is fastened round the neck by two gilt buttons. Their hair, which is esteemed a great ornament, is black; and to obtain this, they keep their daughters heads shaved till they are eight or ten years of age, leaving only a little hair on their foreheads to distinguish them from the boys. They wash their heads and hair in water, to make the latter thick and long. and let it hang loose that the air may dry it; after which they perfume it with an odoriferous oil. When this is done, they stroke all the hair backwards from the forehead, and tie it behind in a knot, to which they add a large lock of a man's hair; and the whole is curiously ornamented with flowers of various sorts. The common people have houses built of cocoa-wood, and covered with leaves sewed one within another; but the superior sort build their houses of stone, which is taken from under the flats and rocks in the following manner: among other trees in this island, is one called candou, exceedingly soft, and, when dry, and sawed into planks, is much lighter than cork: the natives, who are excellent swimmers, dive under water, and, having fixed upon a stone for that purpose, they fasten a strong rope to it: after this, they take a plank of the candou-wood,

wood, which, having a hole bored in it, is put on the rope, and forced down quite to the stone : they then run on a number of other boards, till the light wood rises up to the top, dragging the stone along with it. By this contrivance the natives weighed up the cannon and anchors of a French ship that was cast away near their coast about a century ago.

The Maldivians, in general, are very polite, particularly those on the island of Male ; but they are very libidinous, and fornication is not considered as any crime ; neither must any person offer insult to a woman that has been guilty of misconduct previous to marriage. Every man is allowed to have three wives if he can maintain them, but not more. The girls are marriageable at eight years of age, when they wear an additional covering on their necks : the boys go naked till seven, when they are circumcised, and wear the usual dress of their country afterwards. These people are very abstemious in their diet, their principal food consisting of roots made into meal, and baked; particularly those called nell-pou, and elas, the latter of which they dress several ways : they also make a pottage of milk, cocoa, honey, and bread, which they esteem an excellent dish ; and their common drink is water. They sit crofs legged at their meals, in the same manner as in other eastern countries. The floor on which they sit is covered with a fine mat, and they use banana leaves instead of table cloths. Their dishes are chiefly of china, all vessels of gold, or silver, being prohibited by law : they are made round with a cover, over which is a piece of silk to keep out the ants. They take up their victuals between their fingers, and in so careful a manner as not to let any fall ; and if they have occasion to spit, they rise from the table and walk out. They do not drink till they have finished their meal, for they consider that as a mark of rudeness ; and they are very cautious of eating in the presence of strangers. They have no set meals, attending only to the call of nature, and all their provisions are dressed by the women, for to cook is accounted disgraceful

graceful to a man. Being naturally very cleanly, as soon as they rise in the morning they wash themselves, rub their eyes with oil, and black their eye-brows. They are also very careful in washing and cleansing their teeth, that they may the better receive the stain of the betel and areca, which is red, a colour they are particularly fond of. They present betel, which they keep always about them, upon occasional salutations, as we do snuff..

They have many pagan customs, though they profess the religion of the Mahometans. When they meet with any disaster at sea, they pray to the king of the winds; and there is in every island a place, where those who have escaped danger make offerings to him of little vessels made for the purpose, in which they put fragrant woods, flowers, and other perfumes, and then turn the vessel adrift to the mercy of the waves. They dare not spit to the windward, for fear of offending this aerial deity; and all the vessels that are devoted to him, are kept as clean as their mosques. They impute crosses, sickness, and death to the devil; and in order to pacify him, in a certain place, make him banquets and offerings of flowers. Each of their mosques is situated in the center of a square, and round it they bury their dead: they are very neat buildings, have three doors, each ascended by a flight of steps: the walls within are wainscoted, and the ceiling is of wood beautifully variegated. The floor is of polished stone, covered with mats and tapestry; and the ceiling and wainscoting are firmly joined, without either nails or pegs. Each mosque has its priest, who, besides the duties of his office, teaches the children to read and write the Maldivian language, which is a radical tongue: he also instructs them in the Arabic tongue, and is rewarded for these services by the parents. Those of the people, who are very religious, go to their mosques five times a day; and before they enter it, they wash their feet, hands, ears, eyes and mouth. They who do not go to the mosque, may say their prayers at home; but if they are known to omit doing one or the other, they

are

are treated with the greatest contempt, and every body avoids their company. They keep their Sabbath on Friday, which is celebrated with great festivity; and the same is observed on the day of every new moon. They have several other festivals in the course of the year: the most distinguished of which is called mau-lude, and is held in the month of October, on the night of which Mahomet died. On this occasion a large wooden house, or hall, is erected on a particular part of the island, the inside of which is lined with the rich-est tapestry. In the middle of the hall is a table co-vered with various sorts of provisions, and round it are hung a prodigious number of lamps, the smoke of which gives a most fragrant scent. The people af-semble about 8 o'clock in the evening, and are placed by proper officers appointed for that purpose, ac-cording to their respective stations. The priests, and other ecclesiastics sing till midnight, when the whole assembly fall prostrate on the ground, in which posture they continue till the chief priest rises, when the rest follow his example. The people are then served with betel and drink; and when the service is entirely over, each takes a part of the provisions on the table, and preserve the same, as a sacred relic, with the utmost care. When two persons enter into the state of mar-riage, the man gives notice of his design to the pandiare, or naybe, who demands of him, if he is willing to have the woman proposed for his wife: on his answer-ing in the affirmative, the pandiare questions the pa-rents as to their consent; if they approve of it, the wo-man is brought, and the parties are married in the presence of their relations and friends. After the cere-mony is over, the woman is conducted to her husband's house, where she is visited by her friends, and a grand entertainment is provided on the occasion. The bride-groom makes presents to the king, and the bride like-wife pays the same kind of compliment to the queen. The man does not receive any dowry with his bride, and he is not only obliged to pay the expence of the nuptial ceremony, and to maintain her, but he must alfo fettle a jointure upon her, though, if fhe thinks proper, fhe may relinquifh it after marriage. A woman cannot part from her hufband without his confent: but a man may at any time divorce his wife ; however, if her affent to the feparation is not obtained, fhe may demand her jointure ; yet as this is confidered as a mean act, it is feldom practiced.

When any one dies, the corpfe is wafhed by one of the fame fex, of which there are feveral in each ifland appointed for that purpofe. After this it is wrapped up in cotton, with the right hand placed on the right ear, and the left on the thigh. Then it is laid on the right fide in a coffin of candou wood, and carried to the place of interment by fix relations or friends, and followed by the neighbours, who attend without being invited. The grave is covered with a large piece of filk, or cotton, which, after the interment, becomes the property of the prieft. The corpfe is laid in the grave with the face towards Mahomet's tomb; and when depofited, the grave is filled up with white fand, fprinkled with water. In the proceffion both to and from the grave, the relations fcatter cowries, for the benefit of the poor, and give pieces of gold and filver to the prieft, according to the circumftances of the deceafed. The prieft fings continually during the ceremony ; and when the whole is over, the relations invite the company to a feaft. They inclofe their graves with wooden rails, for they confider it as a fin for any perfon to walk over them ; and they pay fuch refpect to the bones of the dead, that no perfon, not even the priefts, dare to touch them. On this occafion they make little difference in their habits: the mourners only go bare-headed to the grave, and continue fo for a few days after the ceremony of the funeral. If a perfon dies at fea, the body, after being wafhed, is put into a coffin, with a written paper, mentioning his religion, and requefting thofe who may meet with the corpfe to give it a decent interment. They then fing over it, and after having completed their ceremonies, commit it to the waves on a plank of candou wood.

Male,

Male, the ifland where the king refides, is fituated in the center of the reft, and is about five miles in circumference. The palace is built of ftone, and divided into feveral courts and apartments ; but it is only one ftory high, and the architecture very infignificant : however, it is elegantly finifhed within, and furrounded with gardens, in which are fountains and cifterns of water. The portal is built like a fquare tower ; and on feftival days the muficians fing and play upon the top of it. The ground floors of the refpective apartments are raifed three feet, to avoid the ants, and are covered with filk-tapeftry, fringed, and flowered with gold. The king's beds are hung, like hammocks, between two pillars ornamented with gold, and when he lies down his attendants rock him to fleep. His drefs is ufually a coat made of fine white cloth or cotton, with white and blue edging, faftened with buttons of folid gold : under this is a piece of red embroidered tapeftry that reaches down to his heels, and is faftened with a large filk girdle fringed, with a great gold chain before, and a locket formed of the moft precious ftones. On his head he wears a fcarlet cap, which is a colour fo efteemed, that no other perfon may prefume to wear it. This cap is laced with gold, and on the top of it is a large gold button with a precious ftone. The grandees and foldiers wear long hair, but the king's head is fhaved once a week ; he goes bare legged, but wears fandals of gilt copper, which are worn only by the royal family. When he goes abroad, his dignity is diftinguifhed particularly by a white umbrella, which no other perfons, except ftrangers, are permitted to ufe. He has three pages near his perfon, one of whom carries his fur, another his fword and buckler, and a third his box of betel and areca, which he almoft conftantly chews. He goes to the mofque on Fridays in great pomp, his guards dancing, and ftriking their fwords on each others targets to the found of mufic ; and is attended on his return, by the principal people of the ifland. He either walks, or is carried in a chair by flaves, there being no beafts of burden. When the

queen appears in public, she is attended by a great
number of female slaves, some of whom go before, to
give notice to the men to keep out of the way; and
four ladies carry a veil of white silk over her head, that
reaches to the ground : on this occasion, all the women
from the several districts meet her with flowers, fruits,
&c. She and her ladies frequently bathe in the sea for
their health, for the convenience of which they have a
place on the shore close to the water, which is inclosed,
and the top of it covered with white cotton. The only
light in the chambers of the queen, or those of the
ladies of quality, is what lamps afford, which are kept
continually burning, it being the custom of the country
never to admit day-light. The drawing-room, or that
part where they usually reside, is blocked up with four
or five rows of tapestry, the innermost of which none
must lift up till they have coughed, and told their
names. The guards appointed to attend on the king's
person consist of six hundred, who are commanded by
his grandees ; and he has considerable magazines of
arms, cannon, and several sorts of ammunition. His
revenues consist chiefly of a number of islands, appropriated to the crown, with certain taxes on the various
productions of others ; in the money paid to purchase
titles and offices, and for licences to wear fine cloaths.
Besides these, he has a claim to all goods imported by
shipping; for when a vessel arrives, the king is acquainted with its contents, out of which he takes what
he thinks proper, at a low price, and obliges his subjects to purchase them of him again, at what sum he
pleases to fix, by way of exchange, for such commodities as best suit him. All the ambergris found in this
country (which produces more than any other part
of the Indies) is also the property of the king ; and so
narrowly is it watched, that a person would be punished
with the loss of his right hand, if detected in convert-
ing it to his own use. Most of the nobility and gentry
live in the north part of this island, for the convenience of being near the court ; and so much is this
quarter esteemed, that when the king banishes a cri-

minal,

minal, the fending him to the fouth is thought to be a fufficient punifhment.

The government here is abfolute monarchy, every thing depending on the king's pleafure. Each attolon, or province, has a naybe, or governor, who is both a prieft and doctor of the law. He not only prefides over the inferior priefts, and is vefted with the management of all religious affairs, but he is likewife intrufted with the adminiftration of juftice, both in civil and criminal cafes. They are in fact fo many judges, and make four circuits every year throughout their jurifdiction; but they have a fuperior, called the pandiare, who refides in the ifle of Male, and who is not only the fupreme judge of all caufes, but alfo the head of the church: he receives appeals from the governor of each province, but does not pafs fentence without confulting feveral learned doctors; and from him appeals are carried to the king, who refers the matter to fix of his privy council. The pandiare makes a circuit once a year through the ifland of Male (as does every governor in his refpective province) and condemns all to be fcourged who cannot fay their creed and prayers in the Arabic tongue, and confrue them in that of the Maldivian. At this time the women muft not appear in the ftreet unveiled, on pain of having their hair cut off, and their heads fhaved, which is very difgraceful. They have various modes of punifhment for crimes. If a man is murdered, the wife cannot profecute the criminal; but if the deceafed has left any children, the judge obliges him to maintain them till they are of age, when they may either profecute or pardon the murderer. Stealing any thing valuable is punifhed with the amputation of a hand, and, for trifling matters, they are banifhed to the fouthern iflands. An adultrefs is punifhed by having her hair cut off, and thofe guilty of perjury pay a pecuniary mulct. Notwithftanding the law makes homicide death, yet a criminal is never condemned to die, unlefs it is exprefsly ordered by the king; in which cafe he orders his own foldiers to execute the fentence.

The chief articles exported from thefe iflands are

cocoa-

cocoa-nuts, cowries, and tortoise-shells, the latter of which is exceeding beautiful, and not to be met with in any other place, except the Philippine Islands. The imported articles are, iron, steel, spices, china, rice, &c. all which, as has been observed, are ingrossed by the king, who sells them to his subjects at his own price. They have only one fort of money, which is filver, called lorrins, each of which is about the value of eight pence. It is two inches long, and folded, the king's name being set upon the folds in Arabic characters. One thousand two hundred cowries make one lorrin. In their own market they frequently barter one thing for another. Their gold and filver is all imported from abroad, and is current here as in all other parts of the Indies, by weight.

The Maldives are happily placed, with respect to each other, for producing mutual commerce, to the respective inhabitants; for though the 13 Attolons are in the same climate, and all of them very fertile, yet they produce such different commodities, that the people in one cannot live without what is found in another. The inhabitants have likewise so divided themselves, as greatly to enhance this commercial advantage; for all the weavers live in one ifland, the goldfmiths in another, and the like of the different manufactures. In order, however, to render the communication eafy, these artificers have fmall boats, built high on the fides, in which they work, fleep, and eat, while failing from one ifland to another to expofe their goods to fale, and fometimes they are out a confiderable time before they return to their fixed habitations.

(5.) Bombay. This is feated on an ifland near the weft coaft of India, in 19 deg N. latitude, and in 72 deg. E. longitude. It is an excellent harbour, from whence the Portuguefe, the firft poffeffors of the Europeans, gave it the name of Boonbay, now corruptly called Bombay. The ifland on which it ftands, is about 20 miles in circumference: the chief town is a mile in length, meanly built; the fort ftands at a diftance from it. The ifland is inhabited by Englifh,

Portuguefe,

Portuguefe, and Moors: there are three or four more fmall towns on the ifland. The foil is barren, and the water bad; they preferve therefore the rain water in cifterns; and there is a well of pretty good frefh water about a mile from the town. The king of Portugal transferred this ifland to Charles II. king of England, as part of the portion of the Infanta Katherine, whom he married in the year 1662, and the king afterwards gave it to the Eaft India Company. The fort has been befieged both by the Mogul and the Dutch, but neither of them were able to take it. Notwithftanding Bombay lies within the tropics, yet the climate is not difagreeable to the conftitution of Europeans; there being but few days in the courfe of the year, in which the weather is in any extreme. The fhort hot feafon precedes the periodical return of the rains: the night dews, however, are very dangerous, therefore great care fhould be taken not to be expofed to them. If people would but live temperately in this place, they need not be afraid of the climate, which is far healthier than in any other of the European fettlements; and there are fome good phyficians on the ifland. They have wet weather at Bombay about four months in the year, which is commonly introduced by a very violent thunder ftorm: during this feafon all trading veffels are laid up. The rains begin about the latter end of May, and continue till September, when the black merchants keep a feftival, gilding a cocoa-nut, which they confecrate and commit to the waves. What they abound in moft is their groves of cocoa-nut trees, their rice fields, and onion grounds. Their gardens alfo produce mangoes, jacks, and other Indian fruits; and they alfo make large quantities of falt, with very little trouble, from the fea-water.

The town or city of Bombay is a mile long, and furrounded by a wall or ditch; it has alfo a pretty good caftle: fo that it is well fecured, and efteemed one of the ftrongeft places belonging to our Eaft India Company. The houfes of the Englifh confift, in general, of a ground floor, with a court both before and behind, in which

which are out-houses and offices. Most of the windows
are of transparent oyster-shells, which admit a tolerable
good light. The flooring of their habitations is a sort
of stucco, composed of shells that have been burnt; this
they call chunam, which being well tempered, and becoming hard, receives an excellent polish. The English
church is a very neat building, situate on a pleasant
green, round which are the houses of the English; as to
those in which the black merchants reside, they are, in
general, ill contrived structures; and the pagodas of
the gentoos, are most wretched edifices.

The government is entirely English, subordinate to
the India Company, who appoint by commission a president and council; and the maritime and military force
is under the immediate direction of the president, who
is stiled commander in chief. The common soldiers
are of many nations; but what are called topasses, are
for the most part black, or of a mixed breed from the
Portuguese. There are also regular companies of the
natives, who are called seapoys. Any popish priest,
except a Portuguese, may officiate in the churches of the
three Roman catholic parishes, into which Bombay is
divided; but the English formed an objection against
the Portuguese, from an apprehension that those fathers
might have rather too close a connection with others of
their own country, in the adjacent settlements belonging to their master: however, there are no disputes in
this town about professions in religion, all alike being
tolerated. Liberty of conscience, freedom of speech,
riches, and honours, distinguish the people and clime.

Bombay is inhabited by a mixture of all nations;
English, Portuguese, and Indians, amounting, as it is
said, to 50 or 60,000. The president of Surat is usually
governor of the place, who has a deputy here, and courts
of justice, regulated as in England. The governor,
when he is upon the island, appears in greater state
than the governor of fort St. George, being attended,
when he goes abroad, by two troops of Moors and
Bandarins, with their standards. The natives, and
those who are seasoned to the country, enjoy a tolerable
good

good state of health, and, if they use temperance, live to a good old age. Near Bombay are several islands, the chief of which are Butcher's Island, Elephanta, and Salsette. The first took its name from great numbers of cattle being kept in it for the use of Bombay; and the second from the enormous figure of an elephant cut in stone, and which, at a distance, has the appearance of one alive, the stone being exactly of the colour of that quadruped. On this island, which is nearly one entire hill, and about three miles in circumference, there is a temple hewn from the rock. This real curiosity is supported by two rows of pillars, and is 10 feet high. It is an oblong square, about 80 feet in length, and above 40 in breadth, and its roof is formed of the rock cut flat. At the farther end of this singular structure stand the figures of two giants, the faces of which, however, have been much mutilated. The Portuguese, when they became possessed of this island, disfigured and injured these pieces of antiquity as much as possible. This curious fabric has two doors, which front each other; near one of them are several images, much disfigured, and there is one image standing erect, with a drawn dagger in one hand, and a child in the other. The other door, which opens on the left-hand, has an area before it; at the upper end of which is a range of pillars, or colonade, adjoining to an apartment ornamented with regular architecture, round the cornices of which are some paintings. The whole of this temple differs from all of the most antique gentoo-buildings; but with respect to the æra when genius and labour produced it, no discoveries have yet been made.

Salsette lies northward of Bombay, being about 26 miles long, and 9 broad. Here is a ruinated place called Canara, where are several caverns in rocks, which considerably gratify the curiosity of such Europeans who visit them. The soil is extremely fertile, and great plenty of game is found in this island, which, it must be acknowledged, is a most agreeable situation. It was originally comprehended under the regality of Bombay, and of consequence became the property

perty of the English crown when Bombay was given to King Charles the second ; but the Portuguese defrauded us of it ; they, however, lost this island by the invasion of the Marattas, who inhabit the continent bordering on Bombay: they are a very formidable tribe of Gentoos, who have extended their dominions by dint of arms. Their chief, or king, resides generally in the mountains of Decan, at a fort called Raree ; reported to be the strongest place in the universe: it is so well and powerfully guarded by nature, that no enemy can approach it, being surrounded by steep, inaccessible rocks. In this fort the king, or mar-rajah, holds his court, and lives in great splendor. He has long been the avowed foe of the Moguls, Subahs, and Nabobs ; making war, and concluding treaties, just as he thought his interest might be best promoted. The Marattas are all bred to arms and agriculture: the use of the former they learnt from the Europeans, though they depend greatly on their targets, which will turn the ball of a pistol, and even a musquet from a distance. Their swords are excellent, with which they do great execution, but their musquets are very indifferent. Their horses are small, active, and will go through much fatigue. European arts and manufactures receive little encouragement among these people, who prefer those of their own country to the most curious that can be shewn them from foreign parts.

(6.) In 15 deg. 20 min. N. latitude, and 74 deg. 20 min. E. longitude from London, on an island, about 20 miles in length, and six in breadth, stands the large and strong town of Goa, which is the principal place belonging to the Portuguese in India : it was taken by them A. D. 1508. It has the convenience of a fine salt-water river, capable of receiving ships of the greatest burden, where they lie within a mile of the town. The banks of the river are beautified with a great number of handsome structures, such as castles, churches, and gentlemens houses. The air without the town is very unwholesome, for which reason it is not so well inhabited as formerly. The viceroy's palace is a noble building,

building, and stands at a small distance from the city, which leads to a spacious street, terminated by a beautiful church. Goa contains a great number of handsome churches, convents, and cloisters, with a stately large hospital, all well endowed, and kept in good repair. The market-place takes up an acre of ground; and in the shops about it may be had the produce of Europe, Bengal, China, and other countries of less note. Every church has a set of bells, some of which are continually ringing. Their religion is Roman Catholic, and they have a most horrid cruel inquisition. There are a great number of Indian converts, who generally retain some of their old customs, particularly, they cannot be brought to eat beef. However, there are many Gentoos in the city, who are tolerated, because they are more industrious than the Christians, and better artists. The clergy are very numerous, and illiterate; but the churches are finely embellished, and have numbers of images. Their houses, which are of stone, are spacious and handsome, and make a fine shew; but they are poorly finished within. The inhabitants are contented with greens, roots, and fruit, which, with a little bread, rice, and fish, is their only diet, though they have hogs and fowls in plenty. They are much addicted to women, and are generally weak, lean, and feeble. Captain Hamilton, when he was in this island, stood on a hill near the city, and counted above 80 churches, convents, and monasteries, and he was told, that there were about 30,000 priests and monks. The body of St. Francis Xavier is buried in St. Paul's Church, and, as they pretend, performs a great many miracles. None of the churches, except one, have glass windows, for they make use of oyster-shells instead of glass. The town itself has few manufactures, or productions, their best trade being in arrack, which they distil from toddy, the sap of the cocoa-nut tree. The river's mouth is defended by several forts and batteries, well planted on both sides with large cannon; and there are several other forts in different places. This settlement is 250 miles N. by W. of Cochin.

(7.) The island of Diu or Dio. This is situated in 21 deg. 45 min. N. latitude, and in 68 deg. 55 min. E. longitude; and is three miles long, and two broad. The town, which bears the same name, is pretty large, and fortified by a high stone wall, with bastions at convenient distances, and well furnished with cannon. The harbour is well secured by two castles, one of which is made use of for powder, and other warlike stores. It was one of the best places in those parts, the structures being built of free stone and marble. It contains five or six fine churches well embellished within, with images and painting, built by the Portuguese; but it is much decayed of late years, not one fourth part of it being inhabited. In 1670 it was taken by the Arabs, who plundered all the churches, and other places, of their riches, but were driven away with the loss of 1000 men. There are not now above 200 Portuguese inhabitants, for the rest are Banians, who may amount to 40,000.

(8.) The Johor Islands. These lie to the N. E. of Cape Romano, but produce nothing fit for the carrying on of commerce. Pulo Aure, one of them, is peopled by Malays, who are said to form a kind of republic, headed by a chief. In this island are several mountains, on which are many plantations of cocoa-trees. Articles of trade are purchased here with iron, and the people have the character of being very honest, friendly, and hospitable.

(9.) Sincapour, or Sincapora, is an island and town, which lies at the southermost point of the peninsula of Malacca, and gave name to the S. E. part of Malacca Straits. Here is a mountain which yields excellent diamonds; and sugar canes grow to a great size. The soil of Sincapour is fruitful, and the woods produce good timber for ship building.

(10.) Pulo-Condore, the only one inhabited of several islands in the East India sea, lying off the coast of Cambodia. It is situated in 107 deg. 40 min. E. longitude, and 8 deg. 36 min. N. latitude. It is about 13 miles in length, and nine in breadth, but in some places not
above

above a mile over. The inhabitants of this island are of a middle stature, and well shaped, but their complexion is exceedingly swarthy. Their hair is strait and black, their eyes are remarkably small, and their noses high : they have thin lips, small mouths, white teeth, and in their dispositions are very courteous. They go almost naked, except on particular occasions, when they are dressed in a long garment girded about the waist, and ornamented with various coloured ribbands. Their houses are built of bamboos, covered with long grass; but they are very small. They are raised several feet from the earth, on account of the dampness of the ground; and they have neither doors nor windows; so that one side is left open as well for convenience of light, as for the entrance of the people. They are very free of their women, and will bring them on board the ships, where they are kept by the sailors while they stay. These people are idolaters, but of what kind is not known ; however, they have images of elephants in their temples, which are mean edifices built of wood : on the south-side of the island is one of this kind ; within it is the figure of an elephant, and without is that of a horse. The soil of this island is a blackish mould, but the hills are somewhat stony. The trees are not very thick, but large, tall, and fit for any use. The principal fruits are mangoes, a sort of grapes, and bastard nutmegs. The principal animals are hogs and lizards. There are fowls of various kinds, as turtle doves, pigeons, wild cocks and hens, parrots, and parroquets, and several sorts of birds, not known in Europe. The sea produces great plenty of turtles, limpets, and muscles. The chief employment of the inhabitants is to get tar out of the very large trees that grow here. In 1702, the English settled in this island, after the factory of Chusan, on the coast of China, was broke up. However, they continued here but a short time; for having made an agreement with some Macassars, natives of the island of Celebes, to serve for soldiers, and assist in building a fort, and not discharging them at the end of three years, (for which term they

were

were engaged) they rofe in the night, and murdered
every Englifhman they could find on the ifland. The
Englifh had purchafed this ifland of the king of Cambodia, to whom, after this event, it again reverted. Few
remains of the fort are now ftanding, it having been for
the moft part demolifhed. There are feveral other
fmall iflands in thefe feas, namely,

(1.) Pulo-Dinding, near the continent of Malacca,
which belongs to the Dutch where they have a fort.

(2.) Pulo-Timon, on the eaftern coaft of the penin-
fula of Malacca, in 3 deg. 12 min. N. latitude, and
105 deg. 40 min. E. longitude. It is pretty large,
covered with trees, and the valleys are very pleafant.
It is often touched at for wood, water, and other refrefhments, and there is great plenty of green turtles.

(3.) Pulo-Way, near the ifland of Sumatra : it is
fituated in 5 deg. 40 min. N. lat. and in 21 deg. 47 min.
E. long. It is the largeft of all thofe iflands which form
the entrance of the channel of Achem, and is peopled
by culprits who are banifhed from thence.

(4.) Puna, 120 miles north of Patay. It lies at the
entrance of the bay of Guiaquil, in 3 deg. 15 min. S.
latitude, and 100 deg. 5. min. W. longitude.

Having given this copious, geographical, defcriptive,
and hiftorical account of the moft remarkable iflands in
the Indian fea, we fhall now return to the Swallow
Sloop, which we left at anchor off Prince's Ifland, in
the Strait of Sunday.

Friday the 25th of September, we weighed, and got
under fail ; for we could not get a fufficient quantity of
wood and water at Prince's Ifland, to complete our ftock,
the wet monfoon having but juft fet in, and confequently not rain enough had fell to fupply the fprings.
We would have departed from this part of the ifland
fooner, but we had the wind frefh from the S. E. which
made a lee fhore ; but it being this day in our favour,
and more moderate, we worked over to the Java fhore.
We anchored in the evening, in a bay called by fome
New, and by others Canty Bay, which is formed by an
ifland of the fame name. In thefe parts New Bay is
the

the beſt place for wooding and watering; the water being ſo clear and excellent, that, in order to get a freſh ſupply, we ſtaved all that had been taken on board at Batavia and Prince's Iſland. It is to be had from a fine ſtrong run on the Java ſhore, which falls down from the land into the ſea, and by means of a horſe it may be laded into the boats, and the caſks filled without putting them on ſhore, which renders the work very eaſy and expeditious. There is a ſmall reef of rocks within which the boats go, not in the leaſt dangerous, and the boats lie in as ſmooth water, and as effectually ſheltered from any ſwell, as if they were in a mill-pond; and if a ſhip, when lying here, ſhould be driven from her anchors by a wind that blows upon the ſhore, ſhe may, with the greateſt eaſe, run up the paſſage between New Iſland and Java, where there is ſufficient depth of water for the largeſt veſſel, and a harbour, in which, being land-locked, ſhe will find perfect ſecurity. Wood may be procured any where, either upon Java or New Iſland, neither of which at this part are inhabited. In our preſent ſtation, we had 14 fathoms water, with a fine ſandy bottom. The peak of Prince's Iſland bore N. 13 W. The weſtermoſt point of New Iſland, S. 82 W. and the eaſtermoſt point of Java that was in ſight, N. E. We were diſtant from the Java ſhore a mile and a quarter, and from the watering-place a mile and a half. In a few days having completed our wood and water, we weighed, and ſtood out of the Strait of Sunday, with a fine freſh gale at S. E. which continued till we were diſtant from the iſland of Java 700 leagues.

On Monday the 23rd of November, we had in view the coaſt of Africa; on the 28th, at day-break, we made the land of the Cape of Good Hope; and, in the evening, caſt anchor in Table Bay. Here we found only a Dutch ſhip from Europe; and a ſnow belonging to the cape, which was in the company's ſervice, for the inhabitants are not permitted to have any ſhipping. This Bay, in ſummer, is a good harbour, but not in winter; on which account the Dutch veſſels lay here no longer than the 15th of November, after which they go to Falſe Bay, where they are ſheltered from the N.
W. winds,

W. winds, which blow here with great violence. At this place we breathed a pure air, had wholesome food, went freely about the country, which is exceeding pleasant; and found the inhabitants hospitable and polite; there being scarcely a gentleman, either in a public or private station, from whom we did not receive some civility; and Captain Carteret observes, " he should ill deserve the favours they bestowed, if he did not particularly mention the first and second governor, and the fiscal." We continued near six weeks at the cape, in order to recover our sick.

On Wednesday the 20th of January, in the evening, we set sail, and before it was dark cleared the land. After a fine and pleasant passage, on Wednesday the 20th, we anchored off the island of St. Helena, from whence we again sailed on Sunday the 24th. On Saturday the 30th, we came in sight of the N. E. part of Ascension Island, and early in the morning ran in close to it. We sent out a boat to discover the anchoring-place, and in the afternoon came to an anchor in Cross Hill Bay. To find this place, bring the largest and most conspicuous hill upon the island to bear S. E. When the ship is in this position, the bay will be open, right in the middle between two other hills, the westermost of which is called Cross Hill, and gives name to the bay. A flag-staff is upon this hill, which, if a ship brings to bear S. S. E. half E. or S. E. by E. and runs in, keeping so till she is in 10 fathom water, she will be in the best part of the bay. In our run along the N. E. side of the island, we observed several other small sandy bays, in some of which our boat found good anchorage, and saw plenty of turtle. At this place, where we lay, they also abound. In the evening we landed a few men to turn the turtle, that should come on shore during the night, and in the morning they had secured 18, from 4 to 600 weight each. There being no inhabitants on this island, we, according to a usual custom, left a letter in a bottle, with our names, and destination, the date, and a few other particulars.

On Monday the 1st of February, we weighed, and

A. D. 1769.

I   set fet fail. On the 19th, we came in fight of a fhip, in the fouth quarter, which hoifted French colours; and on Saturday the 20th, fhe tacked in order to fpeak with us. Her commander we, after fhe had left us, found to be M. de Bougainville, whofe frequent traces of the Englifh navigators had very remarkably occurred in the courfe of the three voyages, which they made round the world. This gentleman made a voyage to Faulkland's iflands, called by the French, after the Dutch, Mauritius, in the year 1765, and was feen by commodore Byron, in the Straits of Magellan, as we have related in our hiftory of that voyage. Soon after his return home, he failed from port L'Orient, in November 1766, on board the Bourdeufe frigate, attended by the Etoile floop, on a voyage of difcovery, and to encompafs the world: but being baffled in his attempts to pafs the Straits of Magellan, he returned to the eaftern coaft of South America, and wintered at Buenos Ayres. On the return of the feafon, he renewed his attempt with better fuccefs, touched at the ifland of Juan Fernandez, where he ftayed two months, followed Captain Wallis and Captain Carteret, in the manner already related, and, by fuccefsfully completing his defign, became the firft native of France, who had gone round the world, at leaft in one continued voyage. At this time he was on his return in the Bourdeufe, having left the Etoile at the Mauritius: he had alfo touched at the ifland of Afcenfion; and after having hailed us, fent an officer on board, in order to receive fome letters, which were to be conveyed to France, who, under colour of general converfation, endeavoured to obtain information concerning the route and incidents of our voyage, while by a ftring of plaufible fictions he concealed their own; but Captain Carteret could not be brought to be communicative, fo that all the endeavours of the Frenchman proved fruitlefs: on the other hand, the crew of the boat in which the officer had arrived foon imparted all they knew to thofe of our failors who converfed with them. Capt. Carteret obferves very juftly on this tranfaction, " that an artful attempt to draw him into a breach of his obligation to fecrecy, whilft

the

the French commander impofed a fiction, that he might not violate his own, was neither liberal nor juft."

We had now a frefh gale, and all our fails fet, when the French fhip, though foul from a long voyage, and we had been juft cleaned, fhot by us as if we had been at anchor. On Sunday, the 7th of March, we paffed between the weftern iflands of St. Michael and Tercera. As we proceeded farther to the weftward, the gale increafed, and on the 11th it blew very hard from W. N. W. with a great fea, which blew our fore-fail all to pieces, before we could get the yard down; this obliged us to bring to; and having bent a new fail, we bore away again. On Tuefday, the 16th, we were in latitude 49 deg. 15 min. north, and on the 18th, we found ourfelves by the depth of water in the channel. The next day we had a view of the Start-Point; and on the 20th after a fine paffage, and a fair wind from the Cape of Good Hope, to our great joy, the Swallow came to an anchor at Spithead: and to what can we afcribe her arriving fafe at laft, after having gone through, apparently, infurmountable difficulties, but to the merciful interpofition of a particular Providence. In following her and her brave crew, through this voyage, our aftonifhment is excited, not fo much at the number and importance of the difcoveries made, but that fuch wants, fuch embarraffments, and fuch dangers, as thefe neglected and devoted people had to encounter, fhould have been overcome, in a fhip that had been thirty years in the fervice! It is alfo no lefs furprifing, how it came to pafs, that fo able and gallant an officer fhould have been fo cruelly treated, when fent upon a fervice, which, in almoft every other inftance, has been particularly attended to, and received the moft ample fupplies: and, to conclude, if we confider the many impediments which lay in the way of Captain Carteret, beyond what any other navigator had to ftruggle with, we muft acknowledge that this voyage does great honour to him as the conductor of it: indeed this fenfible officer feems to have been animated with the true fpirit of difcovery, and to have poffeffed fuch an uncommon fhare of fortitude and perfeverance, as nothing fhort of death could fubdue.   A NEW,